A
MALEVOLENT
MANNER

William Scott

The evil that is in the world almost always comes of ignorance, and good intentions may do as much harm as malevolence if they lack understanding

   - Albert Camus

* * *

Chapter 1

Each year in Canada's capital there comes a time when life seems to crawl slower and slower, until one might swear to it halting completely. Nothing seems to grow and the winds of change are ushered in, a feeling of melancholy with them. The jet streams of the North descend with cold air, like heralds of an impending invasion of brutality. The once multicoloured arbor, an inspiration to artists and residents alike, drop and perish before the onslaught. Their remains become a skeletal form of warning for those who travel beneath them. Their apparent demise ushers in a slow and hesitant period between the seasons. The comfort of autumn in the afterglow of summer slowly recedes and the sun no longer shares its warmth. The days become gray with indifference and with them the people who must endure through it. The only thing to do, it seems, is to wait for the eventual cold and frost of the long dark winter.

Within these gray thoughts walked a civil servant among many, abandoning the halls of government within the city center. He forced his way up a pair of city blocks, through the throng of workers eagerly trying to get home before the impending cold rain. Despite the fact that his leather jacket and boots would offer minimal resistance against the impending hard rain, he wasn't in a similar rush for shelter. It was the end of another work week, with nothing to celebrate or look forward to, save a drink or two on his way home. As the street came to an end, he turned east along the roadway bearing the name of the Iron Duke of Waterloo. The crowd thinned out noticeably as he passed the gothic towers of Parliament, as most people made their way towards the bus stations further south. From there they would board the bumping and screeching vessels of the road which eagerly waited to spirit them to their identical suburban homes.

As the Peace Tower chimed the quarter hour, he stopped to look over the national war memorial. He guiltily conceded to himself that he'd stopped due to repetition as much as respect or reverence. If confronted he'd argue that he was not a man of habit, but deep down he knew it was an argument he would lose. Everyday he woke up at the same time, ate the same thing for breakfast, walked the same route to the office, took breaks at the same time, ate the same thing for lunch, and then took the same route home from the office. Every Friday he stopped at his favourite pub on the way home and had the same drink.

With this in mind he grabbed the letter out of his pocket. Here was something outside the ordinary clockwork of his life and he was intrigued. It was addressed to *Commandant Pierce* in an elegant hand of black ink, with no return address and no postage stamp. The letter had appeared during the last mail run of the day, however when questioned, the mail clerk had no memory of dropping off the letter. Even more perplexing than the appearance of the letter, was the name inscribed upon it. He couldn't remember the last time he'd heard the word commandant, let alone used it himself. As the rain began to fall he replaced the letter in his pocket, lowered his head, and trudged onwards.

The warmth of the pub hit him as he passed through the second set of doors. Passing the threshold, one was immediately hit by a feeling of passing back in time. The sturdy dark oak walls were adorned with gilt framed hunting prints. Large oaken pillars lined the room, like ancient trunks in a druidic grove. Mingled beneath them were a variety of brown leather loungers and crimson encased chairs with matching tables. Near the door stood the bar itself, a gleaming monolith of polished oak and brass. Its brilliance embellished by the twinkling of numerous bottles lined in front of a large mirror. The fireplace on the opposite end of the room was spitting flames and he welcomed the chance to dry off beside it. But before he could do that he needed to get himself a drink. On his way to the bar he nodded to some of the regulars he recognized and shared the odd pleasantry. For the most part he tried to avoid speaking for no real purpose. He could talk for hours upon numerous subjects; however he found short banter regarding the weather or other inane subjects tiresome. He couldn't help but think of that now as he reached the bar and placed his order.

"What can I get you Pierce?" asked Talbert the bartender, a squat man who always acted as though he was on the inside of a shared joke.

"The usual," he replied to the bartender.

"Are you sure you don't want to branch out, try something new?"

"The usual's fine thanks."

"You know there's a wide world of spirits and ale out there, all waiting to be discovered. You've been coming in here for ages and have always ordered the same thing. You know what that tells me? It tells me tha-"

"I know what I want and more importantly," placing money on the bar, "always pay for it."

With that he grabbed his drink and walked away before the bartender could continue. Talbert was a decent enough type and was always in extra good spirits on Fridays. The impending weekend revellers always meant profits.

Luckily there were still a couple spots available near the fireplace. Some of the patrons probably couldn't handle the heat it was giving off. Pierce on the other hand welcomed the crackling blaze. Having just escaped the rain outside, that was well on its way to becoming a storm, the intense heat would be comforting. He picked a leather lounge chair near the hearth that also allowed him a view of the window and the street beyond it. The soaked leather jacket was removed and placed to dry on a nearby clothes tree and he dropped into the chair, weary from the week, the day, the walk, and the rain.

Taking a drink from his full pint, he remembered the strange letter that was sitting in his jacket pocket. Placing his drink on the small table beside his chair, he leaned over and removed the letter for further inspection. With relief he noticed that the letter had been unaffected by the rain, though he was still no closer to comprehending the strange title written upon it.

Commandant? Surely this letter couldn't be for him. The name itself sprung to mind old World War Two movies of cookie cutter villains with horrendous German accents. Thankfully concentration camps no longer existed, besides anyone put in charge of a similar lock-up was called a warden these days. Either way, he couldn't think of any conceivable reason why anyone would bestow him with the title of *Commandant.*

It's a prank or joke. Pierce could think of no other possible explanation for this singular letter and its appearance at his desk. But even this revelation could not entirely shed light on the letter. He had never been a practical joker and Pierce was not close enough to any of his colleagues to invite this type of joke. Besides, it didn't even seem like a good one.

Without any real resolution, Pierce decided to open the letter and see what explanation the contents could provide. Sadly the contents of the letter turned out to be just as unhelpful as the plain envelope that had carried it. He removed a postcard sized piece of cream paper, clearly expensive from its weight and thickness. It had a thick black border with a golden inner line. Within this bold boundary was again the ominous and mystifying title, *Commandant Pierce.* Flipping the card over, he found more writing. This however was not in the bold print of the main side. Here in a more elegant and fine scrawl were what appeared to be directions. *November 18th, 11am, 111 St. Patrick.*

Pierce held the card between his fingers, staring at it thoughtfully, while taking sips of his drink. He was now more certain that this was some kind of a prank. The letter was clearly meant for him, since he knew of no other Pierce on his floor. The jokers probably dropped it off at his desk, as the clerk had no recollection of delivering it. Unless he was in on it, in which case his initial hypothesis was still correct. He didn't recognize the exact address, but downtown Ottawa wasn't that big. He knew that St. Patrick Street was nearby and well within walking distance.

Finishing the dregs of his drink, Pierce donned his jacket, nodded his farewell to Talbert on his way to the door. Stepping into the rain soaked street, he turned up his collar and began his journey to find what clues the unfamiliar address on the mysterious card in his pocket might tell.

The knitted rug offered little protection against the cold floor as she gingerly stepped out of her bed. The flagstone floor of the lower level of Ravenwood Manor seemed to suck the cold from the ground and disperse it into the many rooms above it. She had left her slippers just out of reach when she got into bed, necessitating a pair of steps on the floor before her feet were safely tucked in. With her feet now protected and warming, she donned her robe and tied it tight around her. She left the flashlight in her bedside drawer, as her night vision was good enough. Besides, she thought, it would be terribly inconspicuous. She did however grab a letter that was underneath the flashlight. Thrusting it into her pocket she made her way to the door, opening it as quietly as possible before departing.

Although Jane's mission this night was neither personally nor professionally risky, being caught would nonetheless be uncomfortable. The staff were given more freedom than was usual to walk around the Manor, though very few abused the privilege for fear of it being revoked. What did concern Jane was the letter she had in her robe pocket. The staff were regularly instructed to stay out of the affairs of the Manor and the club that inhabited it. But she was used to completing tasks outside of her normal duties and felt the risk worthwhile.

The instructions she'd received that morning had seemed easy enough to fulfill. All she had to do was take the envelope hidden in the Study and place it in the outbound dispatch box located within the Secretary's office.

While the club members were having their midday meal, she had gone to the Study to carry out the daily cleaning of the room. The letter was exactly where she had been instructed it would be, in the secret drawers behind the volumes of the *Encyclopaedia Britannica*. She grabbed the letter and hurriedly placed it under her apron, quickly closing the drawers and returning to her room. The letter was then placed in her bedside table for safe keeping for the duration of her daily duties.

With both hands in her robe, Jane made her way through the darkened hallways of the Manor. She was walking slowly and quietly, but at the same time refraining from taking dramatic tip-toe steps one would expect from a thief. She made her way to the office of the Secretary. From here the business of the building was conducted. Within minutes she found the cabinet that held the dispatch boxes. It was a tall gothic affair, constructed of ebony hued wood with multiple spaces in it. Each one contained an equally ebony coloured dispatch box, bound in brass. She went along two shelves before she found the correct one; embossed with a series of letters and numbers she'd been provided. Luckily the box was not locked and the closures yielded to her easily enough. She placed the letter in the box and placed it in the space reserved for deliveries.

With her task accomplished, Jane retraced her steps to her room within the bowels of the Manor. She wondered why secrecy was needed for the delivery of this letter. To her knowledge these letters were sent out very rarely, but it had never been a secret before. Getting into bed she couldn't help but wonder at the strange request she had just fulfilled. Why did the letter need to be sent this way? What did it mean? Who was *Commandant Pierce*?

*

"Touché!" exclaimed the white clad fencer, as he made his final hit with a quick jab. His opponent, caught off guard stepped backwards leaving his own epee to hit nothing but air. As both competitors lowered their weapons, the loser began to laugh.

"Touché? Pat, nobody says that anymore."

"Sorry, I guess I just got too into the match," replied Pierce beginning to chuckle himself. "I was probably too busy beating you that I couldn't think of something cleverer. How about next time I don't say anything and just raise my hands up in the air in triumph, walking back and forth in front of you?"

"Funny. So what have you got planned for the rest of the day? Some of us were going to go over to Sam's. He picked up a new game, supposed to be really gory."

"New game eh? Sounds like a riot."

"Well, do you have something better to do?"

Unlike most days, Pierce actually did have something better to do today. Not that the absence of the letter would have changed his mind. He enjoyed fencing with this group, but spending more than the usual two hours every Saturday morning with them seemed unnecessary. Armed with an epee or saber in the confines of the gym, they were poised and confident. Without them in the outside world they were nervous and juvenile.

"I'll let you know, but I've got an appointment around noon." With that attack parried, Pierce went to the locker room to shower and change.

Patrick Pierce had started fencing at a young age. Shy as a boy, he had always avoided team sports. The idea of making a mistake in front of groups, or letting down teammates always made him uncomfortable. His parents, who encouraged him to keep a low profile, found new sports for him to participate in.

He immediately took to fencing. Fencing came naturally to him, as it does most young boys. Travel down any street in any city in the world, and you will find young men armed with a myriad of sword like objects. Pierce enjoyed being his own team and he enjoyed the uniform, mostly the mask. With the mask on he was indistinguishable from everyone else. Thus he continued to devote Saturday mornings to fencing, becoming very proficient to say the least. Some at the club believed he could have even made it to the Olympics, if he had had any ambition.

Leaving the recreation complex, he walked quickly to his car in the parking lot. The rain clouds from the day before seemed to be stuck in place and the cold droplets continued to stream downwards. Reaching his car, a non-descript neutral-toned sedan, he dropped his gym bag in the trunk and climbed in behind the steering wheel. He pulled out of the lot and headed towards the parkway, enjoying a nice leisurely drive along the canal back to Lower Town.

After parking behind his apartment building, Pierce walked into the foyer and shook the water off him like a waterlogged dog. Through a security door, down a hall, up two sets of stairs, along another hall, he finally arrived at his door. Putting the key slowly into the doorknob, the events of the night before came streaming back into his mind. He entered cautiously, looking round his apartment and dropping his gym bag on the floor. Everything seemed to be in its original place.

"You've got yourself into something deep Paddy me boy," he uttered to himself, echoing a line his long dead Irish Grandfather loved to say.

*

The warmth of the pub behind him, Pierce stood on the sidewalk on St. Patrick Street staring at number 111. He felt like a fraud desperately trying to see the genius of a Van Gogh. But the longer he looked at 111 St. Patrick, the more perplexed he became.

Having been a victim of cruel pranks in his younger days, Pierce now remained alert for them. So he'd expected the address to be some kind of obvious joke. Like a sex shop or something of similar juvenile hilarity.

This was not the case. Standing in the early night rain, Pierce was staring at a two story red brick building with three storefronts and four doors. Each door corresponded with a store, all of them very tame and not humorous in the least. There was a convenience store, a butcher shop and a bookstore. However the last door on the far right had no corresponding window, no sign, and no advertisement of any kind. The only thing on the door was a simple brass plate with *111* stamped into it.

Having decided from the outset that the letter was a joke and just needed a quick inspection to settle his mind on the matter, Pierce had been prepared to continue home and forget the whole situation and enjoy the weekend. However things had now changed slightly. He felt uneasy and yet curious at the same time. Eleven in the morning on a Saturday hardly seemed the time of day to pull any shenanigans. So standing in the rain, staring at the blank door, he decided he'd return the next morning and find out what this business was all about.

The walk home turned out to be more an exercise in swimming than walking, as the rain continued its gravitational duty. Certain sections of road were quickly becoming urban ponds and the sidewalks provided only moderately better protection. His fellow pedestrians performed feats of athletic prowess to avoid the water. One trench-coated businessman cleared a puddle in one giant leap that would have made a decathlete proud. Another teenage couple, clearly not prepared for the rain, tip-toed across expanses of water with such precision and speed one might have thought they were recreating a scene from Swan Lake.

Twenty minutes later Pierce was sitting in his leather lounge chair, highball of Irish Whiskey in hand, with a recap of the day's events playing on the news. Another nightclub overseas had been bombed, provoking competing feelings of sadness, frustration and anger in his mind. Clearly some new strategy had to be employed to combat the ideologues, however he felt that any new plan could possibly reverse matters and simply escalate the situation. In his weaker moments he was glad to be a simple mid-level public servant, not required to solve the world's problems. With this reassuring thought he slowly drifted off to sleep, weary from the work of the week and the alcohol flowing through him.

The sound of wooden wind chimes awoke him in the early hours of the morning. Instantly he knew something was wrong. Not encumbered by wealth, Pierce had to devise alternate methods of home security. Amongst the many inexpensive and unusual systems in place, was a set of wooden wind chimes placed inside the balcony door. It wasn't that Pierce was paranoid; he just didn't trust people to stay out of his apartment. Little did he realize, upon waking suddenly in his leather chair, that he had a very real reason to believe this.

Staying completely still, he watched two dark shapes slide in through the balcony door. They were both fairly large, draped in long black leather jackets. Directly in front of them stood a dining room table, which forced them to part ways in order to reach the open space of the apartment. From his vantage point in the living room Pierce watched the two intruders formulate their plan with hand gestures. He guessed that these were not ordinary burglars and they were not interested in his television. Pierce watched as the farthest intruder disappeared down the hall toward his bedroom and the closer one moved towards the front door. This one passed by him intent on the door. Figuring he was going to open it for possibly more intruders, Pierce suddenly felt indignant to this invasion of his space. Grabbing a large coffee table book adorned with famous pictures of the past century, he slowly removed himself from the soft cushions of the leather chair.

With a swift swing he struck the intruder in the back of the head, dropping him to his knees. With his fencing skills taking over, he took a step back to plant his feet for his next attack. The intruder, dazed from the surprise attack, seemed to recover quickly with the appearance of a telescopic asp from his sleeve. From his kneeling position the intruder rose towards Pierce, taking an uppercut shot with the asp in the same motion. Prepared for the attack from below, Pierce sidestepped him and delivered his counter blow with the book to the side of the head. This shot dropped the intruder again allowing Pierce to provide the final blow downward to the back of head, knocking him out.

Pierce quickly grabbed the asp, preferring it to the now destroyed book in his hands. He knew the other intruder would have by now realized that his bed was empty and would be returning to confer with his confederate. He gripped the asp with anticipation beside the entrance to the hallway. He figured surprise would again work in his favour and planned on taking a swing at the intruder once he returned to the dining room.

The footsteps from the hall quietly approached closer and closer. The second intruder had probably heard the noise from the encounter in the living room and deduced the presence of the homeowner. However stepping from the hallway into the dining room, he was surprised to see the crumpled form of his associate. Unprepared, he took a solid shot from the asp in the back of the head, dropping him immediately.

Staring at the two black figures on his floor, Pierce backed slowly towards the phone in the front hall. He knew that the closest police station was well manned at night, combating the ceaseless shenanigans of the local university population. He could still feel the adrenaline rush of the encounter, but it was leaving just as quickly as it came. He was utterly confused and shocked by the situation he was in. He now had two dangerous, albeit unconscious, men in his apartment with no possible explanation at hand.

Suddenly he felt a hand fall onto his shoulder, the shock shooting his heart into his throat. Without feeling much pressure, he knew that the hand clasped on his shoulder was a powerful one.

"A fine show Mr. Pierce," uttered a dispassionate voice, "however we have much to discuss and we can't have you waving a metal baton at everyone in the room. In the interest of fairness I believe we should all start the conversation from equal footing. Therefore if you would be so kind as to drop the baton, I will place you in the company of my felled compatriots."

Confused Pierce dropped the baton.

"I don't really understand. They're both uncon-"

Before he could finish his sentence he heard an electric clicking followed by a sharp shock to his side. His body convulsed for a second before dropping to the ground unconscious.

Chapter 2

Pierce awoke is a confused daze, his mind slowly trying to make sense of scattered memories and sore muscles. But it was the continued darkness that caused him the most anxiety

After a few minutes of slow breathing and blinking he finally realized that his vision was not impaired, but that the lights were off and the blinds drawn. As his eyes began to adjust to the darkness, two forms began to take shape in front him. Clad in black, they had blended into the darkness of the wall when he first came to. When they finally became clear he realized they were the intruders he had incapacitated earlier. Both were young looking, athletic, and wearing their long black uniform-like jackets. If it weren't for their illegal entry and confinement, he would have thought they were military types.

Now fully coherent, he began piecing together his situation. He was sitting on one of his dining room armchairs, facing the darkness of his living room. Strangely his hands and feet were not bound. Looking to his right he saw nothing down the hall towards his room.

Drawn by movement to his left, Pierce turned to watch one of the intruders leave his vigil in the living room and approach the previously unseen third intruder staring out of an opening in the balcony door blinds.

Seeing this third person, Pierce remembered how his

triumphant victory over the first two had been negated by the mysterious appearance of the third. Although dressed similarly to the other two, this one had the bearing of leadership. He stood motionless with his hands clasped firmly behind his back as the one guard leaned towards him and muttered some inaudible information. Offering a single nod in response the leader turned slowly from the window, offering Pierce with the first view of his assailant.

Comparing the guard to the leader he found that they were not only dressed similarly, but completely identical. His initial impression of the military was further influenced by the metal symbols that the leader alone wore on his lapels. However, no military uniform he had ever seen looked like the clothes they were wearing. His voice however, had the tone of one that was used to being obeyed; strong, confident, and deliberate.

"Very impressive Mr. Pierce. You gave my men quite a hard time, which is very uncommon. I can understand why you've been chosen. Brute force is often not enough. One must rely upon skill and resourcefulness."

This last word was uttered while lifting the damaged coffee table book from the dining room table. Looking at it the leader allowed himself a small smile.

"You will notice that you have not been bound to the chair you now occupy. This should be a sign to you that we don't wish to harm you." At this Pierce rubbed his side in a mock salute. The leader continued, "if you do not believe that, then allow the absence of any bindings to be a sign that we will do what we wish, whether you are bound or not."

"Listen, there must be some mistake," Pierce mumbled with wide eyes. "Who are you guys?"

"Who we are does not concern you at this time. Sufficed to say we are part of a group that has an interest in you. Earlier today," pausing to pull out a pocket watch, he restated the time, "that is yesterday, you received a letter. You needn't deny this, as its presence is beyond debate. We took it from your jacket."

Nodding towards the dining room table, the leader

motioned for Pierce to observe its presence. It was indeed there, though Pierce was now just as confused as the first time he had laid eyes upon it.

"What we need to know is whether you intend to keep the appointment as stated on the back of the card."

"I wasn't really sure to be honest," replied Pierce, returning the gaze of the leader, hoping to project his honesty.

"Hmm," ruminated the leader for a moment. "Either way, I shall deliver our message. This invitation is like a wormed hook to a trout. Bluntly, it is a trap. The group that wish to meet with you are evil. They will make you offers that seem impossible, however they will deliver them. To your everlasting detriment." This last sentence was uttered in such a quiet, forceful fashion, that Pierce couldn't help but feel the danger involved.

"But who are they?" inquired Pierce, now totally out of his depth, not really sure if he would understand the answer.

"There is no way for me to describe to you in any way that you might understand. My suggestion to you is to not even show up at the address written down. If you indeed keep the appointment, keep my warning in mind. If you are foolish enough to accept their offer, you and I will see each other again, to your dismay.

With the threat offered, the leader turned and left towards the front door with his minions following. Pierce was left watching in stunned silence.

*

Looking at the card and destroyed book on the dining room table in the light of day made the events of the night before all too real. Clearly it had not been a bad dream caused by indigestion or alcohol.

Despite the echo of the warning, he was still curious about the meeting on the card. Being a well adjusted young man, he believed that if the situation arose, he would know an evil proposal if he heard one.

He continued to debate the issue with himself as he changed clothes and ate a quick meal. Finally he found himself standing in the hall, staring at his boots and jacket in the closet. Like a diver on the edge of a cliff he took a deep breath and plunged in, deciding to see where events would lead him. For too long he had deferred various offers, never wanting to take a chance on the unknown. Too many potential opportunities, both professional and personal had passed him by through his inability to act. This time he would do something.

With a new found determination he walked through his front door, down the hall and stairs of his building, exiting upon the sidewalk of the street outside.

The storm outside continued undaunted by time. Although the rain had settled to a slight drizzle, the winds had grown stronger, causing the rain to mimic the bow spray of a ship at sea.

Rather than take his car Pierce decided to walk the minimal number of blocks to his destination. The hydrated air seemed exhilarating and added to his already anticipatory mood. Each step he took towards the mysterious building on St. Patrick Street, the more determined he was to follow through with the invitation.

After several blocks of brisk walking he turned a corner and sighted the building. It was halfway down the street and still as ordinary as the day before. The stores on either side were open and seemed to be doing a standard amount of business. Parents with their children going into the bookshop intent upon raiding the children's book section, professionals buying cuts of meat from the butcher for dinner parties, and hung-over students grabbing liquids and snacks from the convenience store. It was an altogether normal scene of midday Saturday shopping. None of the impending danger prophesized by the intruder of the night before seemed present.

Without hesitation Pierce went up to the door marked *111*, prepared to enter. With a quick glance he noticed the absence of a doorbell or doorknocker. Shrugging, he decided he would have to simply knock, hoping that his host would hear him inside. Deciding that three forceful knocks would be appropriate for the situation, Pierce raised his fist and began knocking. Upon the second knock the door creaked open and continued to part, leaving him staring into the void with his arm held up in midair.

The feeling of determination that had imbued his walk started to slowly drain from his body. Trying to maintain his composure, Pierce decided he should call out.

"Hello?" he called into the void, conscious of his deliberate attempt at keeping his voice from cracking. "Hello, I received a letter yesterday. It gave this time and address."

The silence was broken by footsteps from above him. Stepping inside the foyer, Pierce was presented with a single narrow staircase leading directly up to the second floor. Finally the door at the top of the stairs opened and a balding gentleman in a three-piece pinstriped suit appeared.

"Pardon the state of the door, you were right to knock and enter. Please come up." The voice was well educated without the hint of an accent.

Ascending the staircase Pierce felt as though he were climbing an oak tree from the inside. The stairs and walls were all build from dark wood. Although not apparent at first glance, the walls were finely made with mouldings and carvings.

Upon reaching the top of the stairs, Pierce noticed that the man appeared much smaller than from below. Despite a protruding gut pushing against his waistcoat pockets, he was short and weak looking. Both shook hands as a pair of businessmen on a first meeting.

"Good day Commandant Pierce, so very good of you to show up on such short notice. I trust you found us without trouble?"

"Yes... No trouble at all... Pardon, but you just called me..." Pierce tried to answer his questions affably before he realized he had received that strange title again. Before he could continue the man interrupted.

"Yes, well I suppose it is the weekend. I can address you as Mr. Pierce if you prefer. Please take a seat." He spoke quickly, but not rushed as they entered the room at the top of the stairs, finally motioning to one of a pair of chairs in front of a fireplace.

The fireplace was filled with a pile of glowing embers, projecting heat but very little light. The room itself was a continuation of the staircase; solid oak paneling, with bookcases surrounding the room, broken only by a pair of windows flanking the fireplace. Beneath the chairs was a crimson carpet, with faint designs along the edge. There was a table with a couple chairs in the corner. Behind that stood two doors, presumably the washroom and closet.

"I would like to thank you again for being so prompt and accepting the offer of this interview. Furthermore I would like to congratulate you on being offered said interview. The offer itself is very rare and we bestow it with great deliberation." Noticing that Pierce was about to question what was being offered, the man raised his hand. "Please, all will be explained in due time."

"First I will introduce myself and my organization. I am Percival Drummond, Secretary of the Black Tower Hunt Club. It is based on the traditional English hunt club, though with some modern differences. However it is mostly a club for like-minded professionals with the right mixture of credentials and characteristics."

"What kind of credentials and characteristics would these be?"

"Well you needn't worry about that, as you clearly have them. Otherwise we wouldn't be having this conversation, wouldn't you agree?"

"Uhh, clearly, yes of course," uttered Pierce trying to sound more confident than he felt. So far there seemed little to be concerned about. Perhaps the evil the men in black had earlier alluded to was in fact be the hunting of animals. Perhaps the intruders were animal activists. He decided to find out, as he had no wish to kill animals or have activists hound his every move.

"Now, what exactly do you hunt? I'm not sure I…"

"You needn't worry. Foxhunting has been banned for years. We no longer hunt to kill animals. It is more of a sport now. But I wouldn't be fixated on the hunting aspect. We're more of a club now, and unlike your traditional gentleman's club, we also recruit female members.

"Now I must ask you, have you told anyone of the letter we sent you or our present interview? Since this is a rather exclusive club we would prefer discretion on the part of our members."

Now fully convinced of the nature of the nights intruders, Pierce decided not to inform his host of them. Besides, he had not told them about the interview. They already knew.

"No I did not."

"Splendid, I think you will fit in nicely. Now if you agree to our offer I th-"

"But what exactly are you offering," interrupted Pierce.

"Well I shall tell you," replied Mr. Drummond, irritated by the interruption. "You will be offered a place in the club. This entails access to all of our facilities, invitations to all of our events, and all the subsequent benefits. In addition there are other members whom you will become acquainted with. I do not think I exaggerate when I say they are all unique people of influence and intelligence."

"Who are these members and what exactly are the benefits you alluded to?" inquired Pierce, straddling the line between curiosity and suspicion.

"I cannot possibly divulge their identities," replied Drummond quickly, his calm veneer cracking into a frown. "And the benefits are too numerous and staggering to provide here."

Startled by this sudden change of tone, Pierce began to protest the response provided. Seeing this, Drummond's demeanor immediately returned to its previous gentle state.

"You will have to excuse me. I am not used to having so many questions during the recruiting phase. Usually prospective members are more than eager to join."

"I am interested in your proposal, but it just seems so

outlandish. I haven't accomplished nearly enough to be included in the type of club you seem to be promoting."

"That is understandable, however one must sometimes look for potential rather than experience. We have a complete dossier on you and believe you have great potential."

With that he lifted a black attaché case from beside his chair and placed it on his lap. From within he removed a manila file folder and began to read from it.

"Your name is Patrick Pierce, born at the Ottawa General at 7:26 in the morning. You attended Brookville High School, despite the fact that your family is Catholic."

"How did you know that about my family?"

"What, their being Catholic?" inquired Drummond peering over the file folder. "You needn't worry about that. Our members have many different faiths." Returning to the file he continued, "I see they emigrated from Shannon Ireland, though they were originally from Belfast in the North. Your father a soldier, your mother…"

"You made your point," Pierce shot testily. He still found the mention of his parents a sore subject, despite their passing almost ten years ago. They had had an impact on him that he continued to discover everyday.

While they had been alive, his parents had been quiet about their past and lived a moderately sedate and anonymous life. They had imparted these qualities on young Patrick, teaching him to blend in and observe others closely. Together they had played games that Pierce later realized were meant to teach him the ability to think logically and to stay calm in distressing circumstances. He had thought nothing of his curious upbringing until after they had died in a car accident. He had been in his second year of university when the accident happened, shattering the simple routine of his life. At the small wake he met his maternal grandfather for the first time, reanimating his dormant familial curiosity.

Despite displaying the hardiness of a farmer working tough land, he was quick with a joke and even quicker with a smile. The old man took an instant liking to his grandson, inwardly ashamed for having not seen him before then. So when Pierce asked about his parents, he found himself divulging their long kept secrets.

To begin with Pierce was not his father's real last name, it was actually Wallace. He had been an officer with the 22 SAS Regiment, assigned to Northern Ireland during the Troubles. He had been a born a leader and natural soldier, earning the respect of his men and adversaries alike. One rainy night in Belfast he came across a young woman being attacked by a group of drunken soldiers near a checkpoint. Their excuse was that the woman was a known IRA sympathizer and potential member. Their colourful response to Wallace's order to place themselves in his custody for court martial was met by instant action. Within minutes they were all face down on the ground, arms bound, and bleeding from their faces.

The girl was Bridget McPhee, Pierce's mother, and she fell instantly in love with the soldier before her. It was true that she was a member of the IRA and had been responsible for some daring but little known assassinations of senior officials. She rationalized her love for a British soldier by the fact he was actually Scottish. However this proved of little consequence to the local IRA Commanders who viewed the young couple as a danger to be dealt with. When they refused to leave each other, a bounty was placed on both of them. Due to their training and respective professions, the pair easily procured money, passports, and way out of Belfast before the hunt truly began.

They crossed the border into Ireland with little difficulty, stopping by Bridget's father's farm for a day on their way to Shannon. Unlike his Fenian brothers, old McPhee saw the love between the young couple and realized their fighting days were over. They flew from Shannon to New York and slowly made their way North to Canada. The young couple settled in Ottawa as Mr. and Mrs. Pierce, raising a son in peace. Patrick had appreciated discovering the truth to his past and had stayed close to his grandfather from then on.

As Drummond continued speaking, Pierce knew that it was only because of his parents and his upbringing that he had stayed moderately composed so far.

"You now have the ability to make a change in your life. I am providing you with the ability and means to do great things. All you need to do is sign on and become a member of the club. Once you have done this we can immediately travel to the Manor. I can have some people collect your things and have them delivered, though truth be told you will not require much of them."

"Manor, what are you talking about?"

"Sorry I must have glossed over that. Membership includes a set of rooms at Ravenwood Manor, a large staff to look after your needs, and a considerable allowance."

"What if I don't want to move out?" replied Pierce suddenly wary.

"Why would you not?" Mr. Drummond replied in confusion. "However, if you feel more comfortable remaining at your current lodgings, that is your prerogative. I would suggest that you at the very least take a tour of the Manor."

Pierce was now at a crossroads of opinion. If this offer were nefarious in any way, surely Drummond would have provided a take-it or leave-it attitude, forcing him to accept despite his reservations.

"I know this is a lot to accept in such a short time, but we are anxious to have your response to our offer," he said while removing some paper from the attaché case. "Are you ready to sign the membership so we can begin? The car is down on the street at this moment, waiting to take us to the Manor."

"Well," replied Pierce with newly acquired apprehension, "I would like to read those documents first if I might, then take a day or two to decide if that is alright."

"Of course," offered Mr. Drummond courteously and without apparent disappointment. "We wouldn't have it any other way. It is obviously a big decision and one must not be rushed into these things. What do you say to a quick drink in celebration, as I'm sure you will inevitably realize the magnitude of the offer you have just received."

With that he rose from his chair and moved to the

sideboard where numerous glasses and decanters sat.

"Irish Whiskey satisfactory?" inquired Mr. Drummond over his shoulder.

"Absolutely," replied Pierce. Looking around the room he added, "this is a strange place to do business out of. From the outside you'd never realize what kind of rooms where inside. Plus it is a very strange part of town for a club such as yours to have offices."

"We find the setup discreet and the area sufficiently anonymous," he replied handing over the drink. Saluting with the glass he proceeded to take a drink. After the first sip he noticed Pierce had yet to raise his glass and was staring at him.

"Surely you don't think I would be so melodramatic as to do anything to your drink," he said, obviously offended.

"Of course not. Sorry I was just lost in thought for a second." The fact that, that was precisely what he had been thinking made Pierce blush slightly and take a quick drink from his glass.

Mr. Drummonds gaze turned from one of indifference to one of intensity. Slowly a smug smile began to appear as the edges of his mouth raised slightly.

"Well now that you're drugged, I hope that you will accept our offer with slightly more enthusiasm."

Pierce chuckled and was about to say something in response but found himself unable to speak. Slowly his vision began to blur like the view from inside a windshield immerging into water. The last thing he saw was Mr. Drummond walking over to one of the two doors, opening it slowly.

"We really must stop meeting like this."

The gravelly voice was familiar to Pierce and as he opened his eyes he was slowly able to focus on the man occupying the chair opposite of him. Sitting comfortably with a highball of whiskey and ice was the leader of the intruders from the previous night. He was an imposing figure draped in his long black leather jacket. His hair was a similarly dark colour and his tanned face was tough looking, with the hint of a scar above his left eye. But despite his dangerous appearance, Pierce felt that he was not a malicious thug. There was a calculating alertness behind the man's eyes, but it was not threatening. He grabbed a second glass for the side table and leaned forward, delivering it to his prisoner.

"Take this, it will help you regain your senses. This one is not drugged, I assure you," continued the man in the dark leather coat, sensing Pierce's disbelief.

"I'm sorry Percival had to resort to the drugs, but you were not easily convinced."

"You told me not to come here!" retorted Pierce after swallowing a mouthful of whiskey.

"Yes, and you passed the test admirably. We wanted to see if you had the nerve to ignore a threat and follow through. You arrived here as planned."

"So you broke into my house as a test?"

"Obviously we don't want someone who would shirk at the first moment of danger, would we?"

"I have no idea! I don't know what's going on!"

"Surely you must have gleaned something during your interview this afternoon?"

"I'm afraid that wasn't possible Tiberius." The voice came from Drummond as he appeared from one of the two doors. "I've discovered he has been tapped early and we couldn't go into detail. However due to the apparent necessity of his recruitment I was forced to rely on the drugs. He was not easily convinced."

"I see," ruminated the man known as Tiberius. "Very well, shall we tell him then?"

"Tell me what? What's going on?" Pierce asked in exasperation.

"I think not. It is too early," said Mr. Drummond, ignoring Pierce.

"Well we must explain some things. We cannot keep drugging him."

"Very well if we must," replied Mr. Drummond pulling one of the chairs over to the two occupied by Pierce and Tiberius. "Well Mr. Pierce, what would you like to know?"

"What am I doing here?"

"I explained that earlier."

"You mean everything you said before about this club is true?"

"Every word."

"What did you leave out then?"

"More than I can possibly explain in our short amount of time. But none of it should cause you to worry about your wellbeing."

"Except the fact I've already been drugged once," Pierce retorted quickly. "What about this Manor?"

"There is a manor where you will live, just as I said earlier," explained Mr. Drummond.

"What about this hunting business?"

"The hunt is a pivotal part of the club. As I said I am the Hunt Secretary. Tiberius here is a Whip," and then motioning to the two other men at the door Mr. Drummond continued, "and these two, whom you've already met, are the Hounds."

"Hounds?"

"Yes. You see, you really are joining a Hunt Club. As a member you will become a Huntsman along with your fellow members. They are all well educated, professional, and sophisticated people. They range from doctors, to lawyers, to military men. However the actual hunt excursions are very few in number. The rest of you time is spent in the Manor or the surrounding countryside. If I may say, it is a life of luxury."

"Are either of you members?"

"No, we are both employed by the Manor and its Club. I have worked there for years and would give anything for the opportunity before you."

"So let me get this straight," began Pierce, "I have been recruited to join a hunt club and live in a mansion, being catered to every hour of the day? Not only do I not believe you, but I think you're both crazy. I'm leaving!"

"Very well leave!" exclaimed Mr. Drummond. "This has been a waste of time and I for one am glad you're not going to become a member of this hollowed Club!" The distaste for Pierce that Mr. Drummond had kept at bay throughout the two interviews finally shone through. Although seated, he was able to give the impression of looking down his nose at Pierce. Again that smug look began to creep onto his face.

With that Pierce got up and headed for the door he had entered that morning. As he got closer to the door, the two guards blocked his way, stepping in front of it.

"I'm afraid I can't let you do that," came the voice of Tiberius from behind him. "You might not realize it, but you must come with us."

"Why?" screamed Pierce in exasperation, turning to face Tiberius who had also risen from his chair. "Why do you want me to come, while Mr. Drummond over there could care less?"

"It's not my place to tell you. You must enter into this with an open mind. But know this, it is necessary," pleaded Tiberius.

Mr. Drummond then came over to add, "if you don't come with us, you will be unable to get the antidote for the poison that is now coursing through your veins.

Chapter 3

"You poisoned me! I thought you said I was just drugged!" exclaimed Pierce with rising anger and frustration.

"Do not be offended, it's not personal," replied Mr. Drummond. "I assure you it is standard procedure."

"Well so is this!" With one swift motion he punched Drummond in face, immediately breaking his nose and releasing a flow of blood.

Before he could move away, the two guards by the door were behind him with each grabbing an arm. Instinctively he began trying to counter the restraint, struggling back and forth. Finally realizing the uselessness of struggling he relaxed.

"Sorry," Pierce said in mock sincerity, "but that's also standard procedure when someone poisons you."

Drummond removed a blood soaked handkerchief from his face and moved towards Pierce and his two captors. Muttering an incomprehensible insult he wound up to deliver a back-handed slap. However before it could land, a strong hand from behind stopped it in midair.

"That is quite enough," growled Tiberius, slowly letting go of Mr. Drummond's hand after the smaller man started to wince in pain. He then turned his attention to Pierce. "We will now depart for the Manor, you can either come peacefully, drugged up, or kicking and screaming. The choice is yours."

Suddenly ashamed of his violent strike and realizing the hopelessness of the situation, Pierce knew there was only one choice.

"I will come peacefully of course," Pierce allowed after a brief moment, knowing it was the best option. Making the decision for himself made Pierce feel as though he still had a bit of control over the situation. However the little voice inside his head told him he'd lost control the moment the letter had appeared at his desk.

"Very well follow me."

Tiberius went to the two doors behind the table and chose the one on the right; the one Mr. Drummond had appeared from earlier. He opened it and entered. Pierce was next in line and followed him into a long dark corridor, followed immediately by the two guards and finally Mr. Drummond.

Although the corridor was not terribly long, Pierce was confused as to how it could fit over the three stores below them. From the outside, the building that housed the bookstore, butcher, and convenience store did not look to be this long or large. When they reached the door at the end of the corridor, Pierce began to feel a strange and fearful sense of foreboding. Despite the home invasion, the incredible proposal, and the subsequent drugging, the situation was becoming as dark as the corridor.

This suspicion proved correct immediately after Tiberius opened the door. The only option that would have made physical sense would have been a fire escape leading down to the street. After all, they said a car was waiting to take them to the Manor. Instead, peeking over Tiberius' shoulder, Pierce could clearly see a large circular stone room, illuminated by torches.

"What did you poison me with?" Pierce mumbled as he rubbed his eyes, unable to process what the opened door had produced. "This isn't possible."

Tiberius ignored him and crossed the threshold without any apparent trepidation. Pierce could find no such confidence, his feet were like stones and he was stuck in place. Even if he wanted to move forward, his brain was too busy trying to make sense of the situation to order any movement. This was impossible. The building was too small. Who builds round rooms? Who uses torches?

The noise of throat clearing from behind him made Pierce shake his head clear. Up ahead, Tiberius was looking back at him and waiting. Although he still felt a sense of foreboding, the look on Tiberius was not menacing. In fact he looked like he understood the swirl of thoughts and emotions flooding in Pierces' mind.

"Well I'd rather walk into this on my own steam, than dragged in drugged."

With a deliberate step, Pierce crossed the threshold. The moment was anticlimactic. There was no feeling of his body tingling, no sudden head pain, not even a pushing or pulling sensation. Getting off an escalator felt more bizarre.

Before he could fully appreciate his surroundings Pierce was moving quickly behind the departing figure of Tiberius. The group moved together across the flagstone floor to a circular staircase. At the top they went through another door that in turn led to another corridor. This corridor was a complete opposite to the one they had just exited. Rather than an oak paneled hallway, this one was made entirely of stone and lined with numerous doors. The flicker of the torches along the corridor produced shadows on the doors, giving them a lifelike character with menacing expressions.

The corridor led out to a small landing. This appeared to be the crossroads of a larger floor. Behind them was the torch lit corridor filled with doors. To the left and right were a pair of staircases and in front lay another long corridor.

"Where... I mean... We can't possibly... I..." stuttered Pierce, unable to form coherent thoughts or speech.

Without a response from any of his companions, the group continued forward through the next corridor. Pierce felt like he was no longer walking. He was floating in place and the building was moving around him. Nothing was making any sense.

The next corridor was stone like the previous one, however this one had no doors along it. At first Pierce thought it was lined with mirrors, but with a second glance he realized they were windows. This wasn't a corridor at all, but a long covered bridge. They were quickly through it and into a slightly larger hallway in a completely different building.

"Good night Tiberius," called Mr. Drummond as he went to the first door on the right.

Tiberius merely nodded without looking back. Pierce did look back, but all he saw were his two guards. They continued down stairs, through hallways and across galleries. Upon reaching an enormous hall, Pierce finally had to stop and try to organize his thoughts. Although not scientifically inclined, he had the distinct impression they had all just defied the laws of physics. His mind struggled with the Sisyphean task of understanding what the hell was going on. Just when he felt he was coming to terms with everything, something new toppled him backwards in confusion.

"Wait a second, where are we?"

"Ravenwood Manor."

"But… But we didn't take the car?"

"No."

"Why not"

"Ravenwood is not really accessible by car."

"So its more accessible by a hallway."

"So it would seem."

"What?! Where are we really?"

"This will be hard to explain and I'm not the one to do it. I suggest you follow me to your room. After some rest you will be better prepared to understand the situation."

"What if I don't want to? Will your goons continue to force me?"

"Goons? Oh you mean Morgan and Dufresne. They left us some time ago."

Shocked Pierce spun around to see no one behind him.

"You're free to try and find your own way," then motioning around the large hall, "but as you can see there is a distinct possibility of getting lost."

Pierce followed Tiberius' hand as it swept the hall and understood. There were two large staircases leading up to galleries full of doors and hallways. On the level under the galleries were more doors and two large corridors. However his gaze finally fell upon the largest door he had ever seen. It wasn't so much a door as a gate. Constructed of what appeared to be wood and iron, he figured it would take ten men to open it. But more importantly it was probably the front door, and a way out.

"Lead on then," uttered Pierce.

An equally disorienting tour finally led them to a large dark door. A brass plate with the name *Commandant Pierce* embossed upon it was on the door.

"These are your rooms. You should have everything you need within. If you require anything there are multiple bell pulls that will bring a staff member to you."

"Anitdote?" Pierce asked hopefully as he rubbed his shaking hands together.

"Sorry?"

"Can you have someone bring up the antidote for the poison Drummond gave me?" Pierce elaborated with a stronger voice. He couldn't tell if he was reacting to the shock of his new circumstances or from the poison, so he wanted to eliminate one of the possibilities.

"Yes, the poison," Tiberius allowed slowly, the hint of a smile breaking out across his face. "The truth is that there was no poison. It was Drummound's little trick to push you in the right direction. I apologize if it caused you any additional anxiety. Good night."

With a quick bow Tiberius turned then retreated back down the corridor, vanishing around the corner. Stifling a string of curses, Pierce instead took a deep breath and opened the door to enter, not feeling any less anxious.

*

Pierce awoke with a start, only to discover he was still in the giant four-poster bed. Grudgingly he accepted that he had not been dreaming and was still living in a reality he couldn't comprehend. The only positive thing to be found was that it was still night. When he first arrived in his bedroom he had tried to peer out the window, to get an idea of the surroundings. However the darkness of the night was impenetrable through the windows. The idea then came to him to make a break for the large door in the main hall. However a brief moment of relaxation on the bed had quickly turned into a nap. But there seemed to be no harm done, as the sun had yet to begin its slow rise.

Sitting up, he started to grope for his clothes. He didn't remember taking them off, but here he was, missing his pants, shirt, and jacket. What had happened to them? Looking around for something to wear, he saw a robe hung on one of the bedposts. Throwing it around himself, he made his way to the dressing room. There he found some pants, a shirt, and some soft soled shoes.

Quietly Pierce stole out of his room, looking back and forth down the hall for any other late night ramblers. Slowly he made his way towards the main door, doubling back when he made wrong turns.

Finally he came to one of the large staircases. In the dark, the hall looked like an enormous cave. Subconsciously he kept looking upwards for bats on the ceiling. At the bottom he moved swiftly towards the front door, not sure that he'd even be able to open it.

A quick inspection of the door didn't produce a mechanism to be unlocked. Pierce couldn't believe it. Surely the main door would be locked. With a shrug he grabbed the handle, turning it slowly. Setting himself, he started to move the door.

Instead of it being an exercise in hopelessness, the door moved freely. In fact it glided open without a sound and with the least amount of effort. Not waiting to be discovered, Pierce quickly bounded out the door. He made his way down some stairs and a dozen yards along a gravel drive way before he stopped. Looking out over the horizon, the sun was beginning to rise. Rays of orange, red, and purple started to shoot upwards, but it wasn't the beautiful sunrise that stopped him.

Looking forward, then side-to-side, Pierce's heart sank. There was no city here, Ottawa's footprint was nowhere to be seen. In fact there were no buildings to be seen at all. All around him were rolling green hills, sharply rising mountains, and what appeared to be the beginning of a very dark lake. All he could think about was the impossibility of it all. So stunned was he by this revelation that he didn't hear the crunching footsteps behind him. He just stood there staring into this otherwise beautiful scene.

"Sir?" said the voice behind him after a few minutes of silence. "Sir, it's rather cold, I think you should come inside."

"Cold… Ya… I uh…"

Taking him by the arm, the newcomer turned a dazed Patrick Pierce around and led him back towards the Manor. Back inside the confines of the building, Pierce began to regain his awareness. He blinked rapidly and shook his head, clearing it of the fog from the outdoor scene he had just witnessed.

"Who are you and how did you know I was outside?" Pierce finally asked glancing at the man helping him up the stairs. He was roughly the same age, though somewhat shorter and with lighter hair. He was dressed in a dark suit jacket, white shirt and tie, with grey pinstriped pants.

"My name is Melrose sir. I am your valet."

"But how did you know I was outside? I thought no one followed me."

"It is my duty sir, to look after you."

Mulling over this new information, Pierce continued with his valet up to his rooms. Within minutes they were back where he had started and Melrose was pouring him a drink.

"Take this sir, it will steady you."

"You should have one as well," replied Pierce accepting the glass and sitting down on one of the chairs facing the hearth. The fire jumped and crackled exuberantly with its rebirth.

"I couldn't possibly sir."

"Well I don't want to drink alone," Pierce countered, seeing the flicker of uncertainty on the valet's angular face.

Nodding in assent, Melrose poured himself a small drink and moved over to the fireplace standing upright. When Pierce motioned for him to sit, he acceded, though slowly in protest.

"I want you to know that I feel somewhat uncomfortable with this situation. It's nothing personal, but I've never been in a position that requires a servant. What am I supposed to do?" bowing his head into his hand he uttered. "This is turning into some sort of messed up Victorian melodrama."

"If I may sir, everyone has a style for dealing with difficulties. You will find yours."

"Right. Well if I start acting like an imbecile, I trust you will be good enough to ignore it and do whatever I say."

Melrose reacted somewhat more quickly than his training would presume, raising an eyebrow in disbelief, before he could return to a neutral expression.

"Good," chuckled Pierce, "I see you can pick out irony."

"Irony sir?" he replied dryly, "I can't say I've ever experienced it."

"Sarcasm as well, we'll get along alright."

Melrose allowed himself a smile, and then finished his drink. He started to get out of his chair, but Pierce waved him back down. Grabbing the bottle, he poured another set of drinks.

"I need to know what I've gotten myself into," said Pierce staring directly at his valet, "and you're going to tell me."

Melrose didn't initially react, but then drained his drink and held out the empty glass.

"This could to take some time."

*

"So you're telling me, that this castle…"

"Manor."

"Right, manor, is stuck in time?"

"Or out of time."

"In time, out of time... What does that mean?"

"I have no idea. You should ask the Russian, she's a scientist."

"The Russian?"

"Nevermind. The point is that the Manor is in some sort of li...(hick)...imbo."

"What?"

"Limbo."

"But what does that mean? Everything stays the same? Or is the Manor trying to slowly move underneath an ever lowering bar to Caribbean music?" Pierce then began laughing as the description took shape in his mind. Melrose joined him almost immediately.

Both were still sitting in Pierce's lounge, the fire slowly dying, its embers barely lighting the space. Between the two chairs was a pair of empty glasses and the corresponding bottle, equally empty.

"All I know is that I have been here for many years but I don't know how many. I can truthfully say that I have witnessed at least fifty winters."

"What?"

"Hand to heart sir. By my estimate I should be close to eighty, but here I sit a young man of thirty."

"So the seasons still pass by; winter, spring, summer, fall..."

"But no one living in the Manor ages. Even those living on the island age slowly, however they eventually do become old. Funerals for the elderly are very uncommon, but do happen. It's as if the island were keeping people alive."

"That's impossible."

"More inconceivable rather than impossible I should think," corrected Melrose, slightly slurring his words.

"You mean it's possible, but that I can't understand it?"

"None of us can." Then adding soberly, "everyone simply accepts this phenomena as fact and continues on. I won't presume to tell you what to do, but I wouldn't delve too deeply into this sir."

Pierce accepted this advice uneasily. He wanted to know, to understand what was happening. Normally he wasn't an inquisitive type, but these were exceptional circumstances.

"All right I'll follow your advice, for now."

Pierce began to try and form his thoughts with this new insight into his situation. So deep was he in thought that his eyes began to close, almost shutting completely. Thinking that his master was falling asleep, Melrose began once more to rise from his chair.

"How did I get here?" whispered Pierce behind closed eyes. "One moment I was in a room above a butcher shop in Ottawa. Then I was in some old section of the Manor." Opening his eyes he stared at Melrose, stopping him in place.

"The North Tower."

"The North Tower?"

"That's where you entered the Manor. It's forbidden for anyone other than members of the Hunt to enter."

"Why is that? What goes on in there?"

"It's supposed to be secret, but I like to stay informed," Melrose replied, gently touching his nose knowingly. "From what I've discovered, the Hunt uses the portals within the North Tower to travel to different hunting grounds."

The answer seemed too simple to Pierce, but he'd been though too much to think things through properly. He decided to curb his curiosity and surrender to his need for sleep.

"Well it's a starting place I suppose." With a yawn and stretch he continued, "You can leave now Melrose. I'm half drunk, all the way tired, and heading to bed."

"Very good sir."

*

The note left in her stall with instructions to see the Secretary that morning did not arouse any suspicion or anxiety in her. As a member of the Manor's private staff, she regularly met with the secretary. These meetings ranged from routine interviews to special requests. Her discretion and efficiency made her a regular recipient of these requirements. Jane accepted these requests and completed them with zeal, as they were a nice break from her otherwise monotonous duties.

Like the rest of the servants at the Manor, Jane was from the island. Her parents had scratched a living fishing in the nearby town of Rooks Bay, barely providing for Jane and her siblings. But unlike the rest of her family, Jane had not been satisfied with the simple but content lives they lived by the dark waters of the large lake. From the moment she first saw a Lord from the Hunt confidently strolling through town and heard about the Manor, she knew she wanted to be a part of it. Always a sly one, Jane wrangled herself a position as a chamber maid at the Manor when she turned thirteen. She simply showed up and started working. By the time anyone noticed, the head housekeeper decided to keep her on.

It was from that time on that Jane truly grew up, amid the intrigue and secrecy of the Manor. She was a skilled and diligent worker, but the real reason Jane quickly rose through the ranks of maids was her ambition and cunning. At fifteen she'd placed an expensive diamond ring in the room of a Hunt member at the behest of another. She never knew the reason or what resulted from the action, but she'd received an expensive present for her troubles. It slowly became unspoken knowledge that Jane was both capable and willing to assist Hunt members in their constant feuding with each other. She'd spy on members for the Hunt Secretary, spy on the Secretary for the members, and pass notes between all of them.

The fact she did not run afoul of anyone at the Manor in completing these secret tasks came down to three things; she worked hard as a maid, she never informed on her fellow servants, and she served all the Hunt members equally. Her loyalty was to her colleagues, the Manor, and to herself, but never to one single person in particular. Thus her usefulness outweighed anything negative she did in the eyes of the Lords and Ladies of the Manor. So she continued working and continued receiving special requests.

Sitting down to breakfast in the staffs' dining room, Jane noticed the other workers were alive with conversation. Normally breakfast was the quietest meal of the day. The efficient running of the Manor required that work commenced early. This in turn meant that the staff were awake, although not entirely alert, at early hours of the morning. Therefore the usual breakfast conversation was merely a collection of grunts, wheezes, and single worded questions and their direct responses.

Today, being Sunday, meant that everyone was able to begin the day a little later. Saturday nights at the Manor were often liquor-filled late nights for the members. Since this required more sleep than normal to recover from, many did not awaken till late morning. This enabled the staff to also indulge in some much needed sleep Sunday mornings. However the extra sleep was not enough of a reason to explain the cacophony of conversation swirling around the tables.

"He looked a proper worker in those clothes. Not very appropriate," declared one of the waiters disapprovingly.

"Yes indeed, leather jacket and boots. A proper hooligan," agreed one of the older housekeepers.

"Well I think he looked a proper rogue," countered a younger maid with a hint of admiration.

"A proper rogue is it? I should say so, but not in your way of meaning. Apparently he broke Mr. Drummond's nose with his fist!"

At the mention of the Manor's Secretary, Jane became more attentive to what was being said.

"I heard he also beat Morgan and Dufresne the night before!"

"What?" "Really?" "Barbaric!" exclaimed many of the staff eating their breakfast at various tables within the room.

"I heard from Geoffrey the doorman," continued one of the stable boys. "When they went to his house he went into a rage, pulled out a club and beat each one. They both had bumps and bruises on their heads when they came back last night."

Two of the groundskeepers nodded in appreciation of the supposed work done by the mysterious subject. Seeing this, the matron clucked their way reproachfully. Seizing a moment of quiet in the conversation, Jane waded in.

"Who is this horrible person?"

"Apparently he's a prospective member," answered a valet from behind her. Everyone turned to listen to the newly entered member of the staff. "He seems a bit young to be a member, but you never can tell. However I wouldn't believe these stories of brutality. From what I saw of him, he's not terribly large nor imposing."

"And clearly not a gentleman," chimed in the waiter.

"Clearly. From what little I heard from his speech, I'd say he's an American."

"Like the Colonel?" inquired a stableboy.

"I should say not. More northern than the Colonel I think, which should prove amusing."

"Do you know his name?" pushed Jane, hoping to sound indifferent.

"It's odd. Mr. Drummond was furious upon returning to the Manor. He exclaimed that the man couldn't be *Commandant Pierce*. So either he's not the commandant, or something has gone wrong."

At the mention of the name, Jane's heart sank. That was the name on the letter she had moved during her night time mission. Had she been discovered? The letter containing her instructions had been written in Mr. Drummond's handwriting. Now she knew her impending interview with the Hunt Secretary was not routine and worthy of the rising anxiety she started to feel. Passing secrets between Hunt Members was one thing, but interfering with the recruiting process without the Secretary's knowledge was something completely different. If she was discovered, she'd be lucky to leave the Manor in one piece.

*

Jane finished her dusting of the library and looked over to the clock. The ancient grandfather clock chimed the quarter hour, unnecessarily reminding her she had to meet Mr. Drummond at half-past. She grabbed her supplies and exited the book-lined room, gliding down the halls to a staff stairwell. Like the numerous other stairwells reserved for the Manor's staff, the entrance was hidden in the corner of a stone alcove. Although not completely hidden, and by no means a secret passage, it nevertheless allowed the staff to appear and disappear almost magically to carry out the duties with the least amount of intrusion possible.

Once below stairs, Jane made her way to a storage room to deposit her supplies and more importantly, to compose herself. Technically she hadn't done anything wrong by delivering the letter to the dispatch box. She had been given an instruction and had followed it. Keeping this thought in mind and ignoring the particulars of the instruction, she set off for the secretary's office.

Jane found herself retracing the steps she had taken the past night. This time it was during the day and the halls were full of people, many of the servants coming and going on their own errands. Without being too obvious she examined the faces of her colleagues for signs of her impeding chastisement. None seemed to pay any extra attention to her than was normal.

The secretary's office was at the entrance to the North tower, though still part of the main building. It acted as the gatehouse to the tower, used exclusively by the members of the Hunt. The hallway was lined with windowed office space, used by the secretary's minions. Although nominally part of the staff, Jane always felt they acted above their position. Therefore with haste she passed the gauntlet of peering office workers to the Secretary's office.

The office took up two floors; the bottom was an anteroom that accessed the servants' floor, and the top served as the office, accessible to the members on the main floor. In this way, the Secretary's office was the neutral part of the Manor, accessible to staff and members alike. The sole passage to the North Tower was by an enclosed stone bridge that started just outside the Secretary's office.

Jane entered the office anteroom at the bottom level. She was surprised to see that the Secretary's assistant was not at his desk as usual. As far as any of the staff at the Manor were concerned Mr. Drummond's assistant lived at his desk. Undeterred and without reservation she headed toward the iron circular staircase that led to the second level. When she reached it she heard voices coming from above, though the words were muted and incomprehensible. Thinking that Drummond was merely passing along instructions to his assistant, Jane started up the steps.

After taking three slow steps, Jane got closer to the opening to the second level. The voices were now completely audible and one of them clearly did not belong to Mr. Drummond's assistant.

"I hope you will accept my apology. I won't pretend that hitting you was an accident, but I regret it in retrospect."

"No apology is necessary sir," replied Mr. Drummond with as much deference as he could muster. "Tempers will flare from time to time."

"I suppose I get agitated when I discover I've been poisoned."

"Yes well, hmph…"

Realizing that the subject of the mornings' gossip was upstairs, Jane quietly moved up the stairs, hoping to catch a glimpse of him.

"Well if that is all sir…" continued Drummond, hoping that it was, when he saw a head and pair of eyes from the staircase behind his guest. Before she could lower her head, the mysterious newcomer turned around to see the object of Mr. Drummond's attention.

Rogue was not the word she'd use to describe the man before her. She couldn't even come up with a word to describe him. He was a blank; medium height, medium build, light brown hair, and nothing too distinguishable. His immediate expression of surprise at her appearance was quickly replaced by indifference. Though he didn't seem to outwardly pose a danger, there was something about his blankness that troubled and intrigued her. Most of the Hunt Members were anything but bland, some almost cartoonish, making them easy for her to read and determine their motives. But her quick examination of this Commandant Pierce gave her little to go on. His body language and his voice were as neutral as his appearance. But then she looked at his eyes and she became more uncertain about him. *He's intelligent and he's examining me just as thoroughly as I'm examining him.*

"Ahh, Jane," said Mr. Drummond, "I haven't forgotten our appointment." Then looking to the man and motioning towards the door, "if there is nothing else sir…"

"No… I… Yes, I'll…" He replied awkwardly looking from Drummond to Jane then the door. He turned towards the door to leave, narrowly missing a vase on a side table.

"Now to business my dear. Please take a seat. We have a few things to discuss."

Closing the door behind him, Pierce looked down and cursed his feet. Place him in a fencing match and he turned quick, athletic, and even graceful. But put him in the company of an attractive woman and he could barely take two steps without stumbling into something. He'd been at the Manor for less than twenty four hours, but he hadn't magically transformed into a suave gentleman.

A grumbling from his stomach reminded Pierce that it was close to lunchtime. Deciding to clean up before the meal, he headed back towards his rooms. He tried to take the same route that had carried him to the Secretary's office that morning. From what little he'd seen of the Manor, it was a huge labyrinthine building. Castle would be a much more apt description than manor.

Down a long portrait lined gallery, right along a columned hallway, and finally out to the Main Hall. He took a large set of stairs down, once more marvelling at the size and majesty of the hall. Huge stone columns rose from the marble floor holding up a massive domed ceiling, its carved figures staring down at the mosaic designs on the floor below.

He walked across the main floor, his new shoes silent against the hard stone. This made him reflect on the silence of the hall and building as a whole. He was currently the only one present in a hall as big as a train station. He whistled a short tune, the sound and its echo slicing through the air. He fought the urge to yodel and thoroughly disrupt the peaceful atmosphere.

Glancing to his left he appraised the large main door. A behemoth of wood and iron, he could picture it being assaulted by a battering ram and mail clad intruders. There was something truly medieval and historic about the building, an air of past inhabitants flowed through it. Maybe it was haunted?

He shook his head clear of these flights of fancy. Pierce continued to another staircase on the opposite side of the hall, the twin to the one he had just descended. Retracing his earlier steps, he made his way back along galleries, staircases, and halls to his rooms.

From what he could tell, his apartment was isolated from the other members. He had yet to pass another door with a brass plaque on it. His rooms consisted of a single floor within one of the Manor's many towers. Entering inside he immediately found himself in the foyer, which then led into a comfortable lounge. This held a large stone fireplace, surrounded by leather club chairs. Paintings and tapestries depicting events in history adorned the walls. An arched opening led to his more private rooms; a well stocked office, a dressing room, and a bedroom. All of these areas were equally decorated and furnished in a rich though utilitarian fashion. And it's all mine, he thought with a growing smile.

Pierce kept wondering why he'd been recruited and what they really wanted from him. Nobody just hands you a new luxurious life out of nowhere just for being yourself. The whole ordeal had been a confusing whirlwind so far. But taking in the obvious richness of his environment, Pierce decided to just go with it. He would stay alert to everything, but he'd try and look as though he were a willing participant and follow along. It would actually be pretty easy, since that was how he usually dealt with things; he kept his head down, blended in, and brought as little notice to himself as possible.

Chapter 4

Pierce had actually taken his first step in blending in to life at the Manor earlier that morning. He knew that he couldn't afford to make any new enemies, especially if some unknown ones already existed and were the reason for his presence here.

Thus, after breakfast Pierce had travelled to Mr. Drummond's office for a quick apology. Pierce didn't feel bad about breaking his nose in the least. However, he felt it was best to try and get on Mr. Drummonds good side. Although sometimes ignorant in interpersonal situations, Pierce could nevertheless always perceive where power lay. From what he could tell Drummond held an inordinate amount of power for the position he held.

Reminiscing on one of the plush leather chairs in his lounge, he could not help but feel his morning trip had been futile. The look on Drummond's face during his apology would have done a poker player proud. He didn't flinch, smile, or sneer. The stony veneer had only slipped after the appearance of the girl.

That Girl. Drummond had called her Jane and despite her uniform she'd seemed like more than just a simple maid. She had been a welcome change after spending a solid five minutes with Drummond. She was a black haired beauty with clever eyes that had scanned him with more than just passing curiosity. Maybe he'd try and track her down in the afternoon if he didn't end up drugged again.

Pierce's reveries were broken by a small cough from behind him, followed immediately by the crisp voice of his valet.

"Sir, the members are still out on a hunt. Shall I bring your lunch up and serve it in your office?"

"Sure. I think it would be pretty awkward eating lunch in a giant room by myself. But I suppose I can't just grab a sandwich from the kitchen, can I?""

"No sir, that simply wouldn't do. I'll ring the kitchen and your meal should be up momentarily."

After a quick wash in his bathroom, Pierce made his way across the hall into his private office. Sitting in the leather office chair, he swivelled back and forth, taking in the room for the first time. In front of him was a massive cherry desk; its size seemed to double by the absence of anything on it. There was a collection of well-stocked bookcases surrounding the room, each adorned with a bust of the world's great thinkers. The windows were large floor-to-ceiling affairs that provided the same view that he had witnessed in the early morning. Apart from that, it was the same type of office one might find in any number of great houses spread across Europe. Much more elegant and rich than anything he was used to.

Eyeing the window once more, Pierce moved over to it to see the offered view. If the idea of escaping through the window with a collection of bed sheets tied together like a rope had ever been in his mind, the view before him dispelled it immediately. By his reckoning the window was easily forty feet above the ground below. The height his window provided actually made the view more spectacular than the one he had witnessed earlier. The hills seemed to roll more, the mountain peaks were closer and jagged, and the lake was larger and darker. Looking closer he thought he could see a collection of buildings in a bay off the lake.

Seeing Melrose enter into the room from the corner of his eye, he decided to inquire about it.

"Melrose, am I seeing things or is that a village down by the bay?"

"You have a good eye sir, that's Rooks Bay," he replied placing the tray of food on the desk. Then coming up beside Pierce he continued, "I grew up there. It was quite pleasant." Then he added while motioning toward the tray on the desk, "lunch sir?"

"Yes of course," he said, turning slowly from the window. Despite having lived a very middle class life until now, Pierce found that he was not opposed to some of these new luxuries. Smiling, he returned to the large desk in his new office, rubbing his hands together hungrily. "So what have they made for lunch?"

Pierce buttered the second half of the roll and ate it with slow deliberation. The bowl of stew had been delicious, filling, and was completely gone. The rolls had been an unnecessary addition, but they were also too good to ignore. Finished with lunch he leaned back into his chair in contentment.

After a quick knock at the door Melrose entered the office.

"How did you know I was done eating?" Then looking around in mock suspicion, "there aren't any cameras in here, are there?"

"Cameras sir?" Melrose responded with sincere confusion at the word. "No sir, although since you are done, I will take the tray. I came in to inform you that you have a visitor." With that he covered the tray and exited with precision.

As Melrose exited a new gentleman appeared through the doorway.

The man who entered looked completely at home in this environment. He could have just stepped out of a thirties British drama. He was dressed in a perfectly cut tweed suit, with the necessary mustache and parted hair for the role. He was roughly the same size as Pierce, but nearly twenty years older. When he spoke, his upper class English accent did not disappoint.

"Good day Mr. Pierce. I see you've settled in to your rooms and trust you've been made comfortable. I imagine you've had a whirlwind of a weekend."

"To say the least," then rising to shake hands with his visitor, "and you are?"

"Of course, where are my manners," taking the offered hand he continued. "My name is Dr. John Cleaver, Master of the Hunt here at Ravenwood. I'm also the acting Master of the Manor at present, as the current Master, Lord Victor Lodge, is convalescing in his own rooms for much needed rest and solitude. So if you have any special requests or requirements, feel free to ask either Mr. Drummond or myself."

"I can't think of anything at the moment. I'm still trying to get my bearings."

"That is entirely understandable."

"I've got a few questions."

"I'll try and answer them to the best of my ability."

The Doctor seemed pleasant, and more forthright than Mr. Drummond. However there seemed to be an indecipherable quality about him that Pierce did not entirely trust.

"Where exactly are we? Ravenwood Manor appears to be in the country; however, I got here through a hallway in an Ottawa apartment. That's impossible."

"Not impossible, merely improbable." Looking around the office, the Doctor found what he was looking for at the liquor cabinet. "Things might be easier explained with a small drink."

He moved to the liquor cabinet and removed a strange black bottle with a raven on it. There were at least two other bottles like it on the shelf. From the shelf below he grabbed two glasses and returned to the desk, pulling up a chair for himself.

"The water of life," he toasted after pouring two small drinks.

"Slainte."

"The Manor seems to be, inexplicably, in a different step than the rest of the world. I'm not sure what you have heard but people do not age normally here."

"What about the village down below?"

"There and everywhere else on the island."

"We're on an island?"

"Yes, although it's quite large. There are many villages and towns scattered throughout the island."

"So where is this island? It looks like we're in Scotland or something."

"Something is about as accurate as you can be, as we have no idea. Some time ago people left to find the mainland, but never returned."

A hint of caution came with this last statement. Pierce felt as though any further searches would be equally unsuccessful. The Doctor seemed in no rush of finding the mainland, or the mainland finding them.

"So we don't know where we are. Is it still the same date as when I left?"

"I rather doubt it. We seem to have a different timeline than the rest of the world."

"But how can you know that if you're not in contact with the rest of the world?" Pierce asked in confusion. The more he tried to decipher the mechanics of this place, the more he found himself running in mental circles. His mind told him that what he was experiencing was impossible, but the whiskey flowing down his throat seemed to disprove this.

"We are in contact, just not as you might think. It's the way that we are in contact with the rest of the world that we know our timeline differs. How do you think we picked you up and brought you back here?"

"Honestly, I have no idea."

*

"So each doorway in the halls of the North Tower is a

gateway to another time and place?"

"Not quite. The gateway is held within the room beyond each hallway door. You might remember that you entered a stone room, then up some stairs before you passed through a door into the hallway."

"Yes, that's right."

Pierce and Dr. Cleaver had left his office and were now walking along a path that led from the Manor to the village of Rooks Bay. Dr. Cleaver had suggested that they take some air while Pierce attempted to come to terms with the strange circumstances of his current situation. The gravel beneath their feet crunched as they spoke.

"So if I were to go through the doorway I entered last night, I would find myself in the same room as before?"

"Right after you had exited. Almost as if you walked in to a closet, turned around and left immediately."

"That's incredible."

"Just so."

They continued walking in silence. Dr. Cleaver believed the silence was due to Pierce's attempt to reconcile this incredible development. However Pierce was really looking at his way back home. If he could get back to the North Tower and remember which door he had come in from, he could make it back to Ottawa, like nothing had happened. That was if the Doctor was telling the truth.

"So where do you come from?" Pierce asked, attempting to deflect any potential suspicion arising in Cleaver's mind from his silence.

"I remember the time and place exactly. It was a stormy day in London, Seventeenth of November, 1888."

"So if you returned through your door, it would take you back to that exact date?"

"Not quite. It would take me back to the date the portal was last used. I've gone back many times since then."

"So I could go back?" he uttered too quickly. Before he could try and mask his true meaning the Doctor replied.

"You can and will, the Manor isn't a prison," Cleaver

laughed as his hands displayed the horizon. "But why would you want to leave this place? This is your new home."

"It's just a bit of a shock," Pierce replied with a slight shake of his head. But at that moment he felt more worry than shock. In the back of his mind he remembered a quote that said the best prison was one which the inmates didn't know they were in.

"Of course everyone feels that way when they arrive," Cleaver continued, oblivious to Pierce's inner misgivings. "But they all end up staying in the end. Nobody leaves."

"Everyone? So there are others here from different times?"

"Of course. Members are recruited from locations throughout time; from America to Russia, and from the Middle Ages to the Twenty First century. You will meet them all in due time, as they are presently on a hunt."

They had made their way down the hillside and had reached the long dark lake. A roadway of similar gravel lay between them and the lakeshore. As they stood admiring the sunshine reflecting off the lake, a horse-drawn cart approached. It was loaded with wooden barrels, with an older man driving. He had a wide honest face, bulbous nose, and the slight hunch of a working man. A boy with undoubtedly the same ancestry was perched on the topmost barrel. Seeing the two distinguished men on the side of the road, the old man slowed down, lifted the brim of his cap and uttered a quick *m'lord*. The cart resumed its speed after passing, heading towards the village.

"I have some business to conduct in the village, if you care to join me," offered Cleaver. "I am meeting someone at the pub. The ale is quite good; however I cannot provide the pies with a similar endorsement."

Nodding in assent Pierce fell into step with the Doctor as they leisurely followed the road to Rooks Bay. As he walked along the lakeshore, he was surprised at the size of the lake. He could barely see the other shore and the sails of the numerous fishing vessels appeared like flecks on the horizon.

The village of Rooks Bay was similarly altered as they drew near. What first appeared to be a scattering of buildings from his office window, transformed into a busy market town upon passing the first set of cottages. The docks were full of activity as fishing boats disgorged their nautical harvest or departed with baited lines. The streets bustled with movement as handcarts, wagons, people, and their animals jockeyed for position on the cobblestones.

Pierce had the immediate feeling he'd walked back in time to Victorian England, which he supposed was possibly true. The stone buildings were both charming and sad; owing to the combination of their simplicity and weather beaten facades. No electrical or telephone cables ran from poles to the houses and no gas engines could be heard or seen. Similarly none of the townsfolk were glued to cell phones or listening to any modern music devices. They were all dressed in wools and cottons, with black and grey being the dominant colours. It was all he could do to refrain from poking them to make sure they were real.

Despite the seeming chaos of the scene, Pierce and Dr. Cleaver were able to maintain their pace and proceed without incident. In fact the townspeople seemed to part ways for the pair naturally. They neither rushed nor stopped completely for the distinguished pair; however Pierce could tell they were making an effort to stay out of their way.

"The townsfolk have always treated us with deference when we descend from the Manor," whispered Dr. Cleaver smugly, sensing Pierces curiosity. "As they should, of course. We have provided them with much from our travels that they would not ordinarily have. I do appreciate it when people show respect to their betters." Although this seemed to be pointed towards the townspeople, Pierce sensed the warning and that he too was included in this group.

Within minutes they reached the heart of the village, where a nondescript fountain dominated a square surrounded by three storied grey stoned buildings. Their destination was on the other side of the square, forcing them to pass a group of children splashing in the pool. The children immediately stopped upon their approach, but instead of the respect and deference showed by the adults of the village, the children were cowed and ill at ease. They ceased their games and the younger ones hide behind their older peers. Pierce could feel their suspicious and wary eyes on his back as he passed, prompting a shiver of his own.

"Ahh, the *Fish and the Feather*," remarked Cleaver as they reached the pub, oblivious to the effect they'd had upon the children.

Pierce looked up at the pub's sign as it swung under the pressure of the afternoon's breeze. Along with the name of the pub, the sign was also emblazoned with the picture of a fish fighting with a feathered fly-fishing line. The sign and the name carved upon it seemed very fitting to Pierce as he made his way into the pub. The walls were adorned with various prized catches and the lures responsible. The pub itself had the customary heavy wood bar in front of a large mirrored wall filled with glasses of various shapes and sizes. There were wooden chairs and square tables in the center surrounded by benches and large tables along the walls. They all had the worn look that only comes with age and regular use, a characteristic shared by the few customers within. They had clearly worked hard during their lives and were now content to spend their remaining years with a pint in their hand.

"Good afternoon my Lord, you are expected. Your appointment is waiting upstairs for you," a soft voice said from behind Pierce while he took in the room. Turning around he found himself facing the beguiling Jane from Drummond's office. She in turn was wide eyed with surprise by his appearance beside Dr. Cleaver.

"Jane, have you met Mr. Pierce?" Asked Cleaver casually, despite the recognition he sensed between the two younger people. "He is the newest member of the Hunt. So new in fact, that this is his first visit to this establishment."

"Is that so sir? Then I shall show him to the Manor's reserved seats."

"Very well. You may bring me up a whiskey when you're

finished."

Without speaking she led Pierce to a secluded snug at the back corner of the pub. Its dark oak half walls were ornately carved and had a small door with a frosted glass window with the Hunt's coat of arms etched in. Leaning over the half wall Pierce took in a completely different scene than that of the rest of the pub. In place of the worn wooden furniture there were two marble topped tables with bronzed legs, one sitting between a plush cushioned booth and the second surrounded by high backed leather chairs. The floor inside the snug was the same as the rest of the pub, but was highly polished and devoid of any dirt or dust.

"So this is how the other half lives," muttered Pierce under his breath, then immediately feeling guilty as Jane waited for him to enter. He was now the other half.

Dr. Cleaver stood with his hands clasped behind his back, staring coldly through the window overlooking Rook's Bay as Jane entered with his glass of whiskey.

"I can't be sure, but somehow he was able to effect this recruitment during my brief absence. I have questioned Drummond and while his honesty can be lacking, so too is his cunning. He is ruthless and cruel, but only like a child playing with insects, giggling as he burns them with a magnifying glass. When dealing with superiors he is cowed like the small man he is. It's actually one of his better qualities." Dr. Cleaver mused over the problem sitting in the pub below.

Jane knew better than interrupt him when he was in one of his dark moods, so she merely stood silently beside him. Her anxiety from the morning turned to pure fear as she felt the growing anger emanating from Dr, Cleaver. If she wanted to get through this unharmed she'd have to keep her composure and be as helpful as she could. She'd always been careful to never work against Lord Cleaver and she had no intention of starting now. Plus if she were able to assist him in resolving this issue without her part becoming known, the rewards could be very impressive indeed.

"Clearly he was able to persuade one of the servants to aid him in this, and Drummond followed protocol like the mindless bureaucrat that he is. Don't you agree Jane?" He asked as he turned to face her, accepting the glass of spirits on her tray.

"It seems like the best possibility. Shall I discreetly question the servants for you? If we can find his accomplice…" Cleaver cut her off with a sharp wave of his hand.

"It is too late for that. Most of the servants have even less guile and I don't believe any of them are truly in league with *him*. They undoubtedly assisted him without knowing his mind. If he can get the help of one of the servants while locked away in the Manor, then he will surely coerce others for similarly small tasks. The problem is that when added up these small tasks could have monumental consequences."

"Then he cannot be left in the Manor," offered Jane shrewdly. "That is why I am back at this Pub is it not, my Lord?"

Cleaver appraised the maid and felt confident in his choice of accomplice. Here was a woman equally gifted with beauty and cleverness, a very useful ally indeed. However he did not wish to reveal his confidence in her with praise. Better to leave her feeling off balance.

"Of course that's why you're here," he exhaled with feigned exasperation. "My men will conduct the transfer tonight under the cover of darkness and bring him to the room on the top floor. They shall enter in by the back door, so you must ensure it is open so as not to arouse unnecessary suspicion. He shall have no contact with anyone save yourself and my men. No one is to know of his existence in this place." With this final proclamation he drained his glass and started towards the door, only to stop upon reaching for the handle.

"There is another thing. The anomaly sitting downstairs that could unravel everything."

"He doesn't seem like a threat."

"That's precisely the problem. He doesn't seem like anything. He has the appearance of a soft, reserved young man. However he bested two of the Hounds without a weapon. He is an unknown quantity and that makes me apprehensive. I feel confident in my ability to predict the actions and motives of the rest the Hunt. I have researched and lived with each and every one of them for some time." He was now pacing the length of the room, airing his dilemma in its entirety. "But this Pierce, he was recruited too soon. Our files on him are incomplete; he should be another 15 years older! Instead of the heartless official with blood on his hands we have a young man without even a parking ticket to his name."

"Shall I look into his character for you?"

"Yes. Please do, but nothing too conspicuous." Dr. Cleaver had now recovered from his brief lack of composure. "But you must be mindful of the fact that he was brought here for a reason. We do not know his true purpose, perhaps he doesn't either."

"Perhaps you could devise a test of some sort," offered Jane thoughtfully, eager to show her usefulness. "You might be able to discover his intentions if not his direct motivation."

"Your thought intrigues me, pray continue."

"The next excursion is placed under the control of Pierce and some other members of the Hunt. But they return to his time," She explained slowly, the plan still forming in her mind. "If he is conscious of the reason he was recruited, he will undoubtedly return to the Manor when the excursion is complete."

"Go on," Cleaver ordered.

"However if he is truly here by mistake or does not know the reason for his presence at the Manor, he might make use of the opportunity to return to his home."

Dr. Cleaver recommenced his pacing, however this time at a pace more suitable for analytical thinking rather than airing dissatisfaction. Jane silently watched his procession from the corner of the room. His face was the picture of concentration; brows furrowed, a steely stare beyond the room, a twitching frown upon his face, and again his hands clasped tightly behind his back.

When he stopped pacing he released his hands and turned toward Jane with deliberation. His eyes focused on her and his frown relented momentarily.

"Very well, I shall implement your proposal. Meanwhile you shall seek him out and discover the reason for his presence amongst us."

Jane nodded in agreement then hesitantly enquired, "what happens if he returns from the excursion?"

"Leave that to me, my dear," he responded as a sly look crept upon his face. "He will find more obstacles in front of him if he dares return.

"I'm going back to the Manor, but I don't feel like having him trail behind me like a lost dog. Please make some excuse and entertain him. I'll leave out the back." He turned and slowly walked towards the door, stopping briefly to inspect himself in front of a mirror. From the reflection he looked at Jane behind him, the slyness replaced by a hard and dangerous veneer.

Chapter 5

Pierce was able to make his retreat along the hallway and down the stairs before Dr. Cleaver opened the door. He quickly sat back down in the Manor's reserved snug ready to act as nonchalant as he could. However the Doctor did not appear. Pierce waited a few more minutes, fighting the urge to see what was keeping him.

He took another drink of his ale, trying to calm himself and slow his racing mind. It was swirling from the information he had overheard. He had felt an immediate curiosity for Dr. Cleaver at his first appearance and their subsequent walk to the village. That curiosity turned to suspicion when the doctor had mentioned a meeting in town. Surely he was the type of man that had people visit him, especially in the grandeur of the Manor where he could project his superiority and make a mental impact on his guest. So when the meeting turned out to be taking place in the secluded upstairs room of a pub, he had decided to find out more.

Despite being both an outsider and a new member of the Manor, Pierce had found no difficulty in quietly slipping away from his place in the pub and following Jane up to the meeting place.

That girl again, he thought. She had seemed many things during their previously brief encounters, but never the devious underling that he had just overheard. At first he had felt ashamed creeping up to the closed door to eavesdrop on the interview. That feeling immediately changed when it became obvious that the meeting was between Jane and the Doctor. But he had only been able to hear the sound of voices at first, followed by their discussion about him when Cleaver had been beside the door, then muffled voices again.

From the time he had arrived at the Manor, Pierce's only thought had been to get back home. But after overhearing their plans, he wasn't convinced such drastic action was in his best interest. There were obviously powerful forces at work trying to both keep him here and get rid of him. Crossing one group might be just as harmful to him as crossing the other. The best thing to do was to stay vigilant and get a complete appreciation of his situation. To do that he'd stick with his plan of going along with whatever was presented to him while he tried to figure things out.

With that decided he finished off his drink and prepared to leave. But blocking his exit was Jane holding a pair of drinks.

"I hope this isn't too forward sir, but I took the liberty of pouring you another drink and thought I could join you. I imagine you're still feeling a little lost and maybe a friendly face could help you out." She beamed a smile at Pierce that made him doubt the conversation he had just heard.

"Yes. I mean of course. You can sit and join me I mean," he replied with his usual sophisticated banter. "But please call me Patrick if that's easier. I don't think I could stand being called sir. I don't even know what I'm doing here."

"Well you've been awarded a great honour. The Hunt has very few members and it's very exclusive. People around these parts have always called the Hunt members lord or lady."

"Well don't let the clothing fool you, I'm no duke or anything," he said taking a drink.

"So what are you planning on doing?" She enquired taking a sip of her own drink.

Pierce was shocked by the quickness and subtlety of the question. The sincerity of her voice made him almost believe the question was asked benevolently. Had he not overheard the conversation of a few minutes ago he would surely answered truthfully.

"Well, can I tell you a secret?" he asked hesitantly. "I'm planning on leaving as soon as the first chance comes up. I was kidnapped and brought here against my will. I'm sure everyone around here is very nice, but I'm a little freaked out. Plus I heard something about poison…"

"Yes, the poison story," she said leaning back slightly, attempting to convey a sense of openness. "I can tell you it's nothing but a foolish tale and I don't believe a word of it. I have worked for many years at the Manor and I've never heard the members speak of it with anything other than contempt or humour."

"Yes, but what is the story?"

"Well, like any tale, there are many versions of it. One says that to maintain the loyalty of the Hunt, the Master poisons each new recruit and hides the antidote, providing it only at designated times. Another one is that the island itself poisons those who live here in exchange for long life. If you leave the island your life is halved and cursed."

"From everything I've seen so far, it doesn't sound that far fetched," voiced Pierce. However Jane was now fully engrossed in her recounting of the many poison tales.

"But the best one is that the poison is actually a vampiric bite and the members are all vampires. The antidote is of course blood and they must travel through portals to feed on people in the outside world. One of the parlour maids really believed this and tried to convince the rest of the staff. But the Manor is full of mirrors, the cutlery all silver, and garlic is a regular ingredient in their meals. Silly girl."

"Drummond himself told me I had been poisoned. That's why I punched him."

"Sounds like a bluff to me. Why would they poison someone they just recruited? It makes no sense."

"I guess that's fair. Well if I make it back home and die of poisoning I'll blame you."

"But I didn't... I wouldn't... Ah you're joking," she recovered awkwardly.

"Sorry, I guess it wasn't that funny." They both sat quietly sipping at their drinks, then Jane started to chuckle and had to put hers down.

"It really wasn't that funny, you don't have to laugh," Pierce said self-deprecatingly.

"Oh I'm not laughing at your joke," she replied still chuckling. "I'm thinking of how you punched Mr. Drummond. I had a meeting with him afterwards. He was trying to be serious and conduct himself in his usual condescending fashion, but his nose was taped and is eyes were bruised up." The chuckle started to turn to regular laughter. "He looked like a raccoon that had been caught in a trash bin and whipped for it."

Remembering his own meeting with Drummond where he had offered his insincere apology, Pierce thought the description apt and started laughing himself.

They continued to share similarly humorous stories as they finished their drinks. When both glasses sat empty upon the table, Jane stood up and collected them.

"Well, my break is over. I had better get back to work; the evening rush will soon be here. And if you don't hurry you'll be walking up to the Manor in the dark."

Pierce turned and looked out the window and saw that dusk was indeed fast approaching.

"Will you be here if I wanted to visit you again?" inquired Pierce, losing the timidity that would ordinarily silence him. He remembered watching many film noires where the hard boiled detective falls for the femme fatale, despite knowing she's up to no good. He'd always thought it a Hollywood contrivance and that no man with a half a brain would act that way. Until now.

"I'd like that," she replied quickly, forgetting the cool reserve she needed to employ. In order to cover the slight slip she turned towards the bar to drop off the empty glasses and continue her work.

*

The sound was like an explosion and simultaneously a loud thump emanated from a tree as a branch shattered near him. Pierce immediately dropped to the ground like a heavy sac, his body rigid in shock. His wide eyes darted around the area as he looked for danger. Dusk had fallen and a mist was forming, hiding the smoke that would tell him from where the sound originated. Was someone trying to shoot him? It hadn't sounded like a gunshot, but his only experience with guns was from television, which couldn't be used as a baseline. To his left he heard footsteps approaching, so he covered his head with his arms in meager defence.

"Sir, it appears that you have killed one of the villagers," stated a calm and passionless voice, "again".

"Damn, what in the hell was he doing this far from the village," replied a more passionate voice with a southern accent. This same voice continued but much louder and in the opposite direction. "You're lucky this time Willy! This should have been you!"

More footsteps approached and Pierce could feel that a group was starting to gather near him.

"If you were to kill me Colonel," replied a cool voice, "who would you duel with?"

"Hmph. Bunch of no-good, honourless…" The voiced started to trail off as it moved away.

Sensing that he probably wasn't in too much danger, Pierce removed his arms from around his head and looked up. The motion made a man beside the wounded tree immediately look down at him.

"Not dead sir!" he exclaimed and Pierce recognized the first voice he heard.

"Not dead indeed," replied the voice he associated with Willy.

Standing up slowly, Pierce started to take stock of his surroundings and the people filling it. Beside the tree a man was prying something out of it with a metal tool. Just to his left a much larger man stood motionless. Upon closer examination Pierce thought they were wearing the same outfits as the men who attacked him in his Ottawa apartment. They must be from the Manor, he reasoned.

"What the hell are you doing breaking up a duel boy?" questioned a man quickly approaching from behind the two near the tree. "Willy!" he shouted in Pierce's direction, making him look backwards at the man who must be Willy. "Willy, this ragamuffin's appearance disqualifies the duel. I demand we restart!"

"It's late Colonel, very close to dinner," Willy replied with a yawn and a shrug. "Perhaps we can reconvene tomorrow?"

"Very well, but my honour will not stand a longer delay." Turning towards Pierce, he regained some of his fierceness. "So just who the hell are you? You're a long way from the village boy."

"I'm a long way from the village," Pierce replied equaling the Colonel's tone, "because I live here. My name's Pierce." Then taking in the Colonel's attire; a light grey suit, white shirt, and a black string tie he continued. "And you appear to be Colonel Sanders."

The Colonel immediately changed his demeanor, but instead of becoming more furious, he turned genial. Pierce decided he was the type to bluster and berate servants for the smallest infraction, but allowed more latitude to his peers.

"I'm afraid you've mistaken me for someone else. My name is Colonel Buford, from Georgia. Where was this Colonel Sanders from?"

"Kentucky," deadpanned Pierce, wondering if anyone understood the comparison.

"I served with many Kentuckians, but never a Sanders. Good riflemen those lads, but much better horses. I had a horse named Spirit that was raised in Kentucky…"

"I have found it sir," interrupted the servant by the tree, displaying a set of large tweezers presumably holding the fired bullet. The Colonel walked over to him to inspect it, continuing his story of the majestic and unequalled horse.

"You'll have to excuse the Colonel," offered Willy as he approached to stand beside Pierce, "he's a lunatic."

"Why would you have a duel with a lunatic?"

"Because he's a lunatic with crooked dueling pistols. The safest place to be when those monsters are loaded is directly in front of them." Extending his hand he introduced himself, "I'm Wilhelm Schell. Please don't call me Willy, I allow the Colonel to because…"

"He's a lunatic?" added Pierce with a raised eyebrow.

"Because he'd continue to call me that even if I corrected him," replied Schell with a smile. He motioned Pierce to join him on the walk back to the Manor as they followed the Colonel and his man across the clearing.

The group made their journey through an impressive arboretum in the failing light of dusk. Enormous trees dotted the vast grassy expanse surrounding them. Their path seemed to consistently meander up a slight grade, though the going was not so difficult that they couldn't speak to one another. Noting his name, his straw haired and blue eyed Nordic appearance, Pierce enquired on his origins. Schell acquiesced and told him he descended from an old Prussian family and had grown up outside Berlin. Pierce explained that he had just arrived at the Manor from Ottawa, where he had grown up. Overhearing the two, the Colonel jumped in with his own questions.

"I've never heard of Ottawa myself, but from the sounds of you I'd say it's from the North. You're not a Yankee are you?" He eyed Pierce narrowly, awaiting the response.

"Canadian, actually."

"Canadian? Well that's nearly the same thing as a Yankee."

"I'll grant you there are similarities," accepted Pierce with sarcastic graciousness, "much like a Texan and a Georgian are nearly the same."

"Exactly," agreed the Colonel too quickly. "No, wait… That's not what I…" He trailed off knowing his argument was lost and decided to abandon it to another diatribe on Canada. An old neighbour of his had lost a handful of slaves that had jumped on some mysterious train to Canada.

"Apparently the tracks ran underground, but damned if we could find them anywhere. You'd think that the construction of an underground railroad would have left more of a trace…"

Pierce looked over to the shrugging Schell. "The Colonel's a very literal man."

"…Piracy, that's what it, was. Simply stealing property is what they were doing. Stealing it and storing it in Canada out of the owners reach. You were lucky we were fighting a war, or we would have marched straight up to Canada and brought back what was ours." He finished the speech pointing accusingly at Pierce.

"Never fear Colonel, the South will rise again," replied Pierce, unable to help himself.

The Colonel seemed to calm down and a mischievous grin spread across his face. He was no longer a wound up toy soldier, bouncing from one subject to another. He emanated the silent power of a confident leader, one born from the carnage and chaos of battle.

"How very prophetic Mr. Pierce. I agree with you and plan to see that day myself."

*

The scotch from the raven emblazoned black bottle was sharp, smoky, and the best he'd ever tasted. Melrose had insisted on pouring him one upon returning to his lounge after dinner. The meal had been pleasant and shared in companionable silence with Schell. Buford was absent and the other members of the Hunt had already eaten, apparently unwilling to wait for the duelists to return. Pierce was glad he had run into the duel, allowing him to finally meet some of the other residents of the Manor. Watching Melrose add another log to the fire, Pierce asked what he knew of the two men he had just encountered.

"Not very much I'm afraid," he replied honestly. "The Colonel is American, from Georgia as you must have discovered. He was rich, though not aristocratic, I should say. However he either lost it all or was about to lose it before he was recruited here. It was due to a war he fought in, one which I believe his side was losing. I imagine that is why he's so temperamental and quick to anger."

"Still upset over the past, believes he was cheated, can't take revenge on those responsible…"

"Just so sir. However the German master…"

"Schell?"

"Yes sir, Schell," continued Melrose, "he has a very similar past as the Colonel, but is very different."

"I had noticed."

"He is also from a rich family, although with slightly better lineage. He was also involved in a war, but not as a soldier I think. Again on the losing side, but he seems to have accepted it and his place at the Manor. He was the newest member before you arrived."

"Not a soldier, but he served in a war?"

"From what I understand sir."

"Has everyone here been recruited under the same circumstances? From the losing side of a war?"

"I don't think so, but I'm not entirely sure. What are you driving at sir?"

"I'm still trying to figure out why I'm here. I have no special talents, skills, or knowledge I'm aware of. So maybe I should look at it from another angle, the method in which I was brought here."

"You were not a willing recruit I take it?"

"Not at all," he snorted, "I was attacked, concussed, drugged, poisoned, drugged again, and then forcibly brought here. Meanwhile the others I've met seem to have been eager to join from what you've said."

"As far as I know sir."

"Exactly, they recruit members when they are vulnerable and see no other alternative. I on the other hand had no such problem. Why was I different…" he trailed off staring at the fire, his fingers drumming along the side of the crystal tumbler of scotch.

After a few minutes Melrose bent down to check if his charge had drifted off to sleep. He was incredibly still and unblinking.

"He said I was early," whispered Pierce, fully coherent. Due to his training Melrose straightened back up smoothly, despite being surprised.

"Early, sir?"

"That's what Drummond said when we first met. He said I was tapped early. I took it to mean he hadn't been waiting long or something like that. But what if he didn't mean that?"

"You mean that you were recruited too soon?"

"That's exactly what I mean," he said, quickly getting up from his seat and rushing into his dressing room. The sound of clothes and drawers being rummaged through emanated through the door, soon followed by Pierce. He held a white piece of paper that appeared to be an envelope.

"What is that sir?" enquired Melrose, now totally engrossed in the discussion.

"It's the envelope that contained my invitation to the recruitment meeting. I wasn't sure if I still had it, but it was wedged in the inside pocket of my old jacket." He enthusiastically thrusted it towards Melrose's incomprehensible face. "What does it say? Read it."

"Sir?"

"It's addressed to *Commandant Pierce*."

"Yes, I see that. But that's your name. I don't see how…"

"That's not my name," responded Pierce with exasperation to Melrose's quizzical look. "I have never been called Commandant in my entire life. I've only ever heard the word commandant a handful of times."

"Perhaps it is a case of mistaken identity?" offered Melrose weakly.

"Impossible. During the interview, Drummond had a file on me. It had information on me, my parents, my childhood…" He flopped back down into his chair and stared at the envelope. He reached for his glass of scotch to try and slow his mind and organize his thoughts.

"How did they, I presume we're dealing with more than one individual, recruit you early? I'm not entirely familiar with the process, but the Master of the Manor is very deliberate with the selection. There is much to be considered when dealing with changes to Time."

"The how is commonplace! A file moved from one pile to another, a slip of paper changing hands. But the why, that is where the heart of this lies. Why was I recruited early and to what purpose? Who stands to gain from my early appearance?" Now that he had finally stated aloud the questions that had been rebounding within his head, Pierce was able to think more clearly. "You may be right Melrose. We might have to look at the how in order to reach the why. Who can tell us about the recruiting process? If we can find out what's involved, we may be able to see who could have influenced the outcome. And that person should know why I'm here early."

"There might be a problem with obtaining that information," replied Melrose. "I assume that this must be looked into with the utmost discretion?"

"Of course. Apart from you, I don't trust anyone here" As he said this, Pierce watched Melrose straighten in pride.

"You may have complete confidence in me sir."

"I felt as much and truly believe it," replied Pierce feeling somewhat abashed. "So who else we can trust with this task? Is there anyone that can tell us what's entailed with recruitment?"

"Drummond cannot be trusted, nor his assistant," counted off Melrose on his fingers. "The Master of the Manor has locked himself away for the past few weeks. Then there's the Master of the Hunt, Dr. Cleaver. However I would caution making any inquiries directly to either of them."

"You have a good sense of judgment Melrose." Sensing his valet's confusion, Pierce explained the meeting at the Fish and the Feather, and the bits that he had been able to overhear. Melrose had a sudden crestfallen look on his face during the explanation. Pierce attributed it to his valet's disappointment in his ungentlemanly eavesdropping. Like Cleaver, he had found that the servants and residents of the island seemed to be stuck in the Victorian age. The technology, sensibilities, and pace of life from the bygone era seemed the norm here.

"I know I should have acted more appropriately…" he offered with an upheld hand.

"You mistake my reaction sir," Melrose interrupted. "I would never question your actions or motives, unless you were in the wrong sir."

"I'm glad to hear it, especially that last proviso."

"The problem sir is that Cleaver was meeting with Jane."

"I agree with you. I was shocked and disappointed as well. She seemed so nice…"

"I have always found that to be true."

"And I thought from our first brief encounters that she was interested in me. That I intrigued her."

"Naturally."

"But to find out she's actually trying to spy on me, well it's disappointing."

"I agree sir."

"So why did you look disappointed when I mentioned her meeting with Cleaver?"

"Because she was the other person I could think of to help us."

*

The rain had started after midnight; the wind had arrived an hour later, and the thunder and lightning were soon to follow. The ugly weather hurled itself at the tough stone buildings of Rooks Bay. The hardy folk of the town slept easily despite the storm, allowing a single figure to stand unobserved beneath the eaves of the Fish and Feather Pub.

Jane was cold, wet, and thoroughly upset. She had been standing outside for only fifteen minutes, but felt like she had just crawled out of the nearby lake. Her apprehension at not following the Doctor's orders to the letter was the only thing keeping here from returning to the warmth of the pub.

The sound of carriage wheels grabbed her attention and she turned to look down the back lane. A solid black carriage with a team of four equally black horses was making its way down the narrow passage. There were two men on the front plus another two on the back, though none of them wore the livery of a footman. They were all dressed in identically long black leather jackets.

"It's about time you arrived," she uttered as the carriage cam to a halt, "someone could have seen me."

"You needn't worry," responded a steely voice from within. "Although you look as though you're made of sugar, we both know you're not in danger of melting." The voice belonged to a tall dark figure emerging for the carriage. The flowing black jacket was similar to the drivers, but more ornate. His dark mass was completed by a long mane of black hair, curled mustache, and a black goatee that followed his jaw line into a prominent point. The gaze he affixed upon Jane was as equally hard as his voice.

"I was not informed that you would be taking part Malicio…" began Jane, clearly off guard.

"Surely you didn't believe the Master would place the success of this little operation in the hands of a maid?" retorted Malicio, cutting her off.

Regaining her composure, Jane lifted her head up and opened the back door to the pub. Malicio descended from the carriage and walked past her into the building. They were immediately followed by his four accomplices, two bearing a stretcher with the form of a person with dark cloth draped over it. With military precision Malicio led the procession down the hall and up the stairs, with the two unburdened men taking position to block off any curious or unwelcome intruders. The group made their way to the top of the building and into a suite that made up half of the top floor.

Malicio moved to one of the windows facing the main street and watched for any signs of movement, but saw none. "Put him on the bed and we'll be done with it." The men unceremoniously lifted the body and swung it onto the bed.

They quickly folded up the stretcher and departed from the room, leaving Jane, Malicio, and the body alone in the room.

"He is now in your custody, ensure you follow your instructions to the letter," he ordered as he walked past her. At the door he turned and slowly appraised her body from head to toe with dark covetous eyes. "I'd hate to have to return to this dank hole to remedy any of your mistakes, I daresay you'd hate it as well."

Once he exited, Jane made a face of defiance at the closed door, acting more confident than she really felt. She'd avoided the unwanted advances from men before, but he was different. Malicio made her feel angry, disgusted, and frightened all at the same time. After a few moments she went to the door and opened it a crack. She could see the shadow of what she presumed was one of Malicio's men at the bottom of the stairs. After a slight shudder, she pulled her shawl closer around her shoulders.

"You are right to feel threatened Jane," pronounced a firm yet gentle voice from inside the room, making Jane jump in shock. "I'm afraid I might have put you in unnecessary harm. Malicio is as violent as he is cruel."

Chapter 6

Pierce slept poorly, bombarded by the cracks of lightning from the storm outside and the memories of his near death experience from the duellists that the noise elicited. He only managed a handful of hours of sleep in the early hours of the morning once the storm had passed. His mood was soon buoyed by the scent of breakfast wafting in from outside his door.

A knock at the door was soon followed by Melrose, who entered with a serving tray filled with domed silver and glass carafes. He headed toward the bed with it, but was stopped by Pierce's gesture towards a side table in the room.

"I will gladly accept breakfast delivered to me, but breakfast in bed is crossing a line I think. Just set it on that table by the window and I'll get up and eat it there."

"Very good sir, is there anything else I can get you? I took the liberty of getting you an assortment of what was offered downstairs, not knowing what you favoured."

"Thanks Melrose, but I was just about to get up, and could have made it down for breakfast myself," Pierce said gratefully.

"I'm afraid that would have been difficult. You see the kitchen stopped serving breakfast an hour ago. I didn't wish to disturb you this morning so I let you sleep and took the liberty of absconding with some food from the kitchen for you."

"I hope you didn't have to battle the cook too hard."

"I was very covert my lord. A little slight of hand and they didn't even know what had happened."

"I'll have to keep that in mind." Pierce lifted the silver domed lid off his plate and took in Melrose's foraging skills. Everything he needed and more was present on his plate; eggs, fried potatoes and onions, mushrooms, tomatoes, toast, and even a small cup of baked beans. "This is enough to feed a small family."

"I thought you'd need your energy today sir. You have been assigned your hunting party and it could turn into a long day."

"My hunting party?"

"Yes sir. Each member of the Hunt is given a hunting party, generally called a pack. Each pack consists of their leader called the Whip and several men called Hounds. I'm not entirely sure their exact duties, but I imagine they are there to help you in the hunt. The Hunt staff and the Manor staff do not generally mix, so I'm afraid I can't be more definite."

"I see," said Pierce falling into a contemplative silence. After a few moments Melrose cleared his throat in an unobtrusive attempt to regain his master's attention. Pierce slowly looked up at him questioningly.

"Sorry sir, however I was just thinking about your predicament. The one we discussed last night…"

"Great minds, Melrose," replied Pierce, "I was thinking the same thing. Can these new men be trusted? Or have they been sent to watch me?"

"Precisely my thought sir. If you approve, I'll make some discreet inquiries throughout the day. Complete discretion of course."

Pierce nodded assent and returned to his meal, hardly tasting anything as he concentrated on this new puzzle. With every new person he met, the possible conspirators and co-conspirators seemed to increase. Was he becoming paranoid or was the threat to him actually increasing? The only option at this point was to continue forward and gain more information.

Within a half hour Pierce had cleaned up, dressed, and was following Melrose through the dark winding passages of the Manor. Eventually they made their way to the galleries adjoining the large staircase that led down to the Great Hall.

"Generally the Hunt Secretary introduces the hunting party to the new member, however, circumstances as they are…" Melrose trailed off, with a glint of amusement in his eyes. "He asked that I show you to the rooms of the Brown Pack, your Pack sir."

"They're not mine yet. I don't even know what I'm doing." Speaking the words aloud made Pierce suddenly feel the full amount of anxiety he'd been repressing. Despite the fact that the upcoming meeting would probably shed more light on his current situation, he was in no rush to get there. Walking the long halls of the Manor, he felt like a child making the long dreaded walk to the principle's office.

They made their way across the hall and walked towards a set of doors past the opposite stairwell. Through the doors were passages just as dark and windy as the previous ones. They passed few people, mostly servants at the Manor, who all diligently stopped what they were doing as Pierce passed.

Finally they came to large foyer where the ceiling became much taller and long glass windows let in small amounts of light from the late morning gloom. The foyer was a large square devoid of any furniture. The entranceway offered a view of the airy space, each side of the room had a large set of double doors.

These doors were magnificent pieces of workmanship, intricately carved and designed. He toured the foyer going from one set of doors to another. The first set was made of ebony and was completely black. At eye level, where a door knocker would normally be, there was an impressive emblem of a raven carved into the door. This was repeated on the second set of doors, but this one was made of out of a golden hued wood and contained the emblem of an eagle carved into it. The third set of doors was made of a lustrous brown oak and contained the emblem of a majestic stag.

Pierce looked over to Melrose who nodded, "That is your door sir, here's the key Mr. Drummond gave me. It should open it, but I can't follow you in."

*

The door opened silently and matched the quiet of the foyer he stepped into. Unsure how to proceed and slightly nervous on what awaited him, Pierce decided to close the door as loudly as possible without slamming it. With a slight thump and loud click the door was closed, quickly obtaining a response of sound beyond the door. Chairs squeaked and boots thumped on the floor in the adjoining room. Muffled voices soon changed to silence, and Pierce was unsure if he should call out or await a further sign. Surely someone would come and see to the door? Before he could make a decision, the answer came in the form of heavy metronomic footsteps.

The footsteps materialized into the form a large man, who nearly filled the doorway he stepped into. Pierce instantly perceived the military manner of the man in both his bearing and his attire. His large black boots were highly polished and solidly planted to the floor. His brown tunic was wrinkle free and perfectly sized for his frame which was currently ramrod straight. After a slight pause, he walked towards Pierce, his kilt of black tartan and brown leather sporran swinging rhythmically to his precise steps.

"Lord Pierce," Uttered a strong voice that matched his uniform and manner. "It is my honour to welcome you to Ravenwood Manor and the Hall of the Brown Pack." Although his tone was even and unemotional, his eyes held no such disinterest. They were an intense blue; searching, clever, and alert.

"Pierce will do fine," Patrick replied, still uncomfortable with the new formalities.

"I'm afraid it won't my Lord," countered the large man. "I am MacDuff, your Whip. With your permission I will show you the rest of our Hall and the remaining members of your Pack."

Pierce nodded in assent and walked towards the doorway that had momentarily been occupied by MacDuff, who quickly fell in step with him.

"MacDuff you said? Surely you're not the one from the Bards play? You didn't slay MacBeth did you?" Pierce asked looking at his companion. He looked to be less than middle age and without a speck of grey in his thick reddish brown hair. But as he was finding out, time no longer held the same rules he once thought.

"No sir, a little before my time," came the reply breaking through the thick beard in what Pierce assumed was a quick smile. "I do come from the same stock, but a little later."

They walked into a large room with a giant fireplace that sat prominently at the far end. The same stag emblem was carved into the stone over the mantle. An array of weapons hung from the walls in between arched windows. Along with columns in the corners, the room had the effect of a church, but one devoted to warfare rather than prayer. The church effect was also somewhat muted by the array of brown leather furniture and the polished oak dining table reflecting the light from the windows. The table held what appeared to be the remnants of a meal.

Pierce soon realized that the meal had been interrupted, as MacDuff guided him to his right and presented him to two men. They were dressed similarly to MacDuff, however with black pants rather than kilts. Although they were dressed the same, the similarities ended there. The man on the left was tall and lean, with cropped red hair. Meanwhile his companion was short and muscular, with wild black hair attempting to cover his ears and eyes. Walking up towards them, Pierce found that he was probably an average between the two of them in terms of size.

"These are your Hounds my Lord," announced MacDuff. "This is Sean and this is Liam," pointing to the taller man first, then to the shorter one.

"Please excuse my ignorance MacDuff, but what exactly

are your duties here? Dr. Cleaver said that members from the Manor are part of a Hunt Club, but I must confess I feel I'm still in the dark."

"Surely you have been part of a hunt before sir?"

"You mean like a fox hunt?"

"Precisely."

"No I haven't."

"Deer, grouse, boar, big game?"

"None of the above."

"You mean you've never hunted anything?!" exclaimed Sean with exasperation, before quickly regaining his self-control.

"Never. I'm not much of an outdoorsman," replied Pierce, ignorant of the accusatorial tone of the question. "I've never even fired a gun."

MacDuff was unmoved by the declaration, but Sean couldn't hide his incredulity, rolling his eyes and looking towards Liam.

"Christ, they've saddled us with a bleedin' tosser," murmured Liam in response.

Before Pierce could respond, MucDuff had wheeled around and was now staring both men into quiet submission. When he turned back towards Pierce he did not have the expression of embarrassment or anger one might have expected. Indeed Pierce thought he caught the quick look of someone enjoying themselves.

"As I was saying sir," continued MacDuff, "As the Whip it is my responsibility to drive the Hounds and maintain the pace of the hunt. The Hounds in turn work to flush out the game. The three of us work together to get you the perfect shot, before one of the other Hunt members gets the opportunity. Each member has a hunting party similarly formed."

"I see." Seeing that the men were still standing to attention he asked them to relax.

"I have a question, *sir*."

"Yes, it's Sean right."

"Aye, what did you do before being recruited to the Manor? If you don't mind my asking."

"Why should I mind?" replied Pierce good naturedly. "I was a public servant, a government employee. I worked in an office writing policy papers for various departments, mostly procedural type documents. Why do you ask?"

"Just curious, *sir*," he replied, this time not trying to hide his sarcasm.

"Curious Sean?" Questioned MacDuff stonily.

"Curious MacDuff," countered Sean turning towards Pierce. "Curious that we have a new Huntsman that doesn't hunt, hasn't fired a weapon, is not an *outdoorsman*, and doesn't look like he could fight off anything tougher than a common cold!" Then bowing to Pierce with a great flourish he added, "my Lord."

Pierce had been ill prepared for this outburst and still had a pleasant smile on his face. Up until this point everyone he had dealt with, even Drummond, had been professional, if not pleasant. At least to his face. The fact that what the man said was all true made a rebuttal slow in returning. MacDuff had no such delay, although his rebuttal was not as robust as Pierce expected.

"Careful Sean, looks can be deceiving."

"Only if they've been deceptively created," countered Liam coming to his friends' side of the argument. "I see nothing deceptive about this one."

"Is that so? "

"Aye, it is. This man is about as dangerous as a newborn and I wouldn't trust him with a picnic basket, let alone my life."

"You forget your place, both of you…"

"If you don't mind," cut in Pierce having regained his voice and composure, "but I would appreciate the courtesy of you speaking as if I were in the same room as you."

Both of them stared back at him silently.

"Neither of you believe I am fit for this?"

"Without a doubt" "Aye"

Pierce didn't think he was up to it either, but he suddenly

felt a desire to prove himself. He was tired of being alone and saw before him the chance to change that. Eventually he'd need help beyond what Melrose could offer and three good additions stood facing him. Their honest rejection of him made Pierce doubt their collusion with Cleaver or Drummond. Otherwise they'd surely be more friendly, welcoming and obedient?

Determined to gain their confidence, Pierce realized it would have to be done now. They would be no use to him if they simply nodded their heads at any order he gave, he needed allies not automatons. But for that to happen he'd have to show them something they didn't expect, something to change their minds. When it came to physical endeavours he only had one real skill.

"What would I need to do to disprove you?" Pierce asked, hoping they didn't want to wrestle.

Both men were wary now, not really sure where this was heading. However the answer was so clear that they maintained their stance.

"I don't think there is anything you can do."

"How about a duel then?" he offered, pointing to a collection of swords mounted on the wall like a deadly steel fan.

Both men sniggered. Pierce thought it had been an admirable solution and hoped they'd ignore the pistols mounted on the opposite wall.

"I'm serious."

"I'm sure you are, but we've already heard from the Red Hounds. How you stumbled into a duel already. However I promise you, our pistols are not bent like the Colonel's. Plus it would be an unfair advantage, you never having fired a pistol. I couldn't fire on a helpless man with a clear conscience."

"Swords then," Uttered MacDuff, ending the conversation and heading towards the door at the far end of the room, not waiting for the others to follow.

*

The three men followed MacDuff's lead to the door, which opened up to a set of stairs leading down. The staircase circled down until they reached the bottom, where it opened up to a great cavern of a room. Stone columns lined the space like an ancient greek temple. There were training mats, more collections of weapons and even modern exercise equipment.

"This is our training room my Lord," explained MacDuff with his back to the others as he continued to walk towards an unknown destination.

"What sort of things do you train for?" inquired Pierce, trying to make out shapes in the darkened space.

"Hunting, fighting, and killing," offered Sean.

"We're pretty good at it," added Liam.

Pierce's heart began to beat a little quicker, feeling like he might have made a mistake. If time stands still in the Manor, how long had these men trained at hunting, fighting, and killing? His years of fencing now seemed paltry in comparison and his ploy at acceptance might be unravelling with every step he took towards this duel.

"Aye they're good," stated MacDuff, bringing Pierce's attention back. "But you can always learn more. For no matter how good you think you are, there's always someone better."

With that pronouncement, MacDuff reached a door that led into a second hall flanked with more doors. The group made their way to a door on the left and entered into a room clearly designed for swordplay. The floor was painted with various shapes, designed to practice various sword fighting styles. The walls held a myriad of swords; from a centurion's gladius to a samurai's katana.

Pierce was taking in the room and its many weapons when his attention was brought back by the stern voice of MacDuff telling them they weren't on a break and to choose their weapons.

Sean calmly walked over to the far wall and grabbed a basket hilted claymore from a weapons stand. Pierce stared at the giant sword; it's long thick blade reflected the light of the room, the basket seemed solid enough to crush a man's skull, and the red velvet within mimicked blood that could soon be his.

Pierce quickly pushed these thoughts from his head. This had been his plan and he would only have one shot to prove himself to these men. This was the only thing he was moderately good at that they would respect. He looked over at Sean again, this time deliberately assessing his opponent. Sean had chosen a large weapon, meant to hack in a wide sweeping motion. Although it could be used to stab, Pierce felt that Sean would not use it for that purpose. His only chance was to offset the power of his opponent's weapon with speed and cunning. Seeing a collection of French rapiers behind him, Pierce walked over and grabbed one of middling weight and length.

With their weapons chosen both men squared off and awaited instructions.

"First blood gentlemen," announced MacDuff simply.

As Pierce aligned himself into his fighting stance, Sean quickly drove towards him sweeping his claymore in a giant arc from the right. Pierce dodged this easily, circling to his left and raising his sword for the next blow. His training paid off as Sean quickly stopped his motion and wielded a backhanded slice, striking Pierce's raised sword. The ringing sound of steel filled the room and Pierce's hand vibrated with the shock of the attack. His rapier was not designed to defend direct hits from the larger claymore. He therefore began to move around Sean, using his trained footwork to keep his opponent off balance. He realized he needed to end this soon, before Sean realized he was not the metaphorical sheep sent to slaughter.

Sean's next blow came from above, forcing Pierce to jump backwards. It was a shot not meant for duelling, it was meant for battle. With the weight of the claymore, any hit from above would either take off an arm or imbed itself inches into the brain. Pierce looked over to the others, hoping they would say something to keep Sean from trying to kill him. Seeing no response from MacDuff and laughter from Liam, Pierce realized he had to end this soon in order to merely stay alive. Pierce backed away from the next two swings from Sean, trying to look scared and succeeding due to his actual fear.

Despite the weight of the weapon, Sean seemed to control it with ease. However Pierce had noticed a flaw in his opponents' technique. Sean appeared to be unconcerned with any counter from his opponent, erroneously believing he was happy to avoid attacks and not make any of his own. This was to be his downfall.

Sean again charged forward and attempted another blow from above, however he had telegraphed his move and Pierce was waiting for it and ready to take his first shot. As the sword came down, Pierce shifted quickly to his right and raised his rapier. Using Sean's momentum against him, he merely spun in place and sliced a quick cut in his opponents' cheek with little effort. Unable to stop himself in his moment of victory, he finished his spin with a solid whack to the backside of his opponent with the side of his sword.

Instead of yielding defeat, Sean turned in a rage and brought his claymore up once more, screaming as if in battle.

Chapter 7

Before he could bring the sword down for the killing blow, Pierce's rapier flicked upwards and was at Sean's throat in an instant.

"I understood we were fighting to first blood," called Pierce over his shoulder to the other two.

"Indeed you are my Lord," replied MacDuff.

"Well if you want to fight to the death Sean, I'm game," said Pierce calmly, turning back towards his opponent. "But I don't think it will make this duel last any longer."

Sean closed his eyes and dropped the claymore to the ground. Pierce kicked it away and lowered his own weapon. Backing away slowly, he was shaking slightly and not prepared for what followed.

All three men, brave and proud, lowered themselves to one knee and uttered in unison, "my Lord, we are yours to command, obedient to the end" Pierce was speechless and moved by this display. Without further instructions the men stood up and gathered by him.

"Instructions my lord?"

"I don't know about you guys, but I'm hungry enough to eat a skewered boar," said Pierce staring at Sean, hoping they'd get his poor attempt at a joke. Although he appreciated the reverence they'd all just showed, it also made him feel uncomfortable.

There was a brief silence until Liam broke out in laughter, soon followed by the others and finally Pierce himself.

"I forgot that I had interrupted your meal. Hopefully it hasn't been spoiled."

Sean and Liam turned for the door, saying they would get something else from the kitchens for all of them.

MacDuff came over and leaned down to pick up the dropped claymore. He straightened up, feeling the weight and balance of the weapon, looking every inch the ancient Scottish warrior. He peered at Pierce then nodded.

"You did well my Lord. I think they got the message."

"Did you know how this would turn out or did you really want to see if I had any worthwhile skills?"

MacDuff just clicked his tongue and turned, moving to the far wall to replace the sword.

Although it wasn't much of an answer, Pierce was glad for the acceptance. He felt that MacDuff was honest, honourable and could be trusted. He had nothing to base it on other than a gut feeling, so he needed to know more.

"Did they mean what they said? That they would follow me?"

"They said they'd obey you," replied MacDuff gruffly. "A man can obey another for many reasons; fear, riches, duty, and so on. But for a man to follow another there needs to be mutual trust, respect, honour, and leadership. You displayed today that you can wield a sword. Therefore it can be argued that you indeed belong here and are a member of the Hunt. We are sworn to obey the members of the Hunt. But for them to follow you and for you to lead them, that has yet to be decided. My lord."

"MacDuff, you also said that you'd obey me. Right?"

"Aye."

"Then stop calling me that, I'm not royalty and I'm no lord. I'm just some poor Canadian kid in over his head. My name's Patrick, feel free to use it."

MacDuff smiled and walked over. "You're a good lad.

We'll train you up right. But first let's eat. The boys should have scrounged up something by now."

"Good then, lead on MacDuff."

He looked at him with a raised eyebrow, shook his head and led the way out.

*

Jane brought the tray of food into the suite at the top of the pub after the guard had inspected it. She wasn't sure what he was looking for, but he hadn't found anything.

"Here's your breakfast my Lord," she said laying it on a table by the door.

A tall slim man with dark hair slicked back turned from the window he was looking out of to take in her presence. He had a hawk like face and intelligent eyes that could be both piercing and genial at the same time.

"It seems my little breakfast has been approved by the guard dog," he observed in a well educated English accent, looking down at the tray.

Jane looked down at it in confusion and couldn't see that anything had been disturbed. The guard was a flight of stairs down and couldn't be seen from this room.

"You don't see it?" he asked chuckling. "Very well a quick explanation to put your mind at ease. First, since I was drugged and brought to this little holiday house in the dead of night, I have to presume that I am to be kept here, against my will if it comes to that. Therefore moving someone against their will without placing a guard to ensure he doesn't leave seems like the actions of thoughtless mind. And I know that the main perpetrator is a very clever man."

To this Jane stared straight ahead without responding.

"So you agree? Good," he replied sitting down to eat. "Second, I know that you have been working at the Manor, were trained there in fact. I know that the training there is exacting and the lessons learned stick. Therefore when I look over this expertly prepared breakfast tray, I know if something is amiss it wasn't due to your negligence." During this oratory his hands had flowed over the tray like a conductor. He stopped suddenly and picked up the napkin, then opening it in a flourish.

Confused Jane was about to ask how this told him anything, but she was silenced by his voice.

"This napkin my dear, placed below the plate," he continued. "You would never have placed it there. Therefore it could only have moved after you had prepared the tray. Had it moved when you brought it here you would have noticed and fixed it prior to presenting it. However being preoccupied with the presence of the guard, you did not notice that he moved it during his search."

"You mean to say you devised all this from a moved napkin?" she asked incredulously.

"I can tell many things from the seemingly inconsequential. Keep that in mind my dear."

"I'll do that," she retorted with more defiance than she felt.

"Good. Now tell me about the newest member of the Hunt, I believe you met him a short while ago."

"How…" she began to ask, but thought better of asking the question. That he knew of Pierce's presence was obvious, although how much he knew remained to be seen. She had not been instructed to refrain from speaking to the gentleman, however if she could pull him into a conversation she could possibly extract some information from him.

"I'm really not supposed to talk to you," she began innocently. "However if you promise to stay in this room and not try to escape I will visit you daily for a good chat. Deal?"

"On my word of honour, I shall remain in this room," he pledged raising a hand to his chest.

"Very well. I've only met him once, but he seems pleasant enough."

"Strange. Pleasant is not the usual term employed when describing members of the Hunt."

"Well he was. Or seemed to be at any rate. I doubt he was

putting on an act, I would have noticed."

"Really? Hmm."

"Yes really. Do you want to hear more or shall I leave you to the rest of your tea?" she replied calmly, although not attempting to rise from the chair she had taken up opposite of him.

"Pray continue, and don't allow my little editorials to interrupt you."

"As I was saying he seemed pleasant, although he was also very confused about his appearance here. He was not terribly interested in his new position and seemed at a loss at what to do about it. To be honest he was very underwhelming. I don't know how he was even invited to join the Hunt."

"Don't you?" inquired the man knowingly as he raised his tea cup.

This unexpected observation made her flinch before she could try and control her expression. Knowing any possible explanation would prove fruitless she decided to employ an age old tactic: denial.

"I don't know what you're alluding to."

His response was a slight shrug and a wave to continue her dialog.

"Well there's little else to tell. I only met him briefly." They continued their conversation as he ate his meal. He explained how he knew of the letter that link her to the new member and Jane found herself unable to deny it. At that moment the fact she was indeed playing a very dangerous game was confirmed. When he finished she stood up and collected the tray with its collection of emptied plates and cups. She expertly held the tray with one hand as the other opened the door. On her way out, she heard his farewell.

"Thank you Jane for our little talk. Let me know how our friend is doing after his next visit. I'd be very surprised if he doesn't appear sometime today."

She closed the door behind her and had the sudden feeling that she had just had her fortune told by a gypsy. He had seemingly seen through her, a feeling she had never experienced before. She worked hard to either hide her thoughts and feelings, or to project whichever ones she decided would suit best for the situation. But she was sure he had seen right through her. Not only that, but she couldn't see what his true goal was. Was it simply to lull her into a false sense of confidence, or provoke and unsettle her?

Passing the guard at the bottom level of the stairwell she realized her extended period upstairs would be noted. She would have to dispel any concerns of Cleaver's before he approached her or sent his dog Malicio. A quick letter describing her brief encounter would suffice.

She dropped the tray off in the kitchen for the washers to clean up and made her way to the little office in the back. Here she took out a piece of paper and pen, composing her news to Cleaver. She would continue to meet the prisoner in order to obtain more info on this Mr. Pierce. However she did not mention in the letter that she recognized the prisoner, inwardly wishing she hadn't. Jane had no idea what the goals of these two adversaries were, but she knew they'd probably crush those around them like fighting titans of ancient myths.

Having finished she put the note in an envelope and made her way to the front of the inn, passing the doorway to the pub. At the front she called over one of the page boys and gave him the envelope to deliver to the Manor, adding a coin for his trouble. Seeing the shiny coin in his hand, he shot out the door at a run.

*

"Let's try it again sir," ordered a kind and patient voice with a hint of a Highland accent, "but this time try to not blow yourself up."

"Well, that's the trick, isn't it?"

"It is indeed, my Lord. But you're lucky, you get to learn without being hunted through the heather by a horde of murderous Redcoats."

"I don't see why I have to learn how to shoot this old

relic, I don't plan on fighting any redcoats."

"I wouldn't be too sure about that. You practice so that you're ready when the plan falls apart. Besides, this old relic was advanced technology at one time and a good reason why Bonaparte was defeated."

Pierce nodded and began the process again of loading, priming, aiming, and firing a Napoleonic era Baker rifle. The process was slow for an expert, being able to fire three rounds a minute in good conditions. Pierce was averaging one round every five minutes, twice forgetting to load the ball and the last time leaving the ramrod in the barrel. However this time he was able to get a shot off in his best time, remembering all of the correct steps.

"Very good!" exclaimed his tutor slapping his back, "now all you need to do is hit the target." Following the pointing finger, Pierce observed that the past hour of target practice had left the target miraculously unharmed. In fact, judging from the pock marks on the opposite wall and the black sooted appearance of himself and his tutor, the target was probably the safest place to be in the room. Remembering Schell's description of the Colonel's bent duelling pistols; Pierce hefted his rifle up and stared down the length, searching for any inconsistencies.

"You won't find anything wrong with that barrel lad," observed MacDuff, apparently clairvoyant. "A solid piece of craftsmanship that. Why compared to the muskets I learned on and used on the battlefield…"

"Understood Duffy," said Pierce, stopping him with a raised hand.

"Well, since I believe we've exhausted the use of black powder weapons for today, shall we turn to the use of more modern pieces?" Taking the Baker rifle from Pierce he turned and handed it to one of the assistants for return to the armoury. He then ushered Pierce through the door of the practice range out into a hall filled with tables, weapons, wrestling mats, and combat dummies. They were once more in the Brown Packs training facility.

Upon reaching the far end of the room they entered an adjoined hall, this one containing multiple doors facing each other. They walked to the second door on the right and entered into a modern firing range, complete with firing lanes and mechanical targets at the far end. As he had for the past two days, Pierce walked over to a stall with his name inscribed above and opened it. He took out a pair of safety glasses and ear plugs, but hesitated before putting them in.

"Why wasn't I wearing these before?" Inquired Pierce to his tutor.

"You didn't ask," replied Duffy, "plus you don't really need them if you only fire once every half hour."

Ignoring the good natured jibe, Pierce donned the protective gear and walked up to the first firing lane. A 9mm semi-automatic pistol was sitting on a small shelf at the firing line, along with a group of filled magazines. He got to them and started his safety check, then loading the gun as he had been taught.

He slowly raised the weapon to eye level, concentrating on the sights and the target beyond them. He scarcely heard the instructions calmly emanating from behind him; "remember your breathing", "squeeze the trigger, don't pull it", "aim past the sights"…

The pistol jerked in his hands as he let off his first shot, maintaining control, and aiming again as it automatically reloaded. A second shot then fired, immediately followed by a third. A brief pause was followed by another secession of three shots. This routine continued until the pistol locked open, denoting the end to the supply of bullets. Pierce lowered the pistol to a safe position as the target made its way to him along a small overhead track.

"Well done, my lord," came the voice from behind him. "Significant improvement from yesterday, look at your groupings." He pointed to the clustering of the holes throughout the target. "You're starting to feel the weapon, not just shoot it."

"It just seemed so much easier after using that old rifle."

"Now who could have foreseen that?"

"How many of these little tricks do you have?"

"Tricks? I don't use tricks my Lord," replied MacDuff indignantly, quickly followed by a knowing grin.

"You don't? Then pray tell me what you would call the incident at our initial meeting, if not a trick?"

"So you caught on did you? I figured you for a clever lad. That was not a trick, just a well timed lesson. For everyone involved in fact."

"How did you know what the outcome would be? Nobody in their right mind would have bet on me against Sean."

"That's exactly why the lesson worked so well. Plus I followed one of my most important rules: I cheated. Mr. Drummond had shown me your dossier when I was given the title of your Whip. So I knew you were an expert with a blade. Now reload and let's try this again. This time try and keep your eyes open when you fire. You'll find that significantly improves your chances at hitting the target."

*

Pierce entered his rooms to find Melrose emerging from his dressing room to meet him in the foyer.

"I've laid out a suit for you to change into, sir. I see you've been attempting the musket again."

"Rifle Melrose, not a musket," he corrected good naturedly. "And to be honest I am very close to graduating from attempt to use."

"Of course sir."

"You don't believe me?" asked Pierce, sensing his valet's disbelief. "Ask MacDuff the next time you seem him."

"Have you hit the target yet?"

"Speaking of MacDuff," continued Pierce, ignoring the question. "I think we can trust him and I doubt he had a hand in recruiting me."

"I agree sir. I've known him for some time and he's always been honest. Besides I believe he's more in Lord Lodges camp than Dr. Cleavers."

"Is there is a rift between the two Masters?"

"You wouldn't know to watch them, as they are both gentlemen and conduct themselves as such. However it is well known that they are very much opposites, and antagonise each other, however covertly. Most people at the Manor choose sides between them, whether they know it or not."

"Interesting. Seeing as Dr. Cleaver is behind this, I should try and meet Lord Lodge. He might be able to help me…" Pierce trailed off as he said this by the look on Melrose's face. "Bad idea?"

"Not at all sir. In fact that would have been my suggestion from the beginning."

"However…" Waited Pierce.

"However, Lord Lodge has not been seen for weeks. Well before you arrived here in fact." Leaning in closer, he continued in a conspiratorial tone. "At first the Doctor said he was taking a break from his Manor duties and was relaxing in his rooms. However I heard from the head cook that the Doctor informed her that Lord Lodge would no longer be requiring any food prepared."

"That sounds ominous."

"Indeed sir. Do you think he's dead?"

"No. If he were we would have been told. No I think the Doctor is playing some kind of game, and needs Lodge alive, for now. So he's either still in his rooms and the food is being brought in to him. Or…"

"He's no longer in the Manor," finished Melrose. "What shall we do sir?"

"You said that the order came to the cook this morning?" Seeing Melrose nod, Pierce continued, "then quietly ask around the staff if anything out of the ordinary occurred last night. Meanwhile I think I'll take a stroll down to the village."

Pierce quickly changed out of his training clothes and put on a perfectly tailored tweed suit. At the door he grabbed a cloth cap of similar material and picked up a wooden walking stick. It was made of a knobby black wood and reminded him of a similar piece his grandfather used.

"Aren't we just the image of a country gentleman," he uttered softly, mimicking the flowing Irish accent of the old man. "I hope to Jesus you know what you're about Paddy boy."

By now Pierce was fairly familiar with the layout of the Manor and made his way to the front door without any detours, emerging to find a gray but dry afternoon. He decided to stay to the gravel drive that led to the main roadway and the village beyond, still a little nervous from his previous bullet filled walk in the arboretum. This decision proved justified as he immediately heard the crack of weapons fire, shortly followed by small plumes of gray smoke.

Pierce passed the large stone and wrought iron gates that signalled the extent of the Manor grounds and took the road to Rooks Bay. The road was quiet, with no traffic to watch out for. This enabled Pierce a chance to figure out what he'd do when he reached the pub. If it weren't for overhearing Jane for himself, he would have doubted her having any dubious intentions. From the very first time he had seen her, he hadn't felt suspicious of her. Although the fact that she was also beautiful and interested in him should have signalled her questionable intentions from the start.

However he couldn't shake his gut feeling that there was more to her. Upon meeting Drummond and Cleaver he had instantly felt their animosity, the Doctor hiding it better, and knew they could not be trusted. Nevertheless he had overheard everything she and Cleaver had said and it was beyond question. He would simply have to keep his misinformation flowing until he could figure her out better.

By the time he reached this conclusion, Pierce arrived at the outskirts of the village. Again he was able to walk unobstructed through the streets and the square, despite the bustling crowd. When he reached the pub door, it was held open for him and he was immediately led to the Manor snug, the barman finishing off with a nod and a dutiful "m'lord". Despite a reticence towards classism learned from his native land, Pierce thought he could get used to this treatment.

No sooner had he removed his hat and sat down, Jane swung open the door with her hip and placed a pint down before him.

"How did you know I was here," exclaimed Pierce, surprised and impressed.

"I was upstairs tending to one of the guests when I saw you down on the street walking this way."

Pierce replied with a raised eyebrow and was quickly rewarded with a playful flick of Janes towel.

"Nothing like that," she said playfully, "he's an older gentleman that hasn't been feeling well. He's on the top floor and can't make his way down to socialize. In fact that gives me an idea."

"Sounds ominous," replied Pierce taking a sip of his drink.

"Well seeing that he's not had any visitors apart from me," she continued, ignoring him, "would you be able to go up and visit with him?"

Before he could object, she beamed him a smile that he knew he couldn't refuse. No matter what schemes she was up to. Speechless, he simply nodded his assent and stood up to go.

"No, no," Jane exclaimed, waving him back down. "I'll be done in a couple minutes and we'll go up together."

*

Pierce sat in his study with the remnants of his dinner before him, having returned from the village too late to join the rest of the diners in the dining room. Melrose entered with the black bottle of whiskey and poured him a drink and began to remove the dishes.

"Leave those for a minute," Pierce instructed him, then waved him to take the seat across from him. "I had a very interesting meeting in the village today. I'd like to get your opinion of it."

"Of course sir."

"I went to the village to see Jane. She's intriguing; although I heard her conspire against me, I don't feel threatened by her." Pierce held up a hand before Melrose could debate this irrational feeling. "I know, the trusting innocent young man gets duped by the beautiful woman and never sees it coming. I understand the concept of a femme fatal and will not be taken in. That she's hiding something is beyond debate, but we can't be sure as to her ultimate motive."

"Very well sir," replied Melrose without confidence.

"As I was saying, I had hoped to meet Jane to try and get more information out her. Even faulty stories could provide clues to follow. Plus I figured to provide some misleading facts of my own; that I continue to plan an escape, that I met my new pack and distrust them, etc."

"And did your trip prove fruitful sir?"

"I'm not sure. Before we could sit down together she told me of an elderly gentleman staying at the pub who had not been out of his rooms for some time. She asked me to look in on him, provide some company. It was odd."

"In what way sir?" asked Melrose. "It seems very straight forward to me."

"By itself yes, but there is more going on at that pub than what's on the surface." Seeing the questioning look on Melrose's face, Pierce continued. "For starters what's an old infirm man doing on the top floor when we passed a handful of empty rooms on the way to see him? Surely it would be more convenient for him to be closer to the main level.

"Second, though the man was indeed old, he didn't seem infirm or sick. His limbs were not frail and he exhibited no signs of pain when he moved his joints. I could be mistaken, but I doubt it. So why the deception? I would have easily accepted a case of misanthropy as an excuse to stay away from the crowd of the pub."

"Are you suggesting he's a prisoner there?"

"It appeared that way. At the bottom of the stairs there was a chair and table with a half eaten meal on it. Like someone was watching the stairs and was quickly ushered away before we went up. But I'm not convinced. Why go to the trouble of hiding someone, only to have them visited?"

Melrose thought intently, but could offer no thesis before Pierce began again.

"Then there was our conversation. Most of these things I've pointed out did not immediately strike me when I was there, but later on as I walked back. Something felt odd and not quit right when I was there, but I didn't feel in danger. It felt thrown together, as if they weren't expecting me."

"In what way sir?"

"Well, if it had been set up like some sort of elaborate and subtle interrogation, it did not really succeed. Jane and I spoke for a short time and I believe we both walked away empty handed. I tried to find out more about the Manor and the surrounding island and she responded as if she hadn't lived here her whole life. I answered her questions as I told you I had planned; deception, falsehood, and outright lies. But our exchange would have been the same with or without the presence of the old man. I kept waiting for him to start some sneaky interrogation, but it never happened. In fact the old man didn't so much ask me questions about myself, but told me. It's as if he had studied my biography before meeting me. Isn't that strange?"

Upon hearing this Melrose immediately faced Pierce head on and stared right into his eyes, momentarily losing his professional detachment.

"What did he tell you? What did he say?"

"Well nothing ground breaking, but it was extraordinary. He was able to tell where I came from, that I worked in an office at a desk job, that I studied fencing, and a myriad of other little tidbits. He explained how he had reached his conclusions, and to be honest his deductions seemed very straightforward. I suppose in a way he did interrogate me, only he provided me with the answers instead of asking questions. Why do you ask?"

"I was asking around the Manor today as you instructed.

Something out of the ordinary did happen last night. Apparently one of the servants was taken sick and the Doctor's Pack, the Black Pack, rushed him to the village."

"Why is that so strange?"

"Sir, Doctor Cleaver is a medical doctor and more proficient than anyone in the village. Plus his Pack would not escort a servant to the village, they'd have a groomsman or stable boy do it. And finally, I heard of no servants missing from the Manor… This old man, was he tall and thin? With a pointed face, long nose and piercing grey eyes?"

"That's him exactly!" exclaimed Pierce, slightly confused. "Do you know him?"

"He's no servant, I served him for many years as I serve you now. He is the most observant and logical man I've ever met. How he ended up in that room in the pub is mysterious indeed. One we will need to discover quickly in order to get him out."

"Why, who is he?" Inquired Pierce.

"His name is Victor Lodge, Master of Ravenwood Manor."

A sharp knock sounded on the outer door before Melrose could continue. He looked to his master who nodded for him to answer it while he tried to process this sudden revelation. Melrose returned to the room, transformed back into servant from conspirator.

"That was a footman sir; the members have retired to the salon and billiard room. Lord Schell has invited you to join him if you are available."

"I suppose it would seem unnatural to decline the invitation," replied Pierce before trying out his new *lord of the manor* voice. "Have the footman send my regards to Lord Schell and inform him I'll be down momentarily."

Holding back a laugh, Melrose nodded and left the room, returning seconds later.

"I will prepare your change of clothes sir."

"Change?" inquired Pierce, looking over his current garments. "This suit seems perfectly fine to me. I didn't drop one piece of my dinner on it."

"As astonishing as that is sir, since the rest of the members will be dressed in their dining clothes, you will have to reciprocate to fit in," countered Melrose. He turned sharply towards the door, hiding a quick smirk, and made his way to the dressing room.

"I think I liked him better when he didn't speak," muttered Pierce sarcastically. "Me and my liberal sense of equality."

Melrose already had the new suit out and was collecting the highly polished shoes. After setting them out he left to provide his master with a small amount of privacy to change. After waiting a few minutes he returned to the dressing room and was greeted by quiet curses as Pierce struggled with a set of cufflinks.

"Allow me sir," instructed Melrose and he easily fitted them on. With this task finished, he removed the black dinner jacket with its long tails from the hangar and moved behind Pierce to help him into it.

"A perfect fit sir," offered Melrose, stepping back as both of them inspected Pierce in the long cheval mirror.

"I look like an overgrown penguin," countered Pierce.

"That means it fits sir. Sir?"

"Yes?"

"Now that we know his true whereabouts, we have to get Lord Lodge back," Melrose gently pleaded.

"I was just thinking about that. Although we know his location, we don't know the circumstances of why he's there. Until we know that, any action would be premature."

"Very well sir. But I don't like it."

Chapter 8

Pierce followed the footman along the gallery of the west wing of the Manor in silence. The darkness of the moonless night had seeped into the Manor, save for the small islands of light emanating from the uniformly spaced lamps along the corridors.

This sense of desertion was washed away as they walked under a large stone arch that opened on to an immense column lined hall. The white marble floor reflected the vibrant light and sounds emanating from a large room to the right. The footman pointed towards this room as he led Pierce across the hall, pronouncing it to be the main salon. Pierce quickly glanced at the room from across the hall and was provided with a view of fashionably dressed revellers absorbed by the exertion of a talented pianist. The menace of the Manor seemed to slip away with this new scene of camaraderie and joy.

The footman continued to a door across the hall, pronouncing it to be the billiard room. But before Pierce could walk in, the door swung open and Colonel Bufford appeared, hollering in the direction of the salon.

"Harold, you darn well better cut off their liquor," he admonished the footman pointing a pool cue towards him. "That off key piano wheedling is distracting my game and cost me another match!"

The footman stood stonefaced and waited for the Colonel's diatribe to conclude before bowing slightly and turning towards the salon.

Pierce made his way inside, looking over another new room. Unlike the hall that led into it, there was not a speck of white marble inside. However, this did not make it any less welcoming. The cherry panelled walls and carved white ceiling created a warm and inviting space. There were two billiard tables in the center around which the Colonel's adversary was counting his winnings. A bar stood past the tables, where a beautiful woman with light brown hair and a tight fitting crème gown leaned against it, casually smoking a cigarette. Beside her stood Wilhelm Schell, speaking to the bartender before noticing the new arrival.

"Patrick, Good of you to join us," he exclaimed coming over to shake Pierce's hand. "You already know the Colonel, so let me introduce you to some of the other members."

He led him towards the pool player and Pierce was immediately glad he had followed Melrose's advice and wore the penguin suit. Just like those in the salon, everyone in the billiard room was immaculately and elegantly dressed.

"Patrick Pierce, allow me to introduce Herr Josef Zeidt," Schell said good naturedly, then adding, "a prolific Swiss banker."

"Welcome to the Manor Herr Pierce," he offered, taking Pierce's outstretched hand. His chiselled angular face showed no emotion as they were introduced. Zeidt had the cold good looks often seen in male models advertising obnoxious cologne.

Sensing the conversation over and not wanting to force a greater welcome, Schell manoeuvred Pierce away from Zeidt towards the bar. A barman wearing the livery of the Manor efficiently began making a pair of drinks when Schell motioned him as they approached.

"And this beautiful woman is Mademoiselle Veronique Laflamme," Schell said as he grabbed the drinks, giving one to Pierce.

"Patrick Pierce, mademoiselle," said Pierce introducing himself. He stood motionless, deciding if he should shake hands or try to kiss hers in the Parisian fashion. He really didn't know what the protocol was and felt that he would end up picking the wrong one. However she didn't offer either, but simply kept smoking with a bored look on her face.

"Another ghastly American," she muttered after taking another drag.

"Ah, the accent," rescued Schell looking over his shoulder from the Colonel to Pierce. "Mais non, I'll est Canadien."

"Vraiement?" responded Laflamme with slightly more interest.

"Oui vraiement," answered Pierce for himself. "Puis je parle Français aussi."

With this discovery the three of them settled into a conversation in French. As an ice breaker they talked about how they had learnt the language. Veronique was born in France and had spoken French her entire life, however she provided a few amusing word plays she had learnt from her Father growing up. Schell explained that he had learned to speak in French in school, as his parents had insisted. In his time French had been a language of diplomacy and the aristocracy, and he had been a member of both. Luckily, he exclaimed, he had been good at languages and not math or science. Since neither of those had ever been needed for diplomats or aristocrats, he had been in luck. Pierce meanwhile echoed some of Schell's story, telling them he had learned French at school as well. His parents hadn't forced it upon him, since French was part of the school curriculum. His education had not been easy and he proclaimed that if he were required to compose a rescue letter in French he would never be saved.

"Vous êtes drole," gushed Veronique at the end of his story.

"I guess…" replied Pierce confused by her sudden interest in him. He knew his joke was weak at best, so he figured that maybe she was the type who liked new things. But when she placed her hand on his shoulder, Pierce decided he could live with filling the role for as long as it lasted.

Always suspicious of attractive women paying attention to him, Pierce continued to observe Veronique as they sipped at their drinks. She kept darting glances towards Schell. It was as if she was waiting for him to react or say something. Great, thought Pierce crestfallen, she's just trying to make Wilhelm jealous. He had no wish to get involved in her little games, but then thought better of it. I wonder how far she'll take this charade?

The appearance of a new member entering the room broke his hopeful train of thought. He was by far the oldest looking member of the Hunt Pierce had seen so far. The black and grey hair surrounding his balding head was ruffled and wild. His creased mouth was drawn into a frown, which Pierce imagined never altered shape. A pair of dark squinty eyes glared at the group at the bar from across the room as he approached. "Who's that? I wonder what happened to him, he looks pretty pissed off."

"He's always like that," said Veronique, discounting the new arrival with a wave of her hand. "Pay no attention to him,"

This was meant as a hint to her two male companions to return their attention to her, as she corralled an invisible hair back into place.

"I shall introduce you," offered Schell, too well bred to ignore Pierce's question.

Pierce nodded in agreement, needing a brief escape from the growing awkwardness he felt at the bar.

"Signor Diego De la Gena, may I present the newest member of our fraternity, Mr. Patrick Pierce."

"Please to meet you," said Pierce with an outstretched hand.

"Hmmph," replied De La Gena turning towards the bar, deliberately ignoring the newcomer. "They have certainly started scraping the bottom of the barrel. Vino tinto, Serge".

"Diego, a little civility," admonished Veronique half-heartedly. She pushed her glass towards the bartender and lit another cigarette, trying to regain her previous air of studied boredom. Her boredom was matched by De La Gena's disregard for the others.

Ever the diplomat, Schell moved to intercede when an argument broke out between the billiards players. So Pierce found himself standing in awkward silence between the two of them, wondering who would break first and speak. The Spaniard seemed content alone with his wine and Veronique probably wouldn't talk to him until Schell returned.

"I suppose I could offer something close to acceptance," broke De La Gena first, turning from the bar to face Pierce and Veronique. When neither seemed to comprehend, he sighed heavily and said, "sharing gossip of course."

"I find gossip to be tiresome," countered Veronique unconvincingly.

"And you …?" He asked turning to Pierce, pretending to have forgotten his name.

"Pierce," he said, filling the blank. "Well… I…" he replied haltingly, not really knowing where he stood on gossip.

"Very well I shall not…"

"Well if you must tell us," objected Veronique before De La Gena could continue. De La Gena smiled, feeling he had just won an argument.

"Prior to joining you here, I had an interesting conversation with Mr. Drummond."

"And pray what did the weasel have to say?"

"We had a very thorough discussion on the current situation of the Hunt," he continued, ignoring Veronique. "He told me, or rather showed me, about our newest recruit."

After taking a sip he ever so subtly touched his eye with the index finger of the hand holding the glass. Pierce looked down in embarrassment, as they had clearly discussed Pierce's right hook.

"But more importantly, he told me something of Lord Lodge."

"I assume he had nothing good to say about the Master of the Manor," assumed Veronique.

"Not at all. He's very concerned for him in fact.

Apparently Lord Lodge is very ill, perhaps terminally. Dr. Cleaver is attending to him as we speak."

"Dreadful. But what is to happen if he dies?" she asked, without very much sympathy. Pierce could tell she actually wanted to know how his death might affect her.

"Drummond assumes that Dr. Cleaver will take control of the Manor. Whether someone takes his place as Master of the Hunt remains to be seen. The situation is unprecedented."

"Really? I assume people have died here before," questioned Pierce.

"My dear boy, Lord Lodge is the founder of the Hunt and the first of us." Seemingly exhausted from his conversation with Pierce, De La Gena moved over to one of the lounge chairs grouped in the corner around the room's sole fireplace.

His departure was quickly replaced by Schell, returning from his diplomatic interlude between Bufford and Zeidt. He showed significantly more emotion than the others when finding out about Lodge's condition.

"That's terrible, though not surprising. I can't even begin to figure out how old the man must be. Plus he hasn't been seen around the Manor for some time, it must be really serious."

Pierce was initially confused by the news, knowing it to be false. But then he quickly began thinking of the consequences of such a lie and realized that any potential outcome would be bad. He didn't know what kind of power struggle he had wandered into at the Manor, but he did know that Lodge presented the best way for him to find out why he was here. Despite this fact, Pierce found his quick decision to act surprising. Usually he took ages to decide on a course of action.

"Sorry, you were saying?" Pierce asked after hearing distantly hearing his name. He was so engrossed in thought that he didn't register Schell's question.

"I asked if you had ever met Lord Lodge?" repeated Schell. "But of course you didn't, seeing as you just arrived."

"You're right, I've never met him," covered Pierce as casually as he could. He finished his drink with a final gulp and placed the empty glass on the bar, while motioning the bartender to him.

"Another drink sir?"

"Please. And could you direct me to the... uh...," asked Pierce sheepishly.

"Of course sir. Out through the hall, the corridor on your right and it is the second door on the left."

Pierce nodded his thanks and excused himself from the others, walking past the billiard players and out the door. In the hall he noticed that the music had stopped from the salon, however the murmur of multiple conversations echoed in the large space. Pierce looked around and found the real reason for his departure, a footman standing at attention beneath the large arch.

"Can you fetch my valet," requested Pierce as he approached the man. "I'll be in the billiard room when he arrives."

The footman nodded and left, walking with the same methodical pace he had witnessed all the servants of the Manor use. Turning to the right he saw the door the bartender had directed him to and decided to use the facilities, unsure when he'd get another chance.

*

"How could you be so foolish!" exclaimed Dr. Cleaver to Jane, once again in the room at the Fish and Feather.

"I only thought..."

"That was not a question," rebuked Cleaver, levelling a violent stare at her. "I sent him here in order to be secluded from the Manor. And the first day he's here, you arrange tea with the newest member. Incomprehensible!"

"I was only trying to use him as a way to gain more information from Pierce. I thought it would put him at ease with another person in the room. I was there the whole time and Lodge never tried to deliver a message of any kind. He simply sat there, mostly silent."

"And what pray tell did your little scheme pry from Pierce?"

"As before, he still plans to flee the Manor at the first opportunity. Apparently his pack did not greet him well, in fact they almost took up arms against him."

"Really? Well that is encouraging."

"He is also convinced that his valet is stealing from him," continued Jane, warming to the subject.

"Hmm. I suppose you haven't bungled things completely. Though I'm sure you could have gained this information without involving Lodge and putting the entire plan at risk. If Lodge had been able to get a message to Pierce..."

"But he didn't! I told you I was in the room the whole time. They didn't even come in physical contact with each other," she pleaded.

"Very well. Despite your error in judgement," he said raising a hand to stop her rebuttal, "we have some useful intelligence. However Lodge must be moved from this location. Small though the chance might be, he could still get a message to the Manor from here. That is a chance I simply can't take. All signs of his existence here must be removed."

"I will take care of it," Jane pronounced, seeing the look on Cleaver's face and trying to mitigate his judgement of her. Having Pierce meet Lodge had been foolish, but necessary in the end. When Lodge had asked to meet the newest member of the Hunt, she'd decided that she could comply and potentially end up allied with both him and Cleaver. It had been a dangerous gamble, but she didn't want to simply choose one side of this subtle battle. What if she chose the losing side?

She began to feel slightly more at ease as Cleaver sat in the brown leather club chair.

"Start the preparations immediately. I will remain here," he stated, his calm precise demeanour returning. "Have some food sent up and when you are finished we shall have some tea together and discuss the next stage."

Jane nodded in assent and quickly left the room. She first went down to the kitchen and made Dr. Cleavers order. She then climbed the stairs to the top floor and Lodge's suite.

When she entered, Lodge was sitting in a straight backed wooden chair, gazing out the window upon the square below.

"I think I've spent too much time secluded in the Manor. I never realized the stimulation provided by the casual comings and goings of the villagers of Rooks Bay."

Jane didn't respond, but began gathering the few items that had accompanied Lodge on his journey. When this was accomplished she began tidying the room.

"I take it I won't be able to continue my observations and am being forced from my perch?"

Jane's silence was all the confirmation Lodge required. Watching her, he deduced her troubled feelings.

"It will be fine," he assured her. "It was the only way for me to meet Mr. Pierce and it had to be done. I'm sorry to have put you in this position, but you needed to choose a side, the right side. Cleaver still needs us, so we should be safe for the time being."

"I'm not so sure. I can't deny I'm worried, but hopefully that will steady me and keep me focused." She had meant it as a lie until she realized how disposable she really was to the Master of the Hunt. Suddenly her worry was no longer an act.

"I'm not concerned my dear. That's why I chose you; you have a bright mind and unyielding determination. Plus your ability at, shall we say, deflecting the truth? I've known Dr. Cleaver for many years and we've been playing this game for most of that time. I always come out on top. That's not idle boasting, but simple fact."

This small speech lightened Jane's demeanour and she left the suite, ready to continue her work and report to Cleaver. She passed the guard on the second floor landing, having moved up from the ground floor to increase security. She let herself in to the room Cleaver occupied without knocking.

"How is he?" inquired Dr. Cleaver as he prepared tea for them.

"He knows he's moving."

"Of course he does. The man is an incredible intellect;

otherwise I would have disposed of him ages ago."

"I don't believe he suspects I'm working for you," she continued accepting the cup of tea he offered her.

"I find that hard to believe, but perhaps not," he replied smoothly. "He seems to have lost a step, so it may be possible."

"What is the plan now? Shall I return to the Manor or stay here in the pub?"

"Drink your tea," Cleaver responded gently, as he sipped from his own porcelain cup.

Jane peered over her cup as she blew on it, observing Dr. Cleaver. He was also watching her, but more serenely, almost nonchalantly. Although she had been initially alarmed by his presence at the pub, that feeling was subsiding. Perhaps he continued to trust her and had not discovered her shifting alliances after all.

"Now, as for the future," he continued as they drank their tea, "you cannot stay here. Returning to the Manor is also out of the question."

"As you say, my Lord," she concurred, starting to feel slightly tingly from the tea. "Then where shall I go?"

"You will go with Lord Lodge."

"I don't understand..." she uttered as the tingly feeling quickly turned to disorientation. Her heart started pounding with fear as Cleaver's face started to blur and blend into the spinning room

"You have outlived your usefulness here," stated Dr. Cleaver has he stood up.

Finally understanding the danger, Jane tried to stand up and attempt an escape. However there was no feeling in her legs and she simply toppled onto the floor. She tried to speak but began to lose consciousness.

"You silly little girl," taunted Cleaver as he calmly finished his tea.

Behind him Malicio appeared out of the shadows, his black coat and dark hair menacing and demon-like.

"Take her and Lord Lodge to the carriage," ordered

Cleaver. "It's late enough no one should see you. I shall return to the Manor, you continue on to the Crow's Nest."

*

Pierce returned to the billiard room to find Colonel Bufford and Zeidt still at odds. Bufford was hollering and blustering so vehemently that Pierce could only piece together the words; cheat, money, and toad. Zeidt remained silent, but kept jabbing his cue stick towards Bufford in an attempt to keep him at a distance and to aggravate him further. This time however Schell did not intervene. In fact he sat lounging on a stool by the bar beside Veronique.

Pierce remained silent, watching the proceeding from the door, awaiting his valet's arrival.

"I am not paying another dog gone cent to you mister!" bellowed Bufford loudly, pointing his finger at Zeidt's face.

"You insult me sir!" replied Zeidt, throwing the cue stick to the floor.

"Do you throw down sir?" inquired Bufford, his rage turning to enthusiasm.

"Well I shall certainly not take any more abuse from you!" he countered indignantly.

Melrose appeared behind Pierce at that moment, distracting him from the scene inside.

"You sent for me sir?" inquired Melrose professionally, ignoring the tempest in the room beyond. Pierce motioned his valet to follow him into the hall.

"I've just heard that Lord Lodge is very ill and that Dr. Cleaver is attending to him in his rooms," Pierce explained, pulling Melrose into a quiet corner of the hall.

"But that's impossible, since you met him in the pub this afternoon."

"Precisely. Something's not right here. He's in trouble, since it sounds like an easy way to explain his death."

"His death?"

"Think about it Melrose. Cleaver's got him locked up and

away from the Manor. He's made up this illness story so that if something were to happen to him, it could be explained away. They would simply need to bring the body back. I'm not sure what the good doctor's plan is, but I intend to get Lodge out. Tonight."

"I couldn't agree more sir, what do you need?"

"I need you to gather the Brown Pack at once, but quietly. No one else can know about this. I will meet you all in their hall shortly." Melrose nodded and calmly walked away.

As soon as he left, those from the Billiard room emptied out into the hall. They were quickly joined by the inhabitants of the salon, creating a noisy exodus. Schell walked over, seeing Pierce's quizzical look.

"Bufford challenged Zeidt to a duel, word spread," he explained waving towards the crowd with a bottle of Champagne. "Since there's nothing else going on tonight, we figured we'd start a bonfire and watch."

"Why is Zeidt duelling Bufford? He doesn't seem like the duelling type."

"It's his turn," offered Schell with a shrug. "Don't worry, eventually we all take a turn. The Colonel is only happy when he's duelling. Will you join us?"

"Perhaps later, my valet just informed me of something I have to look into. It shouldn't take me long."

"Well bring another bottle when you come," he said lifting his. "This can't possibly last me long enough."

Schell turned and quickly joined the crowd walking down the corridor, their excited voices filling the otherwise quiet halls.

Pierce waited for them to get out of sight before setting off to the Brown Pack's lair. Despite the darkness of the Manor he was able to make his way without any wrong turns or detours. Eventually he found himself in the foyer facing the three coloured doors.

He pulled out the ornate key he'd been given to unlock the massive door. The Brown Hall was always locked, due to the myriad of weapons stored inside and because they didn't trust anyone. The key slid in and he turned it effortlessly. He entered quietly locking the door behind him.

In the anteroom he stopped, listening to the voices from the hall beyond. He could clearly hear Liam questioning what was going on. MacDuff quickly told him to wait and find out. He was hesitant to enter, having never been much of a leader before. Leader's had to stand above the rest and he'd always taken the safer route and kept a low profile. But now he felt different, more confident and determined to take charge. A man's life was potentially at risk and he knew he couldn't sit by. Pierce took a breath and then confidently marched into the hall, ready to face his men.

"Gentlemen," announced Pierce from the edge of the room. "I have an urgent request for you. It is not an order, as your discovery could be detrimental to your employment here. I need your help and there is no one else at the Manor whom I trust. If you want out of it, I won't hold it against you."

Melrose stood at attention along the wall, remaining motionless as if his feet were fastened in place. Being privy to the situation, he was prepared for the speech and displayed no emotion.

The pack however, reacted differently. MacDuff stood in the middle of the room, closest to Pierce. He had a wolfish grin, his eyes shining in amusement. Liam and Sean were together and stood slightly behind MacDuff. They looked at each other in mirrored confusion, before nodding to Pierce in unison.

"Good, I'm glad for the help. Here's the situation," Pierce began, quickly explaining his meeting with Lodge and the news from De La Gena. "I believe that Lord Lodge is in imminent danger, and we're going to rescue him."

"There's no love lost between Lodge and Cleaver, that's a fact," replied MacDuff for the group. "I follow your logic, but are you sure lad?"

"If I'm wrong I'll look foolish and everyone can have a good laugh. But if I'm right, than we need to do something."

Sensing Pierce's determination, MacDuff concurred and

started organizing his men. When he was finished they left to gather what was required for the night.

Liam returned first, placing four holsters complete with pistols and extra magazines on the table. Sean arrived soon after, putting a rucksack on the table.

"I've got flashlights, night vision goggles, rope, and plastic restraints. You think we need anything else Duffy?"

"No that'll do."

With this done, the three men retreated to the adjoined cloak room, donning their long dark brown hunting jackets. These were copies of the black ones worn by the intruders that had accosted Pierce in his home when all of this began. After putting on his jacket, Sean looked at Pierce, still in his dinner jacket and turned back. He immediately returned holding another long brown leather jacket, handing it to Pierce.

"This belongs to you sir," he said taking the dinner jacket from Pierce and helping him into the new one.

"The Pack hunting jacket is usually handed over to new members before their first hunt," explained MacDuff. "But under the circumstances…"

"Thank you. Thank you all," replied Pierce with heartfelt appreciation.

"Well we can't have you running around the island looking like a waiter. That white vest and shirt are a dead giveaway on a dark night like tonight. This way the odds of us getting shot at because of you have diminished. Slightly," observed Liam wryly.

"Not to worry, they'll hear us first from those fancy squeaky shoes," joked Sean, glancing at Pierce's patent leather shoes.

"Not enough time to fix everything," countered MacDuff. "So what's the plan Patrick?"

"Well, I hadn't really thought it out too much. Melrose stays at the Manor, keeping an eye on the doors. The four of us run down to the village. Horses would draw too much attention and I haven't ridden a horse in ages. We break into the pub through the back door, race up the stairs, knock out the one guard, and get Lord Lodge. We return the way we came." They all nodded while they donned their holsters and did up their jackets.

"Good enough for me!" laughed MacDuff when he finished. "We go as a group; if anything happens we split in pairs. Liam and Sean together and I'll team up with our leader here."

They all nodded in agreement and headed out for the door. Melrose led the way through the Manor, detouring when people approached. They followed slightly behind him, but walking casually in case they were observed. Melrose led them to a side door, opened it, and whispered good luck.

The night was indeed a very dark one with no hint of a moon or stars in the sky, with a fog creeping up from the lake below. Liam passed around the NVG's, and each man's world immediately turned from darkness to various shades of green.

They quickly made their way through the Manor's immediate grounds, crouching and looking out for any observers. As they approached the arboretum, they all saw a bright green flare of light on their goggles' displays. MacDuff held up his hand and they all stopped and dropped to the ground.

"I forgot to tell you," whispered Pierce, creeping up to MacDuff. "There's a duel tonight. They headed out before I met up with you."

The group got up and began jogging through the arboretum, giving the duellists and revellers a wide birth. Within a short time they reached the roadway that led to the village. After a quick look in both directions they crossed and resumed their jog towards the village.

It was late, so there was no traffic along the road, much to Pierce's relief. He was about to say this when his companions threw themselves into the ditch. Liam had barely reached up and pulled Pierce down before a four horse carriage sped past, moving as if it was being chased by the devil.

"Thanks," acknowledged Pierce self-consciously. He was feeling a little out of his element, but tried to ignore the feeling as the others approached.

"That was Cleaver's coach," whispered MacDuff as they regrouped in the ditch.

"With his Pack riding shotgun. Literally," agreed Sean. "They were armed to the teeth."

"Probably terrorizing the countryside," offered Liam.

"I wouldn't bet against it."

"Let's go," ordered Pierce eager to get Lord Lodge and get back.

They all took off at a greater pace, Pierce managing to keep up despite the slippery dress shoes. When they reached the first set of buildings they removed their NVG's. The light from the lamps and windows would make the goggles troublesome at best, a hazard at worst.

Liam took off first, leading them through the back alleys of Rooks Bay, weaving them closer to their destination. Having only reached the pub by the main road and front door, Pierce was totally lost. They finally stopped at the corner of a shop.

"That was a sneaky way Liam," commented MacDuff.

"How many angry husbands did it take you to figure out all those shortcuts?" inquired Sean with a smile.

"Didn't you know, I'm a geographer of great renown," countered Liam with his own mischievous smile.

"Sure, but you're no locksmith," countered MacDuff. "Sean, your skills are up next. You pick the lock on the back door. Patrick and I will be at each side of the door. Liam, you back us up from across the street. When the doors open I go in first, then Patrick and we head up to the top as fast as we can, taking out the guard along the way. You two follow us in and secure the ground and second floors. I don't want any surprises popping out behind us."

Quietly they all removed their pistols and screwed on silencers, except for Sean who took out his lock picking tools.

MacDuff held up an open hand and started to count down. When his last finger closed in, they all charged towards the back door of the pub.

Chapter 9

Pierce wanted to scream, but had to hold it in, lest he awaken the owners of the pub. Vainly, he rechecked the room and found the same thing as when they had first entered. Nothing, no sign of Lord Lodge.

Their entry into the building had been perfect. Sean had opened the back door within seconds, letting MacDuff and Pierce silently rush in and start up the stairs. They met no one on the flight up and had quickly reached the top floor suite. MacDuff had motioned for Pierce to open the door and he would go in first. Nodding he understood, Pierce gingerly turned the knob. When he had turned it fully he looked at MacDuff, took a deep breath, and then pushed it open as quietly as he could. This had proved unnecessary as the pair were confronted with an empty room. A quick search verified this.

"We've got to go," whispered MacDuff, pulling Pierce back to the top floor landing.

The pair descended the stairs rejoining the others at the bottom. Both shook their heads, signalling that they had also found nothing.

Unable to accept this failure, Pierce began stalking around the ground floor, looking for anything that could provide a clue. At the entrance to the main pub, a floor board creaked as he stepped in. Looking down at his feet, he suddenly thought of the basement. It was a much more natural hiding place and must surely be where they moved Lodge to.

Pierce spun around and pointed down at the floor to his men, indicating that he believed this to be the next place to search. However Liam shook his head in response, having already searched it as the ground floor sentry. MacDuff looked at the others and pointed towards the door, signalling their need to exit and regroup outside. Pierce sullenly left the building, feeling defeated.

"You're sure he was there lad?" voiced MacDuff, back in the relative safety of the alley across the street. Pierce responded with a black look. "Sorry, but I had to ask. What do we do next?"

"Nothing we can do. Return to the Manor and try and figure out what happened here."

They extracted themselves from the village and returned to the Manor the way they had come. The trip proved uneventful, although they had to be particularly careful when they reached the Manor grounds. The bonfire alluded to by Schell had reached epic heights and had gathered a large crowd, judging by the shadows of revellers that they could see.

"What a bloody mess," spat Pierce as they re-entered the Brown Hall.

"What happens now, to Lord Lodge I mean," asked Liam.

"I have no idea. Maybe I got it wrong. Maybe he wasn't in danger at all and they took him to some mountain retreat or seaside resort. But I doubt it."

"I as well," agreed MacDuff. "The carriage that almost ran you over on the lake road belongs to Cleaver and was filled with his Pack. I'd be willing to bet that it also contained Lord Lodge."

"We probably missed them by minutes," uttered Sean, rubbing his face wearily. They all sat in silence around the large table, refusing to continue. A knock at the door broke the stillness of the group and MacDuff motioned for Liam to get the door. He was followed back into the room by Melrose, although his training forbade any great signs of emotion, Pierce could tell he was as similarly disappointed as the rest.

"I watched your return from the second floor balcony," offered Melrose.

"Do you think anyone saw us?" asked Pierce, not knowing what else to say.

"I believe not my Lord. You picked a good spot, as mine was the only perch that provided a clear view."

"Well that's something."

"I took the liberty…" said Melrose, displaying two bottles from behind his back.

One was immediately opened and passed around without glasses. Unable to witness a second ill-mannered pass, Melrose went in search of glasses. He returned with five, allowing himself a drink, feeling like part of the team. No one objected when he poured out five glasses and handed them out.

"Anyone have a plan?" inquired Pierce, scanning the room.

"Get rip roaring drunk," offered Sean lamely.

"Then regroup and formulate a new plan," seconded Liam.

"That's as good as anything I've thought of," agreed Pierce. He got up and took the second bottle. "But you guys are on your own. I've been invited to the festivity of fire out there and they're expecting me. So good night gents, and thanks for your efforts. This does not end tonight."

He moved to the door after picking up the second bottle. Melrose followed him, grabbing his master's forgotten dinner jacket. Pierce looked down at his odd attire and removed the hunting jacket, handing it to Melrose and then shrugging into his original formal wear.

"I won't need you for some time Melrose," Pierce instructed his valet. "Feel free to grab another bottle from my stock and share it with the Pack. They've earned it."

"Very kind sir."

"Kind nothing, I assume that's where the first two bottles came from."

"Indeed."

"I'm heading to the party by the bonfire. Come get me if I don't return by sunrise."

*

The carriage barrelled along the gravel road, heedless of mud filled puddles and the pot holes they filled. Jane awakened with a start after the carriage met a group of these holes in succession. The carriage lamps provided an ethereal glow within the cabin that hindered her attempts to focus and discover her surroundings.

Jane was finally able to make out the interior of the cabin, however the window only provided a canvas of dark shapes flying past outside. Across from her sat Lord Lodge, presumably asleep, although he could have been similarly drugged. The throbbing in her head provided the proof to Jane that she had been drugged and that this was not a dream.

"I see you've awoken," uttered a grave voice opposite her in the cabin. She could only make out a dark figure facing the other window. However when the figure turned to face her, she saw the menacing face of Malicio smiling cruelly.

"Where are we?"

"I told you to follow your instructions," he replied with growing pleasure at her discomfort, ignoring her question. "But you just had to ignore me."

Jane remained silent, unwilling to provoke him further. However he continued his quiet attack, his deliberate and calm voice more threatening than wild shouts.

"You had the chance to be a part of something special, but you threw it all away. The Doctor's plans always rely on strict adherence. I might have enjoyed your company in our little conspiracy."

"Where are we? Where are you taking us?" Jane mumbled, finding the courage to ask a second time.

"Us is it? You truly are doomed," he replied amused. "We have just crossed the Talon Pass and are on the West Mountain

Road. Our destination is…"

"The Crow's Nest," she sighed, completing his sentence. Malicio simply smiled in reply and turned to continue his vigil out the window.

The carriage began to slow as the surrounding country became too treacherous for its previous speed. The road snaked along the side of the mountains that gave it its name. Dense woods engulfed the road as it made its elevated progress.

After an endless amount of time in the monotonous darkness, Jane suddenly felt like the world opened up. The forest thinned out quickly and the moon finally broke past the thick black clouds of night. She sat staring out the window in awe; rolling mountain pastures, jagged peaks, and the white caps of a rolling sea in the distance.

However this magnificent view soon became equally disheartening, as Jane could see no signs of civilization. A huge dark expanse was laid out before her; she could see no light or smoke. There were no buildings to be seen anywhere, no chance of help in an escape.

"This is your first time at the Crows Nest, isn't it?" asked Malicio.

Jane nodded, not trusting her voice to maintain its composure.

"Well then you won't want to miss the view," he replied pointing out his window as the road turned sharply. Jane followed his glance out the window and she was again struck with feelings of both awe and dismay.

Thrusting out from the sheer face of the mountain, the Crow's Nest sat kinglike on the sole level piece of land in the surrounding area. The terrain to the rear and the side turned into steep cliffs within feet of the buildings walls, leaving the roadway as the only means of approach. This approach was only made possible by the crossing of two stone bridges that crossed deep ravines. The Crows Nest itself was an imposing hall built of stone and timber, reminiscent of the great Viking strongholds of Scandinavia. The light coloured stone seemed to glow from the moonlight in comparison to the dark woods and mountains surrounding it. The building was all alight and smoke billowed from the chimneys, creating an even more enticing view.

Jane sat back as the carriage took another turn that placed a hill between it and the fortress, obscuring the view. As welcoming as the Crow's Nest appeared from the cramped confines of the carriage, she knew it would be a prison. Built far away from any populated area on the far side of the mountains, it was not easily accessible. Additionally it was built where the only real means of escape was by the front door.

The carriage stopped at the first bridge, where an iron gate forced one of the men on top to descend and unlock it. This was repeated soon after as they reached the second bridge. Blazing torches lined the drive from the bridge to a circular courtyard, illuminating the grandeur of the hall. Roughly the first twenty feet of the building was expertly crafted of stone; square, smooth, and flawless. If it weren't for the light gray shade of the stone, one would think it had been carved right out of the dark stoned Cliffside. Solid log beams continued where the stone ended and were just as finely crafted. Shapes and designs were carved into the walls where the corners met and seemed to be painted in with silver, allowing the building to shimmer in the moonlight. The sheen appeared to run from the roof, as it was also constructed of silver flecked stone.

"Out," ordered Malicio as the carriage halted in front of a sweeping staircase that led to the main doors of the hall.

Jane stood up slowly, stiff from the long and brutal ride. She reached over and gently shook Lord Lodge's knee, awaking him slowly.

"Have we reached our destination so soon?" inquired Lodge, yawning and stretching his extremities.

"As you very well know," countered Malicio. "You've been awake since before the Talon Pass. I'm not some boy, easily fooled by your trickery."

Lodge merely glanced at him and let Jane help him down from the carriage. They were immediately welcomed by a stiff cold breeze that threatened to topple them before they secured their footing.

"Enjoy your stay!" yelled Malicio as his fellow Black Pack companions took the recently emptied spots in the carriage. When they had all gotten in, the door was slammed shut, muffling the laughter emanating from within.

Jane looked over the vast dark valley beyond and shivered. For the first time since she had delivered the letter, she was at a loss for a plan. Lodge came up beside her and joined her gaze into the abyss before them. Glad to not be alone, she linked her arm with his.

"My dear, you're shaking," he replied with concern.

"Don't worry my Lord," she replied calmly. "I might be a little cold and scared, but I'm shaking with fury. This isn't over."

*

"You're a cruel bastard," Pierce uttered in pain, "and I won't forget this."

"What was that?"

"Nothing. I think I said it was a nice day." He then uttered another curse under his breath.

"You're a terrible liar."

Wilhelm Schell looked back over his shoulder, watching his companion struggle up the slight grade of a hill. He pulled the reins of his horse to stop and turn around. Pierce finally reached him, wincing in pain.

"I can't feel my ass, I think I might be bleeding."

"Stop complaining, this was your idea."

"All I said was that I hadn't been riding since I was a child," retorted Pierce sharply. "You're the one who said we should take the horses out."

"Yes, but you agreed."

"But I was drunk!" exclaimed Pierce.

"So was I!"

Both began laughing at the ridiculousness of their

conversation and the situation they found themselves in. Schell grabbed a bottle of water from his saddle bag and passed it over, sensing Pierce's greater need. They polished it off within minutes between them, neither satisfied.

"I think there's a creek further up, we can give the horses a break and refill our canteens."

"I doubt the horses need a break, since we've only gone about two kilometres," chuckled Pierce.

Pierce urged his horse to follow Schell's as they continued along the path. His head was pounding and his muscles ached. Scenes from the night before flashed in his head; a bonfire, scotch, dancing around the bonfire, more scotch, some champagne, mistakenly walking up to an amorous couple, and then more fire and scotch. He didn't remember how he got back to his rooms and could hardly remember waking up this morning. However his attempts at recollection were halted by Schell announcing their arrival at the creek.

"Watch out when you dismount," warned Schell, "you probably won't be able to use your legs properly."

Pierce was able to dismount without much trouble, although it was not graceful. He led his horse over to the creek, casually wrapping the reins around a tree branch. The horse leaned down to take a drink of water and Pierce followed suit with his canteen.

Taking a pull from his bottle, Pierce surveyed their rest stop. The land rose steadily, but there were no big ditches or rocks surrounding the area. Indeed, there didn't seem to be any real natural obstacles anywhere, despite the wooded environment. Growing up in the woods of the Canadian Shield where the bush was dense, rocky, and chaotic, this place seemed almost groomed. When he mentioned this to Schell, his partner nodded in agreement.

"When I first arrived and began my equestrian excursions I asked the same question," explained Schell. "Apparently this is the old hunting ground when the Club was first created. They had the groundskeepers remove the rocks, fill in holes, and trim the trees. They used to ride their horses through the forest at speed so that, like their prey, they weren't confined to the paths."

"Hardly seems sporting," observed Pierce with mild conviction.

"The Hunt is not terribly concerned with fair play," responded Schell with a shrug.

Pierce was intrigued, but his head was too sore to delve too deeply into the statement. Instead he found a solid tree to sit against and continued to empty his canteen.

"How come you're not a hung-over mess?" asked Pierce relaxing into his spot.

"I am, trust me," he replied with a smile. "I'm simply better trained to deal with it than you." Pierce raised an inquiring eyebrow, forcing him to continue. "First, I've been at the Manor much longer than you. What you witnessed last night was a fairly regular occurrence. Of course we don't always have large bonfire parties every time the Colonel duels someone. Otherwise these woods we're enjoying would have been cut down long ago.

"The second reason is that I was a diplomat for some years. When I wasn't in meetings I was drinking at receptions. There's nothing diplomats like better than to drink. But you always had to be ready to go into a meeting the next morning and sit through hours of deliberations without falling asleep or being sick on the floor."

"You didn't have to drink."

"Of course I did, it would have been bad manners to refuse. Besides, getting the other side drunk was the best way of getting information. And nobody trusts a sober person."

"Words of wisdom," toasted Pierce raising his canteen to his companion.

"I think we've rested long enough," he announced after a few minutes of silence.

"I still feel awful."

"Well then another bit of wisdom to follow," offered Schell walking over to his horse. "The best cure for a hangover is greasy food and more alcohol. We'll ride down to the village and stop in at the pub and get both."

Pierce nodded slowly in agreement. The thought of food or beer made him feel queasy; however he wanted to return to the pub to renew his search for Lord Lodge.

*

Both men sat down in the Manor's snug at the Fish and Feather with a sigh, sinking into the soft leather club chairs. A young girl cam over and took their drink orders before quickly moving back to the bar. She returned within seconds with their drinks.

"I certainly enjoy the perks of our position," announced Schell having a drink and taking in the private snug. "On one of my excursions back to Germany I got a good beer recipe from a local brewer and brought it back. So now they make my favourite beer."

"I wondered why they offered it to me the first time I came in here, since nobody else was drinking it," joked Pierce.

"Cretins, the whole bunch," he laughed in reply.

"So where in Germany are you from?" inquired Pierce, taking a drink from his own beer.

"Berlin, well a suburb outside of Berlin," answered Schell easily. "Although my family had land throughout what was once Prussia. But I imagine you don't want to know where in Germany I'm from, but *when*."

Pierce had merely meant to make small talk until he could track down Jane and figure a smart way of finding out what happened to Lodge. He would have to ask it in such a way that she wouldn't realize he knew Lodge was no longer here.

"I keep forgetting everyone is from both a different place and time," Pierce said, bringing his attention back to his companion.

"Some people think it matters more when you came from than where. They believe when you lived can provide a better insight into who you are."

"And what do you believe?"

"That people are people," shrugged Schell taking another drink.

"So *when* were you a German diplomat?"

Schell sized up Pierce from his seat opposite of him, thinking quietly. When he began speaking it was casual, as if he was talking about the weather and seemingly hadn't just made a tough decision.

"It was in the 1930's," he started, looking for a reaction. Seeing none he continued, "I joined the Foreign Department after University during the Weimar Republic. It was a golden age of diplomacy. War had gone out of fashion; therefore dispute resolution became the sole domain of the diplomat. I was able to travel to many places."

"Then..." said Pierce knowingly.

"Yes, I thought you were clever," he replied. He stood up and waved at the waitress. When she came over he ordered another round and a pair of beef pies. The drinks came quickly as before, soon followed by the food which she placed at the empty table. Both men moved to the table from their club chairs in order to eat.

"I'm sorry if the subject is troubling," offered Pierce slightly embarrassed.

"Don't be, it's not a problem for me," he replied taking a forkful of beef before continuing. "Correct me if I'm wrong, but I believe you were alluding to the appearance of Hitler and the Nazi's in the German government."

Pierce nodded once, hoping he hadn't touched a sore spot.

"I met the man you know. He had a certain charisma, an attraction even, in those early days. If we had known then..." he trailed off shaking his head. "Well, after they took power I stayed on for a little while. But it wasn't the same. People started being replaced by hacks, so I left before they could get rid of me. At that point many of us felt powerless, sensing the oncoming war with no possibility of avoidance."

"So what did you do?"

"I kept my head down and survived."

"But you weren't a…?"

"A what? A Nazi?" He replied amused. "Patrick, we were all Nazi's, whether we admitted it or not. The Nazi's didn't invade Germany. They rose up from within; democratically elected amidst large popular support I might add."

Pierce didn't know how to take this statement, so he just finished eating his food. Schell finished first, leaning back from the table.

"I don't know why Dr, Cleaver dislikes this place. The food is delicious." He placed his napkin beside his empty plate and excused himself.

The waitress appeared to clear their table before Pierce could figure out a plan to see Jane. So he found himself asking her where she was, without so much as an excuse.

"Jane, my Lord?" She responded thinking, "why she went back to work at the Manor this morning. I'm not sure the circumstances."

This made sense to Pierce, since she was obviously sent here to look after Lodge while he was in the pub. However he couldn't help but feel as though Lord Lodge was in even more trouble now that she had been dispensed with. Perhaps she knew where he had been taken or at the very least could provide a clue.

When Schell returned they both donned their riding jackets and made their way to the stable where they had left their horses. They rode back to the Manor along the road in companionable silence, with Schell answering the odd question posed by Pierce about the surrounding countryside.

After arriving at the Manor, Pierce thanked Schell for the afternoon and made his way to his rooms as soon as the groom took his horse. He was met by Melrose at the top of the staircase in the main entrance hall.

"How did you know I was back already?" inquired Pierce. "Are you psychic?"

"Part of the training sir," deadpanned Melrose in response. "However in this instance I saw you and Lord Schell returning along the drive."

"Have you heard any more rumours about Lord Lodge?" asked Pierce quietly as they turned to make their way up to his rooms.

"Nothing of any consequence."

"What about Jane? Have you seen here yet?"

"No sir, should I have?"

"One of the barmaids told me Jane had returned to work at the Manor this morning."

"Not that I've heard," replied Melrose shaking his head. "I'll ask around, but if I haven't heard about it yet, there's only two options."

"And they are?"

"That I've either lost my ability to remain informed of the Manor's activities or she has not returned."

"I hate to contemplate either of those options," Pierce said quietly. "Find out where she is Melrose. She is our only link to Lord Lodge."

Chapter 10

Dawn was peeking through the thick paned glass as Jane's internal clock woke her up. Despite the tiring trip and late night arrival, a lifetime of waking up early took precedence over her need for sleep. Despite her wakefulness and uncertainty as to what was required of her, she decided to remain in bed. A sweeping glance of the room provided a view of solid wooden walls, a bland red tapestry and fur rugs. The room was slightly larger than her old one at the manor, but equally sparse in its furnishings.

Laying back down she stared at the ceiling and tried to piece together how she ended up here. She knew Dr. Cleaver had drugged her before she hit the ground. That he didn't trust her was nothing new, as she was pretty sure he didn't trust anyone. But why had he sent her to this mountain retreat, surely not for a vacation. But if he had wanted to rid himself of her, it would have been easier to swap the drugs for poison and have his men drop her body on the way here. Clearly he wanted her alive, but to what end and purpose?

The noises of a rising house echoed from down the hall, bringing her back to reality. She rose from the blankets, but before she could get out of bed the door inched open. The round rosy cheeked face of a middle aged woman poked through.

"Good you're awake already," she said neutrally. "I'm Mrs. Hobart, housekeeper and cook at the Crows Nest. As Lord Lodge didn't bring his valet with him, you'll have to fill in. He requested an early breakfast, so be ready to bring it up to him in ten minutes."

Without another word or glance the door was closed and Jane was left to scramble into whatever was available in the closet. The selection appeared to be various sizes of the same uniform worn by the staff of the manor, albeit made of slightly warmer material. Within minutes she was dressed and made herself presentable with the help of a small mirror. Looking at her reflection, she was disappointed to be filling the role of a servant. The whole point to working with Lord Cleaver was to eventually move up to something new. Well it could be worse, she thought; those drugs could have been poison and I could be dead right now.

Pushing that dark thought aside, Jane found her way to the kitchen easily enough by following the sounds of banging cooking implements. Despite the sounds she heard from the hallway, she was surprised to find only Mrs. Hobart in the kitchen.

"There's only Lord Lodge staying here at the present," offered the cook, sensing Jane's curiosity. "So there's only myself, Mr. Hobart, and a couple groundskeepers."

"I see," replied Jane with the only response that felt right.

"Ordinarily meals are served in the main dining room upstairs," continued the cook without turning from the stove. "However since Lord Lodge is the only guest, he will likely be eating in the study adjoined to his room."

"Where is that exactly?" inquired Jane. "I don't really remember the layout of the building from last night."

"Through the hallway you just walked down to the end and up the stairs. Turn left at the top, then down the corridor to the entrance hall. Go up the main staircase and turn right at the top. It's the second door."

The cook had rifled of these directions in quick order, finishing as she turned to deliver the breakfast tray to Jane. She returned to her work without another word, focused on her next task.

Jane's trepidation at getting lost or forgetting the directions was dismissed as she reached the main floor. Though imposing from outside, the building was simply laid out and easy to navigate. The stone of the basement level gave way to large intricately carved timber walls. She passed by the dining room and then a couple large rooms adorned with hunting trophies. There were no wrong turns to make, as this hallway exited to the main entrance hall. It was a large open room with a big circular fireplace in the middle, disgorging its smoke into a metal bell-like device above it. This was apparently the chimney, as the top traveled up to the ceiling high above. The second level was visible, with a balcony circling the space above. She picked out the second door from her position and hurried up the stairs as quickly as she dared, holding the tray steady.

Luckily there was a small side table beside the door that she could set the breakfast tray on as she knocked and opened the door. The room was empty, though a fire had been started in the small fireplace on the wall to the right. There was a door beside it, which she assumed connected to Lord Lodge's bedroom.

She was barely able to set the tray on the desk before one of the logs in the fire suddenly fell over, dangerously close to falling out of the fireplace. She jumped nervously as it banged down and would undoubtedly have dropped the tray if it were still in her hands. Leaning down to move the log into a safe position in the fire, Jane noted that the fireplace serviced both rooms. In fact she could see into the other room, though only clear enough to see a pair of polished leather shoes walking towards the door. This gave her just enough time to set the poker down and stand up to receive Lord Lodge.

"Good morning Jane," he said cheerily.

"Yes my Lord."

"I think it is," he replied to her neutral response. "The sun is up, we've got this wonderful hunting lodge to ourselves, but most importantly we're still alive." This last sentence was delivered with nonchalance, though Jane could tell it was not a general statement.

"Is there anything else sir?" She asked quickly.

"Please sit," he gestured to an empty chair. "Have you eaten yet? No? Then please join me, I feel like eating with company. Try the fresh buns; Mrs Hobart is a terrific baker."

They divided up the meal, and began eating in companionable silence. Jane realized that she hadn't eaten in some time and was thankful for Lodge's offer.

"This is your first time at the Crows Nest I believe?" asked Lodge over his tea cup before taking a sip. Jane nodded in assent, as her mouth was filled with a buttered roll.

"What's your impression of it? I have been here so many times I forget what it must be like your first time."

"Honestly it's unsettling," replied Jane after taking a moment to clear her mouth and give the question some thought. "It must be different when it's full, but empty like this, I feel like the ghosts of previous visitors are all around. And then I think about the scene from last night. It's so remote and formidable, like a prison."

"How very astute of you my dear."

"What are we doing here?" inquired Jane to no one in particular, while staring out the window. She looked back to find Lord Lodge staring at her intently, though without malice.

"That's the very question I was going to ask you," he replied. Before she could protest the question he held up a hand. "I will do you the courtesy of not spending unnecessary time trying to get information from you in an innocent way, and you can reciprocate with telling me the truth."

Jane was not prepared for this and the sudden shock of the direct statement stunned her. Feeling helpless in this desolate location, far from any friends or allies, she succumbed to honesty.

"It seems we're in this together," she allowed. "But in the spirit of reciprocation, when I've finished you'll tell me what I've gotten myself involved in."

"That seems only fair," Lodge responded, refilling her tea and passing it across the table to her. She accepted it gratefully, taking a small sip and closing her eyes.

"Where should I start? I suppose you'll interject if you need elaboration?"

"Indeed," Lodge assented. His gaze then turned from affable dining companion to something different entirely. His hawk like eyes became extremely focused, cataloguing the slightest change in his companion's expressions. "I'm well aware of most of your activities at the Manor. However I'd be most grateful if you could begin with your task to deliver the letter addressed to Commandant Pierce."

"Nothing?"

"Nothing sir, no trace whatsoever."

"This is not good Melrose. We need to find her."

Pierce was sitting in his study, having just finished reading on old manual on flintlock pistol operations. It was midday and he had hoped Melrose would have been able to find some information on Jane. He hadn't stopped thinking about the potential danger she might be in since his return from the village the day before

"I suppose the rest of the staff still believe the original stories?" inquired Pierce.

"Yes sir, without arousing suspicion I was able to conclude that everyone at the Manor believes Jane is still employed at the pub and that Lord Lodge remains an invalid within his rooms here. Should we try and force a situation to expose these falsehoods?"

"I don't think so," Pierce responded thoughtfully. "Forcing the issue will not help our cause at this point. We need to find them first, deal with those responsible second."

"As you say sir."

"We'll keep our eyes open, but we'll have to be sneaky about it," Pierce decided lamely. "It's not a great plan, but what else can we do? Other than that we carry on business as usual. So what's the rest of my day look like?"

"There is an excursion planned for this evening. Those taking part are to meet in the Hunt Room at 7 sharp."

"Well if there's nothing else planned for the afternoon I think I'll wander the Manor. I've never been to that room, so I think I should track it down before I'm expected. Has the Pack been informed of this excursion?"

"Yes sir. They will be preparing the required equipment."

"Good, then I might stop by and see them as well."

Nodding, Melrose retreated from the study and returned to his duties. This left Pierce to don his jacket in preparation for his exploration of the mazelike expanse of the Manor. He picked up the book he had been reading and vainly tried to correctly replace it in the imposing bookcase.

The size of the Manor was registered by Pierce after walking within it for a quarter hour. Despite knowing that there were numerous people living and working in the Manor, he had only passed a handful in the halls. Although these had mostly been servants, he had expected to see even more of them going about their routine functions. The rooms he passed were all picture perfect, the fires well stoked, and the hallways were immaculate. Surely there would have to be a large staff to accomplish this?

Despite the size, he felt as though he was starting to understand the layout better. He was able to use waypoints to recognize his location; certain statues, specific plants, even elaborate suits of armour. It was at one of these pieces, a statue of Apollo, that Pierce discovered a corridor he had not yet travelled. It was a couple steps lower than the foyer he presently occupied, wide and dark, though not menacing.

Pierce looked around, trying to take a mental photograph of the location for his internal map. He was suddenly aware of a maid passing behind him, appearing as though out of thin air.

"Excuse me?"

"Yes my Lord?"

"Where did you just come from," he asked kindly. "I was

sure I was alone here a second ago."

"From the passage door, sir. Behind the curtain on the other side of the statue," she responded, pointing to a spot mere feet from where they were standing.

Pierce walked over and discovered that there was indeed a door behind the curtain, perfectly concealed in the wall.

"Holy shit," he approved softly. "Are there more of these doors throughout the Manor?"

"Yes sir. They open to stairwells that lead to the servants' spaces below."

"Cool, almost like a secret passage. Well, carry on I guess."

With a quick bow of her head she turned to leave, only to stop from Pierce's raised hand before she had the chance.

"Wait a second, where does this corridor lead to?"

"To the laboratory sir."

"Of course, just what an old manor needs, a laboratory."

Seeing the questioning look on the maid's face he motioned her to ignore him. She once again bowed and left.

The corridor was dark and wide, and lined with a chequered floor that would have seemed at home in an institution. After walking a short distance Pierce could see an illuminated doorway ahead to the left. Before he reached the opening he heard the distinct clang of metal landing on stainless steel. He was momentarily unsure if he should proceed, but the maid had not warned him off.

He quietly walked up to the doorway and then slowly peaked around the corner like a Saturday morning cartoon. But rather than a wild looking man working on a cadaver, he was looking at beautiful middle aged woman, seemingly radiating in contrast to her dark surroundings. Her hair, skin, and lab coat shared a glowing white hue that was almost angelic.

"Yes?"

Realizing that this was addressed to him, Pierce tried to nonchalantly emerge from around the corner. However he felt decidedly like a child caught out of bed by his parents.

"Sorry, I don't mean to interu…" His apology was

abruptly cut short when he knocked into a metal tray, dumping its contents on the floor. "Sorry again, I'll get these."

"No need, that's what assistants are for," she said raising a graceful hand.

Hearing her speak a full sentence, Pierce was struck by her accent. Although by no means a linguist, he concluded this was the Russian scientist Melrose had spoken of previously.

"What can I help you with?" she asked coldly, but without malice.

"Oh, well, nothing specifically I guess…" replied Pierce awkwardly.

"Well then what are you doing here?"

"Here? Well I was just exploring the Manor and ended up here."

"I see. Take a seat if you wish," she instructed motioning to a stool near her. "I have just finished for the day."

Pierce sat down by her, noticing that she appeared more clinical and less angelic with proximity.

"I've just arrived at the Manor and am trying to find my bearings…"

"I assure you they're not here," she answered literally. Then taking some instruments from a nearby tray she moved towards him questioningly. "Do you mind if I…?"

Unsure what was happening, Pierce simply nodded in assent. She grabbed a large calliper and began measuring his head.

"I meant that I was exploring the building," replied Pierce uneasily as she moved around him measuring. "I'm the new Member of the Hunt."

"Really?" She said momentarily stopping her work. "So you are Commandant Pierce. Did you run a Gulag?" Seeing no comprehension she elaborated, "a prison, a jail, a work farm?"

"No, I just worked for the government," Pierce answered somewhat abashed. "I hear you're a scientist." He immediately felt foolish asking this question as she was clearly wearing a lab coat in a lab. However she did not seem fazed by the obvious statement.

"Da, I am Dr. Elena Sirinova." She continued her measuring, and then had Pierce hold out his hands as she prodded him with new tools.

"As a scientist would you be able to explain how we came to be here? At the Manor that is. Did we travel through time, space, or both? How do those doors in the North Tower work?"

"I am not that kind of scientist," she replied succinctly. "I study biology, the human body. Although I doubt if physics could even answer your questions. Sometimes I think there is more witchcraft than science at work here."

Pierce wanted to smile and point out the apparent contradiction as she sat back down and started writing notes. But thinking better of it he stood up and started to wander the lab, looking at the strange gadgets that lined the immaculate walls and tables.

"Be so good as to bring that clear bottle over," ordered Sirinova, pointing to a bottle by a sink.

While he grabbed it, she gathered a pair of clean beakers from a wash stand. She took the bottle from Pierce and poured two drinks into it.

"You've been so good to allow my little intrusions, let us have a drink together."

She seemed to be warming her cool appearance, so Pierce nodded and took the offered beaker. He looked at it closely but refrained from sniffing it, not wishing to insult his host.

"I know vodka is supposed to be taken cold," she explained pleasantly. "But you have to make do."

"I'm sure it will be fine," answered Patrick, starting to feel more comfortable. His comfort level increased as they clinked glass and drank from the beakers.

"It is passable," agreed Elena. "How do you find it?"

"Ith's velly goo…" mumbled Pierce. Suddenly startled, he tried to move his mouth as it was beginning to feel numb, making him unable to speak properly. Wondering how strong the vodka was he looked up at Elena to see how she was fairing. However her warm look had once again turned cold and clinical. She raised a small flashlight and began looking into his eyes. Pierce tried to blink, but he could not move his eyelids. In fact he couldn't move anything!

*

A knock at the door. Although he couldn't move, his hearing and eyesight were not diminished. Pierce watched Elena look up from her notes with shock.

"My lord, I've come to collect you for the Pack meeting," announced the firm voice of MacDuff from behind him.

Sensing no response, MacDuff looked from Sirinova to Pierce, and then to the glasses and bottle between them.

"Sir, if you haven't taken the paralytic vodka, raise your hand." No arm raised, but Pierce let out a snort. "I see. Comrade Doctor, would you be kind enough to administer the antidote."

"There is none," she responded calmly. "The effects will wear off over time. You may take him MacDuff, I've got all the information I need."

MacDuff nodded and walked over to Pierce, leaning down and then throwing his lifeless body over his hulking shoulders.

"Here we go then lad," he said brightly. "Let me know if I bounce you too much." Pierce replied with a throaty growl. "Didn't your mother tell you not to have strange drinks with strange women?"

Their voyage through the Manor was uneventful, but more importantly to Pierce, unobserved. By the time they reached the foyer outside the Packs' doors he was able to walk again, though still supported by MacDuff.

"Wait a second," said Pierce, stopping MacDuff from opening the door. "I'd like to get a little more composed before we go in."

MacDuff nodded and leaned against the door, tired from carrying his leader.

"What happened back there?" asked Pierce while he stretched his limbs.

"The Doctor is interested in the human body, obsessively so. She's been known to experiment on the unsuspecting. Just little tests, nothing terribly dangerous."

"I feel like that could have been useful information when I arrived."

"Do you mean to tell me when she smiled so sweetly and batted her eyes you would have ignored her?" countered MacDuff sceptically. "No you would not. Nor any warm blooded man for that matter."

"So have you ever fallen for her tricks?" inquired Pierce feeling less naïve.

"Of course not. I'm too experienced and cunning," he replied with a wink.

Pierce laughed and rolled his eyes. MacDuff opened the door after getting an approving nod from his leader.

"How did you know I was even there?" asked Pierce as they walked into the now familiar lair of the Brown Pack. "I didn't even know I was going to be there five minutes beforehand."

"I'm no witch my Lord, but I'm no fool. You'll have to learn there are many eyes and ears around the Manor. I have some of the servants keeping an eye on you. One of them happened to be the maid you asked directions for in the corridor. Fearing she had sent you to the laboratory unprotected, she came to see me."

"And you rushed to my aid? I was there for a good ten minutes before I drank the drug and spent another ten minutes as stiff as a board. We just made the trip back in five minutes with me on your back!"

"I was busy with a very important sandwich my Lord," responded MacDuff lightly, realizing that his masters accusations were made in jest. "Had I rushed to your side and stopped you from drinking the drug, you would have eventually made your way back to her and ended up in the same position, but without anyone coming to your rescue."

"So another part of the learning process then? Another lesson?"

"You see, I told the others you were bright."

"I bet they weren't fooled," laughed Pierce as Liam and Sean emerged from the lower training area, bags in hand.

"Good afternoon my lord," nodded Sean as the pair joined them.

"I hear you were in the clutches of the black widow," observed Liam. "Looks like you made a daring escape. I hope you haven't set up a second date."

"Very funny," replied Pierce. "I hope you all got a good chuckle. But I'd like to have a little bit more warning about issues that could pose a danger to me."

"Of course sir," acknowledged MacDuff for the group.

"So what's in the bags? What's the excursion for tonight?" inquired Pierce looking to the bags on the main table.

"Actually pretty much the same as what we packed for the assault on the pub," answered Liam. "Pistols, goggles, flashlights, and so forth."

"All modern equipment, so we'll be going somewhere close to your time," concluded Sean.

"But we don't know the specifics?"

"No sir. We receive the general requirements in order to pack the gear and have it ready. The specifics will be announced in the Hunt Room, when the Hunt members participating are present."

"Speaking of which," Macduff interjected looking at a clock on the wall, "you need to return to your rooms and change. I sent up the various clothing you will need to Melrose. He will get you ready and I'll meet you in your rooms to escort you to the Hunt Room."

Though the footsteps in the hallway were faint, his hunter trained senses were easily able to discern their approach. As they got closer their whispered voices became audible, though only with extreme concentration. He remained in his fortuitous hiding space once he recognized the owners of those voices.

"And you believe her my Lord?"

"I have no reason not too," responded a cool voice. "She was too afraid to cross me."

"Then why have her exiled?"

"She had outlived her use to me where she was," the voice replied with the hint of an implied threat. "I couldn't have Lodge killed, nor am I sure that is what I want. However by sending her with him, she might again prove useful."

"She'll wish to regain your favour and continue to play Lodge for a fool?"

"Precisely," he said, stopping and looking around for any eavesdroppers.

"I have to say I am somewhat sceptical that he told her the truth when he said he would jump at the first opportunity to leave the Manor and return home."

"She can be very persuasive and appear trustworthy to simple men. I also believe that when he said those things, he believed it would be a difficult and lengthy task."

"But instead we have created the opportunity for him," observed Drummond. "So we are to open the door and he will leave us of his own will, never to return?"

"That Drummond, is a necessity," ordered Cleaver. "However it must be non-violent. I cannot risk the death of a Hunt member. It must be his decision to leave."

"Understood my Lord. Whom shall we send with him?"

"Send one person he trusts and someone he has already met. However inform both those members of Pierce's wish to leave. I don't want any heroic attempts to bring him back."

"It shall be as you say my Lord," obeyed Drummond following Cleaver as they continued their journey through the Manor.

Tiberius emerged from the servants' passage behind a Norman tapestry hanging in the corridor. He checked to see if his emergence was observed, then continued down the ornate corridor in the opposite direction of the conspirators. His plans for a quiet night by the fire were now impossible after hearing the devious conversation. He quickly formulated a plan as he negotiated the halls of the Manor towards his room. He needed to get some supplies, a change of clothes, and a key to the North Tower as quickly and quietly as possible.

Chapter 11

Pierce stood on a side street, his shoulders slouched and slightly shivering in the rain. He was looking up at an apartment building. His apartment building. He shook his head in disbelief on how easy his plan had worked so far. He hadn't been sure where Jane's allegiance had been when he had passed her the lie of getting home as soon as possible, but he was sure now. For within a week of uttering the need to return home, he was staring at it.

He remembered how suitably shocked he was, sitting in the Hunt room, when he learned his Pack's excursion was going to be through his portal.

The knock on the door was answered by Melrose and he escorted MacDuff into the foyer of Pierce's apartment. He was dressed in a long brown leather jacket with a high color adorned with some sort of metal insignia.

Pierce emerged from his dressing room similarly dressed, though his jacket was slightly more elaborate and with a different insignia. Both men looked at each other approvingly in their respective hunt uniforms.

"I can't believe you wear the same thing in every era and in every country and don't get pegged as out of place," stated Pierce taking in the uniform.

"Is that a fact my Lord?" replied MacDuff in mock surprise. "I can count the number of hunt staff you passed on the street in this very outfit prior to your recruitment on one hand. Including both myself and Tiberius and with you none the wiser."

Pierce stood astonished, waiting for MacDuff to laugh it off as a joke. But he didn't.

"Please close your mouth sir," uttered Melrose from behind his master. "The look of shock and disbelief does not become you."

Pierce threw him a black look over his shoulder, to the utter enjoyment of MacDuff.

"Don't worry lad," offered MacDuff with a smile. "It's the same for everyone else. Now we'd better get over to the Hunt Room or we'll be late."

Having never found the Hunt Room during his previous travels through the Manor, Pierce followed MacDuff through the numerous shadowed halls and corridors. Passing an open gallery, Pierce looked out to see that they were high above the floor of the Main Hall. The vista proved more imposing from above than below, as the floor's mosaic design became fully recognizable.

The view was fleeting however as they continued their journey. At the next corner they turned left into an imposing space in its own right. This hallway was double the width of the previous corridor, with an ornate iron and glass skylight running its length. Between the floor and the skylight were evenly spaced and intricately carved wooden archways. Walking below them, Pierce felt as though he were walking within the skeletal ribcage of a long dead monster of great proportions.

As imposing as the corridor was, its length was not terribly great, which enabled the pair to reach the double doors at its end quicker than Pierce had expected. Just as they approached, a pair of footmen opened the doors for them.

Apparently the corridor was simply a prelude to the magnificence of the Hunt Room itself. Pierce had visited the House of Commons and the Senate a few times throughout his education, but they paled in comparison.

The wooden archways continued from the corridor into the main room, though they were larger and even more impressive. This was due to the room itself being another two sizes larger and taller than the corridor. The skylight also continued from the corridor into the Hunt room, but it again became more impressive in this space. The iron formed various designs and some of the glass was coloured.

Just like the Houses of Parliament there was tiered seating on each side of the room facing each other, separated by a thick rich carpet. The carpet in this case was blood red and ran from the doorway that Pierce now stood, to a raised platform on the opposite side of the room. This platform contained the two largest and most decorated chairs in the room, one slightly larger than the other. A desk and chair of plain design faced it from the middle of the carpet.

"Good, we're the first ones here," observed MacDuff. "As you can see there are twenty seats in the first row. These are for the Hunt members. The small desk in front of each chair bears the emblem of their pack and designates where you sit. You will also notice that the chair also has the pack's emblem carved on top of it."

Pierce walked to the middle of the room on the carpet, inspecting the various emblem carvings. Not finding his, he doubled back and found his was the first one on the right from the entrance. He figured this made sense since he was the newest member.

"Behind each member's chair there are three more, one for the pack whip immediately behind," continued MacDuff pointing. "And two behind it a level above for the pack hounds."

"This place is incredible," uttered Pierce as he continued to absorb the space.

"Apart from the North Tower, this is one of the oldest

parts of the Manor."

The sound of approaching voices made Pierce turn his head as the footmen opened the doors to admit a group headed by Schell and Zeidt. They were speaking in German, though they seemed to be simply exchanging pleasantries. Behind them trailed men and women who were presumably their Whips and Hounds, all of them dressed similarly in the Hunt uniform. Although of similar design, the uniforms had slight variation in colouring for each pack.

"Patrick, they're letting you out of this prison?" exclaimed Schell amiably as he approached Pierce.

"Only on parole," returned Pierce in the same spirit.

"Just so!" answered Schell. "I believe you've met Herr Zeidt," he said motioning to the man beside him.

"Of course, you introduced us."

"Really? Was I drinking at the time?" Schell asked searching his memory.

"You're always drinking," Pierce replied with a laugh. "Good evening Herr Zeidt."

Pierce received a curt nod in response, and then Zeidt left them to find his seat.

"I suppose we should take our seats as well," said Schell as the doors again opened to admit Dr. Cleaver, Mr. Drummond, and a gang behind them.

Pierce found that Schell had the seat beside him and was the leader of the Red Pack. His pack's jackets were made of dark red leather and their chairs bore a carved wolf head. Looking behind him, he also noticed that both Liam and Sean had silently and invisibly taken their position behind him and MacDuff.

Drummond took his post in silence. As Hunt Secretary he sat at the desk in the middle of the room. Cleaver continued to the platform and stood in front of the smaller of the two chairs. Surrounding the base of the platform stood five black leather clad men. Once everyone was placed, Dr. Cleaver sat, immediately followed by everyone else in the room.

As he sat down he could sense MacDuff leaning towards

him.

"Hounds without a pack serve the Hunt and wear the black uniform," whispered MacDuff. "They're not all loyal to Cleaver, but those are all Cleaver's men and they were all on the stagecoach outside Rooks Bay."

Pierce nodded his comprehension, not wishing to interrupt Cleaver's opening.

"As Master of the Hunt I pronounce this session open," he began grandly. "Your mission tonight is for requirements for the Manor. Although not particularly dangerous, this is a vital exercise that will require a certain amount of skill and discretion."

The various Hunt members looked to each other in anticipation, while the packs' faces remained impassive.

"You will be travelling to 2010. The location is Ottawa, Canada," the Master continued. "Your target is a new solar power system being developed at the University of Ottawa."

Schell gave a quick eyebrow raised glance to Pierce before returning his attention. Pierce was shocked by this pronouncement, but battled to remain as calm as his men.

"Mr. Secretary please continue with the brief."

Drummond stood up and passed out paper pamphlets to the Hunt members and their packs.

"If you turn to page 1 you will see a map of the area," began the Secretary. "Further pages will show maps of the campus along with a list and diagrams of the requirements. Please read through this and I will answer questions when you've finished."

*

The briefing was quick and efficient, ending without incident. The packs had come prepared with the equipment required for the task, so the groups filed out of the Hunt Room heading towards the North Tower.

"Did you know this was coming?" MacDuff quietly asked his master.

"No."

"What do you plan to do?"

"I'm not sure, but I'm not leaving and I'm not giving up."

"Good."

They walked the rest of the way to the tower in silence, though the other packs were not as sombre. It appeared that this excursion was more a fun diversion. However everyone became silent as they passed the Secretary's office and crossed the bridge to the North Tower.

The procession passed door upon door and down sets of stairs. The torches lending a suitably medieval air to the ancient building. The Secretary finally stopped at a door with a series of letters and numbers on it. Pierce had noted the markings on the other doors and assumed it was some sort of location system. Knowing this was his door, he quickly memorised the combination.

"Good luck gentlemen, ladies," offered Drummond opening the door for the Hunt. Everyone passed by him, with the odd member nodding to the Secretary.

Pierce followed MacDuff along a short hallway and then down a circular staircase to a round room with one door. The three participating packs had divided themselves up, so Pierce walked over to where the Brown Pack had gathered. Everyone was armed with pistols and had removed them from their shoulder holsters to inspect them one last time.

Understanding the Canadian disdain for handguns, Pierce had no intention of using his and left it unchecked in his holster.

As the senior Hunt member present Zeidt looked to see everyone was ready and led the way through the door. His pack followed him, then Schell's, and finally Pierce led his pack through.

The small room looking out over St. Patrick Street in Ottawa quickly filled up as all twelve members emerged from the Manor's portal.

Zeidt's pack had been tasked with the actual incursion into the university, so they left first. This eased the tension in the room as the Red and Brown Packs were on relatively good terms with each other, though not with the departed Gold Pack.

"What do you say we head over to a nice little bistro I found the last time I was here?" offered Schell. "Our packs know what they're doing and we'll probably only get in the way."

Schell's pack was in charge of transport and was making their way down to the back alley, which housed a garage with a panel van. Pierce's pack was held in reserve in case something went wrong. He could sense that the Red Pack was used to the absence of their master.

"Sounds great," replied Pierce. "I'll meet you down on the street. I just have to talk to my guys."

"Don't take too long, it sounds like a downpour out there," he said as he went down the stairs.

"I'm going with Herr Schell," Pierce explained walking over to his pack. "I can't go into everything, but I've got to find a way to return to the Manor without attracting attention. Cleaver thinks I'm going to stay in Ottawa. That's why we're here. If I'm not back here when the task is complete, return to the Manor without me."

The pack looked dubious, but decided not to argue.

"As you say my Lord," answered MacDuff for the three of them. "Take care. We'll take our positions as arranged and will be on channel 4 if you need us."

Pierce nodded and turned towards the stairs, descending to the front door of the building. When he emerged he almost ran into Schell on the doorstep, huddled from the storm in the doorframe.

"Let's get out of this mess Patrick!" he yelled while he headed down the sidewalk. "Keep up; I don't want to catch cold!"

They took off at a quick pace, just under a run. The long leather jackets proved very efficient against the rain, though their lack of hoods had their heads wet within seconds.

Pierce was struck with a strange thought as they dodged

puddles and avoided passersby. Dr. Cleaver had said that when you leave your time through the door, you return at the exact moment. As if you never left. But he had left Ottawa during an overcast afternoon and it was now raining at night. He didn't know what to make of it, but something didn't seem right.

They finally came to the bistro and Pierce recognized it as a place he passed from time to time and never entered due to its extreme expense. He continued to benefit from the perks of his new found life.

"They do a passable crème brulé," observed Schell under the shelter of the bistro's canopy. "But it's more than made up for by the extensive wine list."

"I've just noticed we're very close to my house," observed Pierce with mock surprise. "I hadn't planned on it, but being so close I think I'll stop in and pick up some things." He said with a slight inflection at the end, hoping Schell would take it as an invitation to join him. He did not want the company, for his newly formed plan would not allow it. But to ignore his companion might be suspicious.

"Capital idea," observed Schell with enthusiasm, causing Pierce to pause. "I will be waiting for you in the comfort of this establishment."

Pierce felt slight relief, though he would never have made the offer if he thought Schell would accept.

"Fair enough," Pierce said turning back towards the street. "I should be back soon."

"Not to worry my friend, I might never leave," he murmured as the door opened, providing a wave of warmth, music and laughter.

*

The plan had worked so far, thought Pierce staring at his apartment in the rain. It had come to him after getting Schell's offer to skip out on the university break-in. Before that he had been stumped on how to return to the Manor without attracting suspicion from Cleaver. But now he had it.

Having separated himself from the rest of the group, he would enter his old apartment. But rather than grab a few sentimental items, he would light the place on fire and immediately pull the fire alarm. This would give him an excuse for not staying in his time and returning to the Manor. He would act distraught and melancholy, hopefully gaining some more time to figure out the reason for his presence as a Hunt member.

Armed with a lighter and newspaper from the convenience store around the corner, Pierce started to cross the empty street, but stopped after a step. For a minute he thought he noticed someone further down the street in a long black jacket. He had been on guard since leaving Schell, sensing he was being watched and tried to spot a follower. Pierce looked again, but no one was there. He figured it was nerves and that no one from the Manor would possibly be following him. Besides, he thought, the person down the street had been going in the opposite direction. It was probably just some college kid getting out of the rain.

Shaking his head at his new found paranoia, Pierce continued his trek across the water logged street. As he reached the other side, a high pitched sound started emanating from his building, shortly followed by its residents. Although not sociable by any means, Pierce recognized some of the people grouping together on the sidewalk.

Before he could register the strange coincidence of this situation, an explosion erupted from the top floor. The windows of the top right apartment shot out jets of flames, sprinkling debris on the crowd below. Without hesitating, Pierce turned and slowly walked away, the cries and sirens filling the night behind him. His apartment had just exploded.

His paranoia returned, but was joined by confusion and a little bit of fear. Had someone just tried to kill him or was it an actual accident? He couldn't accept that on the very night he planned to set his apartment on fire, an explosion would erupt within it. And from what he had seen, his was the only apartment initially affected. Without realizing it, he made his way back to the Bistro without looking.

He walked in to the establishment in a daze, passing the questioning hostess without stopping. The room was gently lit with candles, filling the luxurious crème walls with shadows. A piano was being expertly played, neither drowning out conversation nor inaudible in the far side of the room. Disciplined waiting staff glided effortlessly between tables, depositing dishes and removing them with ease. Pierce watched one waitress magically deliver four plates to a table without apparent effort. While following her journey to another table, Pierce spotted his friend Schell in the far corner.

He was talking amiably with a pair of women at the table beside him as Pierce approached. He was still shocked by what had happened earlier, but was trying to hide it and act nonchalant.

"Ah my friend," exclaimed Schell after taking a sip of wine. "I was worried you wouldn't find your way back here. However theses two ladies have been kind enough to indulge me while I waited."

"That is very kind indeed," Pierce addressed the pair. "You both deserve a medal." Normally he would have only muttered some inconsequential words, faced with a pair of attractive women. However his recent experiences had removed some of his usual timidity.

He was also feeling braver from his new outfit; it felt like a costume that he could use to create this new character he was becoming. As if by telepathy, the more vocal of the pair noticed that his clothing and Schell's were very similar and asked if they were uniforms.

"Indeed they are," replied Schell with practiced ease. "My friend and I are both military attaches with the German Embassy."

Pierce was glad that Schell had such an easy answer at hand, since he would have probably stood there stammering or avoided the question entirely. He was doubly grateful that he had learned some easy German phrases from Schell during their time together, as he was able to understand when his friend told him to sit down.

"Diplomats, really?" asked the girl, now fully intrigued.

"Well Ottawa is the National Capital," answered Pierce, trying out the storyline for himself. "It's absolutely *teeming* with diplomatic riff-raff." He hoped the self deprecating line would make them seem unpretentious and appealing.

"Well then you should probably join us," she answered, fully enticed by the pair of handsome diplomats. "We can keep an eye on you and make sure you don't get into any trouble."

Schell was impressed by Pierce's improvisational skills and was eager to join them. However a warning glance from his friend slowed him down and he changed his response accordingly.

"I'm afraid we must regretfully decline," he said sorrowfully. "As we have some business to discuss. However once we're done…" He trailed off expectantly.

"You know where to find us," she offered, hoping they would finish quickly.

Schell gave them a smile and wink before turning back to the table and giving Pierce a questioning look.

"This had better be good, they are the most promising women here," he said lightly. "I'm not sure how long they will be available. The waiter just brought them their second bottle and two bankers could suddenly seem more appealing than two mysterious diplomats."

"But we're not diplomats," countered Pierce.

"Details Patrick," Schell brushed aside. "So what's so important that we are not currently wining and dining those attractive ladies?"

"My apartment exploded," replied Pierce calmly. "Before I could even get inside the building, the fire alarm went off and everyone came outside. Then a couple seconds later, my apartment exploded into flames."

"That's terrible," offered Schell sympathetically. A few moments of silence passed before he spoke again. "Who would want to blow you up?"

"I don't know Wil! Nobody should," exclaimed Pierce,

trying to keep his voice low.

"Buildings don't just explode by themselves," instructed Schell. "You must have some enemies, all of us do. How do you think we all got recruited? This was a better offer than what we had."

"I've been trying to think, but I don't know." This was not precisely true, as he knew that both Drummond and Cleaver would have gladly lit the match.

"Very strange indeed, considering the rumour I heard before we left."

"What rumour?" asked Pierce.

"That you might leave the Manor and return to your previous life."

"Well I had thought about it," responded Pierce weakly, somewhat taken off guard. "But I hadn't really decided. But I can't now, not with everything I own up in flames."

"Good choice, although I'm sure you would have made it anyway."

"Very probably."

"Under the circumstances I think we should make our way back to the safe house."

"I concur," agreed Pierce. "People might be looking for me after the explosion."

"The explosion?" questioned Schell finishing his glass of wine and rising from the table. "No my friend, the women. Our female companions have left." He pointed to the empty table beside them.

*

"It's been four days, and still no word."

"Do not trouble yourself my dear, I'm not."

"I just think we should have received news from your men by now."

"We are in the middle of a subtle game Jane. Unnecessary haste could undermine our plans," explained Lord Lodge. "I'm sure my men could have gotten word to us the first morning of our stay here. However Cleaver would have discovered this just as quickly. I'd rather have no news than have him wise to our plans."

The pair were taking their regular walk around the grounds of the Crows Nest. The gated courtyard at the entrance to the cliff side lodge was the only place to easily walk around. They stopped by a railing that protected residents from a precipitous drop.

"I've had very little luck with the Hobarts," reported Jane gloomily, as she looked out over the valley below and the sea beyond. It should have been a wondrous and inspiring sight. Indeed many visitors to the Crows Nest found the view breathtaking. But to Jane the empty expanse of land from this prison view was disheartening.

"What of the groundskeepers?" inquired Lodge.

"I've only talked to two of them," she answered. "One is a possible. The other could probably be convinced; however he seems so dim he might be more of a liability. The others are returning tonight, so I should know better by tomorrow."

"Very good, that's better than I had expected." Turning from the view towards the building he continued. "However, we must keep in mind that they all work for Cleaver and are reporting to him directly."

"If that's the case," she asked weakly, "what chance do we have."

"A very good one I believe," he answered heartily. "We have some time before Dinner, shall we continue with your studies?"

Jane lit up hearing this and she nodded enthusiastically. Since they could not leave the grounds, and were the only visitors, Lord Lodge had decided to use the library to extend Jane's education. Though extremely clever and very intelligent, her formal education was incomplete. Lord Lodge found her appetite for knowledge a perfect way to spend their time.

"I had planned on continuing with Plato," said Lodge as they approached the main doors. "But under the circumstances, a change might be in order. Please fetch *The*

Prince by Machiavelli from the library. It should prove more instructive under the circumstances."

Chapter 12

Pierce was once again riding the Manor grounds with Schell, though this time in a better physical, if not mental state than the last time. It had been a week since their return to the Manor from Ottawa and the destruction of his home. His return had gone unmentioned by everyone, though Drummond's face seemed to have turned a more violent shade of red. The day after their return Schell had suggested taking the horses out in the mid morning and it had become a routine both men enjoyed. Pierce had not been a great rider when he arrived, but after a couple days of Schell's instruction he was improving drastically. The same was true of his weapons lessons with MacDuff and the others in the Brown Pack. Already proficient with a sword, he was greatly improving with most of the other weapons.

"Glad you decided to stay?" asked Schell as he halted his horse by the great lake outside Rooks Bay.

"I didn't have much choice in the matter," replied Pierce coming up beside him. "But I am glad to be here. It's starting to feel more real each day."

"That means you're not drinking enough," Schell observed with a laugh and threw him a flask as both dismounted

They had been riding hard, even vaulting a pair of fences,

and both riders were ready for a break. The horses were similarly tired and were led to the water for a drink.

Pierce was indeed glad to be here, though no closer to finding out why. Repeated attempts at finding Jane and Lord Lodge had come up empty. In truth he was almost ready to stop looking for them, fearing what he might discover. Without them he was at a standstill in his investigation and had thus begun to fall in to life as a member of the Hunt.

This proved to be an easy proposition. Every member was free to do as they pleased, with a large staff to ensure they were able to do so. Pierce spent much of his time with his pack, trying to learn new skills and be better prepared for his new life. They spent countless hours in the practice rooms training with a variety of weapons, becoming proficient with most. Pierce learned techniques in stalking prey; within the forests on the Manor grounds and by following unsuspecting townspeople in Rooks Bay. The Pack, Pierce included, were surprised to discover how easily he was picking up these new skills.

Many of the other members however were not as keen and enjoyed following other pursuits. Many could be found in the various salons and halls; drinking, reading, eating, gossiping, etc. From time to time a summons would be made for certain packs to attend a meeting in the Hunt Room and those members would then disappear for a day or two.

The Brown Pack had yet to be called again, but MacDuff had assured him that this was normal. Excursions like the one to Ottawa were a regular occurrence and did not necessitate the entire Hunt's presence. Only the actual hunts included everyone, though gossip had started spreading that another was soon on the way.

"So do you think there'll be another hunt soon?" asked Pierce, triggered by this train of thought.

"Who can say?" shrugged Schell. "Although I hope the next one is better than the last. We spent two weeks mucking around Denmark, in the Middle Ages."

"Sounds delightful," Pierce offered mockingly.

"Doesn't it?" replied Schell in a similar tone. "Luckily my whip Wolfric was a Viking warrior and knew his way around. If it weren't for the mead and wenches we found, I might have jumped into the funeral pyre we witnessed on the ninth night."

"Funeral Pyre?"

"Yes, though not the most impressive I've seen," elaborated Schell. "A village we were passing through was honouring the Chieftain who had just died. They loaded his body and possessions into a longboat, lit it on fire, and set it adrift. Just like the movies"

"Sounds impressive to me," replied Pierce.

"Well it's all in the recounting," observed Schell with a grin. "The village was really a handful of wooden huts, the chieftain a drunk who died from falling off his horse, and the longboat was an oversized rowboat. But that's a not as good a story. A good story beats a true one ninety nine percent of the time."

"So you're saying that most of your stories are exaggerations?"

"I never exaggerate," countered Schell with a straight face. "But others do all the time and you should take what they say with a little scepticism."

Pierce cocked an eyebrow at the irony and Schell replied with a shrug, leading both to have a good laugh.

The sun was close to reaching its pinnacle, the rays reflecting off the waves and pebbled shoreline. The wind was light, but provided just enough power to fill the sails of the fishing boats plying their nautical trade beyond. Pierce had noticed that weather such as this was uncommon on the island. Storms seemed to arrive quickly and last days, keeping only the most adventurous inside.

Though both men stood enjoying the unseasonable weather, the sun's position high above them the approach of midday, prompting them to remount and return to the Manor.

They maintained an easy pace on the return trip, never rising above a trot. Neither rider felt it necessary to spur their mounts any harder as the ground continually rose once on the Manor grounds.

"I believe tonight will be your first official event with the entire hunt," observed Schell as they passed a stream that bisected the expansive grounds. Pierce merely nodded in assent. "At least you've met many of the members already. Plus you've been lucky enough to befriend one the hunt's more popular members."

"Really?" asked Pierce sincerely. "I didn't think Senor De La Gena liked me."

"Very funny," countered Schell. "Count yourself lucky, when I arrived no one spoke to me for weeks."

"So what is tonight all about?"

"It's what we call the Reminiscence. It's a formal dinner where all the hunt members are required to attend. We wear our traditional clothing and discuss our pasts or where we came from."

"Sounds a little too intrusive to me," observed Pierce, feeling a sense of reticence rising within him.

"Don't worry, nobody's going to ask you when you lost your virginity or if you've killed a man," Schell interjected calmly. "We mainly speak about the time we came from and simple things from then. What was popular, what we ate, current events. It's a way for us to retain our old identities."

"And a dinner helps do that?"

"Patrick, some of the members have been here for ages. Many have lived longer here than in their old lives," instructed Schell. "It's easy to lose track of yourself in this environment. Look at yourself now compared to the lost young man who almost got shot in the clearing over there."

Pierce followed Schell's glance to the spot where he had interrupted the duel on his second night at the Manor. It was true he was starting feel different. Usually timid and shy, he always tried to go unnoticed. He'd always felt uncomfortable in groups and around women, generally remaining silent if forced into the presence of either. But ever since arriving at the Manor he was slowly shedding this reserved skin. He joked with

Schell, led combat training exercises with the Brown pack, and even (according to Schell) flirted with Mme Laflamme. The strange thing was that he didn't feel any different, let alone losing his identity.

"From your silence I take it you understand what I mean," observed Schell eyeing him closely. "I've found that this place doesn't really change you though. It creates a free atmosphere for your true nature to emerge."

"Very profound," replied Pierce solemnly. "Who told you that line?"

"Inconsequential," he ignored with a waved hand. "But I've found it to be true. Just keep it in mind."

Pierce and Schell lunched together in the informal dining room after returning their horses. The room was on the ground floor and brighter than most in the Manor. A wall of windows provided diners with a view of the rising mountains behind the Manor. The room itself was large, but not imposing; with a collection of tables and chairs filling it. Mostly empty of diners, save for a pair at the far end of the room and a solitary man by the door.

Sirinova walked in, and observing the pair finishing their meal headed over to their table. She sat down too quickly for either man to stand for her, not one to wait on protocol. As she settled herself, Schell removed his napkin and placed it over his glass, winking at Pierce.

"And how are you feeling?" She asked Pierce brusquely after placing her order with the waiter.

"Very well and thank you for asking," replied Pierce somewhat confused by the women who had drugged him a short time ago. "And how are you?"

"Fine, fine," she said absently. "No sweating, loss of memory, or cramps?"

"I… no, everything's fine."

"Interesting," she muttered thoughtfully. "The other test

subj... people had at least one of those symptoms. I must be making headway." With that taken care of she relaxed noticeably, leaning back and taking a drink of the wine the waiter had left. Schell cleared his throat, making Sirinova jump slightly.

"My dear Wilhelm, I didn't even notice you there," she apologised affectionately. "You know how I get when I'm working."

"Indeed I do Elena," replied Schell just as warmly. "There's no need to apologize."

"Well I have been very busy lately," She continued. "I will have to make an effort to be more social. It seems like ages since we've last spent time together."

"It has, but I'm glad you decided to join us."

"Us? Oh yes. I didn't realize you were friends with the Commandant here," she said noticing Pierce again. "Otherwise I might not have..."

"Used me as a test subject?" interjected Pierce. "Think nothing of it, I'm just glad to be a part of the scientific process," he continued sarcastically.

"What a refreshing point of view," responded Sirinova, oblivious to his tone.

"Rest assured Patrick, most of us have contributed to the comrade's science," Schell offered as Pierce rose from the table.

"Of course. Well, I have some things to attend to," he stated stiffly, annoyed by their cavalier attitudes. "I'll let the two of you get re-acquainted."

He left the dining room and headed towards the stairs, trying to figure out why they had affected him so much. He had a mixture of feelings towards both Schell and Sirinova; jealousy, irritation, humiliation, and some he couldn't put a name to. He had taken her interest in him beyond what she intended, a lab rat. That she was enamoured with Wilhelm did not make the revelation any easier to handle.

He surfaced from his musings to find himself standing outside his door. He wondered how long he had been standing there as he turned the knob and entered.

"I'm glad you've returned sir," said Melrose approaching from his dressing room across the hall. "We were able to find a uniform for your dinner tonight, and I need to make sure it fits properly."

"Uniform?" asked Pierce confused. The brown leather hunting jacket he had received from MacDuff a week ago was the only uniform he had ever worn.

"Yes sir, but perhaps I had better explain. For the Reminiscence the members wear their old uniforms or clothing, something from their old life. I took the liberty of tracking down one for you."

"But I never wore a uniform," argued Pierce.

"Patrick Pierce never wore a uniform, that's correct," explained Melrose tactfully. "However Commandant Pierce did."

"And you think it will be easier for me to be Commandant Pierce at this dinner?"

"Infinitely easier sir. The fewer people that know you were recruited early the better."

"I see what you mean," agreed Pierce, nodding his head in thought. "Hmm, I will need some sort of reliable back story though."

"I've thought of that and believe you should be alright," stated Melrose as he ushered his master in the dressing room. "You see you come from a more modern time compared to the rest of the members. So if you remain vague enough, no one will know if you provide some somewhat inaccurate details."

"Well hopefully no one will want to speak to me. I'm not a very convincing liar."

"You'll be fine sir," calmed Melrose as he pointed towards a uniform hanging up behind him. "What do you think?"

Pierce turned and stood stunned, staring at the uniform before him. He hadn't put much thought towards the uniform, after all uniforms were nothing more than clothing to him. He had foreseen a bland suit or maybe a sport jacket with a crest sewn on the pocket. But that was not what he was presented with. This uniform radiated with dark meaning and he now understood how a uniform could become a symbol and create its own aura.

"Where did you get this," whispered Pierce hoarsely.

"I found the design in one of the books in the library. I had one of the girls sew it up this past week and had the jeweller create the accoutrements. It should be as close to authentic as possible," he added, noticing Pierce's unease. "Is there a problem sir?"

Pierce took a closer look at it, fingering the metal lettering on the epaulettes. "What does RCMS stand for?"

"In the book it said it stood for Royal Canadian Marshal Service," replied Melrose, now wary.

"I think I'd like to see this book," ordered Pierce still staring at the clothing laid out before him.

The uniform was an almost exact copy of the Red Serge worn by the RCMP, although this one was jet black. There were additional alterations to the original version; all of them making it appear more intimidating. The shiny brass buttons and insignia had been replaced by brushed silver. The brown leather Sam Browne belt and riding boots were now polished black, with brushed silver buckles. The gold stripe running down the side of the riding breeches was changed to silver. Everything had been altered slightly from the Mountie uniform Pierce remembered, right down to the insignia on the high collar. The crowned bison surrounded by maple leafs was replaced with a ferocious polar bear.

Despite his apprehensions, he didn't want to disappoint Melrose, who had clearly put some effort into the uniform. He donned each piece slowly, ignoring the mirror across from him.

"A marvellous fit," exclaimed Melrose when Pierce was fully dressed. "Diana does wonderful work; I don't think any alterations are in order."

"I look like a Nazi," muttered Pierce in distaste. There must have been some mistake in the book Melrose had borrowed. He couldn't imagine any Canadian agency approving a uniform that so closely resembled the worn by one of histories most evil organizations.

"Is there a problem sir?" inquired Melrose.

"No, nothing, it fits like a glove," replied Pierce. He remembered that Melrose had no knowledge of the history of the outside world and thus did not see the same thing as Pierce did looking at the reflection in the mirror.

"If you require no changes, I will simply clean it up and prepare it for this evening."

*

"Stop fidgeting dear, they'll get here when they get here."

Jane looked up and smiled at Mrs. Hobart, then put down the wooden spoon she'd been drumming on the table. She was nervously awaiting the return of the two groundskeepers that had left for the Manor a few days ago. Mrs. Hobart believed she was anxious for Philip, one of the groundskeepers, to return because she was enamoured of him. Jane hoped Philip also thought this.

Within a couple days of arriving at the Crow's Nest Jane had found that Philip lingered in rooms she also occupied. At first she had ignored him, not being attracted to the simple worker in any way. However this changed when she discovered from Mrs. Hobart that Philip and one of the others made regular visits to the Manor for provisions and general instructions. From that point on she had accepted his slow and simple advances, cultivating his trust. This had culminated a few days ago with her passing a sealed letter from him to deliver to Lord Cleaver and no one else. He had accepted the letter like an ancient knight on a quest.

Dogs barking in the courtyard signalled the return of the wagon and the men driving it. Jane forced a nonchalant attitude, which brought a knowing smile to Mrs. Hobart. Eventually Philip and the other groundskeeper made their way into the kitchen and were immediately rewarded with some hot tea.

"Safe trip?" Jane inquired of Philip as he tried to casually sidle up to her.

"No problems," he replied. He then glanced around the kitchen, ensuring the others weren't watching them. Satisfied, he took an envelope from his pocket and passed it to here under the counter. Jane smiled at his attempt at espionage.

"So Lord Cleaver..." began Philip hesitantly. "You're not... I mean, you don't... Umm, the both of you aren't...?"

"Us? Oh no, nothing like that," she replied laughing once she figured out what he was driving at. She hadn't thought how sealed letters passed between them might appear to an outsider. The thought of being Dr. Cleaver's lover made her want to laugh and shiver at the same time. Though he was handsome for an older man, Jane knew that he was both dangerous and unfeeling.

"Good," Philip smiled in response. He finished of his tea quickly, burning his tongue slightly, before leaving the kitchen to unload the wagon.

Mrs. Hobart gave her a wink as Jane left the kitchen; having witnessed what she thought was a tender moment.

Gliding down the hallway towards her room, Jane had to fight to keep the letter hidden and not read it immediately. When she reached her room she opened the door and slid in, closing it immediately behind her. There were no locks on the servants' doors, so she leaned her back against it to avoid a surprise interruption.

The letter was quickly opened, breaking the wax seal in the process. Jane scanned it swiftly to obtain its intention, then read it slower a second time, memorising it. She smiled at its contents and let out a sigh of relief.

There had been very little danger in sending the letter. The worst thing that could have happened was for it to be ignored, thus confirming her placement in this purgatory of a hunting lodge. However Lord Cleaver had not only responded, but responded positively. She had once again worked her skills and was feeling the stir of success.

Not lingering in the moment too long, she went to her bedside table and found a small box of matches. She lit one on the first strike and immediately set fire to the letter, before placing it in the fireplace. As she watched it burn, she once again felt invigorated at the opportunity before her. This could be a turning point in her life, one that she had felt only somewhat satisfied with so far. She had always been bright, but after a few lessons with Lord Lodge, she realized how little she knew. He had shown her that however great her skills for survival were, she was capable of much more if challenged. Jane knew that if she were to avoid being the puppet of men like Cleaver, she would have to learn to think critically and strategically.

A knock at the door broke her reverie, forcing Jane to refocus as Mrs. Hobart stuck her head in.

"It's time for Lord Lodge's afternoon tea," the housekeeper reminded her. "We don't want to keep him waiting."

Jane nodded in response and followed her out into the hall and then back to the kitchen. A silver tray was waiting on the counter, fully stocked for the afternoon service. Without another word she lifted it up and made the now routine procession up to the suites on the second floor.

Lord Lodge was comfortably ensconced in his study with a book when she entered. She was able to open the door with one hand and expertly hold the tray with the other, thereby avoiding the clumsy and unprofessional use of her backside. She set the tray down on a side table and waited patiently for him to finish so she could serve him and deliver her news.

"Well you might as well tell me what he said," offered Lodge from behind his book.

"It couldn't have gone better," replied Jane as she began pouring his tea. She had been spending enough time with Victor Lodge to no longer be surprised by his uncanny perception and speedy deduction. "To be honest I was expecting a response to follow much later, if at all."

"Dr. Cleaver is highly clever and an expert plotter," Lodge expounded while setting his book down and accepting the offered tea cup. "However he is also impulsive, most notably when close to the kill. I'm sure after receiving your letter, any notions of duplicity on your part where washed away by the thought of finally beating me."

"Surely it can't be that easy. He must have some doubts about me."

"Probably. I've known Cleaver for a long time, longer than I'd like and longer than I thought at our first meeting," he said as he motioned her to the seat near him. "I underestimated him and find myself in this current predicament. I do not intend to repeat that mistake."

He said this with a cold voice, the most natural emotion Jane had seen him display since their arrival here. She no longer doubted his desire to defeat Lord Cleaver and realized she would never want to become his enemy. But the moment passed as quickly as it came and she found him watching her expectantly. Quickly she realized she had yet to relate the contents of the letter, so she proceeded to do so.

"What should we do next?" She inquired after finishing.

"What do you propose? It was your plan to ensnare a groundskeeper."

"I've put some thought into it since I sent the letter," she started slowly. "But I have to admit I haven't come up with a suitably elaborate plan."

"How so?"

"Every time I think I've developed a plan or even an outline of one, I eventually find holes in it," she continued without confidence. "Dr. Cleaver will never be convinced."

"Well then I suppose there's only on thing we can do," observed Lodge, with a hint of a smile emerging. "You will tell him the truth."

"What?"

"Tell him exactly what we're doing here, every step of a plan we implement." Seeing the confusion on her face he continued. "That is the only way to ensure your safety and possibly mine. Take a moment and think it through, it's the only way this will work."

"If I provide false information, he'll find out and either

get rid of me or ignore me," she said as she began to work through Lodge's suggestion.

"Probably."

"But he will believe me if I provide the information on the real plan."

"Because it is both possible and believable."

"And if anything goes wrong I can say that I was telling him the truth without having to stick to a story."

"Precisely. Plus keep in mind he's probably been spying on us since we arrived. And if he hasn't he will start now."

"There's only one problem with this. At some point we have to escape," she offered dubiously.

"That, my dear, is the most cunning part of the plan," explained Lodge. His eyes were now shining and his mouth straining to contain a full smile. "Cleaver is so devious that he will undoubtedly believe what you send him. He will believe you are being truthful with him, since it will be confirmed by his other spies. However he will not believe that that is the true plan. He can't. He will use your information to discount what he perceives is my true plan. A man such as Cleaver could never understand putting his faith in another person, let alone a servant. If you tell him that I plan to escape out the front door, he will immediately have people posted at every exit BUT the front door. Therefore we will be able to do exactly what we plan, with him in on it, so to speak."

"But can that actually work?" she asked incredulously.

"We shall see. But he expects me to try and escape and he expects you to keep him informed as to the means. We might as well provide him with both."

"Very well," accepted Jane. She felt mildly confident, but also appreciated the risk Lord Lodge was taking for her. Although she was sure he could have come up with a superior method of both misleading Dr. Cleaver and escaping, this was the only one that provided her with some security if it failed. She suddenly felt very close to the older man and hoped that their escape would not be too soon as she was enjoying his company. "So what should I do now?"

"Exactly what we discussed," ordered Lodge picking up his book and returning to his previous page. "Tell him the truth; that you told me the contents of his letter and that I want you to relay my exact plans to him so that he discounts them. As I said, you need to tell him everything."

"But won't that unravel everything if he knows that you know that I'm sending him information?" She asked, her faced squeezed in confusion. "This just turns into a bewildering cycle of logic. I thought the beauty of this was the simplicity?"

"It is," answered Lodge offhandedly, now completely engrossed in his book. "Let him muse over the intricate and revolving possibilities of the truth and of our plans. Meanwhile we carry on with only one plan and one train of thought. Escape."

Chapter 13

The Manor was unusually silent as Tiberius strode along the gallery overlooking the main entrance hall. His boots echoed within the large chamber as each sole rhythmically landed. He enjoyed prowling the halls on most nights, never sure who he would run into or what scenes he would witness. Many of those chance encounters had proved useful to his continued employment. Not due to blackmail, but a healthy respect of his knowledge by those around him. This fact, along with being one of the longest serving members of the staff made him an imposing figure within the walls of the Manor.

He knew the emptiness was due to the Reminiscence that would be starting within the hour. The Members would all be in their rooms, being groomed and dressed by their maids or valets. Downstairs the staff would be rushing to ensure the dining room was equally prepared. The cooks would be the busiest of all, preparing a multitude of dishes, representing food from the many members' own time and country. Having arrived at one of the many passages that connected the upstairs with downstairs, he took a breath and dove into the chaos of the Manor staff.

The passage led into a wide hallway that connected the kitchen to the dining rooms. Immediately he was thrust to the side by a progression of silver domed carts that would have done the Rose Bowl parade proud. Servers pushed them quickly by without even glancing at him, keeping step with those in front.

Once they passed, Tiberius fell into step with some of the staff returning from the dining room to the kitchen. This group had just deposited the china to the dining room and were now ready to collect the silverware. The silver room was manned by the butler and one of his assistants, who Tiberius discreetly nodded to as he passed.

Due to his position within the Manor, most of the kitchen staff ignored his passing through their space as they worked. He was known to wander throughout the entire building at will, usually on some important errand or duty.

He poked his head into the small office of the kitchen manager, grabbing an apple from a bowl she kept stocked.

"Everything progressing well? No problems?" He inquired congenially, then taking a bite of the pilfered apple.

"The only problem I have is people interrupting me," she responded absently without raising her head from the notes she was reviewing.

"Message received. Good luck."

"I don't need luck. All I need is …"

Her voice trailed off as Tiberius had already started walking away, the din of the kitchen filling his ears. There was a cacophony of sounds; knives on chopping boards, steel on copper, shouts and orders, and feet shuffling. It was the perfect place for a quiet chat, sure to be unheard by anyone outside of two feet.

He took a position in the corner, well out of everyone's way and far from any doors, windows or halls that could hide an eavesdropper. He chomped away at his apple, quickly becoming part of the kitchen scenery.

Within minutes the assistant butler made his way over to him, taking time to speak to the odd person along his route. He approached as if he were surprised to see Tiberius there, smiling and holding out his hand.

"Be quick I haven't much time," he said smiling as the

hand shaking ended.

"I need some info on food shipments sent to any of our buildings on the island."

"Why don't you ask the head Cook or the Kitchen Manager?"

"Because I don't trust them and you owe me a favour." Tiberius replied, still smiling like his companion.

"Very well. What do you need to know?"

"I need to know the location of any shipment that contained cod, cornmeal, and cucumber." He slapped the Assistant Butler on the shoulder and walked towards a nearby door that led towards the back courtyard.

*

Pierce descended from his rooms early, not wanting to be late for his first Reminiscence. Upon reaching the ground floor he was directed by a footman to a lounge close to the main dining room. Whereupon entering he discovered it to be empty apart from a bartender at the far end.

If it weren't for the carpeted floor, Pierce would have thought he'd entered a ballroom. The space was airy and bright, the ceiling rising impossibly high with large crystal chandeliers. Occasional chairs and large mirrors ran along the walls, creating the illusion of a larger room.

Unsure how to proceed, Pierce decided that if he were to stand awkwardly, he might as well have a drink in his hand. He approached the bar in the corner, taking in the various bottles to choose from.

"What can I get for you Commandant?" asked the bartender. Pierce almost looked behind him, still unused to his new title.

"I'll have a glass of that on the rocks," he replied after a slight hesitation, pointing to an amber coloured bottle with a Gaelic name on the label. The bartender made it quickly and Pierce soon found himself standing awkwardly with a drink in his hand.

After a couple minutes of staring hopefully at the door, he decided it would be better to not appear so eager for company. After all, the first person through the door might be Colonel Buford and he could quickly find himself staring down a barrel at twenty paces. He took a sip of his drink, which was very good, and strolled to one of the large floor to ceiling windows to take in the view.

Upon closer inspection the windows were actually doors that led to a stone patio overlooking a garden. Stone benches and statues lined a gravel path that seemed to lead towards a hedged maze. On the far side of the patio Pierce could see part of the Manor, twinkling window lights dotting the vast dark stone rising above the ground like a cliff. In the distance he thought he could see the dark mass of the North Tower, even more forbidding by its lack of illumination.

"What a wonderful uniform Patrick! We could have the same tailor."

Pierce was broken away from his examination of the outdoors by a friendly voice behind him.

"I figured you'd be here early," continued Schell from the bar. "So I decided to arrive early and keep you company."

Pierce turned and took in his friend in horror as he approached from the bar with a glass of champagne in his hand. It did appear as though they had the same tailor. Now that Pierce had the original to compare it to, his initial assessment of his own uniform was terribly accurate.

Wilhelm Schell stood looking at him quizzically, dressed head to toe in a black Nazi SS uniform, complete with red swastika armband.

"They are somewhat similar I suppose," offered Pierce after finally finding his voice.

"Similar, why they're almost identical," countered Schell affably. "Although I must admit that I pull it off somewhat better than you."

Pierce smiled in response, still shocked by his friend's appearance. He knew that Schell had been in Germany during the war, and had admitted to being in government. He had even said that he had followed along with the Nazi's, by not opposing them directly if nothing else. But the uniform he was wearing did not support this line of reasoning. The SS only accepted full fledged Nazi's. Pierce was stupefied and sickened by the man standing before him.

"You said that you'd left the Foreign Service when the Nazi's came to power," stated Pierce hoarsely.

"I did. I left and joined the SS," he answered nonchalantly. "I could tell which way the power was shifting and decided to follow. I received a post within the foreign intelligence section of the SS."

"How could you do something like that? You were no Nazi," accused Pierce harshly. "Were you?"

"Not really," Schell shrugged in response. "I certainly did not believe in their superior race nonsense. But what was I supposed to do? They offered me a similar job working abroad and I accepted. I never knew about the camps or the special action groups. I was recruited to the Manor in 1942."

"But you knew how the Jews were being persecuted! The Nuremburg laws were already well in place."

"Of course I knew," Schell replied calmly. "But what could I do about it?"

Pierce was taken aback by his friend's nonchalant attitude towards his past. So mush so in fact that he hadn't noticed the appearance of new members in the lounge.

The pair walked and mingled with the other members, Schell introducing him to those he had not met. The room filled up quickly and Pierce was impressed by the multitude of dresses, uniforms, and clothing. Everyone was wearing their regular clothes from when they had been recruited by the Hunt. He felt slightly overwhelmed by all the colours, faces and voices that were filling in the lounge.

It was not until Colonel Buford arrived that Pierce finally realized the concern that had been nagging him as he had toured the room.

The doors opened and Buford paraded in wearing a flowing white robe. Nobody seemed to take notice of his entrance, doubtless having witnessed it many times before. But Pierce was intrigued by it and walked over to take a closer look. Buford stopped to talk to a woman wearing a luxurious evening dress with a stylized silver brooch when it dawned on Pierce.

Buford was wearing the riding robe of the Ku Klux Klan. Suddenly Pierce knew what was wrong and it became completely evident as he looked around the room. Here were almost two dozen people from throughout time gathered in one place. And they were all wearing the uniform, insignia, or other such signs denoting their membership in histories most evil and malevolent organizations.

The room began to spin around him as his mind started cataloguing this rogue's gallery. Bufford was in his KKK robe, talking loudly to De La Gena in the gear of the Spanish Inquisition. Schell and Sirinova were getting reacquainted by the bar, in their SS and KGB uniforms repectively. Laflamme, laughing with two men, was clad in the reactionary clothing of the French Revolution during the Reign of Terror. They were all, overtly or otherwise, a pageant of humanity at its worst.

It was then that he glanced at himself in the mirror and his heart stopped. He was one of them. Hand picked and recruited like everyone else here. If he had been recruited early, what did this uniform signify and what was he to become in the future to merit the invitation.

"Are you all right?"

Pierce blinked repeatedly and Veronique Laflamme slowly came into focus before him. "Sorry?"

"I asked you if were all right," she repeated warmly. "You appear slightly ill."

"No I'm fine," he replied weakly.

"Very well," she said losing interest. "Aren't you going to compliment my dress?" She then did a quick turn, the movement making her thin dress rise provocatively. She was wearing a classical blue and white silk dress with a felt cap bearing the tricolour of France. The very personification of *Marianne,* or Liberty of revolutionary France, right down to the revealing bust line.

"It's very nice," he said noncommittally, trying to keep his eyes above her neckline.

"Granted it's not as elegant as what some people are wearing," at this she darted a death stare at the women in the ball gown. "However it's what I wore in Paris and I maintain an authentic aura for the Reminiscence."

"Very commendable."

"I must say your uniform is quit imposing," she said taking his arm and angling him towards the bar. They passed Schell and Sirinova, with Veronique not even glancing in their direction. Schell made a quick gesture pointing at himself, then at Pierce, concluding with a wink.

Ordinarily not very perceptive in social situations, Pierce's recent enlightenment must have sparked something in his brain. Because he knew what Schell was alluding to with his simple gesture, he was a stand in. Ordinarily Veronique would have been hanging on Schell's arm for the event. However with Wilhelm and Elena now engrossed in flirtatious conversation, Veronique needed a replacement to complete the visual scene she was trying to convey.

Pierce indeed felt like a prop as they toured half of the room then took a position by the bar. She divided her positions between two favourites; an arm draped over his shoulder while she looked back over her shoulder, and leaning slightly against him and the bar while talking to those who passed by.

The room suddenly quieted down and Pierce turned around to see that the doors had opened and Dr. Cleaver had entered, flanked by two footmen. After realizing the significance of the members' clothing and what they represented, Pierce had wondered what Cleaver would be wearing and who he had really been. Despite the Doctors disclosure of being from Victorian England, Pierce had been hard pressed to decide how he would appear.

"Ladies and Gentleman of the Hunt," he announced to those assembled before him, "we shall dine and reminisce of days past." His appearance was slightly disconcerting and surprising to Pierce. Although dressed in formal dining wear, right down to the tails of his coat, he was also adorned with the accouterments of a secret order. A thick gold collar draped from his neck across his chest along with an elaborately stitched and gilded sash. Pierce didn't know what specific group he'd been a part of, confusing him slightly. He'd always thought of masons, shriners, and the like to be involved with charities and helping others. He'd never thought of them in a negative light, despite the myriad of books by conspiracy theorists.

He followed everyone out of the room through the large double doors and tried to piece this new information together in his mind. He was now more curious than ever to learn what Dr. Cleaver's past was and how he fit into this manor of malevolence.

*

Talk around the dinner table was as innocuous as he'd been led to believe and mostly centered on the food that was passed around. To the delight of those assembled, the cooks had prepared a dish for all of them. Each member in turn praised it and tried to get their neighbour to try it. Pierce had gladly accepted the offer of paella from De la Gena, though had turned down the Borscht from Sirinova. Pierce had been surprised to find a platter of poutine placed before him. Though hesitant to try at first, his dining companions quickly warmed to the dish of rich gravy, creamy cheese curds, and crunchy fried potatoes.

Despite being a new commodity, Pierce found himself doing more listening than speaking. No one appeared to be terribly interested in him or his past, to his great relief. He did however offer the odd comment to conversations, hoping his overall reticence would be ignored.

"I simply adored horse drawn sleigh rides on the outskirts of Moscow," admitted Sirinova. "The white expanses and invigorating air. You must have found the same thing in your Canadian winter's comrade Commandant."

"Yes, invigorating," Pierce replied simply to her question, while De la Gena shivered beside him.

Pierce was able to offer similar single sentence comments to the conversations around him during the first half of the dinner. This proved difficult as the dinner, and the wine, progressed. He had to work carefully to not get drawn into some of the more heated discussions.

"How can you say Shakespeare was a hack," inquired a man in laced collar a few seats down. "The man was a genius."

"Not in German," replied Schell, sitting across from him. He had a smirk on his face that Pierce had seen on his friend before. Schell probably had no views on Shakespeare one way or another, but merely wanted to have some fun at another's expense.

"Of course not, he was English."

"Exactly my point. A real genius is able to transcend simple things like language. Like Beethoven. "

"So then why was he translated into so many languages?"

"The bible has been translated into every known language," offered Schell cheekily. "But it's still a weak piece of literature."

"That's sacrilege!" banged De la Gena on the table.

"Signor, that's not a terribly forceful counterpoint," countered Sirinova, then turning to smile at Schell a few seats down. "Now Marx was very persuasive…"

"You're all missing the point," interrupted Lace Collar, trying to refocus the conversation. "Shakespeare was a genius, even in translation."

"Perhaps he was in other languages," admitted Schell. "Senor, does Shakespeare's genius reveal itself in Spanish?"

"The man was a damned heretic and a favourite of the evil Queen!" spat De la Gena still indignant from the bible comments.

"But was he a genius?" prodded Schell.

"He was nothing of the kind."

"God save the Queen!" sang out Lace Collar, eager to defend his ancient monarch and forgetting his previous argument.

The conversations continued like this as the plates were removed and replaced with port and cheese. Pierce assumed that cultural and historic arguments were being made up and down the table, judging from the animated faces and rising voices surrounding him. The odd cackle and bellow of laughter told him that not all of the conversations were confrontational. This was probably due to the fact that Wilhelm Schell was at only one end of the table.

"Ladies and Gentlemen," Cleaver announced after tinkling his glass and standing. The conversations of those gathered around the long table slowly diminished and fell silent within seconds. "Thank you all for taking part in yet another successful Reminiscence. Sadly, as you may have noticed, our great leader Lord Lodge was not able to join us. He instructed me to pass on his regret for not attending, although his short respite for the Manor has done him well."

"Lord Cleaver!" called out Colonel Bufford as Cleaver paused during his speech. "A question for you sir, if you'll answer it."

Cleaver took the interruption in stride, nodding his head in the Colonel's direction. Bufford took the motion as a sign to proceed and stood to address the head of the table.

"I can't speak for everyone here," he began, as half of those assembled either looked skyward or rolled their eyes. "But I know some of us are champing at the bit so to speak."

"You always are," accepted Cleaver smiling.

"Well, what can you tell us of the next hunt? It's been almost a month and many of us are ready for another." An echo of agreement spread around most of the table.

"Well I can tell you that Mr. Drummond's staff have been hard at work looking for a suitable challenge," he began cautiously as the faces around in the room gave him their undivided attention. "And a hunt is indeed forthcoming."

"Who will we be hunting?" inquired Bufford fully aroused.

"I cannot divulge all the details," responded Cleaver.

"They're still being sorted out. However I can provide you with a preliminary time and place."

With this voices around the table began to murmur and whisper. Everyone was excited to find out any detail.

"The hunt will take place in Twentieth century Portugal and Spain."

This information was like a fuse reaching its end and the room exploded into energetic chatter. Everyone seemed to have a view or something to say about this news. Veronique Laflamme was gushing while she exclaimed that she simply adored Barcelona. Meanwhile Colonel Bufford hooted and hollered, while waving a pair of pistoled fingers around the air.

Pierce was one of the few members without a reaction. At first he believed that he'd been the only one to hear Bufford's question properly and Cleaver neglect to correct him. However as he looked at those at the table and the uniforms they wore, he realized no mistake had been made to correct. Bufford had asked *who* they were going to hunt, not *what.*

Bile began to creep up his throat as the full brunt of the realization hit him. Everyone was excitedly discussing hunting down a human being in Spain. He felt dizzy and sick to his stomach, starting to sway slightly in his seat.

Without realizing it a pair of waiters had come up behind him and helped him out of his seat and out of the room, drawing as little attention as possible.

"Are you alright my Lord?" inquired one of the waiters returning with a glass of water. He handed it to Pierce, who had been deposited on a couch in a hallway outside of the dining room.

Pierce took a sip and nodded slowly. It took all of his power to maintain his composure as Dr. Cleaver emerged from the dining room and approached him.

"My poor fellow," he exclaimed in concern. "Mme. Laflamme just told me you were looking slightly pale before dinner. I hope you haven't over exerted your self."

Unable to speak, Pierce simply took another sip of water.

"All of these foreign foods can create havoc on a person's

constitution. Let me check you quickly." The doctor conducted various examinations in swift succession, finally reaching a conclusion with a series of nods. "Elevated heart rate, quick pulse, pale skin, but no fever. With some rest you should be fine."

Dr. Cleaver instructed the waiters to take him up to Pierce's rooms and to inform his valet. As the one went to fetch Melrose, Pierce stopped him with a raised hand.

"Sir?" he inquired, anxious to complete Cleavers order.

"After you inform Melrose, get MacDuff for me."

Pierce emerged from his dressing room after splashing some water on his face and removing the hideous black uniform jacket when Melrose entered. He immediately rushed over to his master's side to aid him, feeling guilty for having not been there when he fell ill.

"Are you all right sir, is there anything I can get you?"

"Scotch. Lots of Scotch."

Melrose nodded, sensing a side to his master he had yet to witness. He walked to the sideboard and poured the amber liquor from a crystal decanter. When he delivered it, Pierce grabbed it and drank it one gulp. There was a tension in the air that Melrose could hardly stand and was only slightly broken when MacDuff entered the room.

"My lord, the footman said you were ill…" Pierce stopped him with an angry glance and an upraised finger.

"At what point were you two going to tell me?" He asked with a voice shaking between rage and terror.

"Sir?" They both said in unison.

"Don't *Sir* me!" He exclaimed, slamming the empty glass onto a table by the window he stood beside. "Why did you not tell me I had to hunt *people*?! That this whole place is some kind of sick gentleman's club for the homicidally insane!"

"Because I told them not to," announced a familiar voice from the far dark corner.

Pierce recognized the owner's voice immediately, but was still shocked into silence when Tiberius emerged into the full light of the room. He walked casually over to the sideboard and poured three more drinks, then grabbed the decanter to refill Pierce's glass.

"I think you had better sit down, all of you," he motioned the others to the chairs and sofa in front of the fire. When everyone had grabbed their drink and sat down he began to speak, only to be cut off by Pierce.

"Are you going to tell me what the hell is going on?"

"I'll explain everything that I can," he replied calmly. "However I might not have all the answers that you want or need."

Pierce merely stared at him unable to speak not knowing what to say, if he could even find his voice.

"I had better start at the beginning, as I know it," he said after taking a sip of his drink and then looked at Pierce's two men. "This cannot be shared by anyone else at the Manor."

They both nodded and Pierce felt slightly better knowing he was not the only one without a clear picture of what was happening.

"I was born in a medieval village long since destroyed in a country that no longer exists. I was the third son of a minor noble and therefore set on a certain path upon my birth. My oldest brother inherited the land, my older brother was sent to a priory and became a servant of God, and I was given a sword and became a soldier.

"I enjoyed it at first and was very good at it. I was in a good company of fighting men and we travelled, caroused, and generally caused mayhem wherever we went. At this time, in Europe, groups like ours were everywhere. So the kings, princes, bishops, and the Pope decided they could make better use of us somewhere else. Thus began the great crusades."

"What does this...?" Pierce began to ask, his patience waning.

"You must hear the full story," Tiberius cut him off. He refilled his drink and passed the decanter around. "I told my brother the priest that I was going on crusade and he was ecstatic about the idea. However he had heard of some of the ruffians' conduct in the Holy Land and arranged for me to become a Knight Templar. He believed this would further protect my soul for any misdeeds I conducted. Well it didn't.

"The years I spent as a Templar were the most exciting, bloody, enlightening, and dreadful of my life. Some days we would protect caravans of pilgrims and some days we would destroy them. We saved priceless relics and financed the destruction of others. After ten years of fighting I had lost my faith and felt as though I was losing my soul. I was in Jerusalem at that time, surrounded by a Saracen army bent on exacting revenge on us. Although I was ready to die, I knew that I would take too many with me before I did. It was in this morose state that Victor Lodge found me."

The three assembled men sat spellbound to the tale that Tiberius was now weaving. They were hanging on every honestly delivered word. He stood up and walked to the fireplace, placed his glass on the mantle, and then crouched down to stare into the fire.

"Lord Lodge saved me from that fiery battle of dust, steel, and death. But more importantly he saved my soul from the path I had sent it down. I followed him willingly from the tavern he found me in to a small building near Herod's Palace. He told me that he knew all about me and that he had chosen me to help him build a new order, one truly designed to help humanity."

"So how's that going?" inquired Pierce with a snort.

Chapter 14

"That is fair," responded Tiberius with a sigh. "It would appear that the inmates are running the asylum, so to speak. However I'm getting ahead of myself.

"I followed Lord Lodge through a small closet door, in a derelict building in Medieval Jerusalem and emerged as you did, in the North Tower. At that time there was only the tower and a small portion of the Manor you see it now. However, it still seemed like some kind of wicked magic and scared me more than any battle I had fought in. Lord Lodge's powering presence was the only thing that kept me composed as we walked along the portal lined halls of the North Tower.

"He explained to me that he had discovered that the portals were linked to different places throughout time. But when I asked them how he discovered them or where he came from, he remained silent.

"Lord Lodge was always vague about his past, although I sense he was some sort of policeman or something similar. He had a distaste for criminals and crime, though he seemed weary from his battles against them."

"Then why create a club for them?" asked Pierce in exasperation.

"The club was a façade at first," countered Tiberius angrily. "We created a prison for them!"

"Prison?" said a stunned Pierce, looking from Tiberius to Melrose and MacDuff. They seemed as equally surprised as he did.

"There was just a few of us at first, though we slowly recruited more people like us. People with special skills, losing faith with humanity and wishing to combat evil. It all sounds so sappy now, but we believed it then. In short order we built what is now the North Wing that connects to the Tower and it became our headquarters. We also helped the people on this island, by bringing back simple tools from our travels through the portals. This was the best time in my life." He finished in a whisper.

"You said this place was created as a prison," spoke up MacDuff for the first time. "I wish the English had had prisons like this."

"I asked Lord Lodge the same thing when he proposed the idea to me," admitted Tiberius calmly. "He told me that if we made this place like a regular prison, we'd spend more time trying to keep the prisoner's in than finding new criminals. So the Manor was created to appeal to a person's vanity to keep them here. By providing the comforts of a mansion, they would certainly stay contentedly locked away here forever."

"Let's assume that makes sense," offered Pierce standing up. "Which I'm not prepared to accept yet. But say it does, how did you know who to imprison? I notice that there is a SS officer here, but not Hitler or Himmler. Wouldn't they be better candidates for this little club?"

"I'm not sure how recruits were chosen or why," admitted Tiberius slowly. "Lord Lodge said that we had to be careful when influencing the past and future. Some things could be changed while others were set. I'm not really sure."

"Sounds like cheap science fiction to me."

"Nevertheless, that is what happened," continued Tiberius ignoring Pierce's sarcasm. "Lord Lodge would provide me with a name and a door number. I'd travel through the North Tower and collect the candidates. He always found those desperate to join. People that had lost hope in their present circumstances."

Pierce smiled at having his theory proved correct. "Most came willingly and were content when they arrived. To be frank, you were the most difficult recruit."

"So you started collecting these so called candidates," stated Pierce as he started to pace in front of the window. "But they were not all satisfied by the easy country life? They wanted action, excitement, and much more."

"Precisely," answered Tiberius shrewdly appraising the young man before him. "So we started hunting on the Manor grounds. I understand you've seen much of this on your horseback excursions."

"Have you been spying on me?" inquired Pierce stopping to stare at Tiberius

"He spies on everyone," answered MacDuff for him.

"It's my job,"

"What exactly is your job?" Pierce demanded, veering off topic slightly. "You were here at the beginning, personally chosen by Lord Lodge. But you're one of the staff taking orders from Cleaver, one of the inmates. Why aren't you one of the Members of the Hunt?"

"Lord Lodge told me he brought me here to mentor and watch the pack members. In the hierarchy of the Manor, Drummond and I are roughly the same level," Tiberius explained quickly, annoyed at having to detour from his original story. "He needed an ally that could go everywhere and know everyone. As a member of the Hunt I'd be constrained in my movements, unable to travel freely below stairs. Over time I've become accustomed to my place at the Manor and admit that sometimes even I forget the reality of the situation. I suppose the daily routine of the Manor numbed me to the true nature of this place. But I continue to keep up the appearance of my loyal servitude in order to be of use."

"So the *inmates* started hunting on the grounds," continued Pierce as he resumed his pacing. "Deer, boar, and rabbits even?"

Tiberius nodded.

"But again, they weren't satisfied with this? So you

changed things up?"

"We did, though you have to understand the change didn't take place quickly," argued Tiberius. "As you might be aware time seems to stand still on this island. So after who knows how long, people became bored with the same old game in the same old venue. Plus they were getting too curious about the doors in the North Tower. We couldn't risk their returning to their homes. Not with their new found knowledge."

"So you started hunting game in the real world," concluded Pierce. "Bengal Tigers in India, Lions in Africa, Crocodiles in Australia? So why was this not enough?"

"Dr. Cleaver."

"What about him."

"He was recruited sometime later, but he appeared well suited to this type of incarceration," began Tiberius almost guiltily. "From the beginning he was a positive influence on the others. He acted like a gentleman and kept his darker aspects suppressed. Over time however he slowly took over more duties within the Manor, eventually becoming the Master of the Hunt."

"Why would Lord Lodge allow that to happen?" Pierce asked with genuine confusion. "What possible good could have come from that?"

"The position was created specifically for Cleaver and was meant to act as a goal for the other members, something for the more ambitious to strive for. As Master of the Manor, Lodge wielded all of the power and as such he had a large target on his back. He had to watch for possible coups from all directions. But by creating Cleaver's new position, he built a pyramid that the power hungry would have to climb in order to reach him."

"So he gave power to Cleaver in order to make him deal with the intrigue and backstabbing," Pierce summed up. "Plus if one of them succeeded, it's a clean way to dispose of Cleaver. That's actually pretty smart, so what went wrong?"

"Cleaver turned out to be very adept at uncovering conspiracies and dealing with them quietly. As the hunting became more dangerous, members would perish on the excursions thereby created a regular turnover. Eventually the original Hunt members were all replaced with new ones that had only known Cleaver as the Master of the Hunt. With the power structure firmly in place, few contemplated taking his position through violent means"

Pierce looked across the room, the candles and fire providing just enough light for him to see that both Melrose and MacDuff nodded at the statement.

"By the time we discovered that they had hunted their first person, Cleaver had nearly as much power, influence, and followers as Lord Lodge. The Pack Members; the whips and hounds, had been recruited to act as guards for the Hunt Members and to keep them in check as much as to help them hunt. However some of them became too close to their masters. Plus once Cleaver installed Drummond as the Hunt Secretary, we found that the Pack Members being recruited were not of the same moral quality as the originals."

"Malicio and his cronies, the Black Pack," spat MacDuff in distaste.

"Precisely," agreed Tiberius. "That was some time ago and the Manor has been at a stalemate ever since. Between the two camps of Lodge and Cleaver, however it's not an open confrontation. Many don't realize it exists and many don't care."

"But you're hunting people!" accused Pierce, unhappy with Tiberius' explanations. "How can you reconcile with that?"

"You don't understand! Cleaver was cunning," Tiberius replied, walking over to face Pierce directly. "We didn't all wake up one day and decided to charge through one of the portals and pillage a village like a murderous horde. Cleaver set it up gradually, like a long winding fuse just waiting for a spark.

"Drummond went to recruit a new member, a very dangerous gangster. The story he told was that the prospect became upset and killed one of the pack members and escaped. Drummond returned a babbling mess, and before Lord Lodge could decide on a course of action, Cleaver, the Black Pack, and others descended on Chicago to hunt him down."

"So it spiralled out of control from there?" concluded Pierce doubtfully.

"Not at first. That was the first step. Cleaver was no fool and I believe he knew our goal here. Somehow he convinced Lodge that under some circumstances it would be better to kill some of the dangerous people in the world rather than to recruit them."

"I can't believe he would go along with it," spoke up MacDuff.

"Why not?" countered Tiberius. "You're one of the best men I know, and you've been a part of the hunt for ages."

MacDuff had no response for this and looked down.

"I'm sorry my friend," he consoled. "He has played all of us. His suggested targets were dangerous people that had escaped punishment. He proposed we met out justice." Tiberius shook his head at this.

"So everyone just went along with it?"

"Wouldn't you," defended Tiberius. "Imagine being able to hunt down a serial killer let off on a technicality, or a rampant child abuser."

"But you're killing people," Pierce repeated once again. "Sure, even I've sat around with a beer and said *if I could get away with it, I'd kill all of those sick bastards*. But nobody actually does it! It's just something you say when you read something terrible in the paper or see a pedophile's picture on the news. But it's supposed to be just talk."

"What do you want me to say?!" Tiberius shot back, finally tired of Pierce's moral preaching. "That I'm sorry that I've hunted down and killed the scum or the earth? Well I'm not. Would I do things differently if I had the chance? Probably!"

"Ok, ok, I had that coming," Pierce raised his hands in defence, taken aback by Tiberius uncharacteristic outburst. "It's just that after all I've heard about Lord Lodge, I find it hard to believe he agreed and never tried to stop it."

"Of course he tried to stop it," Tiberius replied tiredly. "I was as shocked as you when he went along with Cleaver, so I confronted him about it. Lord Lodge said that he was playing a cautious and long term game against Cleaver. That to act prematurely would only lead to unnecessary violence that would engulf the staff and the people of the island."

"That makes sense, since the Manor is basically an armed camp with loyalties divided between Cleaver and Lord Lodge," MacDuff agreed, finding his voice once again.

"But I think it went beyond that," Tiberius continued conspiratorially. "I think he enjoyed the mental chess game of the struggle, both men using those of us at the Manor like game pieces. He called it a game at the beginning, and I believe that's how he truly felt. But the problem was that Cleaver was no real match for his mental prowess. Lord Lodge always seemed to see five steps ahead and consistently foiled Cleaver's plans."

"It doesn't feel like he's foiled anyone now," Pierce pointed out plainly.

"But like many experts playing a game, I believe he started to lose interest," Tiberius continued, ignoring Pierce' comment. "He was so confident in his abilities that he stopped paying such close attention to Cleaver's activities. He concerned himself about the bigger picture, in a way that only a man centuries old could. But in doing so he ignored the seemingly trivial day to day activities of the Manor."

"That's true," Melrose confirmed quietly, entering into the conversation. "I was one of his valet's some time ago, and he seemed uninterested in the Hunt. He'd spend days at a time reading books and old newspapers. He even created a small laboratory in his office where he'd toil for endless hours at some experiment or another."

"A few years ago he seemed to throw off this cloak of lethargy, around the time of Lord Schell's recruitment. But the damage was done and Lord Lodge was basically the Master of the Manor in name only."

*

Everyone in the room remained silent for many minutes, lost in thought or unwilling to break the silence. Pierce continued to pace and Melrose had collected all of the empty glasses and decanter. Tiberius merely watched Pierce, studying his movements.

"You seem pretty well informed, more than you let on at the beginning," Pierce challenged Tiberius. "So what am I doing here? Why was I recruited early?"

"I don't know everything, I am in the dark as much as you in some respects," he objected. "I don't know why you're here or why you were recruited early. I only know the how."

"The how?" repeated Pierce in confusion.

"Before he disappeared, Lord Lodge instructed me to get you here and to keep you here at all costs," explained Tiberius. "I had to promise to do everything in my power to keep you here and to keep you safe."

"As did I," added Melrose.

"As did we all, it appears," concluded MacDuff to Tiberius' astonishment.

"I didn't know…" said Tiberius quietly.

"I imagine it was a precaution to tell us separately," offered MacDuff to his friend. "Not an indication of his trust in you."

He nodded in appreciation but seemed momentarily lost in his account.

"You said you know how I was recruited?"

"Yes, I organized it after receiving instructions from Lord Lodge after his disappearance," he resumed shaking the cobwebs from his head. "I was able to obtain your correct recruitment letter and had Jane, one of the housemaids, deliver it to the Hunt office out-box. These letters are always written by Cleaver and approved by Lodge. Drummond actioned it immediately and it was on your desk at work that day. You know the rest."

"So that's why you were so insistent I join the Hunt when

you and Drummond recruited me?" Tiberius' nodding reply brought another question to his mind. "Then what was the reason for the home invasion the night before with your goons? Why'd you have to use a goddamned taser?" He rubbed the spot in recollection of that night.

"Look at it from my perspective. My mentor tells me to recruit a potential member early, telling me how important it is that he joins and stays. I wanted to know what you were made of."

"Fair enough. But did you know Jane was in league with Cleaver?" asked Pierce changing the subject.

"Jane?"

"Well, she was Lord Lodge's keeper when he was placed at the pub in Rooks Bay after being spirited away from the Manor," Pierce began counting on his finger. "I overheard her and Cleaver discussing ways of disposing of me. And I informed her of my plan to return home on my first excursion. Only when I got there my house exploded…"

Before he could continue, Tiberius had cleared his throat a couple times.

"I was actually the one who bombed your house."

"You?!"

"I overheard Cleaver and Drummond discussing your plan to return home. So I went through the portal first and made my way to your apartment before the rest of the Hunt emerged in Ottawa."

"So that's why it was night time when we emerged from the portal when it should still have been the afternoon," he reasoned, solving another question that had been nagging him. "I think I even saw you in the road from across the street."

"Possibly. I didn't have much time to install the bomb safely and return to the portal before the rest of you."

"But why did you do it?" Pierce asked, his hands jutting out in emphasis.

"I promised Lord Lodge to keep you here at all costs. I figured you would stay if you were homeless."

"But I wasn't planning on leaving! It was a ruse!"

A silence fell over them for a few seconds until Melrose's quiet chuckling broke it.

"To be fair sir," said Melrose regaining his serious demeanour. "You planned to set your house on fire to reach the same goals."

"But not bomb it!"

"Semantics," retorted Tiberius.

"I think we're all missing the point," interjected MacDuff gravely. "Lord Lodge is missing and we have no idea where he is, why he's been taken, or why Patrick here is so important."

"Well we know Cleaver sent him, and probably Jane, away from the pub."

"How do you know that?" Tiberius asked Pierce eyeing him sceptically.

Pierce and MacDuff then explained their mission to Rooks Bay the night of the bonfire party and the empty room that Lodge had previously occupied. Melrose then informed them of his inquiries with the staff as to Jane's whereabouts. In the spirit of sharing, Tiberius told them his deal with the assistant butler.

"What do you intend to find out with a report about food deliveries?" Pierce raised the question the others were all thinking.

"Despite the situation we now find ourselves, Lord Lodge and I were somewhat prepared," Tiberius conveyed with some renewed confidence. "We knew Cleaver was up to something and Victor believed he might be abducted. So we put together some plans in case that happened. One of them involved him requesting certain food that would be hard to regularly obtain. This would force them to have it sent out from the Manor…"

"And a quick check of the shipping lists would tell you where they were sent and where he was being kept," Pierce finished the explanation, smiling at the elegance of the plan.

"Well if not the exact place, at least somewhere to start looking."

"So that's it then?" asked Pierce looking at the others. "We just sit around waiting for the butler to tell Tiberius where the cucumbers were delivered?"

"Not quite," added Tiberius, looking very serious. "Before his disappearance, Lord Lodge was looking into something else. He believed that Colonel Bufford was up to something, but he never said what exactly. In truth I think he was waiting for you to show up and take over. Now he's gone and I feel as though it's still important. I've been so concerned with finding my master that I have not looked into this myself."

"Which is where we come in?"

"Exactly. I don't believe the Colonel had anything to do with Lord Lodge's disappearance, however it can't be discounted."

"I think we can discount it," snorted Pierce. "The man's a crazed idiot."

"That just makes him dangerous and unpredictable," offered MacDuff sagely.

"Fine, we'll look into him while you wait for the delivery address of the groceries. I don't suppose Lord Lodge had a more precise idea of the nature of the Colonel's scheming?" asked Pierce sardonically.

"Despite his reputation," responded Tiberius, ignoring his tone, "he is not a mind reader."

*

"I don't know how you can stand eating this every day," stated Jane staring at Lodge's platter as he tucked in for his lunch. "Mrs. Hobart is actually a very good cook and has a well stocked pantry."

"I happen to enjoy poached cod with corn cakes and cucumber salad," replied Lord Lodge, pulling out his cutlery from the folded napkin. "It does wonders for your health."

"If you say so," responded Jane dubiously. "But you'll have to do without, as there's no more cod or cucumbers and the cornmeal required for the cakes is running low."

"Unacceptable," Lodge said in the most displeased and haughty manner Jane had ever seen him display. "Inform Mrs.

Hobart that my strict diet requires that I have this food regularly. I don't care how she does it, but I expect to have this same meal in at least three days time."

"Yes sir, I'll inform her."

"Good." He began eating his meal in silence, stopping only to butter his corn cakes. "How do our preparations progress?"

"I've been able to find some large crates in the basement that should suit our purpose," she reported dutifully. "Although I can't think of an explanation for their eventual shipment."

"On the desk behind me you will find a letter," he motioned with his knife. "Read it to me."

She walked over to the desk and was able to find the letter he indicated under a pile of books and blank paper. The black ink flowed across the paper in waves of aristocratic script. At the top was the letterhead of the Hunt.

"To the staff of the Crow's Nest," she began reading from the top. "There are a pair of chairs that I would like delivered from your location to my offices on Loch Dhu Island. Loch Dhu Island?"

"Yes. It's a small island on the great lake," he answered over his shoulder after dabbing his mouth with the silk napkin. "There's a small castle on it and should prove a nice rest stop for our escape. Keep reading."

"You will find these chairs in storage, though I do not know their exact location. They are both large wing back chairs made of black leather and with bronzed studs. I expect them delivered within the week. Signed... How can this be?"

"Read," order Lodge smiling as he rose from his finished meal.

"Signed, Dr. John Cleaver, Master of the Hunt."

"You look surprised," he observed.

"How did you get this?" Jane asked, confirming his observation. Her head was spinning as she stared at the letter that could potentially set them free. She recognized Cleaver's handwriting, but was confused by the contents. The Doctor was not in the practice of dealing with such common matters.

"I wrote it."

"What?!" her head snapped up to face Lodge as he lit his pipe. His eyes burned through the smoke in amusement. "But it's identical to his handwriting."

"Thank you, I am quite good at reproductions."

"But it can't possibly work," she stated without much confidence. But then she started to think it through, logically appraising the situation as Lodge was teaching her. Few people knew his real handwriting, but that didn't matter as the letter had fooled her. The crates were in the basement storage, as were the chairs presumably. So all they had to do was remove the chairs after they were packed and get inside. Then they would be transported to safety. "It could work."

"Possibly," allowed Lodge as he studied her progression from disbelief intently. "What are some of the problems?"

"What is this, a test?" she replied testily.

"This is training," he retorted in kind. "I've provided a problem along with a solution. However I want you to find any potential flaws with our reasoning."

She thought for a short time, moving the sequences of events in her mind. Problems and obstacles began to appear to her as she went through the process.

"First, if one of us is in a crate, the other won't be able to secure the second crate properly."

"Second?"

"Success depends on no one opening the crates during the journey or at the destination."

"Third?"

"We don't know what's awaiting us on the island."

"And fourth?"

"How do we get off the island and then where do we go?"

"Very good, those are the same problems I discovered as well," he congratulated his student. "So what are the possible solutions?"

"Well first we can fashion some sort of handle to hold the crate lid down from the inside so it appears fastened. I would also imagine that they would tie the crate down on the wagon, as they'll want to protect Dr. Cleavers possessions. In that vain, they will probably use some packing material around the chairs. If we're covered with that and if the crates are not opened, we should go unnoticed."

"And the last two problems?"

"I'm not sure," she confessed after a brief silence. "Those appear to be unknown's that we can't possibly theorize from here."

"Capital!" clapped Lodge in appreciation. "It is hazardous to theorize before receiving the facts. We must admit that we have no solution for the last two problems at this time."

He took the letter from Jane and folded it up and placed it in an envelope. Depositing the envelope on his desk, he grabbed a candle and dropped some hot wax along the seal. Then with a wink at his companion he withdrew a metal stamp from a hollowed out book and stamped the wax. After it cooled he placed it back in Janes hand.

"If the handwriting gave them pause, the seal will dispel any doubts."

Jane nodded, realizing their conversation had concluded. She slid the letter in her pocket and then began filling her tray with the remnants of her master's meal.

"Is there anything else you require?" she asked before leaving.

"Nothing at the moment," he replied from the desk. "I need to sit and think. I will see you at dinner."

Jane glided out noiselessly with the tray in one hand, making her way below stairs without passing anyone. The lodge remained largely empty apart from Lodge, herself, and the small number of staff.

"He does seem to go on," observed Mrs. Hobart when Jane deposited the tray in the kitchen. "He must talk the ear off you."

"I don't mind," replied Jane innocently. "Although he does have a request. He'd like to continue his regimen of cod and cucumbers."

"Did you inform him that we're all out?"

"I did."

"And what did his Lordship say?"

"That he didn't care how you got them, but he wanted his meal within the next three days. I must say, I've never seen him cross like that."

"Well if that's what he wants," huffed the cook as she went to a small writing table by the window. "At least he gave me three days. Some of these lords and ladies would give me three *hours* to provide them what they want."

Jane watched her remove a rough envelope from a leather satchel on the table. She realized that this must be the mail bag as Mrs. Hobart scribbled the food order on a list before placing it back in the bag. But when she moved back to the sink, Jane noticed that there was a second bag beside it. She realised that if the first bag was going to the Manor, the second might have come from it.

"Incidentally, the lads just returned from the Manor," Mrs. Hobart said while she tackled the dirty dishes that had just been deposited.

Jane walked over to the window to look outside, much to the amusement of Mrs. Hobart. However the cook did not see Jane smoothly deposit the false letter into the second satchel as she looked out on the empty courtyard.

"When are they going back?" asked Jane innocently as she turned back from the window.

"Not for a few days, so you'll have plenty of time."

"Time for what?" She replied innocently. "I don't know what you're talking about." She did know and she was slightly concerned. Jane knew that using her charms to gain the trust of the groundskeeper was necessary, but how long would her shy flirting act last? Luckily he was content with their slow progress. But she was unwilling to go beyond that.

If she had wanted to escape at any cost, she could have fully seduced him. She would have easily influenced him into helping her and Lord Lodge escape. But that would have caused more problems than it would solve. She was sure he would be severely punished if Cleaver discovered he had knowingly helped them. And she wouldn't be able to live with herself knowing that.

But there was another reason for wishing to avoid any intense personal interactions with him. She had recently discovered she was a romantic. Apart from the books on philosophy she had borrowed from Lord Lodge, she had also borrowed some classic literature. She had instantly become hooked on Jane Austen and read her novels into the early mornings.

So every time she thought of Phillip the groundskeeper, her thoughts would immediately turn to someone else. She didn't even know why she continued to think about him. The first time she'd seen him he'd hardly made an impact on her; he wasn't ruggedly handsome or charmingly suave. But at their subsequent meetings she'd felt a twinge of something within, that somehow they were connected. Her rational side told her it was because he was the dark stranger and the feeling would pass. But the feeling never seemed to pass and her thoughts kept returning to Patrick Pierce.

She knew this was foolish and she should try and stop it. He was a member of the Hunt and she was a servant. Besides, he had probably been bewitched by one of the glamorous Ladies of the Hunt, maybe the Russian or the Frenchwoman. Plus they had only met a handful of times and she probably never registered to him. She concentrated on these thoughts to try and block him out, but knew that it was only a matter of time before he would resurface in her mind.

Chapter 15

Each day there's a new potential for self-discovery and Patrick Pierce had come to that realization in the last few weeks. He had discovered that he enjoyed firearms as much as swords, that he was a decent student of the German language, and that he could converse with attractive women without making a fool of himself. Well, some of the time. But he had not been prepared for the fact that he would enjoy wearing a kilt.

Despite his father being born in Scotland, Pierce had never worn the national clothing. Indeed, he'd never even contemplated wearing it. But that all changed when he woke up the morning after the candlelit conference with MacDuff and Tiberius. A kilt, along with all the accoutrements was waiting in his dressing room when he entered. A quick interrogation of his valet revealed that the Brown Pack had sent it up with their compliments.

"Am I supposed to wear it?" asked Pierce as he felt the fabric.

"That's generally the idea with clothing sir," replied Melrose in his most professional servant's voice.

"I know MacDuff wears a kilt everyday, but I haven't seen anyone else wearing one."

"Sean is also known to wear one periodically, but they're

the only Scots in the Manor."

Deciding to try something new, he had Melrose help him into it properly and was surprised by the ease of fit and the comfort. He looked in the mirror and was impressed by the fact he didn't look like an idiot. In fact he almost looked distinguished.

"It's the Maple Leaf tartan," explained Melrose as Pierce was observing himself. "It's the national tartan of Canada. The brown, red, yellow, and green hues are meant to represent the changing colours of the maple leaf."

Pierce was speechless with appreciation from this pronouncement. He had assumed that the reddish brown coloured tartan had been picked due to his Packs colour. But he had not expected the real reason to be so personal. For the first time since his arrival he felt at home in the Manor.

"I'm blown away," he finally uttered emotionally. "I didn't expect this. Thank you." He could tell Melrose fought to keep his own composure as he passed a brown tweed jacket over for Pierce to complete his outfit.

Looking in the mirror a final time, he was shocked by the transformation. He looked like a Scottish laird, equally ready to tramp around the highland heather or discuss immense matters over a snifter of scotch.

This also seemed to be the consensus throughout the Manor as he made his way to the Brown Packs lair. The staff had always acknowledged his passing with a curt nod, an act that he had initially found unsettling, but had slowly gotten used to. However they had always seemed to do this out of form or duty, and did not really see him as one of the Lord's of the Manor. But as he walked the halls in his new clothing, they stopped immediately and would offer a clearly audible *m'Lord*. After passing the first couple, who showed this respect, he started to walk taller, straighter and with more purpose.

The feeling remained even when he entered the large stag engraved door that guarded the entrance to the Brown Pack's rooms. He had expected to receive some sarcastic comments or some sly grins at best, when he met with his men. But that was not the case.

"You look grand lad," exclaimed MacDuff enthusiastically. He was wearing a matching kilt with his regular uniform. He strode over and gave him the now standard slap on the back.

Pierce was staggered, not physically, but emotionally as he looked from MacDuff, to Sean, and then to Liam. They were all dressed in the Maple Leaf tartan. Sean wore a kilt like Pierce and MacDuff, while Liam wore a pair of plaid trews. Their brown leather uniforms complemented the rustic tartan perfectly, looking as though they had been designed in unison.

It was at this moment that Pierce finally knew what it meant to be part of something larger than himself and to be accepted. He had been a shy child and had avoided large groups and intimate friendships, afraid to open himself up to rejection or humiliation. He was not necessarily a loner or a misanthrope, but he always stayed to the periphery in groups. Despite the welcome he had already received from the Brown Pack after his duel with Sean, it was not a wholehearted display. He imagined they would have made the same gestures to any other semi-qualified Hunt Member. But to make such a symbolic gesture in such a unified way was so foreign to him that he didn't know how to react.

"You all look great," fumbled Pierce after finally finding his voice through all the myriad of feelings. He then decided he had better switch to humour before he was teased for his sentimentality. "Except for Liam. You look like a cheap golf pro at a public course."

"Apologies my lord," bowed Liam theatrically. "But I suppose I'm just not man enough to wear a skirt…kilt…" He finished hurriedly, raising his hands in mock defence.

"Aye, that's about right," MacDuff acknowledged with a smile, turning the tables on his witty subordinate. They all had a quick laugh and both Sean and Liam came over to shake Pierce's hands, unofficially welcoming him into their tight knit club.

"Well isn't this a Gaelic scene," pronounced a dry voice

from the doorway.

The four men turned quickly, not used to having unsolicited intruders in their space. There were few keys throughout the Manor that opened the main door to their chamber and the majority of those keys were on the four men currently within. However they all relaxed quickly, recognizing the owner's voice.

"I didn't know you still had a key Tiberius," observed MacDuff smiling. "We'll have to look into changing the locks. Keep out the riff raff."

"Speaking of riff raff, how are you gentleman?" he asked Liam and Sean as he walked over and shook their hands. Both greeted him warmly, despite his good natured jab at them.

Pierce had found that Tiberius garnered a respect around the Manor that bordered on reverence. He was able to joke, cajole, threaten, and order those around him with ease and without receiving any negative responses. It wasn't just the fact that he was the longest serving staff member of the Manor, it went beyond that. He had a certain innate nobility, charm, and strength that surrounded him at all times, mesmerizing others.

"Not that we don't enjoy the visit," began Pierce with curiosity, "but what are you doing here?"

"I imagined you would be meeting this morning after our talk last night and decided to stop by."

"Talk?" asked Sean, somewhat hurt by being left out.

"Tiberius, Patrick, and I," replied MacDuff hurriedly. "We don't know where Lord Lodge is, though the search has started. Plus we need to find out what Colonel Bufford is up to. There, you're up to date, so stop feeling sore."

"Speaking of Lord Lodge, anything new?" Pierce asked as he sat at the large oak table, realizing that no one would sit down until he did.

"Nothing new this morning," replied Tiberius sitting across from him, followed by the others.

"So why are you here?" repeated MacDuff.

"Colonel Bufford."

"Did he finally shoot someone?" asked Liam lightly, but

only received a dark look from Tiberius as a reply.

"Before he was abducted, Lord Lodge was suspicious of Bufford's activities," answered Pierce solemnly. "But now that he's gone Tiberius has followed Lodge's wishes and passed the investigation onto me. That *me* in turn means *us*, and I assume there are no objections to this pluralisation?"

Everyone around the table nodded their heads, accepting the challenge.

"So what should we know about Colonel Bufford?" continued Pierce inquiringly.

"After I left your room last night I was struck by something that you said. That Colonel Bufford is a crazed idiot. I think we can all agree that it's an accurate description." Tiberius waited a second for an objection, but none was forthcoming. "So the question is, why would Lord Lodge have us looking into his activities?"

"There must be a good reason," added MacDuff. "I've never known Lord Lodge to do anything impetuously."

"Agreed. So I decided to look into the Colonel's file last night."

"He has a file?" Sean asked incredulously.

"We all have a file," Tiberius answered gravely. "Lord Lodge kept a file on all of the Hunt members. He researched their pasts with meticulous detail and kept notes on their activities after they joined."

"But does that also include those of us who are not members?" Sean pushed farther.

"Of course. Though Lord Lodge was not nearly as concerned with the staff as members and kept the files succinct. But Drummond probably added to them, he is nothing if not a busy-body with a bureaucratic need for detailed records."

"Plus I assume that, in general, the history of anyone from the outside being brought here would be delved into in great detail. That would require numerous notes that would have to be kept. Members and staff alike." Pierce's summation was answered by a nod from Tiberius.

"Very grand, we're being spied on from dawn 'til dusk," Liam cut in impatiently. "But what did the file on the good Colonel have to say?"

"If he's a crazed lunatic now, he wasn't always," countered Tiberius looking at those gathered around the table. He leaned back and began reciting the information from memory. "He was born in the United States, in the state of Georgia to be precise. His family were wealthy plantation owners, though poor Nathan received the short end of the stick."

"Youngest son?" MacDuff hazarded a guess, quickly confirmed by Tiberius.

"Third son out of three. So he was packed off to a boarding school in England to be taught like a gentleman. He was kicked out for brawling and sent packing, but did not return home, not immediately. He made his way to the Isle of Dogs in London, where he promptly gambled his savings away."

"Sounds like a real threat," observed Liam with a whistle.

"Remember our lesson on the deception of appearances?" MacDuff sighed like a long suffering school teacher.

"I thought that was Sean's lesson," he grinned in response, while Sean himself felt the spot where Pierce's blade had nicked him.

"So what happened to him in London?" inquired Pierce refocusing the group.

"His descent into darkness."

*

"You spend some time with Lord Lodge don't you?"

"I see him at least three times a day," Jane replied to Phillip's question as they walked in the courtyard. Both had finished their duties for the day and had decided to get outdoors while the weather was mild. A storm was on its way and the Crow's Nest would take the brunt of any inclement weather.

"I know you bring his meals each day," he continued

patiently. "But I mean other than that."

"Really Phillip, I didn't take you for the jealous kind," she replied buying her time. She really didn't know where these questions were heading, but she wanted to be ready to react plausibly.

"I didn't mean…" he stumbled over his words.

"I was just teasing," Jane said affectionately, seeing his reaction. She decided to be as truthful as precaution allowed. "Lord Lodge has been good enough to lend me some books from his library. His only condition is that we discuss them once I've finished reading them."

"Oh."

She could tell from his monosyllabic response that he understood her answer, but couldn't fathom the reason for such an action. She imagined that reading for enjoyment was not one of his pastimes, although to be fair he probably didn't have much free time. Since arriving at this mountain top prison, she had noticed that Phillip and the other groundskeepers were constantly busy. But they had the outdoorsman's blood in them, enjoying the crisp air and the physically demanding tasks.

"Why do you ask?"

"Well he asked me something that seemed strange at the time and seeing that you know him better…"

"You want some advice on what to do?"

"I know he's the Master of the Manor and we're to obey," he stated hesitantly, "but…"

"He's here under strange circumstances," Jane finished for him. He began to nod with approval knowing they were thinking the same thing.

"It's almost like he's a prisoner here. And I don't want to lose this job by doing something foolish."

"Tell me what he asked and I'll tell you if it's foolish or not," she responded logically as their walk led them to the stone balustrade that offered protection against the cliff's edge that dropped off towards the valley below.

"He asked me if there were any ropes and pulleys in

storage."

"So?" She asked pretending to be nonplussed by the question while her mind raced. Knowing that she and Lord Lodge planned to escape by the fake chair delivery, she wondered what this was about. She avoided looking down the cliff face, in case that was indeed the reason for the supplies. Perhaps it was a back up plan in case they couldn't get in the crates?

"So what if he really is being held here and I give him those things and he escapes!" he exclaimed. "He could use ropes and pulleys to get down the cliff."

"You really have the most vivid imagination," she lied dismissively. Realizing he might have a point and needing to keep her accomplice safe she looked over the edge into the darkness. "I can't imagine a man of Lord Lodge's age climbing down that cliff. I bet a strong young man like you would even find it a challenge."

She reached out and held his hand, garnering a smile and an ease in tension from her escort. She hoped a compliment and some physical contact would cloud his mind. She could tell from his reaction it did, he quickly reddened and turned his gaze away from her. Deciding to take in the view, she followed suit.

However as they both looked out over the vast expanse as the stars began to appear, she found her own mind clouded. The hand she was holding began to feel warmer and she started to feel a slight tingle spreading up her arm. She let it happen, having never felt this sensation or this close to someone before. She looked up slowly and found that Patrick and not Phillip was smiling back at her. She smiled back and returned her gaze towards the sea in the distance.

"Of course you're right, there's no way he could get down there," Phillip conceded proudly, breaking the silence.

"Hmm," uttered Jane coming out of her short daze. She blinked a couple times and looked back up to find that she was once again with Phillip. They turned and headed back towards the buildings.

"But I wonder what he wants that stuff for?"

"Who knows?" Jane replied trying to suppress her curiosity. "He's probably building some kind of contraption. He's quite scientific you know."

Phillip offered a shrug, wanting nothing to do with science.

They walked the rest of the way in silence, with only a quick goodbye when they reached the main courtyard. Phillip and the other groundskeepers lived in an out building in the back and he waved to Jane after they parted ways. She let herself in the kitchen entrance and was relieved to find it empty.

Although having Mrs. Hobart a witness to her budding romance made it more believable, she was tiring of the cooks motherly tendencies and advice. She was sure the old woman had started making a wedding menu in her head in the hopes the celebration would be held here at the Crow's Nest.

Upon reaching her room she took in its utilitarian nature and sighed. She'd found some brighter linen in storage and filled a small vase with mountain flowers in an effort to brighten it up. The log walls of the room made it appear slightly warmer than the stone walls of her room at the Manor. But it was at the expense of being infinitely more rustic, which was not her style of choice.

She had spent the majority of her adult life in rooms such as this and it had never bothered her before. So why now? Jane knew the reason before she even had to ask herself. Every time she thought of Lord Pierce she quickly found flaws in such a match and tonight was no different. She looked in the mirror and only saw a servant in a servant's uniform, living in the servant's quarters.

Having finished her daily dose of self-pity, Jane put it behind her and carried on with the real task at hand. Escape plans continued to progress and she had some new problems.

Phillip's revelation gave her a small pause as to Lord Lodge's actual plans. She had believed she'd been privy to his plan up until tonight. However she now wondered what other arrangements he had been making on his own. She couldn't make out what he planned to use the rope or pulleys for, but surely not to descend the cliff face. Nothing else came to mind and she struggled with how to proceed with this new information. Should she confront him about it or ignore it and continue as before?

She knew one thing for certain, that she would not report it to Lord Cleaver. As agreed, she had been sending letters to the Manor, informing Cleaver on the progress of their escape. She had included everything; the forged note, the crates, and even the destination. Every time she tried to figure out how this was going to help them she became confused and just continued sending information. Jane knew it came down to a bluff and a double bluff (or maybe a triple bluff), so she just hoped that Cleaver fell for the right one.

"That's a little melodramatic isn't it?" asked Pierce following Tiberius' pronouncement of Colonel Bufford's London adventures.

"Descent into Darkness," Liam mimicked Tiberius' voice perfectly. "Sounds like a melodrama."

"One day he's a down on his luck teenager in the Docklands," continued Tiberius unfazed by the commentary. "Then he boards a ship bound for the States. Only it takes a quick African stop on the way and it wasn't for the scenery."

"Slavers," spat MacDuff, ever the freedom loving Scotsman.

"The file does not indicate if he knew the real purpose of the ship's journey, but sufficed to say he rejoined the ship after a brief visit to the family plantation. For the next three years he worked his way up the trade, eventually owning his own ship."

"This must have been before the war," added Pierce to Tiberius' account. "We know he was a Confederate Colonel, I guess he wasn't fighting against federal encroachment."

"He spent the first year of the war running arms from the

Continent to the South in a cutter he stole with his slaver crew."

"When did he join the army?" asked Sean now fully intrigued by the tale.

"He returned from sea one day and had a message waiting for him," Tiberius continued, slowly answering the question. "It informed him that there had been a hasty uprising at some of the nearby plantations, including his families'. He raced home to find everything back in order, but with his eldest brother dead. Nathan, now a grown man, lashed out with a cruel fury."

"What did he do?" whispered Pierce, unsure he wanted the answer.

"He paid his respects to his dead brother's body, still out for viewing. He grabbed a silver coin that was placed over the right eye and went to the slave's quarters. He and his crew lined them all up, men on the left and women on the right. He started with the women and flipped a coin in front of each one. Heads they were safe, tails and they were raped in front of everyone. Then he went to the men, only this time those with tails were hung."

Everyone in the room was silent, but there was a growing tension that Pierce could feel. He himself felt conflicting feelings, all rambling around in his head and his soul. Rage, sadness, sickness, they all vied for prominence within him.

"It never changes does it?" uttered Sean with distaste.

"Watch the bastard?" Liam growled rising up from his seat. "I'll bloody kill him and that will make it easier on everyone."

"And then the Grey Pack will kill Patrick in retribution and we've solved nothing," countered MacDuff calmly, signalling him to retake his seat."

"What's a man like Bufford even doing here?" Sean asked after regaining his composure.

With a heavy heart and without any interruptions, Tiberius gave the same speech to Liam and Sean that he gave the others the night before. They remained silent when he was finished.

Both felt a tinge of shame in having been a part of everything. In their minds they could have pleaded ignorance; however in their hearts they had always known something was not quite right at the Manor.

Tiberius softly cleared his throat to regain their attention.

"As heinous as his act was, it was the act of a calculating criminal. From all accounts he was still in full control of his faculties."

"So what tipped him over the edge?"

"The death of his second brother. Not long after he regained control of the plantation he decided to raise his own regiment of cavalry to fight for the Confederacy. Apparently this was normal in the early days of the war.

"They might have worn the grey uniform, but they were soldiers in appearance only. They were actually raiders and they were good at it. With the military knowledge he learned in school he organized the usual guerrilla tactics of such troops and was moderately successful at disrupting the enemy's supplies and communications."

"So what happened to his brother?" Pierce inquired.

"His brother was an officer fighting with an artillery regiment, which befitted his wealthy status. However he lacked the cunning and survival instincts of his younger brother. He was killed in a brothel by Union forces when they broke through the line nearby."

"Helluva way to go," commented Liam with a hint of admiration.

"Not in his case," Tiberius replied soberly. "When the Confederates retook the town the next day they discovered him and his comrades in the brothel. They were all found naked and in the beds they had been killed in, their weapons outside the rooms."

"Killed without a chance to defend themselves," Pierce observed.

"Defenceless were they? Rubbish," snorted MacDuff. "You defend yourself by not getting blind drunk in a brothel a mile away from the front lines in a war."

"Well the Colonel didn't see it like that and he proceeded to lose his mind after he heard the news. Like before he showed up at the brothel and demanded to know what had happened. Some believed the brothel owner had been paid off or was pro-union. Unlike the plantation, he didn't give any of the workers the generosity of a coin toss. He and his men set fire to the brothel and shot anyone who was able to make it out of the smoking carnage."

"I assume he and his men changed their raiding tactics after that?" MacDuff asked knowingly, having seen the worst sides of war.

"Indeed. The Grey Raiders, as they became known, continued to hit supply lines as before. But they also started indiscriminate killings through out the battle areas. They would search out field hospitals and Prisoner of War trains, killing the defenceless. Just like his brother had been."

"Why did nobody stop him? It goes against all of the rules of war," Pierce admonished no one in particular.

"There are no rules in war," countered Tiberius. "The Union couldn't find him and the Confederates had enough problems of their own. The war had turned against them and they needed every able bodied man to fight. Anyway that's what we're dealing with."

"A skilled sailor, soldier, and tactician who is cunning, ruthless, and slightly crazed," Pierce summed up for the gathered group. "What were we saying about not underestimating your opponent?"

"I'm not sure I feel better knowing this new information," admitted Sean. "I liked him better when I thought he was a little mad and eccentric."

"So what's our next move?" Liam asked Pierce. Everyone followed his gaze towards the Lord of the Brown Pack.

Pierce had been thinking about that very question as Tiberius had been regaling them on Colonel Bufford's past. He was glad he'd done it; otherwise he probably would have disappointed them with silence.

"We follow Lord Lodge's instructions. We stay alert to

Bufford and his pack's actions. We try and find out what he is doing or what his goal is. Hopefully we'll be able to find Lord Lodge first and gain more insight. Is there a chance he has something ongoing in the real world?"

"Possibly," acknowledged MacDuff. "But he'd need the keys to whichever portal he was using and be forewarned to plan anything. Excursions and hunts are kept secret, so it's unlikely he's relying on that avenue."

"Kept secret by whom?" interjected Pierce sensing a flaw in his Whip's reasoning.

"Drummond and the Hunt staff," Tiberius replied, realizing the implication.

"So we take nothing for granted. If we go through a portal, we follow Bufford and his pack."

A knock at the door sounded throughout the room just as he finished. Liam automatically rose and went to answer it without being prompted. He returned immediately with Melrose in tow behind him.

"A letter for you my Lord," announced Melrose as he handed a folded piece of parchment with the black wax seal of the Hunt on it.

"Looks like we're going to start the operation sooner than we'd anticipated," Pierce said after reading the document. "The next hunt is set, we leave tomorrow."

Chapter 16

The drumming of rain on the glass ceiling filled the Hunt Room, occasionally drowned out by the crash of thunder. Flashes of lightning augmented the light given off by torches and candles, while simultaneously displaying the intricate designs of the glass ceiling above.

"Very ominous, yes?" smiled Schell, leaning over to Pierce. He agreed with a nod, wondering why it always seemed to storm during momentous occasions. And this seemed like such an occasion.

The entire room was full, awaiting the arrival of the Master of the Hunt. The atmosphere was further enhanced by the uniforms and demeanour of those assembled. The sombre hues of the clothing matched the silence of the majority, broken only by the odd whisper amongst neighbours.

"The lads gathered the required equipment and have it in duffle bags behind them." MacDuff informed Pierce from the seat behind. "Everything is 1930's era. Liam said he even packed a Tommy gun for you if you wanted to feed you inner Capone."

Pierce turned around to shoot a dark glance towards Liam sitting in the top row, but his minion simply smiled back in mock confusion.

"Lords and Ladies, the Master of the Hunt!" bellowed a

black uniformed attendant as the doors drew open, signalling for everyone to stand. As before Lord Cleaver was trailed by Drummond, then members of his own pack as he entered. They took up the same positions as before, sitting after a ceremonious pause. The rest of the room then followed suit and sat back down.

"The Hunt has been called," began Lord Cleaver with a steely voice as he stared out on the assembly. "The Black Pack has answered it. Who else has answered the call?"

"The Gold Pack has answered," Zeidt replied formally.

"The Grey Pack has answered!" hollered Bufford with a wave of his fist.

"The Silver Pack has answered," Laflamme said with theatrical flourish.

In due course the rest of the Hunt Members announced the presence of their pack following the long standing protocol. Even Pierce managed his reply with some dignity, despite the ridiculousness he felt uttering the over dramatic words.

"My Lord!" began Drummond officially, clearly relishing his role in the proceedings. "The Secretary of the Hunt confirms the Call of the Hunt has been answered."

"Thank you Mr. Secretary. Lords and Ladies, you have all answered the call blindly and may defer without disgrace. I can tell you that this hunt is possibly the most dangerous one to date, with a cunning and dangerous prey."

The assembled members began eagerly shouting questions all at once, wishing to know what was ahead of them. Pierce could sense a rising feeling in the room. It started slowly as varying levels of excitement, fury, passion, and intoxication were thrown together. As it reached its peak, Pierce recognized it as bloodlust and they were all getting high on it.

Cleaver's eyes became wide and trance-like, his mouth twitching into a smile, and he gripped the arms of his chair like the talons of a bird of prey. He soaked up the emotions with vampiric thirst, feeding on their energy. It was with slow deliberation and slight disappointment that he raised his hands to quiet everyone down.

"Mr. Secretary please provide the Hunt with the details," he announced dramatically to the hushed crowd. Drummond rose from his desk in the center aisle, nodding assent to Lord Cleaver before turning to each side of the room as he spoke.

"Lords and Ladies, my assistants are now passing out the only documents and information you will receive for this hunt. You will undoubtedly have discovered from your pack that we will be travelling to the 1930's, as that is the era from which they have collected your equipment. You may also remember that the Master of the Hunt let slip the destination." He said this with fake recrimination, which elicited a chuckle throughout the room and a good natured raise of the eyebrow from Cleaver.

Despite having already known this information, everyone in the room was concentrated wholly on Drummond. Everyone save Pierce, who was trying to casually observe Bufford to see what his reactions would be.

"If you turn to page 1 of the file you will see that you will be hunting on new and dangerous ground, possibly the most dangerous you have faced yet. Your incursion will be from a villa in Seville, in the middle of the Spanish Civil War, the summer of 1937."

Again the room erupted with gasps of pleasure and shouts of delight. Schell muttered something beside him, but Pierce was busy watching Bufford's reaction. Rather than the exuberance he expected from the crazed Colonel, it was a more troubling reaction. Colonel Bufford leaned back with a clever smile and tented his fingers together below his chin. It was as if he had planned it, or at the very least expected the news.

"You will find a map of troop disbursements in your package," continued Drummond as he left his desk and began walking the center aisle that divided the seats in the room. "This will be essential as the hunting area will be in the entire Iberian Peninsula, not just the city or it's surrounding areas."

"Is there a possibility of the prey going beyond even Spain or Portugal?" inquired the Lord of the White pack further down the row from Pierce.

"A distinct possibility," he answered swiftly before continuing from memory. "Your target is only known by the name *The Reaver* and there are no pictures on file. As you can see from the physical description, it could fit over half the men in this room."

Rather than be deflated from this news, everyone became even more excited by the challenge. Pierce noted this to his neighbour.

"The last hunt was not terribly challenging," whispered Schell in reply. "It was in 1740's Vienna… again. The prey was a leader of bandits running around the woods with clubs. We could have made the kill within 24 hours, but decided to prolong our stay for the full week. The Viennese Opera was in full form."

"The Reaver is an arms dealer working both sides of the conflict. He is apparently providing arms to both the Nationalists and Republicans alike, therefore he could be anywhere."

Drummond continued providing what limited details on the target he had. Some of the Members took notes, while others simply listened intently. Pierce was doing neither, as he had no intention of hunting some shadowy arms dealer in the middle of the Spanish Civil War. He was planning on shadowing Colonel Bufford instead.

Pierce was once again troubled by Bufford's demeanour as Drummond rifled off information. He seemed uninterested by the conversations around him, sitting back, apparently lost in thought. Even his Pack was busy with their heads together in conversation, paying scant attention to their surroundings.

"They look like their planning something," MacDuff concurred from behind him. "I wonder how long they knew the target and the destination, since they weren't surprised by the news."

The room quieted down immediately as Cleaver stood, prompting those assembled to follow suit. Everyone waited in anticipation for him to speak, eager for the challenge and a change from their lives of leisure.

"The portal will be opened when we adjourn and will remain open for only four hours. Those who miss the deadline will not be able to enjoy the hunt. Mr. Secretary!"

"Yes my Lord," replied Mr. Drummond.

"Unlock the portal and release the hounds!"

*

Despite the thrill of the chase, the various packs exited the Hunt Room with dignity and order. Once outside they all dispersed to their various lairs to collect extra gear or the equipment they had already packed. Pierce noted his group was the only one that brought their equipment with them and were ready to begin.

"I assumed we'd want to be the first ones out in order to be prepared to follow Bufford," MacDuff explained as he walked beside Pierce towards the North Tower. "That is your plan isn't it Patrick?"

"That's the plan Duffy," he replied.

The Brown Pack walked the halls and galleries, trailing behind Drummond far enough to stay out of earshot. Pierce again noticed the lack of people out and about. It was like the servants had retreated into their holes like frightened rabbits in order to avoid the rampaging hunters that had been set loose. Therefore the sound of steps climbing the stairwell ahead seemed out of place and loud despite the carpeting.

"Lord Pierce," called out Tiberius as he stepped up from the stairwell at the same moment the Brown Pack was passing it. He then motioned them to a nearby door that was closed and apparently locked as Liam tried to open it. Tiberius removed a key chain from his pocket and unlocked it, ushering everyone in as nonchalantly as possible.

The room was dark, but a sudden flash of lightning showed that it was a small sitting room. Sean lit a lamp on a nearby table that barely exposed an elegant room filled with cherry wood and scarlet fabric.

"I'm glad I caught you before you left," Tiberius began

explaining. "I just got word from my contact. The list of food has been delivered. Shipment is bound for the Crow's Nest."

"I can't believe that worked," smiled Liam looking out the window.

"What's the Crow's Nest?"

"It's an old hunting lodge high up on a mountain pass," MacDuff began, ignoring Liam's jest. "It's basically impenetrable; cliffs on two sides, a mountain on another side, and a long bridge on the fourth. It's a couple of hours from here by horseback or carriage."

"We can't be sure that he's there though," Pierce observed trying to stay focused. He had felt this same rising anticipation before their assault on the pub, only for it to come crashing down.

"That's true," allowed Tiberius. "But the chances of all those food items being requested by someone not holding Lord Lodge are incredibly slim. That's why he chose that combination."

"Plus it's the perfect place to guard someone without arousing suspicion," added MacDuff nodding with approval.

"Are we able to miss the hunt?" asked Pierce.

"Not without arousing suspicion," answered Sean shaking the duffle bag of equipment he was holding.

"And not without letting Bufford accomplish whatever he's planning," finished Pierce, realizing that they still had job to do. A job that had been given to them by Lodge himself.

"Don't worry, I'll take care of the rescue," said Tiberius. "I wouldn't want you to have to face Lord Lodge after abandoning his orders."

"That's true, ol' Victor would have your head," Liam agreed in mock solemnity.

"When do you plan on going?" Pierce asked.

"Immediately."

"We'd better get going as well," MacDuff advised Pierce. "We want to find a nice perch in Seville in order to follow Bufford when he shows himself."

"Good luck," Tiberius said extending his hand to the

members of the Brown Pack.

"You too," replied Pierce. He left the room as innocently as possible with his men following him.

"I hope he's there," Pierce thought aloud as they continued their journey towards the North Tower.

"I hope he's not heavily guarded," added MacDuff. "They're going to need luck to assault that place."

"We're going to need luck as well," said Sean following behind them. "Walking around the middle of the Spanish Civil War isn't going to be stroll up the Royal Mile."

The basement storage room was dark, though not oppressively so. Its large space and high ceilings made it seem airy despite being largely underground. This effect was magnified by the limited number of items being stored at the Crow's Nest. Jane had only counted a few crates in one corner and a collection of covered furniture in another when she had first entered days ago.

It was largely the same tonight as she hunted through the crates. She placed her lamp down on one when she found what she was looking for. Two large crates were placed beside each other, slightly apart from the rest against the wall. Both were roughly the same size and made from wooden boards, but more importantly they were nailed shut. She tried to open one to verify if they had been packed with the correct cargo. When it didn't budge she sighed with mild frustration and looked around for a crowbar or tool of some sort.

Jane had overheard Mrs. Hobart giving instructions to Phillip that afternoon. She told him to pack the chairs Lord Cleaver had requested and to deliver them to Loch Dhu Island the next day. Realizing their plans were coming to fruition, she had immediately informed Lord Lodge.

So now she found herself traipsing around the basement trying to finalize their steps towards escape. She had to remove the chairs, hide them, and then fashion the lids so that both her and Lodge could keep them shut while inside. But first she needed to get the crates open or their plans would be for nothing.

Phillip was a good worker, but he could also be forgetful. She was hoping this was the case as she looked around the vicinity of the crates. She was rewarded when she found a jar of nails and a hammer by the wall. She had hoped that he would forget his tools once the crates were shut, and she was right. Picking up the hammer, Jane moved to the closest crate and began prying the lid open. He might have been forgetful; however Phillip was very strong and had hammered the lid down tight. She wedged the teeth of the hammer back in, heaved a second time, and was rewarded with a high pitched squeak as the lid opened a hair.

She was about to try a third time when she heard footsteps behind her. She'd been so busy working on the crate that she hadn't noticed the faint light of a second lamp and the presence of someone else. She spun around quickly with the hammer in her hands, eliciting a gasp from her interloper.

"Well I never..." began Mrs. Hobart in breathless confusion.

"You were right to call me Mrs Hobart," said an iron voice blocked from Jane's view by the darkness.

"I knew I'd heard someone shuffling around," stated the housekeeper, puffing her chest out with pride. She then turned back towards Jane aiming a sever glance of disapproval. "What are you doing down her girl? Explain yourself."

Jane opened her mouth to try and explain, but nothing seemed to come out. Multiple stories were swimming around in her head, waiting to be caught. But each one was more unbelievable than the last. This proved inconsequential, for when the owner of the iron voice emerged into the light, her mind went completely blank.

"I imagine she's trying to escape our lovely mountaintop retreat. Isn't that right my dear?"

Jane dropped her eyes to the ground, completely disoriented and confused.

"Mr. Hobart should be down any second. When he arrives please have him escort Jane back to her room. I'll allow you to come up with whatever punishment you see fit."

"As you say Lord Lodge," the housekeeper acknowledged as he turned and left the basement.

Jane couldn't believe what had just happened. It didn't make any sense for Lodge to have turned on her, when he wanted to escape as much as she did. Unless he still didn't believe that she was really on his side and no longer working for Cleaver.

Her thoughts were broken by the appearance of Mr. Hobart in the basement. After speaking briefly with his wife he turned towards Jane and motioned for her to follow him. She'd only seen Mr. Hobart briefly during her stay, mostly eating quietly in the kitchen at the end of a hard working day. He was a hard looking man with a creased leathery face who never smiled or spoke. In fact she couldn't remember him ever uttering a single word. He was not a large man, but a hard life spent working and hunting dissuaded Jane from trying to flee. If he got a hold of her, his powerful hands looked like they could crush her like a vice. She dejectedly led the way out of the storage room, retracing her steps towards the stairwell that led to the servant's area of the lodge.

But before she could take her fist step up, a loud thud sounded from the back of the room. It had sounded like something heavy had fallen and both Jane and her escort stopped. Mr. Hobart squinted into the darkness, and then called out to his wife. When no reply came, he started towards the direction the sound had emanated from. Turning towards Jane, he opened his mouth to issue what she assumed was a warning to not move. However Jane was stunned when his face seemed to freeze and no sound came out.

"Mr. Hobart…" she whispered, taking a step towards him. When he didn't acknowledge her, she reached out to touch him. She raised her hand up slowly, extending her index finger to his face. But before the probing finger could make contact, Mr. Hobart fell backwards creating a similar crash as before.

"Well that took a little bit longer than I had anticipated."

Jane shifted her awestruck gaze from the crumpled body on the floor to Lord Lodge's elegant frame descending the stairs.

"Don't worry, they're not dead," he pronounced as he knelt by the body, finding a pulse. Satisfied he stood up and grabbed one of Mr. Hobart's arms. "Care to give me a hand?"

Jane nodded, needing to do something to calm her racing mind. She leaned over and grabbed the other hand, helping Lodge drag the body to the wooden crates. They laid Mr. Hobart beside his wife, where her pulse was also checked.

"What is going on?" inquired Jane stiffly.

"Start working on those crates again," he replied obscurely, handing her the dropped hammer she had previously been using. "We haven't much time before dawn."

Jane grabbed it from his hand but didn't move towards the crates. She simply stood glaring at him, waiting for a real answer.

"I had to get the Hobart's down here without drawing too much attention. I asked her to watch the basement and have her husband stay ready as I thought there might be prowlers here tonight. I also slipped something into their tea so that they would not leave this basement on their own steam."

"What about the plan?!"

"The plan was too believable," he sighed, grabbing the hammer from her and moving towards the crates. He explained as he worked to remove the lids. "It was a good plan, but it left us vulnerable inside these wooden boxes. Plus Cleaver knew all about it."

"I thought that was the point," she replied in exasperation. "That he would never believe it was the true plan if we were telling him about it."

"But he might still want to cover all the options and have his men watch for these crates." With a final push he opened the second crate. "Help me get these chairs out will you."

They each went to a crate and removed the packing material, and then the chairs wrapped within them. The chairs were carried to a group of old furniture being stored under a heavy canvass tarp on the other side of the room.

"Then why did we even tell him about the chair delivery plan?"

"It had to appear that we were being really clever. Cleaver thinks he's clever and he looks for that in others. More importantly he relishes in being cleverer than anyone else. So we provide him with multiple avenues to keep his mind turning."

"Then to keep it turning you threw in a second possibility," she said, slowly seeing Victor Lodge's genius. "The rope you asked from Phillip?"

"Precisely. We tell him about the crate plan, but not the plan to descend the cliff face with ropes. However I was sure that info would get to him from the groundskeeper. So now he's faced with two escape plans, provided to him from two different sources."

"So what are we doing here if we're not going to use the crates?"

"We are going to use them," he replied lifting up Mrs. Hobart. "We're going to use them as a ruse. Help me get them in."

The pair awkwardly got both bodies into the two crates, closing them with only a couple nails. When this was finished Lodge walked over to another dark corner of the room and dragged back a couple long lengths or rope and box of wooden pulleys.

"So the Hobart's take our place in the crates and we escape down the cliff? That doesn't sound much safer."

"Don't be ridiculous. Neither one of us has the skill to rappel down the mountainside. When the alarm is raised from our escape we need to have multiple avenues for our foes to pursue."

"Divide and conquer?"

"Indeed. There's no direct communications between here and the Manor, therefore Cleaver must have left some instructions to his men anticipating our escape. Instructions that they will not have time to debate when they discover we're gone."

"We give him two options of escape, forcing him to plan for both," Jane thought aloud. "That allows us to predict their reaction. Ingenious."

"When we're gone his men will have two instructions; go to the bottom of the cliff to catch us or intercept the wagon carrying the crates. He has to respect either plan equally, since he won't be here himself to discover any telltale clues as to our real method of escape."

"Which is…?"

"Why, out the front door of course."

"Come in!" Tiberius yelled in reply to the knock on his door. "But make it quick, I'm not staying long."

He was busy filling a saddlebag with supplies and looked up to see one of the Hunt attendants walk in sheepishly. Ordinarily he would have reproached himself for being short with one of the staff, but he had already delayed his departure far too long.

"Pardon sir, but Mr. Drummond asked me to bring you this letter and to bring him back your response," he said, managing to keep his nerve and refrain from stuttering or mumbling.

Tiberius grabbed the offered letter and quickly scanned it, pausing at the end upon seeing Lord Cleaver's signature. It was a request, but more like a demand, to ride to Rivermead and investigate a problem at the distillery. Apparently the latest whiskey delivery to the Manor was delayed, which was very uncommon.

Rivermead was a small village built around a distillery founded by the Manor at its inception. It only created one drink, a dark scotch that was bottled in dark glass, with a black bird on the label. Each member of the Hunt and their pack was fully stocked with bottles and enjoyed a daily belt of the *water of life.* The whispered rumours said it was magically distilled and was the reason those from the Manor lived longer than anyone else on the island.

Tiberius almost snorted in amusement, recalling all of the rumours surrounding the drink. He knew it was delicious, expensive, and thus of intense interest to the Manor. This amusement was short lived however when he realized that Rivermead was in the complete opposite direction of the Crows Nest.

Had Cleaver discovered his plan to rescue Lord Lodge, or was this simply a coincidence? He couldn't be sure either way, but it would be suspicious if he ignored Dr. Cleaver's simple request.

"Inform Mr. Drummond that I will attend to this at once," he told the attendant as he pocketed the letter. "Find Dufresne and Morgan on your way and tell them to come here."

The young man nodded and quickly left the room, eager to complete his task.

Tiberius grabbed a flashlight and a pistol from his desk drawer and put it in his bag before fastening it up. He picked up his long black leather jacket that was folded across the back of his desk chair, putting it on in one fluid motion. The door opened after a quick knock as he swung the saddlebag over his shoulder.

"Ready to go?" he demanded of his men as they entered. Both nodded silently, making him inwardly pleased at their competence and reverence. They had been unruly ruffians with chequered pasts before arriving at the Manor. However Tiberius had seen something in them and eventually worked them into a well oiled machine devoted to him.

The Manor was slowly coming back to life as the last members of the Hunt finally made their way to the North Tower. Years of experience made the staff recede into the lower levels of the building when the Hunt was on the warpath. It had not been uncommon in earlier years for a maid or footman to get injured by overzealous pack members.

With the majority of the Hunt members gone, it allowed the various maids, valets, and servants to continue their tasks without the threat of interruption. Tiberius and his men made their way through the renewed throng with ease, as the staff immediately parted to the side upon the sight of the serious looking black clad men.

They reached the stables within minutes and began strapping the collected gear to their mounts.

"If we're assaulting the Crows Nest I figured we'd need some firepower," offered Morgan as he grabbed a pair of modern automatic rifles and passed them to his compatriots with a grin. For himself, Morgan hefted a long dark sniper rifle and his grin turned into a toothy smile.

"Hopefully it won't come to that," Dufresne observed sensibly as he hefted his weapon and checked it.

"Agreed. But there's been a change of plan, we have to go to Rivermead first," Tiberius replied, then explaining their new task.

"Someone probably broke a wagon wheel," Morgan surmised without much thought. "At least we'll be able to get something to drink for the rest of this expedition."

"I think not," interjected Tiberius without humour. "We should be leaving for the Crows Nest now, but instead we're riding hours in the opposite direction. With Lord Lodge's life in our hands we'll be riding non-stop, without rest, and with clear heads. Let's go."

Chapter 17

The scorching heat of the August sun beat down on the Spanish countryside, forcing the two men to remain under the protective cover of a derelict veranda. A faint breeze made the veranda slightly more tolerable than retreating into the old farmhouse it fronted.

"Anything?" asked MacDuff from underneath a wide brimmed hat. He sat lazily on a chair propped up on its hind legs with the back leaning against a bullet pocked wall in a vain effort to sleep.

"Nothing. Bufford and his men are still trying to fix their truck," reported Sean from behind a set of binoculars. "Without success."

The sound of horses brought MacDuff's chair back down to all four feet as he shook out of his lethargy. He quickly checked for the pistol tucked in his belt at the small of his back out of habit. Seeing that it was Patrick and Liam, he went back to his relaxed state.

"Anything?" asked Pierce as he approached the farmhouse, removing a handkerchief from his pocket to wipe his forehead.

"Nothing," repeated Sean, passing him the binoculars.

"They're still working on the truck?"

"I almost want to go down and fix it for them, just to get

moving again," Liam quipped as he sat down beside MacDuff after seeing to the horses.

They had been camped out at the abandoned farmhouse for the past two days, awaiting their quarry to continue their journey. But a broken truck had put a halt to the chase. What had begun as a challenge in tracking had turned into a challenge to stay patient and vigilant.

"I'm glad we swapped our truck for those magnificent beasts or we'd probably be stranded like them," observed Pierce.

After arriving in Seville, the Brown Pack had immediately begun their preparations for trailing Bufford and his men. MacDuff had sent Sean to *acquire* a mode of transportation, while Liam had wandered off to scrounge for local supplies. Both men had returned to the look out perch Pierce and MacDuff had occupied in time to witness the emergence of the various packs. In randomly timed intervals, a different pack would leave the villa that contained the portal back to the Manor. They all seemed to blend into their environs easily, not attracting any attention from the locals.

Bufford and his men finally exited the Manor at dusk, moving quickly to the back of the building as soon as their feet hit the stone sidewalk. Without any warning they abruptly emerged around a corner in a chugging truck, turning down the narrow cobbled street. Luckily Pierce and MacDuff had been prepared and were able to offer a pursuit, running out to a side street where Sean and Liam were waiting in a car of their own. A difficult pursuit ensued as pedestrians, carts, and wagons clogged up the streets, slowing the progress of both vehicles. This however turned into a blessing, as Sean was able to both keep his distance and maintain visual contact of the truck ahead.

Within an hour they followed Bufford to the edge of Seville and headed north into the dark Spanish countryside. Although the wide empty expanse provided a clear view of their target, Pierce realized that it offered Bufford the same advantage. Noting the full moon and general ineffectiveness of the headlights, Sean turned them off and backed off even further, hoping to stay inconspicuous.

It was initially a good plan, but almost proved calamitous a couple hours later as they drove through a winding stretch of rough road. They had lost sight of Bufford's truck for twenty minutes, slowing to navigate the road safely. According to their map this was the only real road in the area, so they weren't worried about Bufford taking a side road. Finally MacDuff suggested they turn the headlights back on to gain some time, arguing that they would appear like a new vehicle.

Sean turned the headlights on as they rounded the next curve and accelerated from their slow pace. However as soon as they emerged from the curve, they found themselves passing a small cantina on the side of the road. The gravel lot in front of the building contained an assortment of vehicles and patrons. Pierce swore as their car barrelled past, watching Bufford and his men walking towards the cantina from their parked truck.

Unable to stop without drawing attention, Pierce ordered them to continue driving. Consulting their map, MacDuff spotted a village ahead. After a quick discussion they all agreed that following Bufford across this terrain in a car would prove more difficult as they continued. There were too few roads and not enough traffic to blend in for an extended pursuit. So they traded their car and some coins at the village stables for four horses and a mule. They then purchased some food at the tavern and continued their journey on horseback.

MacDuff consulted the map again and found a good observation point which would provide them with a clear view of the road as they waited to pick up Bufford's trail when he and his men passed by.

Although motor vehicles were not new to the area, horses had been traversing the land since time immemorial. Therefore there were only a few roads passable by truck and a multitude of horse trails and paths that crisscrossed the countryside, allowing Pierce and his men to take shortcuts. The road Bufford was taking snaked its way north, sometimes sidestepping east or west for two kilometers for every kilometer forward. Since it was the only main road in the area, Pierce and his men could take an almost direct route north, stopping at intervals to observe the progress of their target's struggling vehicle.

This continued for a day and a half, until Bufford's truck refused to start one morning when they emerged from a quick rest in another small village. Pierce and his men had stopped to rest at an abandoned farmhouse on a ridge some distance north of the village. The spot allowed them to discreetly watch both the village and the road for a few kilometres in either direction.

"Any thoughts on where he's going?" asked Sean as he took the binoculars back and returned to his vigil.

"North," mumbled Liam from underneath his own hat as he mimicked MacDuff's attempt to rest on a leaning chair.

"Where's the map?" questioned Pierce as he searched around the veranda.

"What are you thinking?" Sean asked as he took a map from the bag beside him and handed it to Pierce.

"I'm thinking that Bufford had the truck ready to go when they emerged from the portal. And despite the current setback, it seems he picked one that could handle the terrain. From the look of this map, it doesn't get any easier further north."

"You think he's going to continue north?"

"Well this isn't his destination," observed Pierce, motioning to the small village below them. "North is the only way he can go. So he's got to be going to at least Merida, it's the only thing around here."

"I agree. We pack up and head for Merida while they're stuck here." This came from MacDuff who had roused himself after listening to the pair's discussion.

"We should wait until evening and then head out," offered Sean. "I've seen a couple Nationalist patrols today. Even though we're staying off the road, the added cover will be beneficial."

Everyone nodded in assent, as they had already witnessed the work of the Nationalists on their journey. The very farmhouse they we're squatting in had probably been cleared out by the Nationalists during their bloody march north the year before. The quantity and dispersal of the bullet holes in the walls testified to a very violent and indiscriminate attack.

They were all dressed as civilians, clothed in a myriad of dust coloured outfits. They were also travelling with an array of camera's and notebooks, as they were trying to cover themselves as international journalists covering the civil war. In order to further support this fact, they had been forced to leave their heavy weapons in the villa and travel with just their pistols and knives. MacDuff had argued that since their real goal was to track and observe Bufford, and not kill the mysterious *Reaver*, rifles would only complicate things if they were stopped.

Both Liam and Pierce had warmed to their task and had actually done some journalistic work on their journey. Liam had taken many photographs of the countryside, careful not to take anything that might be too inflammatory to a Nationalist search. Pierce meanwhile was writing notes and phrases, citing the struggle against socialism.

Everyone rested as well as they could through the midday, with at least one of them on guard and watching the village below for signs of activity.

Pierce found himself on duty as dusk followed the setting sun. A multitude of warm coloured rays fought to remain above the jagged horizon before him and the faint appearance of stars began to illuminate the sky. The action of the past few days had prevented him from coming to terms with the enormity of his current situation until that moment. He suddenly felt frozen by the fact that he had travelled through time and space to the Spanish Civil War, and was currently tracking a Colonel of the *American* Civil War. His mind was awash with thoughts of wonder, doubt, and even a little denial. But the impossibility of it all seemed inconsequential as he sat on a hard wooden bench on the bullet riddled farmhouse veranda.

After what could have been five minutes or five hours, he shook himself from his reverie and focused on the present situation. He rose from the bench and entered the main hall of the farmhouse, where the others were sleeping on thin bedrolls. He moved down the line, lightly kicking their feet to wake them.

"If you want to keep that foot lad," uttered MacDuff gruffly behind closed eyes, "you'll keep it to yourself. I'm awake."

Pierce gave a laugh and kicked it anyway, gaining some chuckles from the other two and then MacDuff himself.

"You've got the map and compass Sean, so you take point and head off first," ordered Pierce as they all emerged from the farmhouse. Despite just waking, they were all alert and ready to ride. "Our destination is Merida."

Jane heard the rumbling sound of hoofs beating just soon enough for her and Lord Lodge to get off the road. Within seconds they had crossed a ditch and taken refuge behind a fallen tree. With extreme caution they peered over the trunk and through the broken branches. A pair of black clad riders galloped past, both intent upon the road before them and nothing else.

"I thought it would take them longer to react," admitted Lodge to his companion. "Luckily you have impeccable senses."

"I don't suppose we can risk taking the road anymore?" Jane asked with fleeting hope as she turned to look at the wilderness behind them.

"I'm afraid it's too risky. They'll be watching the roads now, so we're better off travelling cross-country."

Their escape from the plush prison of the Crow's Nest had progressed exactly as Lord Lodge had predicted. Phillip and the other groundskeeper had come to gather the two boxes presumably filled with chairs for Loch Dhu Island. After loading them on the wagon, he had caught sight of ropes lashed to a parapet by the cliff's edge. Immediately suspicious, he completed a cursory search of the lodge and found the two *guests* missing. Without delay he tracked down one of Lord Cleavers men stationed outside the gate and informed him of the escape down the cliffside. His duty done, Phillip promptly returned to the wagon and quickly drove it past the gate and across the bridge, not wanting to incur further wrath from Lord Cleaver for having delayed delivery.

Lodge and Jane meanwhile had witnessed all of this from a window in the coach house. After waiting for a half hour, they had emerged from their perch to find a deserted courtyard, bridge, and gatehouse. Taking a large brass key from his pocket, Lord Lodge walked to the gate and squeezed his hand through the bars. With only a minor amount of effort a click from the lock rang out and he pushed the gate open. The gate on the other side of the bridge yielded to him just as easily, and with a slight flourish he prompted Jane to lead them out into freedom.

Sitting behind the fallen tree, Jane felt all of the exhilaration of the morning evaporate from within her. The full weight of their future prospects was now facing her. As far as she knew, there was no immediate plan of action. A direct return to the Manor was not possible, since Cleaver's Black Pack would easily scoop them up before they could alert anyone. That being said, she had the feeling that there was a plan, but Lodge had still not taken her into his full confidence.

"We're better to be off the road anyway," said Lodge as he pulled a folded piece of paper from his pocket. Unfolding it, Jane could see crisscrossing lines, various symbols, and small writing. A map. Lodge smiled as he sensed Jane staring at what he had just pulled out. "You didn't think I'd spend so much time planning an escape to be lost once I emerged?"

"No, but I've never seen such an illegible map as that," countered Jane peering at the mess of scribbles.

"I can't risk our pursuers finding a decipherable map, or anyone we meet along the route relaying information to them from it."

"You don't even trust me?" she inquired, slightly hurt

after the all the trials they had shared.

"My dear," he said calmly, but with ice cold calculating eyes, "I don't trust anyone. Shall we go?"

He motioned towards the rising ground of the forest beyond and began walking despite Jane's hesitation. Knowing she would never make it alone, she quickly followed his path as they started climbing up the mountainside.

The pair headed east, trudging along deer paths that criss-crossed the wooded hills. Although the ground rose gently, Jane knew they had to be climbing a significant mountain. The Crow's Nest itself was perched on a very high cliff, and they had only climbed upward since escaping. However the dense forest of enormous trees prevented her from gaining a proper look below or above.

Well after the sun reached its apex and began its slow descent, the escapees slowly found the trees surrounding them thinning. Their climb upward had led them out of the forests and onto a stretch of mountain pastureland above the tree line. With the trees finally gone Jane motioned for Lodge to stop so she could take full advantage of the vista surrounding her.

Turning to look back at the route they had travelled, Jane was stunned to see the elevation they had reached. The forest below seemed so steep; she momentarily doubted they had traversed it, as their journey had not been too onerous. But upon closer inspection she could just pick out the glittering roof of the Crows Nest below and the vast dark sea beyond. With a greater sense of accomplishment, Jane then shifted her gaze back upwards at the path ahead.

A small collection of mountain goats were grazing on wild flowers on a swathe of pastureland that cut its way between two peaks rising skyward. The pair of peaks stood like icy sentinels guarding the lush verdant pass with a cold faceless menace. Eager for their journey through the pass to be as quick as possible she nodded to Lodge to continue.

"This is the Janus Pass," explained Lord Lodge as the path they were following led them under the shadows of the mountain. "It's the safest way to cross the mountains for many miles. There's an old stone hut up ahead that shepherds used to use. We'll stop and rest there."

After roughly thirty minutes of hiking, Jane noticed that Lord Lodge had stopped on a small rise ahead of her. Not seeing the aforementioned hut she began to ask the reason for the halt, but she was silenced as she came up beside him. She had spent the better part of a day trudging up a mountain with her eyes peeled to the ground for wood and stone obstacles. But now she stood facing a wide open and near infinite expanse. She could barely see another range of mountains in the distance, their peaks a faint line on the horizon. In between these two stone spines, an enormous patchwork of colours filled a wide valley below.

Jane had lived the majority of her life between her birth place of Rooks Bay and her place of employment at Ravenwood Manor. So in the past days she had seen more of the countryside than she had in all the weeks' preceding it. Jane was shocked to discover the emotional response she felt as the land continued to reveal itself to her. The Crow's Nest, with its dark stone cliffs and stormy sea view, had lent itself to a sense of desolation and despair. But as she looked out on the wide open land of forests, fields, lakes, and rivers, Jane suddenly felt the rising sense of freedom and possibility.

"I've lived on this island my entire life," began Jane in quiet awe. "But I never really knew this place existed."

"That's not surprising," offered Lodge, looking out over the valley himself. "It used to be used exclusively by the Hunt and the Manor. Out of bounds for anyone with sense."

"Why?"

"This is where the hunt used to take place. It was not uncommon for people to disappear after entering the valley. That's why all the older towns and villages are either on the coast or in the hills."

"But it's safe for us?" she asked calmly despite a rising sense of trepidation.

"Oh yes," Lodge replied without hesitation. "The valley hasn't been used as a hunting ground for decades. See those brown and yellow patches down there?"

Jane nodded after following Lodge's outstretched finger pointing an area below.

"Those are farms, and if you follow that blue ribbon of a river you'll see it leads to a small grey area. That's a little village that sprung up some years ago. The entire valley is spotted with farms and small villages now."

They began their descent and soon came upon the old shepherd's hut, a squat stone shack wedged into a ledge of the mountain. Initially they refrained from lighting a fire, simply eating some of the rations they had taken from the lodge kitchen. However night began to fall quickly and both decided some warmth would be needed if they were to spend the night. The glow of the fire, a full stomach and an exhausting trek had Jane fighting off sleep once the sky darkened and the stars emerged. The last image she saw was of a motionless Lord Lodge sitting on a stone, staring out into the night with only the small puffs of smoke from his pipe signally his consciousness.

*

The rescue mission was not going well; in fact it had not really started. Tiberius mused over the meddling of fate and hoped that his mission was not in vain. Similar dark thoughts remained in his mind as he finished a glass of warm cider by the dying fire in a farmhouse kitchen.

Tiberius and his men had left the Manor the night before and travelled as quickly as they could to Rivermead. The road was well known to all of them, so they were able to keep a decent pace through the night. They did not speak, as it took all of their concentration to ride safely in the dark. However during one of their few breaks, while they walked the horses, Morgan reflected aloud what all three had been thinking. They were getting closer to Rivermead, and had yet to see any sign of the delivery wagon. They had all believed that an accident had befallen the wagon and that they would have crossed paths with it during the ride. But the road had been clear and empty.

The answer to their question surfaced as they arrived in Rivermead a few hours later with the rising sun. The first cottage they passed in the village was burned down and the one beside it was missing its door. Signs of a violent disturbance continued as they made their way through the eerily silent village to the distillery on the other side of an ancient stone bridge. The lack of activity on a regularly busy weekday morning made the hair on the back of each man's neck rise up in unease. Outside the heavy doors of the distillery, Tiberius found the slumped body of a man in rough leather with long dirty hair.

"That was one of the ruffians my Lord," announced a thin voice from the distillery doors as they creaked open. The voice belonged to an old man with a grey beard and grey coveralls. Tiberius recognized him as the still master and unofficial leader of Rivermead.

"What happened here?" asked Tiberius, anger rising in his heart.

The old man seemed at a loss for words as the remainder of the village streamed out past them. They seemed shaken and kept their heads down as they hurried to their respective cottages on the other side of the small stream. A young woman, not nearly as silent shoved past the old man, eager to explain.

"Four of them showed up yesterday morning," she began with a steel voice, explaining that they got drunk in the tavern and started making trouble. Things came to a head when they were refused service and kicked out. They tried to break into the distillery for more drink, but were found by the night watchmen. When they approached him, he hit one of them over the head with his club and then retreated fearfully back inside.

"Discovering their comrade dead, they went back to the village square and started screaming and breaking things," continued the old man, having finally found his voice. He explained that they threatened to burn the whole village down, house by house, starting from the outside. When they went to the first cottage, most of the village fled to the safety of the thick stone walled distillery.

"They burnt the first one down without even blinking, but when they moved to the next cottage a scream from within stopped them," said the woman, the fire from the night before lingering in her eyes. "They broke down the door and found my sister. She's just a girl and those bastards dragged her out of the house like a ragdoll!"

Her voiced quivered as her hands wrenched on a balled up part of her dirty cotton dress. But as she related the story Tiberius realized it wasn't fear or shock that was affecting her. It was pent-up anger and rage she was fighting back.

"I just sat in the safety of the damned distillery with everyone else as they loaded Maddie onto the wagon, laughing," she continued, spitting the words out like flames.

"There was nothing you or any of us could have done," the old man countered, trying to console her.

"We could have stopped them instead of huddling together in fear. We could have done something, anything…"

"What's this about a wagon?" Tiberius broke in before their reproaching derailed his questions any further. He had the feeling his quick little errand was turning into a lengthier undertaking.

"The distillery's delivery wagon," the old man answered immediately. "It was bound for Ravenwood Manor… That's why you're here isn't it."

Tiberius merely nodded, expertly hiding the growing rage and exasperation he felt within. Not only had these hooligans attacked a village under the protection of the Manor, but they had stolen the wagon he had been sent to find. He would now have to find it before he could continue his journey to the Crows Nest, with each passing hour putting Lord Lodge in more danger.

"Do you have someone able to ride?" he eventually asked the old man. When he nodded, Tiberius pulled out a piece of paper and hurriedly wrote a note. "Have someone take this to

239

Ravenwood Manor. They will send some people over to look after the wounded and place a guard in case these men return."

With the message dispensed, Tiberius ran over to the edge of the village, following the call of Dufresne. His men were standing at a fence gate, staring at muddied tracks in the ground that led off west.

"They left this way," assessed Morgan thoughtfully. "I'd say about twelve hours ago."

"That matches with their story."

"Did you think they were lying?"

"No," Tiberius answered, turning to look back at the village in the midst of repairing itself. The villagers seemed to be shuffling around in a collective melancholy as they tried to recover for the harrowing events of the night before. "But I don't like leaving anything to chance. Let's get going." They walked back to their horses, mounted them, and then rode back to the tracks.

"What are you going to do to them when you find them?" rang out a voice behind them. All three turned in their saddles and watched the young woman from before approach on her own horse. She no longer had the look of a victim. Her dirty cotton dress and shoes were replaced with tall riding boots and leather leggings. A brown riding jacket flowed behind her as she trotted up to the men.

"That depends on what we find when we track them down."

"But you were only sent here to find the wagon? The Manor needs its booze first and people second?" She replied defiantly, her anger not yet spent.

Tiberius stared at her but said nothing. He could understand her anger and realized she needed someone to aim it at, until they found the men who took her sister. He signalled for his men to head out slowly and followed them, confident he would hear her voice again.

"I'm coming with you, you need me," she stated forcefully, rewarding Tiberius' grasp on the human condition.

"Why is that?"

"I saw them at the pub and can identify them for you."

"I'm pretty sure we won't mistake them for three innocent men driving a wagon loaded with whiskey and a kidnapped girl," Tiberius replied, wondering how she'd answer his subtle dismissal. "Why do you really want to come with us?"

"I'm going to kill those men!" she shot back angrily. "I'm going to kill them even if you let them go when you've recovered your precious shipment."

"As you wish," he replied simply, impressed with her passionate honesty. "What's your name?"

"My name's Katherine, the still master's daughter. You can call me Kat for short; but not darling, or woman, and certainly not wench."

"Very well Kat. My name's Tiberius and these are my companions, Morgan and Dufresne. We travel fast and without many breaks. Keep up if you can, but if you can't..." he shrugged and urged his horse into a gallop, leading the small troop into the wide expanse beyond.

A quiet snore from his riding companion broke Tiberius' reverie. He looked over to see her fast asleep on the bench by the kitchen table. They had indeed travelled fast and far, but had yet to reach the wagon and had decided to rest the night at a farmhouse they passed. She had kept up with them the entire way, displaying a strength he had not been prepared for. Similarly he had not been prepared for her attractiveness to shine through her combative attitude and manly attire. But as he looked at her now, with the faint glow of the fire lighting up her tanned face and auburn hair, he found himself lost in her beauty.

She shifted slightly and Tiberius quickly looked away, not wanting her to catch him staring. He finished the last dregs of his cider and leaned back in his chair, needing some sleep before the morning. Morgan believed they were only a few hours behind their quarry. With luck they would reach them the next day, hopefully with a fully intact wagon and hostage. If they found Maddie in anything less than near prefect condition, he was sure Kat would hold him responsible and never speak to him again. And that was something he suddenly felt desperate to avoid.

Chapter 18

Despite the odd flyover by lumbering bombers and the sporadic sound of gunfire, it was hard for Pierce to believe they were actually in a war zone. Their trek through the Spanish countryside had been uneventful as they made their way towards Merida. They remained within sight of the road, ensuring Bufford and his men couldn't pass them unnoticed.

"There's a stream up ahead where we can stop at and rest," announced Sean riding up to the rest of them. He was once again on point and scouting the area ahead. "Water's good, so we should take the opportunity."

"Well if you're tired..." Liam mocked his friend good-naturedly.

Sean ignored Liam as he reined in beside him. They rode for another couple of minutes before dismounting and approaching the stream on foot, the water snaking its way through a small gully with tall prickly shrubs on either side. The horses were led to the water, where they leaned down and began drinking; meanwhile their riders did the same from their canteens.

"I wonder if they've fixed their truck yet?" Pierce thought aloud as he emptied his canteen in one gulp and proceeding to refill it from the stream.

"Unless they found a mechanic, I doubt any of his goons

would be able to fix anything," observed Liam with a hint of distaste. Without being told, Pierce could tell there was a rough history between his men and those of the Grey Pack.

"We have to assume they did and that their truck is fixed already or very nearly so," replied MacDuff thoughtfully. "That being the case Sean, have you found a good perch for us to wait for them outside Merida?"

Sean nodded and pulled out his map, motioning for the rest of them to gather round. As he began explaining their current location and their probable route towards Merida, their mule began to stomp around and then let out a sharp wail. Pierce immediately sensed a rising tension in his companions, but didn't understand why. He had very little experience with animals, let alone mules. So he didn't know that mules, donkeys, and their kin had been used as guard animals for centuries.

"I should have placed someone on guard," MacDuff muttered in annoyance as he looked skyward. "Everyone remain calm and wait for my signal."

Sean and Liam replied with slight nods, but Pierce was still confused. He tried to ask what was going on, but he was silenced immediately.

"Well we're lost!" MacDuff cried out with exasperation and without his usual accent.

"I'm sure the road is around here somewhere!" rebuked Sean, much louder than was necessary. Pierce looked from one to the other, thinking they had lost their minds.

"You said you knew the way to Seville!"

"I do! It's south, that way!" Sean pointed past MacDuff's head and then jumped in surprise. Pierce followed the direction of Sean's gaze and found three armed men in uniform facing them. All of a sudden Pierce realized the significance of his men's strange act. The mule had sensed the presence of the intruders and MacDuff had immediately begun an act for their benefit.

"Ahh good, soldiers, they should know the way," MacDuff clapped is hands together and then wrenched the map from Sean's hands and approached them. "Do you know where we are? Which way to the road to Seville?"

Pierce had to work hard to keep his face straight. MacDuff's highland brogue had switched to an English public school accent. He was acting like the incompetent aristocratic Englishman abroad perfectly. Despite raising his voice and speaking slowly, none of the soldiers responded to him.

"You," he pointed to Liam, clearly annoyed. "You speak Spanish, get them to tell use how to get to Seville. We haven't got all day."

Liam walked over and began speaking to the soldiers in fluent Spanish. They didn't even react to him until he pointed back at MacDuff and said something that elicited a brief smile from them.

"You said you spoke Spanish," MacDuff complained accusingly to Liam. "Why won't they tell us what we want to know?"

"Because I told them to block your escape and say nothing," announced a voice from the stream. The Brown Pack turned in unison to see who was addressing them. A small man with a clipped mustache and glasses approached from the stream. He was flanked by three more men carrying rifles. The state of his uniform and the fact he bore a pistol in a holster rather than carrying a rifle signified he was an officer and in charge of this small patrol.

"Good you speak English," began MacDuff unfazed and acting oblivious to the threat the officer was trying to convey. "Perhaps you could be so good as to tell me where the road to Seville is?"

"Who are you?"

"Why does it matter?"

"It matters because I say it does. And because I have six men here with rifles that answer to me." He said all of this calmly while removing and polishing his small wire framed glasses. He replaced them carefully and then arched an eyebrow inquisitively.

"If you must know I am Sir Walter Brackenreid-Smith, a

newspaper publisher. This man here is my assistant and those two are my journalists," he explained pointing to Sean, then Liam and Pierce.

"Ahh, so you are here to cover the fight against the socialists?"

"Precisely."

"Then why are you going to Seville? The fighting is in Madrid. Perhaps you are not who you say you are. There has been talk of English socialists joining the enemy."

"Nonsense," harrumphed MacDuff waving the map. "Patrick, show him your notes."

Pierce reacted slowly and nervously, which actually made the officer more at ease. Feeling in control he motioned for Pierce to approach him.

"So what are you writing about?" inquired the officer with a mixture of curiosity and doubt.

"Well it's not so much a piece on the war," he struggled as he removed the notebook from his jacket pocket. "But more about the benefits to Spain without the Republicans in power."

"You're American?" asked the officer hearing Pierce's accent. Not knowing what to do, he merely nodded and handed the notebook over.

"How long have you been here? There aren't many notes written…" Before he could finish the sentence, the officer's head rose up in reaction to the sound of six quick gunshots. His face immediately turned to horror as he looked down upon the bodies of his men, all with single fatal gunshot wounds. He dropped the notebook and struggled to draw his holstered pistol, but was thrown back as a dagger flew into his shoulder. He fell backward onto the ground from the combined shock of the strike and the force with which it was delivered.

"Is this all of your patrol!" shouted MacDuff immediately descending the officer, shaking him with a grip on his collar. When he refused to answer, MacDuff pulled out the dagger, eliciting a shriek in response.

"Yes! Just us! We were on our way to patrol the Portuguese border."

"Are there any other patrols between here and Merida?!"

"I'll tell you nothing you red scum!"

"We're not here to fight with the Republicans," MacDuff answered fiercely, putting the dagger within an inch of the officers right eye. "But you will tell me what I want to know regardless."

"None! There are no other patrols!" he wailed while staring at the blade.

"Do you report to anyone once you reach the border?"

The answer was a simple shake of the head.

"Good. So you won't be missed," replied MacDuff, dropping him and walking away, nodding at Sean as he passed.

"You killed my men you communist bastards! I'll hunt you down and…"

"No you won't," Sean interrupted as he walked up and put a single bullet in the officer's heart.

"Liam, here's your knife," offered MacDuff handing the blade over. "But did you really have to throw it? There was no chance that clumsy prick was going to get his pistol out in time."

"What can I say; I never pass up an opportunity to practice my skills."

"What the hell just happened?" whispered Pierce as he sat down shaking beside his horse, staring at the executed officer. Despite all the training he had received during his time at the Manor, he wasn't prepared to confront death in such a shocking manner. Within a few quick seconds his men had ended the lives of the soldiers whose bodies lay around him. "What the HELL just happened?!"

"Is this the first time you've seen someone killed?" asked MacDuff standing over him.

Pierce tried to reply but couldn't find the words, so he just nodded staring at the lifeless gaze of one of the bodies. He had left the Manor prepared to track Bufford and find information. But he hadn't been prepared for the possibility of serious violence and it showed.

"They were going to execute us," offered Sean

pragmatically.

"You don't know that," whispered Pierce as he finally found his voice. "Maybe they were going to let us go."

"No, my Lord, they weren't."

"But you can't just… What are we doing here? What am I doing here?" Pierce dropped his head into his hands. He heard MacDuff instruct the other two to pack up and head out towards their next checkpoint. The feelings of disorientation he had ignored since arriving at the Manor suddenly crashed down upon him in a powerful wave and he began to shake uncontrollably.

The weight of a blanket placed around his shoulders brought his head up, though it didn't stop the shaking. MacDuff sat down across from him and took a pull from a small flask he removed from the inside his jacket. He then passed it to Pierce, who grasped it with both shaking hands. He lifted it to his mouth with concentrated effort and took a drink, feeling the warmth trickle down his throat.

"When I was fifteen James Campbell stole a cow from my uncle Fergus. My uncle tracked him down, but he was killed while taking the beast back. The Campbell's said he was cattle rustling and the MacDuff's said he was killed in cold blood retrieving his property. So the long standing feud began again and we were off to fight. My father said it was time I learned the ways of battle and I travelled with the rest of my clan to fight our foes."

MacDuff took the flask back from Pierce and put it back in his jacket.

"Were you scared?"

"No, I was proud. I was off to fight with my clansmen, every young boys dream. I was too young and stupid to be scared. I felt exhilarated as we marched along the hills, but it quickly left as I saw our opponents gathered before us. All I could see was the shining points of spears and swords and became afraid."

"So what did you do?"

"What could I do? Run away or hide? I'd have been

shamed out of the clan. No, I charged with the rest of my kin, but I was not prepared for the carnage that ensued. I got knocked out early on and was found by my brother the next day as they collected the bodies. He said that it had only been a hearty skirmish, but it had been a terrifying battle of epic proportions to me. I shook for a week and had nightmares for many weeks after that."

"You were fifteen, I'm a grown man. I bet Sean and Liam have similar tales of induction by fire into manhood. But I don't want to kill anyone and I don't think I could ever get used to it like the rest of you. I mean you killed these men without even blinking." Pierce was over the initial shock and was no longer adrift in a sea of confusion. Instead he was looking directly at his new mentor with renewed awareness. "I don't want to kill anyone, so if that makes me a bad leader, so be it."

MacDuff smiled and slapped him on the shoulder, then grabbed the blanket and pulled it off. He rolled it up as he stood and then leaned over and offered a hand to Pierce to pull him back up.

"The reason you will be a good leader is the fact you don't want to kill anyone. Don't let their bravado fool you, Sean and Liam don't like killing anymore than you. They've had to find ways of dealing with it, as you will. Why do you think Liam's always joking around at the wrong time or Sean boxes? Those are coping mechanisms for the lives we lead."

"So what's your coping mechanism?"

"Alcohol," he replied smiling, then turned serious. "Lord Lodge is the best judge of character I have ever seen. He picked you to come to the Manor and act on his behalf. That means something to me and the others; Sean, Liam, Melrose, even Tiberius. Not wanting to harm others is a noble sensibility; however you have to be prepared to defend yourself and others."

"Sean was right, wasn't he? Those men were going to kill us?"

"Aye."

"But how did you know? What if he was actually going to help us and let us go?" Pierce knew it sounded ridiculously naïve after he said it.

"When you've been around as long as we have, you gain a sixth sense for these things. I don't need an answer now, but for the sake of my men I will need to know if you'll be able to pull the trigger if the situation arises. When we're out here, we only have each other. Our safety rests on the will and abilities of each other. We do not exist, so no police, soldiers, or anyone else can help us without causing more trouble. Leaving that officer alive would have put us all at risk. It was necessary for our survival that he be silenced. Sean knew that and did what he had to do. I need to know, will you be able to kill if necessary?"

"I understand, but I don't really know," Pierce responded with truthful frustration. "We'll just have to wait and see."

*

Morning broke crisp and clear, and despite sleeping on nothing more than a blanket on some old straw, Jane felt energized. After the stress of the escape the previous day, she looked forward to the prospects of the future. A lush green valley of opportunity lay below her and she was ready to begin.

Her positive attitude buoyed her companion and Lord Lodge led their descent from the shepherd's hut after a quick meal. Unlike the thick forests they had climbed through the day before, this side of the mountain was more open with only small pockets of trees. This provided a more dynamic view, which Lodge used to point out various spots he was acquainted with.

"How is it that I've never heard of these villages, or knew of people living here?" she asked after another farm was pointed out to her.

"The valley is still nominally owned by the Manor; those who live here do not advertise the fact. Very few people travel in or out of the valley, as the two mountain ranges create a treacherous wall. There are only a few passes that offer a safe passage, such as the one we just traveled over. There's a gap in between the two mountain ranges, but that is where the Manor is located, so that route into the valley is generally avoided."

Jane nodded, understanding the implication. Though the Lords of the Manor might tolerate a scattering of farmers in the expansive valley, they would not be so kind to travelling caravans passing through their estate.

"Plus I suppose us simple people of the island are content in our ignorance. That we avoid stepping into the world outside our small lives?" She offered astutely, but with a hint of cynicism. "I know you're too polite to say it, but that's also a factor isn't it."

Lodge merely smiled in response, but then decided to say something to diminish her developing frown. "I lent you all those books so you could read them and develop your mind. Take this as an opportunity to continue your education. I know more about this island than anyone else, except perhaps Tiberius."

In that spirit Jane began asking questions about the history of the island, the Manor, and the various villages. They travelled in companionable conversation for the rest of the morning and were so engrossed in their discussions that they eventually realized they had descended the mountain and had reached the rolling hills below. They stopped for a break by a mountain fed creek to refill their canteens and Lodge removed the makeshift map from his pocket.

"Where are we headed?" asked Jane looking around them, ignoring the indecipherable map.

"There's a small farm not far from here that we should be able to reach before nightfall. I know them well and expect a kind welcome."

They ate some of the fruit and dried meat they'd taken from the Crow's Nest, relaxing in the noonday sun by the banks of the creek. But after a half hour they were on the move again, heading east.

Having exhausted Jane's inquisitiveness, the pair travelled

the open countryside in silence. There were some wild animals going about their daily business, but very few signs of any human presence. Jane had seen a couple cabins in the distance throughout the afternoon march, but they had given them a wide berth. She assumed that Lodge either didn't know the occupants, or knew them well enough to not trust them.

The sun was waning and inching closer to the horizon as they emerged from a stand of birch trees and came upon a wooden fence. It ran into the distance in both directions, offering no end in sight. Lord Lodge once again removed his map and pondered it quietly before climbing over the fence. He turned and helped Jane over, despite her initial solo attempt.

"The fence is new from the last time I was here, but I believe if we cross this field the farm should come in sight." Within a few minutes of walking this proved true, as they crested a hill that overlooked the farm and its few buildings.

"Looks very nice. This must have been one of the first farms in the valley."

"It is. They've been farming here for two generations," Lodge said inattentively as he looked around. "Something's not right here. Stay alert and by my side."

As they approached the farm, Jane began to feel the same anxiety as Lord Lodge. Nothing looked particularly wrong, but she felt something was amiss.

"I've only been to a few farms, but isn't there more activity?" offered Jane as they passed a shed and entered the farm yard. No dogs came to greet them and there were no voices coming from the barn or out buildings.

"Take this and keep it ready," said lodge as he removed a small folding knife from his bag and handed it to her. "It's not much, but it might be useful."

As they approached the house, the front door opened and a tall thin man in coveralls and plaid shirt emerged and waved to them.

"Victor! Good to see you, I wasn't expecting you and your daughter until the morning."

Although he had cried out cheerfully, Jane could tell it was forced. Besides that she couldn't remember another living soul, let alone a simple farmer, that called the Master of the Manor by his first name. Lodge gripped her hand tightly, signalling his own unease, as he led them to the house.

"We made very good time, even though we left the horses at home," Lodge replied, quickly transforming into the neighbourly farmer with surprising ease. "It'd be a shame to hurry a journey in such great weather."

They reached the stairs and began ascending them while the farmer continued to talk to them about weather. When they reached the top the two men shook hands like old friends, leaning in close. Jane thought she heard something whispered between them.

"You remember my daughter Jane?" Lodge motioned to her after they broke away from each other.

"Of course I do, though it must be years since I last saw her." Her reached down and hugged her, whispering, "You're not safe here. I'm sorry."

The uneasy feeling in Jane's stomach turned into an icy ball as she heard the apology. Unlike the convivial tone of his greeting, the farmer's whispered warning had been withdrawn and fearful. However despite the warnings, Jane followed Lodge through the front door and into a cramped foyer. There were doorways to their left and right and a staircase that led up to the second floor.

Jane screamed in surprise as large men emerged from around the adjoining rooms and the balcony above. All pointed muskets at the newly arrived guests. The man to the right hit Lodge in the stomach with the butt end of his musket, eliciting a cry as he dropped to one knee. Jane went to help him up but was pulled back by a firm grip on her shoulder, making her wince in pain as he clamped down.

"Wha's all this then Preston!" shouted the third man as he walked down the stairs. "You didn't say nothun' about no guests."

"I forgot all about it until they showed up," grovelled the farmer. "It's nothing. They live in a cottage in the mountains."

"Well at least the old man's harmless," he said upon reaching the floor and giving Lodge a backhanded slap across his head. "And he did bring us some fine sport." He reached up and felt Jane's hair between his two fingers, leering at her and waiting for a reaction.

Not wanting to give him the satisfaction, she tried to just stare straight ahead and ignore him. But the reek of stale booze and sweat made here want to gag, forcing an involuntary flinch.

"Tie them up and put them in the room upstairs," ordered the leader as he walked towards the kitchen. "We'll finish off the last bottles and then have some more fun."

Preston, Lodge and Jane were bound at the hands with some rough twine and then led up to one of the rooms upstairs. They were shoved into the darkness and the door was slammed behind them. A small wimper made Preston run over to the bed and light a candle with his tied hands. The flickering match lit the candle and steady light filled the room, giving Jane the most awful sight she had yet witnessed.

On the bed lay a woman she presumed was Preston's wife. Her hands were tied to the head board and her legs were curled up into the fetal position. She wore nothing but a ripped up dressing gown and a collection a discoloured bruises. Preston began stroking her head and whispering to her, both of them gently sobbing.

"What happened here?" asked Lodge as he sat in a chair in the corner, rubbing his abdomen. When no response came from the bed, he merely looked up at Jane.

Her years working in the Manor and the pub had not prepared her for the scene she now looked upon. However she knew that they couldn't just sit around and wait until their captors returned. Walking over to the dresser she found a clean robe, a washbasin and a cloth. Jane placed them on a tray and brought them over to the bed and then gently touched the husband on the shoulder.

He looked up at her with eyes wide like a hunted animal. She knew his demeanour couldn't be helping his wife, so Jane motioned for him to go and sit by Lord Lodge. After he left she removed the small knife from her pocket and cut the woman's bonds. She then placed the cloth in the basin, rubbed it with soap, and then rung it out. Jane moved it slowly to the woman's face, who clearly fought hard not to flinch when it made contact. She started at the wife's brow and slowly worked down, rinsing and applying soap to the cloth as required.

"Preston, what happened?" repeated Lodge as the farmer sat down on the foot of the bed across from him.

"My Lord…" began the farmer, but was immediately cut off by Lodge.

"My name is Victor. You did well to hide my identity when we arrived. If they were to discover that, matters could certainly turn worse."

"Or better. Surely if they knew the Master of the Manor was here they'd leave right away?"

"Would they?" mused Lodge, mostly to himself. "I'm not so sure. The fact they arrived here when we did must certainly be a coincidence. But the fact that ruffians like these are roaming the valley is not."

"I'm not sure I understand."

"Well my dear Preston," sighed Lodge looking over to Jane as she finished cleaning the wife up, "we're on the lam, as they say." Seeing the incomprehension on the man's face he continued. "We have just escaped imprisonment of our own at the hands of Lord Cleaver."

"How is that even possible?"

"It was carelessness and ennui on my part, however now I see how badly things have become."

"But surely Cleaver couldn't have let these thugs loose after discovering our escape?" asked Jane as she put the wash basin away and unfolded the new robe.

"No the timings are too tight. I believe there has been an unacceptable amount of strife in this valley long before we were sent to the Crow's Nest," Lodge replied to Jane thoughtfully before turning back to the farmer. "Preston, has there been talk in the valley about strange incidents?"

"There's been rumblings," nodded the farmer. "Talk of

things being stolen, barns burned, but nothing like this."

"Tell me what happened, where are your children?"

"Luckily they left yesterday to take some sheep over to the Malloy's, thank heavens. If my daughter had been here…"

"When did they show up?" ordered Lodge, trying to keep Preston talking before he broke down again.

"Just passed midnight, liquored up and singing. We figure they'd move on through but they stopped here. I had my rifle with me when their leader came up to the front door asking to sleep in the barn. Before I could answer he spotted my gun and he barrelled through the door, knocking me down. My wife screamed and the others ran in and grabbed us. They took my guns and tied us up in the kitchen, then helped themselves to our food and some ale."

Jane listened to the story as she helped the wife into the gown and received a brief shadow of what was once a shining smile. A jug beside the washbasin provided some water, which Jane used to pour everyone in the room a quick drink.

"After having their fill and getting drunker," Preston continued staring at the floor unable to meet anyone else's eyes, "they took Alice upstairs…"

Silence enveloped the room, enough that they could hear a renewed ruckus from the revellers downstairs.

"They will pay for this my friend," promised Lodge coldly. "Have they said anything about their intentions?"

"They haven't talked to us directly apart from threats," began Preston as he raised his head to look directly at Lodge. "But I overheard them say they planned to kill us when the rest of their gang arrived and then take over our farm."

Chapter 19

The sound of horses and creaking wagon wheels silenced the captives in the upstairs bedroom. The sounds were faint at first but then became much louder as the wagon approached the house.

"When are your children due back?" Lodge asked urgently, moving to the window.

"Not for another day," replied a slightly confused Preston, before he realized the impact of the question. "My God, they're not back are they?!"

"No, it's not them," he answered as he looked out through the small bedroom window onto the dirt track below. "But it appears that our captors' friends have arrived. Strange…"

"What is it?" questioned the farmer as he joined Lodge by the window. "What's with all the barrels? Is that whiskey?"

"Not just any whiskey," smiled Lodge as he made out the symbols imprinted on the barrels. "Have you ever seen that brand of whiskey?"

Preston squinted below and shook his head and then looked over at Jane as she came to the window.

"I have," she said after a moments deciphering. "That's from Rivermead, best whiskey on the island. The pub I worked at in Rooks Bay could only get a few bottles each year."

"That's correct. Luckily for us their comrades seem to have stolen it."

"Why is that so lucky," snorted Preston. "So they can get stinking drunk tonight and then kill us tomorrow instead? Or maybe you're hoping they drink themselves to death?"

"I seriously doubt they could drink themselves to death, but if they do, so much the better. However if they're distracted and we can stay alive until the morning, then we just might have a chance. I have a feeling that a violent storm is swiftly approaching this farmhouse, to the detriment of the men downstairs."

Preston tried to understand Lodge's reasoning, but gave up and returned to his wife on the bed. Jane also turned from Lodge in confusion and looked back down into the courtyard below.

"It looks like they've also got a woman with them," she announced after seeing a blonde girl, probably no more than seventeen, being forcefully removed from the wagon. Her hands and feet were bound, so one of the men threw her over his shoulder.

They all heard the front door crash open and a chorus of drunken greetings ensued. The noise was so loud that they didn't hear the heavy footsteps climbing the stairs to their room until the door flew open.

"Throw her on the bed," ordered the leader as he followed in the larger man carrying the girl. His eyes were wild from drink as he looked over everyone in the room. "We started the day with one hag, but now we've got ourselves some real girls to play with."

Alice merely stared straight ahead, as she had done since being cleaned up. Jane and the new arrival however merely looked at each other, not wanting to provoke him with the looks of defiance they felt like shooting.

"Don't worry girls, the lads are just getting primed up downstairs and will be up here soon to get you." Both men chuckled and left the room, locking the door after slamming it closed behind them.

"Are you alright?" whispered Alice as she helped the new girl up into a sitting position and worked to remove the gag that had been placed in her mouth. A slow nod was all she could muster before Alice had her arms wrapped around her, once more the mother with concerns greater than her own to attend to.

After receiving a drink of water the new girl introduced herself as Maddie and explained her ordeal; from the attack in Rivermead to her long journey across the valley.

"I know this is hard Maddie," Alice began calmly, "but did they, umm, do anything…?" She couldn't complete the sentence, the pain of her own experience still too fresh.

To the relief of everyone in the room she shook her head, but did not say anything further.

"I counted three on their wagon," reported Jane as she returned to the window. However with night falling and the reflection of the candles on the window, her view became too obscured to see anything else. So she turned back towards the others and leaned on the window sill.

"That makes six and I don't think we can take them on with your little knife," offered Preston with defeat as he used the knife to cut the bonds on Maddie's feet.

"I don't think it will come to that," countered Lodge calmly as he watched Preston move to cut the rope on the girl's wrists. "But we can't do anything to provoke them. That means we all have to keep our hands tied and make them feel in charge."

Everyone around the room nodded with varying degrees of enthusiasm. Jane found herself more inclined to try and escape out the window with the bed sheets, and then making a run for it. But she didn't want to try alone and she knew that the rest of them would follow Lord Lodge, due to his position rather than their thoughts on his plan.

For the next hour they sat quietly in the room and listened to the boisterous activity below. They were all hoping the voices and noises would slowly die down as their captors passed out.

All of a sudden the sounds from below shifted in tone. After listening to the men for over an hour the change from rowdy and high spirited exchanges to concerned shouts was obvious. Everyone in the upstairs bedroom started looking around at each other, hoping one of their number knew what was happening. However the blank stares provided little hope against their own rising concern.

This concern quickly turned to alarm as thick smoke began creeping under the door and into their room. The fear of fire brought screams from Maddie and the older couple. Jane's instincts were more productive and she grabbed a stool to break open the window. However she was stopped in mid-throw when Lodge grabbed the stool.

"Help me with the other's!" He yelled over the shouts and screams throughout the house. "Take these rags; dip them in the water bowl and have everyone tie them around their faces. It will protect against the smoke."

Jane dropped the stool and turned around to let Lodge tie the first rag around her face. The damp cotton rag had a musty smell to it, but she ignored this as she moved to distribute the rest of the rags to the others. Everyone was still tied at the wrists, including herself, which slowed her progress. As she finished her task with Preston, the door flew open, spewing a large cloud of smoke into the room.

"Everyone out!" choked a large long haired figure at the door. "Single file and no funny business!" He stood back from the threshold and pointed down the hall, coughing from the thick smoke that filled the space. Preston led the way, being more familiar with his own house than the rest of them. He was followed by the women and the last to leave was Lodge.

Jane was in the middle of the group, but the thick grey smoke enveloped them all like an impenetrable fog. She could barely see Preston at the front of the line and was holding on to Alice's shoulders for fear of getting lost in the smouldering farmhouse. Luckily the stairs led almost straight to the front door, so they emerged into the crisp night air unscathed with relative speed.

All five of them huddled together and looked back at the smoking house as their captors coughed and hacked around them.

"Who did this!" yelled the leader after spitting and freeing his phlegm filled throat. When none of them responded he removed his pistol and pointed it at Alice. "Who!"

"None of us," responded Lodge immediately. "We're all still tied up." He held up his tied hands and looked back at the rest of them to do the same. When they all followed suit, the leader screamed in frustration.

"Then how come you've all got masks?! Seems to me like you had this all planned!"

"We did this after we noticed the smoke came up under the door."

"You couldn't have had enough time with your hands tied!" he replied with a shout as he wildly swung the pistol in the air. He was starting to become agitated and angry. His comrades seemed similarly upset, though it probably had more to do with the interruption to their festivities.

"There was plenty of time while we waited for someone to let us out."

"I pulled you out of the fire!" screamed the leader coming closer to Lodge, his eyes dark and manacing. "And I can throw you right back in!"

"What fire?" Lodge asked innocently.

"What fire?! That fire!" he answered while spinning around to look at the farmhouse. But as he turned he was faced with the view Lodge already had. Smoke was indeed filling the entire house, muting the glow of the lights within the house. But they were the only things lighting up the dark farmyard in which everyone stood. There was no fire climbing up the side of the house and no flames licking at the gables. The only sign of fire was the smoke, but it was simply hanging within the confines of the house, like a strange fog.

"What is this devilry?!" shouted one of the brigands as he gripped Preston from behind.

"Who did this?! You think this was a good escape plan?!"

shouted the leader as he pushed past Lodge and confronted Preston. "Someone tell me what is going on!"

The prisoners all shrugged with incomprehension, looking at each other and then their captors.

"Well you might have escaped the house," sneered the leader, cocking the pistol in his hand. "But you can't escape a bullet." He lifted the pistol to Preston's head.

"No! You can't!" wailed Alice as she moved to stop the leader, but she was stopped and held in place by one of his men.

"I'll count to three," he ignored the woman behind him and continued. "If I get to three and no one has answered I'll put a bullet in his brain."

"No!" "We don't know!" "Stop!" The captives yelled all at once.

"One…" before he could even finish counting the first number, a loud boom rang out from beyond the farm yard and the leader's head exploded into a red cloud of blood and bone.

"Down!" yelled Lodge to the other captives.

Jane, along with the rest of them, followed his advice and dropped to the ground. Most covered their heads in fear, but she continued to look up in confused curiosity. She should have been terrified and shocked by the sudden disappearance of a man's head, but she wasn't. Something momentous was happening and she had a strange desire to watch it unfold.

Amid distant flashes and gunfire, a second and then a third thug fell to the ground beside her as they tried to raise their weapons against their unseen foe. But they were not smart enough to drop down to provide a smaller target. Jane could tell from the way their legs gave out from under them that their fall was not voluntary. This feeling was verified when she looked over to the closest one on the ground beside her. His lifeless eyes faced her and she could clearly see the large bloody hole that was now located in his chest.

The other pair of thugs similarly dropped to the ground like marionettes whose strings had been cut. One of them fell across Maddie and Alice, prompting them to begin screaming in horror.

The tension of the stand-off and its sudden and violent conclusion had slowed time down for Jane. She felt as though seconds passed between every breath and heartbeat. This feeling continued as she saw two black shapes slowly emerge from the darkness. They walked with purpose, their large impressive rifles pointed upwards into the air. Their ominous approach only increased as the night's breeze billowed their long black jackets.

Upon seeing these new and obviously more dangerous men approach, Maddie and Alice's screaming turned into whimpers as they covered their heads with their arms like Preston had done from the beginning.

Only Lord Lodge seemed calm and cognisant of what was happening. However as the figures came into the faint light provided by the farmhouse, Jane understood and breathed a sigh of relief herself.

"Your timing is as impeccable as always," pronounced Lodge standing up and brushing himself off, "though somewhat dramatic."

"Apologies My Lord," gaped Tiberius, barely able to keep his shock hidden. "How...?"

"Before we get into the story telling, there's still another one of these thugs about."

"That's right there were six of them," Jane added as she got up and counted the dead bodies that surrounded them. "But these only make five."

Tiberius looked from Lodge to Jane and then nodded. He turned to face the darkness and gave a couple hand signals. As he turned around to face them, a few seconds passed before another loud boom echoed around them.

"It's six now," replied Tiberius solemnly.

*

Nearly a year before Pierce's arrival, the city of Merida succumbed to a vicious assault by nationalist forces on their march northwards. Intense artillery and aerial bombardment at the beginning of the battle had left a pock marked landscape that remained as a reminder of the battle.

Having travelled the majority of the distance from Seville to Merida on horse paths away from the road, Pierce was now witnessing first hand the effects of war. It was a sobering scene that left him with a feeling of melancholy.

"We're lucky we weren't here a year ago," observed Sean beside him and reading his thoughts. "At least the bodies have all been buried or cleared away."

Pierce nodded in acknowledgement, not too proud to admit that he did not want to be in the presence of battle ravaged bodies.

After disposing of the nationalist patrol, the Brown Pack had moved swiftly to distance themselves from the scene. A couple of hours riding led them to the western bank of the Guadiana River. Here they found an empty house to use as a perch by the *Puente Romano*, the old Roman bridge that crossed the river and led to the heart of Merida. By nightfall they were all settled in and laying in wait for their quarry to reappear in order to continue the chase.

Although the night and morning brought no change, Pierce and his men were rewarded for their patience when Liam let out an audible sigh of relief from behind a pair of binoculars.

"I'm not going to lie," he began as he watched their distant approach. "But for a little while there this morning, I thought they'd thrown in the towel and headed back for Seville. Leaving us like a bunch of fools dodging patrols in the middle of a civil war."

"Even if that were true, we'd be gaining valuable experience," countered MacDuff, joining him with his own binoculars.

"Ever the optimist Duffy."

"Which way are they going?" Pierce interrupted them. "Not all of us have binoculars."

"Apologies my Lord," grovelled Liam as he dropped to

one knee and held his pair up, while keeping his eyes lowered. After a few seconds he peaked up with mirthful eyes.

"Knock it off. Are they heading for Merida or not?" Pierce said after giving Liam a quick boot to the side.

"Merida," concluded MacDuff, still watching their progress. "I suggest Sean and Liam cross the bridge now and await their arrival from inside the city. You and I will follow them from behind."

"Agreed," approved Pierce after giving it some thought, calculating the risk they'd lose track of each other once in the city if they split up. However it would be easier for them to go unnoticed teamed in pairs. "We could really use some radios for these situations."

"The Manor has strict rules against bringing future technologies on hunts," replied MacDuff. "Besides laddie, that would take all the fun out of things."

Liam and Sean threw their packs onto their horses and led them out and onto the busy bridge, just another pair of travellers heading into the city. Pierce and MacDuff ignored their progress, keeping a closer eye on Bufford's truck instead. When it was halfway across the bridge they left to follow, leading their own horses through traffic.

"Looks like they really came prepared," observed Pierce after catching a glimpse of the men in the back. Sitting in the back of the truck, two of Buffords' hounds sat on a bench brandishing rifles and dressed as Nationalist soldiers. The truck had also been repainted to appear like a military transport and the driver was honking the horn with regular ferocity at anyone crossing their path. This intimidating veneer allowed the truck to pass through the crowds of the city more quickly than they enjoyed in Seville.

"Why didn't we think of that?" questioned Pierce as he and MacDuff struggled to navigate the narrow winding streets while keeping pace with the truck ahead.

"More trouble than it's worth," replied MacDuff in his best instructors tone. "Everyone would have to speak fluent Spanish to start with, which we don't. What do you think would happen if we came upon another patrol, or heaven forbid a full company of soldiers headed by a real officer? Two words of broken Spanish out our mouths and they'd have us hung as spies. Besides that, the nationalist army isn't fighting here and those men remaining all know each other. We could fake passing through a town on the way to the front for a day, but if we had to wait any longer it would become suspicious. Who knows, we could even end up being taken to the front to invade Madrid."

"I suppose the journalist cover is a tad better," acknowledged Pierce with approval. "Looks like they're stopping up ahead, we should hang back and see what happens."

The truck came to a halt on a nameless side street in the middle of the city. The men in the back jumped off and stretched nonchalantly while Bufford got out of the cab and waved for them to follow him. He was dressed like the officer they had encountered briefly, but with significantly more gold braid on his uniform and carrying a leather attaché case. He leaned through the cab window after closing the door and gave some instructions to the driver before the truck continued down the street.

"Liam and Sean will track the truck," MacDuff informed Pierce, who looked undecided between the men in uniform and the departing vehicle. "We'll follow Bufford."

Pierce nodded as the truck took the next left and vanished from their view. He spotted a small track of land across the street that might have been a small park before the war and led his horse there. MacDuff followed and they tied up the horses to a broken bench by a small stone wall. The street was busy, but Pierce didn't think it was busy enough for two men with horses to go unnoticed. He had seen Bufford and his men go into a building after the truck departed and wanted to get a closer look.

"This is the building they went into?" MacDuff asked after they had walked the short distance from the park and stood facing it from across the street.

Pierce nodded has he looked it over. Unlike its neighbours, the building was painted a vibrant yellow rather than the normal off white and beige of the others. However the bright colour couldn't hide the signs of abuse the building had encountered from the elements, age, and war. There were cracks and chips in the stone, broken shutters beside the windows, peeling paint near the roof, and the odd bullet hole dotted the façade. Faded writing etched into the large glass window by the door said it was a hotel and then something about water.

"I wonder why they're staying at a hotel?" MacDuff asked aloud, though mostly to himself. "Surely they'd want to keep a lower profile. Where are you going?" He whispered the question to Pierce's departing form as it crossed the street towards the hotel.

A sudden flash had crossed Pierce's mind and he wanted to take advantage of it before he lost his nerve. Watching Bufford and his men split up from the truck, he was reminded of scenes from a John Le Carré novel he'd read. To throw off a tail; spies regularly left their cars, walked though busy buildings, and then emerged from the other side. A new vehicle would be waiting for them and they'd drive off while their stalkers remained waiting outside like suckers. With this in mind he decided to verify that this was indeed still a hotel and that Bufford was staying there. So before MacDuff could catch up to him, he crossed the street and opened the door to the hotel.

The door creaked closed behind him as he entered a spacious and bright foyer. Despite the seedy appearance from outside, the inside of the hotel was well kept and stylish. A bright tile floor stretched from the front desk at his left to a casual lounge on his right. Beyond the lounge Pierce could see a patio though a pair of French doors, complete with fountain and palm trees. The hotel felt like an oasis in the middle of this busy and dusty town.

A slight throat clearing to his left broke Pierce's reverie and brought him from the patio back to the front desk, where a clerk looked at him expectantly. He walked over to the desk, realizing he must look pretty rough after a long journey on horseback.

"Sprechen sie Deutsch?" Pierce asked the clerk using the German learned from Schell and hoping the answer was negative. He knew that there were Italian and German soldiers fighting for the nationalists, so he hoped he could use this as cover.

The clerk tried to mutter a couple words but then decided on a simple shake of the head.

"Speak English?" Pierce tried again in his most brutal world war two movie German accent. When the clerk nodded he began, hoping that he could keep up the ruse. "Ze Colonel, is he here yet? I am supposed to meet him."

"Colonel just arrive," began the clerk helpfully. "He say not bother him until tomorrow."

"Very well," Pierce replied slightly put out. "How long is he staying?"

"Not sure. He pay two nights advance."

"Danke."

Pierce decided to leave while he had the opportunity and before anyone appeared in the lobby. He walked slowly out the door and then looked for MacDuff across the street. When he didn't see him there, a moment of panic struck him and he began looking down both ends of the street. He was immediately relieved when he saw MacDuff further down the street and away from the sightline of any of the hotel windows. Pierce casually walked over to the Scotsman, who was leaning against the wall of a small shop.

"What the hell do you think you're playing at?" MacDuff whispered crossly as he approached him. "This isn't a game of hide and seek, this is real life. What if you were seen?"

"I didn't see anyone in the window when I walked up," Pierce defended himself. "Besides, we haven't shaved in a week and I'm new enough Bufford and his men probably don't remember me that well."

"Maybe," replied MacDuff grudgingly. "But that's a mighty big gamble."

"Well it paid off. The Colonel is checked in to the hotel for at least two nights. I wanted to make sure he wasn't giving us the slip."

"Giving us the slip?" mimicked MacDuff perfectly. "Laddie this is no gangster movie. There's other ways of finding that out." He pulled Pierce over to the intersection and pointed down the street. Bufford's truck was parked there, with two wheels up on the sidewalk.

"How did you know it was parked there and didn't take off and pick Bufford up from the back?"

MacDuff merely pointed to the other side of the street. Pierce was confused as he turned to look at a small bistro with an array of metal tables and chairs laid out in front. He was about to ask what MacDuff was trying to prove, when he noticed that one of the patrons waved to him.

They both crossed the intersection and made their way to the bistro patio, where Liam and Sean were casually lounged out with their feet up. Pierce turned from them and looked back from where he came. The bistro provided a clear vantage point of both the truck and the front door of the hotel.

"We've done this sort of thing before," MacDuff said, motioning to a seat at his table. He moved a table and a pair of chairs beside the table of the other two so that they could quietly speak amongst themselves.

A waiter brought out a bottle of red wine and a pair of glasses for MacDuff and replaced the empty bottle in front of Liam.

"I still think it was a good idea," muttered Pierce after the waiter had departed. "Now we know he's staying there for a couple days."

"And how did you find that out," asked Sean.

"I walked in and asked the front clerk."

"You did what?!" came the exclaimed response. "I beg your pardon my Lord, but that was very risky. What if Bufford had seen you? What if the clerk tells Bufford that there was some Englishman asking for him?"

"Well I knew he wasn't in the lobby before I entered,"

Pierce repeated himself. "And an Englishman wasn't looking for him. A German was."

MacDuff gave a laugh of approval and raised his glass in salute.

Pierce leaned back with his glass of wine and began to relax for the first time since the farmhouse. He took a sip and closed his eyes as he felt it trickle down his throat.

"Well they didn't waste much time," spat Sean with disapproval. "How long did you say they were planning on staying?"

"The Clerk said a couple days, but he wasn't sure," explained Pierce from behind closed eyes. "Why?"

"No reason, other than they just left out the back door and are climbing into the truck," Sean announced abruptly.

Chapter 20

They all dispersed as quickly and casually as they could, trying to avoid drawing the attention of Bufford and his men down the street. Liam and Sean immediately followed on foot, blending in to the mildly crowded street.

"They won't be able to follow them for long," Pierced observed watching them leave. "Where are the horses?"

"Where we left them," groaned MacDuff reprovingly. They took off running down the street in the opposite direction and quickly found their rides happily grazing on some grass in the park where they had left them. Despite finding their mounts quickly, the delay had been unnecessary and potentially costly. They retraced their path, passed the bistro and continued down the road they had watched the truck head down.

"We're chasing them blind!" Pierce swore as he looked for any sign of his men or the truck. With every step they took, there was the distinct possibility that they were heading in the wrong direction.

"Maybe not," MacDuff replied, pointing over the head of his horses bobbing head.

Liam was at the corner of a busy intersection staring down a street to his right. He looked back and caught sight of Pierce and MacDuff approaching.

"Sean is chasing them down this road," he said nodding

down the street he had been watching. "You can probably still see them further down."

"I see them," MacDuff confirmed as he stood up in his saddle. "Luckily it's almost as crowded as Seville. They're not able to speed up."

"Good work Liam," approved Pierce as he tried to figure out what to do next. Without radios or any other communications devices, the possibility of them getting lost was very real. They had been caught off guard and did not have a rendez-vous or back up plan created. His thoughts were then disturbed by the fortuitous ringing of the local church tower.

"What do we do now?" Liam asked impatiently.

"You go back and get your horses," ordered Pierce before MacDuff could. He then began outlining the plan that was forming in his mind. "MacDuff and I will follow the truck and relieve Sean. I want both of you to head to that Church Tower. You can watch our progress from there with the binoculars."

"What happens if they're heading out of town? They could go in any direction."

"MacDuff and I will wait for you on the outskirts of town if that happens. We should be able to track them easily enough if they leave town."

"If you say so," Liam agreed before racing back to the small stable where they left their horses.

Pierce and MacDuff continued their pursuit of Bufford's truck down the busy streets of Merida. The riding was difficult as they worked to catch up to the truck. They rode quickly; dodging carts, wagons, and pedestrians. They eventually reached Sean at another intersection, where he was breathing heavily from the pursuit. He pointed out the truck's route and Pierce relayed the same instructions he'd given to Liam. Sean nodded and made his way towards the church as the horsemen continued their chase.

"Where do you think they're going?" Pierce asked aloud as they approached a more industrial sector on the outskirts of town.

"No clue, maybe the local whorehouse?" MacDuff winked

before slowing his horse to a trot. "They're slowing down. We'd better do the same."

Pierce nodded in agreement, keeping pace with his companion. The cobble stoned streets of the town were behind them, replaced by dirt tracks littered with small stones and potholes. The change in ground made the horses progress much easier and quieter. However the truck ahead was having an adverse reaction to the change. Pierce watched as the men in the truck bed bounced around as it hit consecutive holes.

"They're going to break their truck again if they don't slow down," Pierce admonished humorously. Another big bounce almost threw one of the men out of the truck, eliciting a sharp cry of discomfort and alarm. The truck stopped immediately and Pierce and MacDuff hurriedly hid behind a crumbling stone wall. The crowd had thinned out considerably, with only a few workers and the odd wagon travelling the road. Although some of the buildings were still in use, business had clearly dropped off in recent times.

"Let's go around the building ahead and get beside them," MacDuff suggested, pointing to a bombed out factory that stretched ahead of them. "We'll track them the same way we did across the countryside. This place is pretty barren and they'll eventually notice us behind them."

They moved out slowly and began following the truck as it started up again. The building ran parallel with the main road, allowing them to track the truck at a much closer distance. Holes in the crumbling walls and shattered window panes provided them the opportunity to observe the progress of the truck in fairly regular intervals. At a window near the end of the building they noticed that the truck had come to a halt at a T intersection. The road forming the top of the T was in front of them as well and had warehouses in even greater disrepair running along it.

"Think they're lost?" Pierce asked peering through a hole in the wall. The truck was still running, but the men on the back had gotten off and were looking down the intersecting road while stretching their legs.

"Can't tell," MacDuff answered quietly. He then held is hand up before Pierce could say another word. "I think they're meeting someone. Quick, get in the building!"

The quiet intensity of MacDuff's order made Pierce move quickly, jumping down from the saddle and leading is horse into the warehouse. MacDuff was immediately behind him, narrowly escaping the detection of the approaching vehicles that he had heard.

Two large dark coloured trucks much like Bufford's followed a dusty maroon sedan convertible. They stopped about twenty yards from the intersection, where Bufford and his men had descended from their own truck. They were still dressed as soldiers, carrying their weapons at the ready.

"I wonder who they're meeting," Pierce wondered aloud as the newly arrived vehicles emptied.

Four men in dusty khakis armed with a collection of firearms emerged from the back truck, casually taking defensive positions. Two similarly dressed men jumped out of the sedan, the first went to the front of the car, while the second opened the front passenger door. A short man with a goatee and light coloured suit got out and removed his fedora to fan his sweating face. He called a greeting to Bufford that was inaudible to the pair hiding in the warehouse.

"I've got to get closer and find out what they're saying," a determined Pierce uttered as he looked for ways to approach.

"It looked like there was a bend in the road this new batch travelled down. It should provide an unobserved way to cross over."

"From there I can get into the building right behind them," Pierce finished as he watched Bufford and the suited man move towards a building across the road with their respective entourages.

"I'll stay here and watch them," offered MacDuff as he removed his binoculars and a metal tin from his bag.

"What's that for?" Pierce asked, seeing the tin as he was leaving.

"I might get hungry. Who knows how long we'll be here."

Pierce was stunned that anyone could eat at a time like this. Between the danger and excitement it was all he could do to keep from vomiting as he crossed the open alley between the buildings.

He moved quickly through two smaller buildings before he found a place where the road veered off at an angle. Spying around the corner, Pierce made sure that there was no direct line of sight to the intersection. Satisfied he looked both ways and sprinted across the road and into a burned out building that had once housed machinery of some type. The wooden floor creaked beneath him as he stepped across a floor littered with the charcoal remains of the rafters. Luckily the shop was not very big and Pierce happily crossed another alley to the next building.

It had probably been a garage of some type. The open space was very long and had a ceiling high enough to rival the entrance hall of the Manor. The floor was smooth concrete and barren of any type of debris. Luckily the walls that ran along the road did not contain any large doors, merely the odd window. However like many of the buildings in the area, this one also had its share of holes in the wall and roof.

Pierce quickly ran the length of the garage, slowing periodically to look out the windows or holes. Within seconds he was near the trucks and was surprised to hear them still running. He carefully looked out a window and saw that the drivers were still inside. *Ready to make quick getaway?* Putting the thought aside he crept onwards with his head down, fighting the curiosity to look out the windows above him.

He followed the murmur of voices until they became audible. Bufford and the other man must have been right beside the building, as Pierce could hear them clearly through a nearby window.

"Everything appears to be in order," rasped a voice in accented English that Pierce couldn't place.

"So everything's in the first truck?" inquired the clear southern drawl of the Colonel.

"As agreed."

"Well that's just fine. Tell you what; you can take our truck in exchange."

"Marvelous," came the response, dripping with sarcasm.

Pierce was fighting hard not to look out the window now. He needed to know what was in the truck and who this guy was.

"Senior, I keep seeing a flash in that building," warned a new voice Pierce had not heard before.

"God damn it, don't look at me," laughed Bufford after a moment's silence. "If I was planning an ambush you'd be dead already."

"Well then you must have been followed! Esteban take two men and check it out."

Pierce's heart sank when he realized that the guard had probably seen the glare off of MacDuff's binoculars. Taking a chance he slowly raised his head to peek out of the window sill above him. Bufford and the other man were indeed close, but were looking in the opposite direction. Pierce looked that way as well, at the building he had left MacDuff in. Sure enough, within a few seconds a reflective flash came from their observation post.

"Get out of there Duffy," whispered Pierce anxiously as he watched the armed men approach from all sides. But the flashing continued as the net tightened. Pierce suddenly thought of trying to make a distraction to give his man time to escape, but he was stuck in place, staring across the street.

The three armed men stormed into the warehouse through whichever means they could, while Pierce shut his eyes helplessly. He slid back down to the floor, his back to the wall, hoping for a miracle.

"Ha, ha, ha," cackled Bufford. "I told you it wasn't me!"

"An old tin can senior," called Esteban as he approached his boss, tossing the can onto the street. "No sign of anyone, probably some bum squatting there."

"Well if there's nothing else, my men will get out of your hair. Pleasure doing business with you."

Pierce couldn't believe their luck, but wondered what had

happened to MacDuff. He slid from his spot and moved to another that would give him a better view of the first truck. If he was lucky he might be able to see what was inside it. He watched Bufford and his men get into the cab, but became confused when they hesitated.

Two military painted staff cars came screaming down the third road that met at the intersection, quickly followed by at least twenty men on foot in uniform and carrying guns. A flurry of shouted Spanish erupted, quickly followed by gunfire.

"You double crossed me!" yelled Bufford from the cab of the truck.

"It was you!" screamed back the small suited man as he ducked behind his car.

Pierce glanced out the window quickly, but was forced back down when bullets shattered the glass and thumped against the wall above him. For some reason a platoon of nationalist soldiers had shown up and were shooting at everything at the intersection.

"Psst," hissed a voice from behind Pierce, freezing him in place. "It's just me lad, relax."

"How did you…?" stumbled Pierce, shocked by MacDuff's emergence behind him.

"Never mind that now. The horses are over by the door. Let's get the hell out of here while they're busy killing each other. You have your pistol?"

Pierce had forgotten all about the small calibre revolver in his waist band when the shooting had started. So he stopped to pull it out, checking it was loaded. Satisfied he started towards the back doors where MacDuff had reached the tethered horses.

Suddenly a small door just ahead of him slammed open and two armed soldiers ran in with their rifles raised. They immediately began shouting at MacDuff as they closed in on him from behind, ignorant of Pierce's position behind them. When MacDuff didn't move, the first soldier pulled the trigger of his rifle eliciting the hollow click of an empty chamber. Cursing he lowered his rifle to cycle the action in order to reload.

Without hesitating Pierce raised his pistol and put a bullet into the head of the second soldier whose rifle was still raised. The soldier crumpled immediately, dead before he hit the ground. Pierce then traversed to the left, where the soldier reloading looked up in shock before he also received a single shot.

Looking at the two dead bodies, a nauseous wave of panic, shock, and disbelief flowed over Pierce. He then unceremoniously dropped his pistol and bent over, vomiting onto the concrete floor. MacDuff was beside him in an instant, pulling him towards the horses.

"Let's get moving," urged MacDuff as they led their horses out the back and onto a dirt path. They raised themselves up onto the saddles and took off down the path heading towards a field beyond that marked the edge of Merida. But when they reached the field Pierce stopped and turned his horse around. He could feel the initial fear and shock of the fight they had just fled slowly leaving him. It was being replaced by frustration and anger. Sure they had tracked Bufford well, but they were no closer to finding out what his plans were. And in that gunfight their first real lead huddled from bullets in a crumbled white suit.

"What are you doing lad? We're not armed for a heavy gunfight. We'll meet up with the boys and pick up Bufford's trail."

"I've got to know what he picked up," replied Pierce jumping down from his horse and running back towards the intersection. "If he's not dead, the small suited bastard will tell us."

"Wait!" yelled MacDuff. "I'm coming with you, you stubborn bastard. Just keep your head down and let's get this over with as fast as possible."

*

"The smoke bomb was a clever trick," Lord Lodge

acknowledged to his loyal assistant, clearly impressed as he sat down in the farmhouse's small drawing room.

"Thank you my Lord. It seemed like the safest way to get all of the targets out in the open," Tiberius allowed with humility. After dispatching all of the thugs, he and his men had entered the farmhouse and checked it for any possible stragglers. Satisfied, they had opened all the windows to allow the smoke to escape.

Everyone had then followed them into the farmhouse to get out of a storm that would soon be upon them. They were all exhausted from the ordeal and fell into separate groups to recover. Preston and his wife retired to their children's room and were sleeping in the single beds, too haunted to return to their own room. Dufresne had returned outside to stand guard, while Morgan had retreated to the kitchen table to clean his imposing sniper rifle. Meanwhile the rest had moved to the drawing room due to the frightful condition the thugs had left the kitchen. The sisters sat on a small sofa by the hearth, their heads together in contented reunion. This left Jane, Tiberius, and Lord Lodge to discuss matters.

"You seemed shocked to see me here; I suppose you thought I'd be at the Crow's Nest?"

"Yes sir. My men and I were on our way there to rescue you when I was summoned by Drummond to look into a missing shipment from Rivermead."

"How very convenient," ruminated Lodge over peaked hands. "I wonder if it was deliberate? Probably, but I doubt this is how Cleaver thought it would end. So with the missing shipment gone and an abducted girl with it, the rescue was put on hold and you followed them across the valley."

"We finally caught up with them here at dusk," nodded Tiberius. "We watched them drink themselves stupid and formed our plan. You witnessed it executed."

"Well put."

Tiberius strangled a chuckle, not prepared for Lodge's attempt at humour. He quickly caught himself and then stared suspiciously over to Jane who was leaning against the wall near

Lodge.

"Despite what you have possibly heard from our new friend, she can be trusted," pronounced Lodge, clearly seeing the thoughts on Tiberius' mind. "She was an integral part of my escape. Our escape to be more precise."

"As you say," accepted Tiberius without another word. He trusted Lord Lodge's judgement as much as his own, possibly more.

"What has transpired since my abduction?"

"Pierce has been searching for you and the woman," began Tiberius slowly, noticing Jane's attempt to look unconcerned. "He has gained the confidence of his pack, quicker than I expected. He's easy to underestimate."

"Did he discover our location?"

"With you missing we pooled our resources and I informed him of the Crow's Nest after I found out."

"So the grocery list worked. I thought it had the right amount of cleverness and simplicity," Lodge congratulated himself. The feeling passed quickly as he bolted upright in the chair. "My God, he hasn't gone there in your place has he?! They'll be running into a trap and he's just desperate enough for answers he might try something foolish."

"Don't worry they're nowhere near the Crow's Nest," Tiberius responded calmly, slightly shocked to see Lodge so agitated. "They're on a hunt in Spain."

"A hunt in Spain hmm..." muttered Lodge, slowly removing his pipe and methodically completed all the required actions to light it. He sat quietly puffing away for a few minutes.

"I told him about Bufford..."

"What did you tell him?" he replied instantly but with more curiosity than intensity. He seemed to barely pay attention as Tiberius explained the search for Bufford's file and its presentation to the Brown Pack.

In all of the excitement of the past two days, the newest member of the hunt had almost vanished from Jane's thoughts. But hearing about him now, she suddenly felt guilty for what she'd done and what she'd been prepared to do on Cleaver's orders. This feeling quickly transitioned to one of tugging apprehension. She knew Colonel Bufford and the thought of Patrick fighting him filled her with dread.

"At least they know who they're dealing with," concluded Tiberius, hoping his actions had been correct in the absence of his master.

"You've done well Tiberius," Lodge nodded thoughtfully. "But it's now up to Patrick Pierce to take care of Bufford, we have more pressing matters."

"Cleaver?"

"Yes. The good doctor has been as busy as I've been neglectful. The crazed Colonel and the bodies outside are simply a symptom of his growing cancer."

"What do you intend to do?" Jane inquired, finally feeling ready to join the conversation despite her inner turmoil.

"Have some rest," he replied simply, rising from his chair and exiting the room without another word or glance.

"Don't worry about Pierce," Tiberius advised Jane as he rose himself. "He's clever and MacDuff will watch out for him."

"I wasn't worried," she shot back defensively, unwilling to admit her true feelings aloud. She hoped she wasn't losing her ability to project false sentiments.

"Sure you are," he replied confident in his appraisal of her feelings towards the new member of the Hunt. "But I'd be prepared for a cool welcome. He still thinks you're working for Cleaver."

"But I wasn't really. I'm not anymore. How did he know?" She blurted out, slightly flustered.

"He heard your conversation through the door of the pub. That's what happens when you try and play both sides."

"I wasn't trying to play both sides," Jane replied just as coldly. "I was trying to survive. Some of us don't have friends with guns following them around for protection." She then turned to storm out of the room.

"Well you do now," Tiberius called after her in a warm

tone, smiling as he saw Jane hesitate slightly as she left. However the smile quickly vanished as he moved to a large window that looked out onto the farmyard. The impending storm was nearly upon them; the wind kicking up dust, the tall elm trees swaying, and the rumble of distant thunder booming.

But it wasn't the weather that concerned Tiberius. In fact he barely noticed it as he stood in solitary contemplation. He was concerned with his apparent dwindling ability to judge and recognize the strength, or weakness, in others. He had underestimated Pierce during their first few meetings and did the same again with Jane. Like some of the Manor staff, he had kept an eye on Jane. In fact he had sometimes used her for delicate assignments within the Manor, including the recent delivery of Pierce's recruitment letter. But he had failed to see her true potential beyond completing simple tasks. She had almost been able to manipulate and thrive in a subtle confrontation between Lodge and Cleaver. An impressive undertaking to say the least.

He had to admit that another reason he had underestimated her was that she was a woman. By no means a misogynist, Tiberius believed woman could accomplish most things and had recruited many of the female Hunt Members and staff. However like many men, he had a hard time understanding the opposite sex. This included his being oblivious to the fact that most women found him very appealing. His rugged good looks, intense gray eyes, and large muscular frame had grabbed the admiration of many female residents of the Manor. However his appeal went beyond mere physical attraction; he had an effortless aura of power, wisdom, and kindness.

These were the characteristics that lured Kat over to him after she watched her sister fall asleep on the couch. She approached silently and sidled up beside him, gently linking arms. For a moment they both stood looking out the window as the rain began falling.

"Thank you," she said quietly, pulling him away from ruminations of his failing skills of perception.

"Sorry?" Tiberius blinked, surprised to find her beside him.

"Thank you," she repeated. "You saved my sister and killed those bastards, just like you said you would."

"I didn't kill them for you," he replied staring straight ahead.

"What?!" she exclaimed, ripping her arm from his and slapping him on the shoulder.

"I didn't save your sister and kill those men for fun, vengeance, or because you told me to," he lectured while taking control of her arms in both his hands.

"I know that!" she replied excitedly, their faces drawing within a foot of each other.

"I saved her because it was the right thing to do. I killed them because I had to. I would have done these things without ever having met you."

"I know!" She repeated in the same tone. "You're a good man!"

Still in his strong clutches, she leaned forward and placed a powerful kiss on his mouth. It only lasted a moment before she moved her head back, slightly embarrassed. But before she could explain her actions, she felt Tiberius' hands move up from her shoulders to her neck. This time he initiated, with more power, and lasting much longer.

They finally took a breathless step back from each other, both equally shocked by their actions. The intensity of the moment, and the past hour, had forced them to succumb to desires both had felt, but would have normally suppressed. The sound of the storm outside filled the silence that fell between them.

A quiet moan from across the room finally made them break their gaze on each other. Kat's sister Maddie shifted on the couch, sleeping fitfully due to the noise outside. Kat went over and knelt by the couch, placing her hand on her sister's head and softly stroking her hair. The familiar touch from her sister calmed Maddie, allowing her to fall back into the deep sleep reserved for the innocent.

"I was afraid if we were too late in saving her you'd never forgive me," Tiberius whispered as he approached the couch and stood over Kat. But before she could look up and respond he headed to the kitchen, unsure why he'd revealed that.

The lights of the kitchen were still bright as Jane and Morgan did their best to clean the room and replace things to the their correct spots. Dufresne had returned from his post outside, confident no one would brave the storm outside. He had taken Morgan's spot at the kitchen table and was cleaning his own weapons.

"Enjoying the spoils of victory?" Dufresne asked innocently while raising the barrel of his rifle, inspecting it closely.

"Shut up," Tiberius responded in mock annoyance. He walked over to Jane and waited for her to replace a few glasses in the cupboard.

"What?" she asked, responding to his inquisitive gaze.

"Are you still working with Dr. Cleaver?" he demanded without preamble. He was still slightly flustered from his brief encounter with Kat and unused to the feeling. So he decided to move onto an area he felt more at home with. Intrigue.

"No!"

"There's a war coming, between Lord Lodge and Cleaver. You're far too involved to avoid it."

"I told you no," she replied more evenly this time, but with no less force. "Lord Lodge is the first person to think of me as more than just a servant or barmaid. He has opened my mind and my eyes. We've had our lives in each others hands. I trust him with my life and I hope he feels the same way." Tiberius remained staring at her for a moment before nodding.

"Accepted. I'm not sorry if I offended you, but I needed to look you in the eye and ask the question."

"So what now?"

"Morgan?" Tiberius raised an inquisitive eyebrow at the man beside Jane. "Did the drunkards leave anything?"

Morgan merely smiled slyly and pulled a black bottle with a Raven emblazoned on it from his bag in the corner.

"What happens now? We all have a well earned drink while you tell us of your escape from the Crows Nest," Tiberius ordered as he led Jane to the now clean kitchen table. Morgan found four glasses and poured equally large amounts in each of them, passing them around as he sat.

"The water of life!" they toasted in unison, clinking their glasses together and then draining them in one shot.

All three men looked over at Jane as she dropped her glass down the same time as they did. Her glass was just as empty as theirs and she showed no signs of its effects.

"What?" she asked smiling at their surprise. "I work in a pub."

Chapter 21

"Are you guys alright!" Sean asked quickly as he emerged from the church.

"I like the car!" added Liam enthusiastically. "Can I drive?"

"Shut up and get your things in the back," ordered MacDuff from behind the wheel of the red convertible. "Unless you two were asleep up there, you know we just stole this car from a shoot out with the army. So I'd rather not sit around for them to find us."

Their gear was quickly loaded into the trunk of the car and they jumped into the back seat, barely sitting down before MacDuff accelerated down the narrow street.

"Which way did Bufford's truck go?!" Pierce asked turning to look at the men in the back of the car.

"He was heading out of Merida, for the road back to Seville," Sean answered evenly, despite having to hold on to the door as the car lurched around a corner. "We lost sight of them shortly after they crossed the old roman bridge."

"What the hell happened down there?" Liam asked as they took another sharp corner avoiding a crowded market ahead. "We watched Bufford stop at the cross roads, then this car and two more trucks showed up. A few seconds after that everything went to hell."

"We were in the bombed out factory across the road," Pierce began, breathlessly explaining everything he witnessed from his hiding place.

"We couldn't see individuals that well, but we saw the explosion."

"That was one of the army staff cars," continued Pierce as the car slowed down behind a lone horse drawn cart. "Apparently the arms dealer's guards had grenades and knew how to use them."

"Arms dealer?" MacDuff shot Pierce a questioning look.

"While you took care of the second guard and got the car, I had a quick conversation with the suited man. There were guns in the back of the truck Bufford drove off in."

"Was he the Reaver, the target of the hunt?"

"I don't know and I don't care," replied Pierce shortly. "Because Bufford now has a few crates of German made submachine guns, with ammunition, and we still have no clue what he's up to."

"Well we know he's leaving Merida, which is exactly what we have to do," offered MacDuff as he honked the horn. They were crawling along behind a slow moving cart, with people walking on either side.

"Relax Duffy, let's not gather too much attention to ourselves," Pierce offered as the cart finally turned and they moved passed it.

"I think we're past a low profile," laughed Liam as he leaned up from the back seat. "Four armed men driving a red convertible riddled with bullet holes?"

"Fair point."

"We don't know how many soldiers made it out of that gunfight, where they are now, or if they're looking for us," MacDuff pointed out as they approached a traffic circle leading to the *Puente Romano*. "Speak of the Devil. Everyone hold on!"

As they had entered the circle MacDuff spotted the second staff car from before, but refilled with more soldiers. He accelerated out of the circle and headed for the bridge, realizing that they had recognized the convertible. The staff car took chase, with the men in the back trying to stand and take aim with their rifles.

The first couple of shots were nowhere close to the convertible, but that didn't keep the Brown Pack from lowering their heads. The firing stopped briefly and MacDuff had enough time to raise his head to see they were about to overtake a rickety hand cart whose owner had taken cover.

"Bugger!" yelled MacDuff as he swerved too late, hitting the corner of the cart and sending it splintering into pieces over them. Sean looked back at the car chasing them and was immediately troubled by what he saw.

The remains of the cart fell in front of the staff car, forcing it to swerve violently. The sudden movement made the two men in the back momentarily lower a medium sized machine gun they were aiming over the windshield. They both fell backwards before they could begin firing.

"Liam!" screamed Sean as he pulled out his pistol and fired a quick shot over the back of the seat. Liam followed his cue and removed his own gun.

"Aim for the tires before they can start firing!" ordered Pierce as he pulled out his own pistol, forgetting it was now empty.

Liam and Sean both popped up at the same moment and fired within seconds of each other before the soldiers could open fire themselves. Both front tires blew out, forcing the driver to over steer as he lost control of the car. It skidded sideways and then slammed into the side of the bridge with a violent screech of metal and Spanish screams.

Everyone in the convertible took a few slow breaths, raising themselves up to a normal sitting position as the car accelerated off the bridge and turned onto the road to Seville. MacDuff pulled out his flask slowly and it was passed around.

"You're a good lad," MacDuff told Pierce as he put the flask back into his pocket after a few moments silence. "You've proven all you need to. I owe you my life."

"I think we're even after that driving performance," Pierce replied lightly, uncomfortable with the solemnity of MacDuff's tone. "How did you know they'd be looking for us?"

"Call it a sixth sense; I've been in this kind of situation before."

"So what do we do now sir?" Sean asked, naturally changing his own tone towards Pierce.

"We head to Seville and back through the portal," Pierce responded immediately, having already concluded the next course of action and wanting to demonstrate confidence in his plan. "I don't know what Bufford's next move is. Neither did the dealer, despite my asking nicely. But I don't think it's going to be in the middle of the Spanish Civil War."

They drove into the night, heading south towards Seville. After a couple of hours and running low on gas, they stopped in a small village frantically looking for a gas pump. When none could be found they siphoned some gas from a parked truck in order to continue their journey.

However by midnight everyone was exhausted, having survived an exciting and dangerous day. Pierce spotted a derelict shed a short distance from the road. They were able to park the car inside and lay their bedrolls on some hay piled in the corner.

"What was all that talk about owing your life to Mr. Pierce?" Liam asked MacDuff when Patrick had gone outside to answer the call of nature.

"That's Lord Pierce," McDuff corrected gently. "When those soldiers showed up shooting at everything that moved we were in the warehouse like he said. But what he didn't say was that two of them came in when my back was turned. They had the jump on me, but he took care of them without hesitation. Bang. Bang."

MacDuff raised his hand in the shape of a gun and demonstrated Pierce's calm shots from the afternoon, eliciting a soft whistle from Liam. It wasn't only the fact that he'd saved MacDuff's life that garnered the most respect from them. It was the fact he hadn't said anything about it in the car. He'd simply done what he needed to do and wasn't about to start celebrating the fact he'd killed two men.

"Then he ran into the street where all the shooting was happening, even when I tried to lead him away," continued MacDuff quietly as the other two drew closer. "He walks up nonchalantly to the arms dealer in the white suit who was hiding behind the car. He puts a gun to his head and asks what he'd just sold Bufford. When the man shook his head he lowered the pistol to his right knee. Again the man refused to answer and even laughed. Lord Pierce shot him in the knee without blinking."

"It's a good story," called Pierce from the shed door, having quietly re-entered. "But you left out the part where I puked my guts out after shooting those two soldiers."

"Creative license," McDuff shrugged.

"Don't feel bad," Sean said as he sat down on his bedroll. "I was a wreck for days after the first time I killed a man. Of course I was a teenager and was forced to defend myself with a rock. It was up close, personal, and very messy."

"You should be proud you vomited," chimed in Liam with his usual bonhomie. "It shows you're not a psychopath."

"Thanks for that. I suggest we all get some sleep. Except for you Liam, you've got first watch."

*

"Unbelievable, he simply walked out the front door," stated Dr. Cleaver with monotonous precision. He was sitting in his study, a large circular room in the largest tower of the Manor. It was filled with a number of scientific and mechanical devices, some of a dubious nature.

The calm statement elicited no response from his two visitors, cautiously sitting in seats across from him. A large black desk separated them; however the distance did nothing to settle their minds.

"It has been two days," he continued, tapping his fingers gently on the arms of his chair. "What developments can you report that would keep me from having you killed?"

"Well, I… You see my Lord…" mumbled Drummond,

clearly unsettled and not used to having to account for himself.

"I believe the housekeeper, her husband, and the groundskeepers were not involved," began Malicio calmly stroking his goatee, ignoring Drummond completely. "I questioned them myself."

"Severely?" asked Cleaver keenly.

"Of course my Lord," he answered smiling. "But they are too simple or too stupid to have had an active part in this."

"I tend to agree my Lord," Drummond spoke up, thankful for Malicio taking the lead. "Lodge would never ally himself with such simple people. Their involvement would offer too great a chance at failure."

"Then tell me Drummond, now that you've found your tongue," Cleaver said in a voice as icy as his glare, "why you employed these simple and ineffective people to watch Lodge?"

Drummond went to reply but closed his mouth, having been tricked into a verbal trap and not willing to fall into another. However the doctor was not yet finished with him.

"What of Tiberius and the whiskey shipment? There's no chance that he has met up with Lodge or helped him escape?"

"None whatsoever," Drummond replied confidently, eager to expound a minor success. "Some men were sent to Rivermead where they confirmed the shipment was stolen and that Tiberius and his men are tracking it. They could be anywhere in the valley and nowhere near the Crows Nest. But more importantly, there's no way that he's with Lodge."

"That is somewhat more encouraging," allowed Cleaver thoughtfully. "Without any support other than that nuisance of a maid he should be easy to contain and dispose of. Perhaps his escape will benefit us. As far as anyone else in the Manor is concerned Lord Lodge went to the Crows Nest for rest and recuperation. However he met with a tragic accident while out walking. Hmmm…"

"Possibly a fall off a cliff or a broken bone turned septic?" offered Malicio innocently.

"Precisely," smiled Cleaver for the first time. "Tell me,

how does the tracking go? Why have your men not found him yet?"

"The terrain has made tracking difficult," Malicio answered directly, knowing Lord Cleaver would not accept evasion. "The rocky ground surrounding the Crows Nest offers very few clues. But we've scoured the roads and the area surrounding the cliffs. Since he's travelling on foot, we can predict the farthest distance he could travel."

"Show me."

All three men rose from their seats and went to a large map of the island that hung on the wall beside Cleaver's desk. It showed the mountains, lakes, roads, villages, and other important points of the island.

"From the Crow's Nest here, he could only have travelled in this sphere" Malicio said first pointing at a small drawing of the building on the map, then moving out in a circular motion. "We believe he's somewhere to the west between the road and the sea, trying to avoid the roads and Talon Pass to the south."

"Why exclude the North and West?" asked Drummond.

"Lord Lodge is an old man and he's travelling with a woman. The mountain range to the North and West is too hard for them to cross. Besides once he makes it over, he's in the valley and many days travel from the Manor. They're travelling on foot without a map, it would make no sense." He answered in exasperation. "Why don't you return to your impotent scheming in that dingy office and leave the tracking to me?!"

Both subordinates stood facing each other in mutual loathing as Dr. Cleaver thoughtfully looked over the map. He hated the idea of having Lodge loose on the island, however he still felt he had the upper hand.

"Drummond, have your men at Rivermead report to you as soon as Tiberius returns with the shipment. I want to know when Lodge's lap dog returns so we can keep him occupied and out of the way. That will be all." Cleaver dismissed him without a further glance or gesture.

"Despite Drummond's ignorance of tracking and hunting," Cleaver motioned towards the map, "I think it unwise to ignore all the possible routes of our prey."

"My Lord," began Malicio, arguing his case. "I don't have enough men to search the island. I barely have enough men to search the most likely method of escape."

"You don't need to search the entire island. As long as Lodge is out on the island alone, he's vulnerable. So we make sure he cannot reach his own allies."

"I see," nodded Malicio, looking at the map again. "If he did make it to the valley, unlikely as that is, he would then head south for the Raven's Vale." His finger stabbed a spot on the map where the two main mountain ranges met, just North of the Manor itself.

"Post a man or two there to watch the northern approach to the Manor," Cleaver ordered. "And Malicio…"

"Yes my Lord?"

"Their orders are to kill Lord Lodge on sight and anyone travelling with him."

"So where are we heading?"

"South."

"You're hilarious; did anyone ever tell you that?"

Their heartfelt embrace from the night before forgotten, Tiberius and Kat had fallen back into their normal routine as the group left the farmhouse. Preston's children were due back sometime in the afternoon and Lodge decided to leave in order to provide them a normal return.

Lodge had Morgan empty all of the bottles out of one of the whiskey barrels and gave them to Preston as compensation. He knew the farmer rarely drank and explained to Preston that the value of the bottles could be used to barter for anything he could possibly want on the island. But possibly of greater importance to the farmer and his family, Lodge promised he wouldn't forget what had happened, and would do everything in his power to ensure it never happened to anyone on the island again.

So they hastily buried the bodies, packed up their few belongings and placed them on the whiskey wagon, leaving the farm in the middle of the morning. Jane drove the wagon confidently with Lord Lodge and Maddie sitting on the bench beside her. Morgan and Dufresne took turns scouting ahead while Tiberius and Kat rode their horses just ahead of the wagon.

"We're going to the Raven's Vale," Tiberius answered after a few moments, making Kat wait. "Then to the Manor, where we'll deliver the whiskey."

"Ravenwood Manor? We're going to Ravenwood Manor?!"

"Yes." Tiberius tried to refrain from smiling when he watched the look of anticipation fly across Kat's face. The Manor was considered a mysterious, almost magical place to the inhabitants of the island. However because of this, any mention of the Manor usually elicited a response of fear, dread, or anxiety. But not to her, thought Tiberius as he looked over at the spirited beauty riding beside him. While she was lost in thought Tiberius stopped momentarily, waiting for the wagon to catch up so he could speak with Lord Lodge.

"Do you think it's wise we approach the Manor so directly?" he asked his master when it came up alongside him.

"I very much doubt they'll be looking for me out here," replied Lodge confidently.

"Probably, but it would be fairly easy for them to hedge their bets and place someone in the Vale to watch the approach from the North."

"Yes but they'll be looking for me," he answered, "not us. Besides I doubt your men will allow us to be taken by surprise. Therefore I should have enough time to hide in one of the empty barrels."

"So that's why you insisted we all travel together when I suggested sending the women and the whiskey back to Rivermead with Morgan?"

"That was one of the reasons."

"And the others?" Tiberius asked warmly, used to Lodges

drawn out explanations.

"I thought you might enjoy the extended company of that wonderful young woman."

Although slightly shocked by Lodge's frank answer, he was no longer surprised by his master's powers of perception. Knowing that the smallest reaction was enough to reveal the truth of the statement to Lodge, he merely continued riding.

The land they travelled on to the south was a vast sea of rolling grass, dotted by islands of small woods. This allowed the wagon to proceed at a decent speed despite the lack of roads or paths. Those on horseback divided into pairs and leapfrogged ahead of the wagon, while it made its slow lumbering progress across the valley. Allowing them to dismount, take a break, and stretch their legs while they waited for the sound for the creaking wheels.

"How long have you worked at the Manor? Is it as fancy as they say? What do you do there? What kind of a name is Tiberius anyway?" Kat rang off the questions quickly during one of their breaks waiting for the wagon. She had been saving them up since they had left Rivermead and could no longer refrain from asking.

"My, aren't we curious."

"Yes I am," she replied quickly without any signs of embarrassment. "And you're avoiding the questions."

"Very well," he sighed in mock exasperation. "I've worked at the Manor for many years, mostly doing jobs for Lord Lodge. As for my name, well it's the one I was born with."

"Well that's real helpful," she noted without much rancour.

Tiberius merely shrugged and then pulled himself back onto his horse as the wagon approached behind them.

"That just means I'll have to keep interrogating you," she concluded, flashing him a wicked smile.

Despite the innocent threat, she didn't continue the conversation as they galloped towards Morgan and Dufresne. The two men had taken position on a small rise ahead and were awaiting the wagon's approach. Both men nodded to Kat with respect as they approached, then turned to Tiberius.

"Nothing ahead of us until that small wood," Morgan reported, pointing towards a stand of tall trees a few miles from their spot.

The land before them began to slowly drop as it headed south. This provided Tiberius with a decent view of what lay ahead of them, made even clearer when he removed his binoculars. Beyond the stand of tall trees Morgan had pointed out, the land became less open. Rocky outcroppings, streams, and denser woods filled the space they would have to travel.

"I suggest we stop at those woods for the night," added Dufresne while Tiberius continued his survey.

Tiberius smiled to himself as he listened to his men's observations. They were well trained, professional, and were simply the best he'd ever led. He knew that he wouldn't find anything through the binoculars that they hadn't taken note of, but that didn't stop him from trying. He knew they wouldn't be offended by this; in fact they'd probably be more offended if he became too lax and simply accepted everything they said.

"I agree," Tiberius concurred as he lowered the binoculars. "The trees should provide us some shelter and cover if needed. Once camp is set up we'll fan out and check the way ahead for tomorrow morning. It might take a while to find a route the wagon can use."

"I seem to remember a path that led through the Vale," offered Morgan looking skyward as he tried to recall the location. "It ended after the land levelled out and opened up. So it should be around here somewhere."

"Hopefully we can find it," Dufresne said, noting the setting sun.

"If we can't find it between the three of us, it no longer exists. Alright, you two stay here and wait for the wagon and then escort it down," Tiberius ordered calmly. "We'll head down and check out the woods and the surrounding area."

"You have a weapon miss?" Morgan asked Kat before they could leave. "It looks clear down there, but you never know."

Tiberius silently reproved himself for not thinking of that himself. He was grateful for his men's attention to detail when she proudly removed a flintlock pistol from her saddle bag.

"We'll call that plan B," Morgan chuckled as he looked at the ancient weapon.

"It's a perfectly good firearm," she shot back, feeling defensive about the pistol her father had given to her years before. "I can hit a target at twenty paces with it as well."

"I've no doubt it's a fine weapon or that you're a proficient marksman," Tiberius said calmly. "But you might need something with a bit more, well, everything."

Kat looked at him in brief confusion before he pulled his back-up sidearm out of its holster from beneath his long jacket. It was a black Walther semi-automatic pistol that seemed like a toy in his large grip. He quickly showed her how to load and fire it before handing it over. She took it in her right hand, moving the flint lock to her left. Staring at both of them in her hands she smiled brightly and then put the old pistol back in her saddlebag. The new Walther went into her jacket pocket after she checked that the safety was on.

"Alright Annie Oakley, let's go," Tiberius ordered, smiling at her confusion to the reference.

They slowly moved down the gradual slope until it levelled off, allowing them to quicken their pace slightly. Using the distance and open space before the woods, they approached in a wide arc. This allowed Tiberius to observe the potential campsite from different angles. He kept his head facing forward while his eyes darted from side to side, missing nothing.

"Relax, there's nothing to worry about up ahead," he observed calmly, noticing Kat's growing apprehension as they got closer to the woods.

"I'm not worried," she retorted quickly, loosening her grip on the reins. "You really think there's no one around?"

"We would have seen something by now," he replied confidently, trying to keep her calm. The truth was that in the failing light menacing shadows were starting to spring up everywhere. But he knew that a display of overt concern in leaders could quickly spread to others in the form of fear and panic.

When they were within thirty yards of the woods Tiberius dismounted and casually removed the automatic rifle that was slung across his back. Kat followed his lead, pulling out her newly acquired pistol as they walked the horses towards the woods. A small elm tree provided a makeshift hitching post for their mounts, allowing them to search the area unhindered.

A rustling from within the woods stopped both of them in their tracks and compelled them to raise their weapons. Motioning Kat to stay put, Tiberius slowly moved forward to scan the area. But within seconds one of the horses whinnied, eliciting the exodus of a group of pheasants from the woods in a flurry of batting wings. Kat cried out in alarm from the sudden noise and movement; however Tiberius coolly raised his rifle and quickly fired three shots into the growing gloom of the evening..

"At least I wasn't the only one frightened by those damned birds," laughed Kat immediately afterwards.

"The only thing I was frightened of was standing near you with that pistol in your hands."

"Don't be embarrassed," she teased in response, bumping up beside him. "Lots of guys shoot off too early."

Despite her innocent face, Tiberius could see the twinkling wit in her eyes. But rather then rise to the bait he simply winked at her and took a couple steps forward and reached down to the ground.

"Don't worry, I always have complete control of my weapon," he said, casually picking up three dead pheasants by their feet. "And I never miss the target."

Kat simply stood astonished, her teasing expression swapped for admiration and attraction. But the sudden sound of quickly approaching horsemen kept her from moving towards him.

Morgan and Dufresne barrelled towards them like the cavalry with their own rifles out. But seeing both Tiberius and

Kat standing safely beside each other they reined in and lowered their weapons.

"We heard gunfire and feared the worst," explained Dufresne surveying the scene.

"Sorry about that," explained Tiberius raising the pheasants again. "I was gathering supper. I remembered you have a delicious recipe for roast pheasant."

Chapter 22

A fire was made by the edge of the woods over the minor protestations of Tiberius, fearing the attention the light would attract. However he was once again overruled by Lord Lodge, deciding the need for warmth took precedence over any dangers the flames might attract.

Everyone in the party pitched in to set up camp for the night. Jane helped Morgan remove a tarp from the wagon and lashed it to some fallen tree branches to create a makeshift shelter. Kat and her sister collected broken twigs and branches from the nearby area and with the help of Dufresne's lighter; they quickly had a fire lit.

Despite the small amount of work that was done, everyone fell down beside the fire in an attempt to relax when they finished. However between the excitement from the previous night and the anxiety of what lay ahead, most of them could not fully unwind.

Jane found herself straining to hear every sound that emanated from beyond the small circle of light the fire produced. She kept imagining a horde of dirty brigands approaching their small camp site, surrounding them in the darkness. But it wasn't fear that kept driving these thoughts. As she looked around their site and observed the men with rifles and black jackets, she knew they'd all be safe. Their captors at the farmhouse had been easily dispatched by these three men and she had no doubt they could have handled many more. No it wasn't fear she felt, it was more a sense of annoyance. She was tired of being kidnapped and held against her will, tired of the jolting transition from safety to danger. But more than anything else she was tired and annoyed at no longer being in control.

For the last few years at the Manor she had always felt in control of her life. True she was a servant and thus did not necessarily have an unlimited amount of freedom. However the secret work she had done there had always been done on her terms and her fate had been in her own hands. But this was no longer the case.

In her thirst for advancement, Jane had waded out into a more dangerous game with much greater stakes. No longer a nameless face in a maid's uniform willing to pass notes; she was now a real player known to the others. Advancing from a pawn into a rook had been her goal, but now she realized the consequences of this. She was now also a real threat and a potential target to someone.

Jane knew that most people in her situation would choose a side in order to gain protection. And looking around at her companions by the fire, she could tell that they were good, honest, and loyal people. Lord Lodge had become a like a second father to her during their current ordeal and she truly liked the man.

But she also knew from experience that the most ruthless usually win over the kind, and there was no one more ruthless than Dr. Cleaver. She was scared of him, knew he couldn't be trusted, and dreaded having him as an enemy.

It was a difficult situation, one that Jane hadn't been prepared for. But after taking a few calming breaths she decided that she would try and support Lord Lodge. The Manor and the Island would be a much better place with him fully in charge and Cleaver dealt with. She didn't want to walk on eggshells around that bastard any longer. But she admitted to herself that she wasn't completely comfortable with burning her bridges. So if Cleaver were to continue winning and he came looking for her help…

Jane hoped it wouldn't come to that and smiled at the prospect of a new life at the Manor with her new friends.

"What are you smiling at my dear?" Lodge asked kindly in between puffs from his pipe.

"I think I just had a revelation," Jane replied quietly, staring into the fire. When she eventually looked up at him, he simply shot a quick and clever smile.

A normal man would have begun firing questions after hearing a statement such as that. They would have been too curious to resist. However Jane knew by now that Lord Lodge was not a normal man. Observing the shrewd gaze of his sharp eyes, she was slightly worried that he'd perceived her entire thought process. But if he did, he wasn't about to bring it up.

"What are we going to do when we get back to the Manor?" she asked trying to change the subject.

"Tiberius says there is a hunt currently ongoing. Hopefully this will still be the case when we return tomorrow. The fewer people around the better."

"I doubt Dr. Cleaver is on the hunt," she observed thoughtfully, "which means we'd still have to deal with most of the Black Pack. Not all of them will support you like Tiberius and his men."

"It's true that the Black Pack have superiority in numbers," Lodge allowed without a sign of discouragement. "However we have superiority in quality. Don't let their current demeanour fool you.

"Look at Tiberius," he pointed with his pipe across the fire. Despite the warmth of the fire he sat quietly with his arm around Kat. Both were quiet but had lazy smiles pasted to their faces. "He's a genius tactician who's seen more battles than anyone I know."

"And the other's?" Jane asked nodding towards Dufresne who was rotating some sumptuous looking pheasants on a spit over the fire. Beyond him Morgan's profile could barely be seen in the darkness as he stood watch.

"Both are master marksmen and accomplished fighters. They are honourable men who will fight deviously if required. All three are thoroughly violent men if the need arises, as you saw at the farmhouse. They understood that those hooligans could not be reasoned with and acted with machine like precision. No, with surprise on our side those three men could take on half of the Manor's hunt staff alone."

"But what if the hunt is over tomorrow and the Manor is full?"

"Then we will have to hope my boasting is justified," he grimaced in response.

*

"Everything seems in order gentlemen," observed the checkpoint officer standing beside the driver's door. He spoke slowly in Spanish, obviously bored with his current duties "But what of these bullet holes?"

Everyone in the car tried to remain clam and not show any anxiety. Their pistols were all within easy reach; however they were hoping they wouldn't be necessary. Unlike the last two checkpoints.

This was the third checkpoint they had come across since leaving the barn they'd slept in after their escape from Merida. Pierce didn't know if their shootout escape from Merida had been the reason for the checkpoints, or if it was a coincidence. Either way they had been forced to shoot their way through the first one even before being asked for their papers. They had escaped the second checkpoint through the grace of a pair of well thrown grenades after the guards had returned their documents and became suspicious. Would their third try be lucky?

"Red Bastards!" spat Liam from the back of the car, continuing to act as the group's interpreter. "They ambushed the last checkpoint we passed. I think your comrades held them off, but you might want to send a patrol to check it out. We were lucky to get out of there alive."

The checkpoint officer cursed and quickly handed their papers back, clearly eager to do anything other than checkpoint duty. As MacDuff drove away they could see a flurry of activity as the men manning the checkpoint prepared to depart.

"You're a clever bastard Liam, I'll give you that!" laughed MacDuff as they sped down the road, quickly approaching the outskirts of Seville.

"Let's dump this car as soon as we can Duffy," ordered Pierce sitting shotgun. "It's served its purpose and it will only continue to bring unwanted attention to us."

MacDuff nodded and another fifteen minutes of driving took them to a quiet side road. Within seconds they had removed their gear and began walking down the road, just another group of journalists touring the city.

"So what do we do now?" asked Sean as they walked towards the center of town. The late afternoon sun reflected off the white and beige stone buildings, heating the streets like an oven. The intermittent groupings of palm trees lining the roads offered minimal respite from the heat.

"I say we steal another car," offered Liam taking a drink from his canteen.

"I could use a real drink. Don't you know a good cantina close to the villa?" Pierce asked MacDuff casually.

"Indeed I do. It shouldn't be more than a couple blocks from here."

After thirty minutes and two wrong turns all four men approached the cantina like it was an oasis. If they had more energy they might have run towards it. However decorum and the weight of their packs prevented such an outburst. The white stone walls glowed and provided the perfect backdrop to the colourful awning that provided shade to a group of metal chairs by the front door.

"I'll just go inside and order us some drinks and food," offered MacDuff as he went inside while the remainder fell into the chairs under the awning, thoroughly exhausted.

Within minutes an attractive young waitress came out with a pitcher of sangria and four glasses, winking at Liam after he uttered a few quick words in Spanish.

"What did you say to her? My Spanish is a little rusty," Sean asked as he poured the drinks for everyone.

"I just asked for something to eat," he replied innocently. "I guess my looks did the rest of the talking."

Sean coughed as he took a sip from his drink and rolled his eyes in disbelief.

"He asked her for something as hot and spicy as her to eat," said Pierce taking a sip of his own drink. "Or something close to that effect."

"And that worked?" Sean asked in disbelief. Before Liam could respond, the waitress emerged with a tray holding four bowls. She handed out each one carefully and returned inside with an order for another pitcher of sangria.

Famished, they all started eating without waiting for MacDuff's return from inside. After the first few spoonfuls, Liam began coughing and drank his full glass of sangria in one pull.

"Looks like you got what you ordered," laughed Pierce, seeing Liam's red face and a few tears rolling down his cheek.

"That's not funny," coughed Liam hoarsely, wiping his forehead with his napkin. He carefully emptied the rest of the pitcher into his glass and even took a bite of some fruit within it. "If I eat anymore of this soup my blood will start boiling."

The waitress came out again with the second pitcher of sangria and another bowl on her tray. She stood in front of Liam with the tray against her provocatively angled hips while he profusely offered apologies. Smiling she swapped his bowl for the one on the tray and grabbed the empty pitcher.

"I guess she's used to dealing with obnoxious tourists," Pierce said between sips after she had left.

"Very funny," Liam countered as he eyed a new spoonful carefully before eating it. "It's actually quite good now that I can taste something other than fire."

They all started laughing as MacDuff finally emerged from inside the cantina. Sitting down, he took a few large gulps of his sangria, draining it in a few seconds.

"Listen to this Duffy," began Sean chuckling. "Liam the ladies man here was trying to flirt with the waitress. *Bring me something as hot and spicy as you to eat*, he says. She winks at him and then comes back out with…"

"Soup laced with the hottest peppers you've ever tasted?" finished MacDuff smiling before Sean could continue.

"How'd you know that?" Liam asked in disbelief.

"Because I told her to."

"Why'd you do something like that? I almost burnt my tongue off."

"Just be glad she took my advice. She came into the cantina cursing about foreigners. Believe me, if I hadn't suggested the hot sauce you might have ended up with something more hazardous in your soup. A place like this always has rat poison on hand."

They all laughed and Liam quickly joined in, being too good a sport to be upset. They finished eating their meal in silence, realizing they hadn't eaten real food in some time.

"So what took you so long in there?" Liam asked MacDuff as he poured the rest of the second pitcher into their glasses. "Ordering food and conspiring with the staff couldn't have taken that long."

"Patrick reminded me that we had set up a spy ring before we left Seville," replied MacDuff easing back into his chair. "I'm waiting for news."

"A spy Ring?"

"We paid a bunch of young boys to watch the villa during our absence and to make note of all the comings and goings," explained Pierce quickly. "Two of them are brothers and their parents run this cantina."

"Young Paolo went to find his brother who's got the watch right now," MacDuff continued. "Before he left he told me that the only activity was a group of four leaving the villa the day the hunt began."

"That would probably be Sirinova's Pack, they're the only ones we didn't see leave before Bufford appeared," Pierce concluded.

They didn't have to wait long for the report on the villa. Within a few minutes Paolo's brother came running down the street, stopping abruptly in front of MacDuff. In halting English he reported that no one had returned to the villa that day. He then shot a wide smile as MacDuff flipped him a gold coin.

"How did we beat them back? I wonder if they had trouble with their new truck?" Pierce observed after Paolo's brother ran into the cantina.

"Or they don't plan on returning through the portal yet," Sean offered, voicing an option they all hoped wasn't true.

"No, it doesn't make sense for them to remain here," Pierce responded confidently. "They were probably delayed, maybe by some checkpoints or something. What do you think Duffy?"

"You're probably right," MacDuff agreed nodding. "I also booked us two rooms upstairs when I was inside. We can sleep here tonight and come up with a new plan if there's still no word tomorrow."

"Sounds good to me," clapped Liam after finishing the rest of his drink and staring at the empty pitcher. "I'll get us another pitcher of this stuff. It's not Jameson's, but by god it's refreshing."

"Better let MacDuff get it," observed Pierce as he finished his own glass. "We don't want it spiked with anti-freeze."

*

"Still nothing my lord," Malicio announced apologetically as he approached Dr. Cleaver walking the Manor grounds.

"By God the man's clever!" Cleaver slammed his walking stick into his other hand violently. He quickly regained his regal manner and calm speech. "I never was very confident we would find him."

"He could be injured or even dead out in the wilderness," Malicio offered lamely, knowing that they couldn't rely on assumptions.

"Lodge's death, though convenient as it might have been, was never a necessary part of the plan. All that matters is that both he and his lap dog are away from the Manor. Plus with the members out on a hunt we have our opportunity to move."

"Shall I recall my men from their search?" he asked glad to have avoided any retribution for his failure to find Lodge.

"How many do you explicitly trust?"

"Six are completely loyal and have the skills we'll need for the next stage."

"Very well," Cleaver allowed thinking his plans through. "We'll take four with us and leave the rest to cause doubt and suspicion. Recall the men from the search area; however leave the guards posted in the Vale."

"In case Lodge still intends to take that route?"

"Precisely," confirmed Cleaver swinging his walking stick carelessly. "If he travelled into the valley he's most likely alone and we are therefore free to eliminate him without the fear of repercussions."

They continued walking in silence, approaching the sloping ground that marked the beginning of the arboretum. Cleaver was clearly lost in thought, mulling over his plans. While Malicio walked slightly behind his master in silence, waiting to be spoken to.

"Your contact in Rook's bay…" began Cleaver slowly, organizing his thoughts.

"Yes my Lord," nodded Malicio immediately.

"The one you used to incite the brigands in the valley," he continued suspiciously. "Can he identify you?"

"Yes of course, he used to be employed at the Manor. But I gave him clear instructions to keep my name out of it when speaking with his contacts."

"Have him eliminated," Cleaver ordered coldly. "Time to remove some loose ends, he's served his purpose and we won't need his services again."

"Yes my Lord."

"Very good. Pick the men you wish to bring with us and have their identity cards created. There are some spare uniforms that should do nicely. Anything else required can be purchased when we arrive. We need to be gone from this place as quickly as possible."

"Yes my Lord."

*

Pierce awoke with a start as strong arms grabbed his shoulders. A quick shake of the head cleared his slumber induced fog. Within a few seconds he recognized the loft above the cantina he and his men had crashed in the night before. He also recognized the face peering down at him.

"Rise and shine m'Lord," smiled MacDuff cheerily.

"What time is it?" he asked noting the darkness and still feeling as tired as when he fell asleep.

"No idea. My watch broke during the shoot-out at the first checkpoint yesterday. But its well before sunrise, call it 3 am."

"That's nice, I'm going back to sleep," Pierce replied stiffly as he began to lay back down. But before his head could hit the pillow, he sprang back up as if prodded by electricity. "Wait, has Paolo reported in?"

Receiving a nod Pierce jumped up and began searching for his jacket within the sheets and his boots on the floor. He quickly put them on while MacDuff made his short report.

"He just showed up and described the truck and Bufford exactly. I imagine they've unloaded their cargo and have gone through the portal by now."

"Where are the others?" Pierce asked looking around the vacant loft.

"I sent them to watch the villa, recon the area before we moved in."

"Good idea," nodded Pierce as they descended the stairs and left the building through a side entrance. It was only a few blocks to the street the villa stood on and they made the trip quickly.

"Anything?" Whispered Pierce as they approached Sean

and Liam huddled in a small alley. It was across from the villa and offered a view of the building and the bisecting street.

"No one has been in or out since we arrived," Sean reported quietly. "I assume that's the truck they took in Merida?"

Pierce looked down a side street beside the villa and recognized the truck that had carried the crates to the meeting with the arms dealer.

"Looks like it. Liam, take a round about route to that truck and check the insides. I can't tell from here if the crates are still in it."

Liam nodded silently and headed out into the darkness behind them. After a few minutes they could see him approaching the truck, checking the cab first then the cargo area. He shook his head slowly after replacing the flap.

"What do we do now?" Sean asked, echoing Liam's thoughts from across the street.

"I want to check out that truck for myself," Pierce replied. "There might be something in there that might be important."

They took off in the direction Liam had taken, zigzagging their way along small streets and alley ways. Just when Pierce was beginning to feel completely lost he saw the hood of the truck ahead of them.

"Did you get lost?" Liam asked leaning coolly against the truck fender.

"We took the scenic route," Sean replied easily.

"I wasn't sure when I'd be back in Seville, wanted to see the sights," Pierce added, knowing he was probably the reason they had taken so long.

"It's completely empty back here," MacDuff confirmed as he emerged from the cargo area. "Just some wood splinters from the crates and some shell casings. They're most likely from the shoot at the meeting."

"What about the cab?"

Sean and Liam entered the driver and passenger doors respectively, their heads swivelling immediately as they searched. Pierce walked over to the driver's door and looked in inquiringly.

"Same story here, shell casings and not much else," answered Sean motioning at the sparse cab he was sitting in."

"Well it was worth a try," Pierce whispered sullenly. He knew their next step was to return to the Manor through the portal. But he had no idea what they would do when they got there. Their mission had been to observe Bufford, since Lord Lodge knew he was up to something. The vagueness of the order hadn't been noticeable when it had been given. But standing in a dark alley in Seville made Pierce realize they'd been running around half cocked, with no end-game planned.

So they had chased Bufford across southern Spain and watched him grab a few crates of machine guns. The fact they hadn't been discovered was a miracle. But Pierce had to admit they had no idea what Bufford was planning or if his plan even had to be stopped. There was a possibility, however slight, that he was actually working on behalf of the Manor. The guns could be for the Manor's arsenal, to be used on future hunts.

But somehow Pierce knew this wasn't true. The evidence on hand might not prove anything definitive but he knew Bufford's character, knew that despite the funny crazed colonel routine, a real devious son of a bitch lurked within. The clincher was where the order to watch Bufford had come from. If Victor Lodge believed someone was planning something nefarious, they probably were.

"Sorry what?" asked Pierce, realizing that the muffled noises around him were voices he'd drowned out while lost in thought.

"What's our next course of action sir?" MacDuff repeated dutifully. Pierce could tell the question was sincere and that his men were as equally unsure on how to proceed as he was.

"I'm not really sure," answered Pierce truthfully, but without sounding lost.

"Do we head back to the Manor?" Sean asked.

"Or do we stay in Spain and hunt down the Reaver?" followed Liam immediately.

"I have the sneaky suspicion there is no Reaver," Pierce

observed as they exited the truck and gathered around. "I would bet that the hunt is on a wild goose chase to keep the Manor empty while Bufford and his accomplices achieve their goal."

"Accomplices?"

"Drummond at least, but probably Cleaver as well," Pierce explained confidently. "Bufford knew where the hunt was going to take place and had probably been here prior to the announcement. How else would he have that truck ready?"

"If that's the case, then there's only one option," MacDuff acknowledged, silently making the decision for the rest. "We return to the Manor, keep our heads down, and sort these buggers out once and for all."

Leaving the truck behind, they rounded the corner and entered the front door of the villa. Everything was as it had been when they been in it last. An air of disuse and abandonment permeated the rooms. Dusty white sheets covered the furniture, heavy drapes were drawn shut, and cobwebs hung amongst the chandeliers and light fixtures. They followed a path ploughed by numerous footprints across the dusty and dirt encrusted floor to the room containing the portal door.

"Nice an inconspicuous," Liam commented as they approached a closet on the second floor, whose door served as the portal to the Manor. The overlapping footprints all merged at the entrance to the closet door. "Ten quid says that at least one street urchin will be found rambling the Manor halls after breaking into this villa and wondering what's so special about this closet."

Chapter 23

Raven's Vale sits at the meeting point of two large mountain ranges on the Island. Despite the rocky and uneven ground, a forest thrives within. Tall trees with heavy foliage create a thick canopy that all but blots out the light from above. Their crooked and unruly branches providing treacherous obstacles along the paths that criss-crossed underneath.

It had not always been such a forbidding place. At one time it had been the main route from Ravenwood Manor to the vast hunting grounds within the valley. But when the hunt had shifted from the island to locations through the portals, it became disused. But the stories of the wild huntsmen were passed through generations, keeping the islanders from encroaching on the forested land.

This made the going tough on the wagon, as it slowly ploughed forward. Jane remained on the reins, expertly driving it through the brush and bramble. Those sitting on the wagon with her had to constantly take cover in order to avoid branches that crossed their path.

The rag tag group had entered the vale that morning, with Lord Lodge hidden inside one of the empty whiskey barrels. Despite his tall frame, he was able to contort himself enough to fit inside.

"How are you doing in there?" Maddie quietly asked the

barrel as she leaned back from the front bench. Two quick taps provided the answer that everything was alright.

"So?" Jane questioned after the young girl sat back upright beside her.

"Two taps, he's still good," she reported shaking her head in disbelief. "I'm already sore and I'm not scrunched up in a barrel."

"He's a very impressive man," Jane agreed, then let out a quick whistle to the riders ahead. When Tiberius turned in his saddle to look back at the wagon, she gave him quick thumbs up.

Tiberius breathed a little easier after receiving the signal, but he was still far from relaxed. They still had a lot of ground to cover in order to clear the Raven's Vale. The path they were currently travelling on was the most direct one to the Manor. Although this offered a greater chance of discovery, he judged it would be worth the risk.

If they were stopped by one of Cleaver's patrols, he would merely say that he was returning the shipment of lost whiskey. The fact that this was the truth would make things easier. As long as everyone remained calm, nobody would challenge him and request to inspect the barrels.

"But what happens if they want to look into the barrels?" Kat had asked him earlier, trying to find a flaw in his plan.

"Well seeing how I am their superior, they shouldn't question me hard, if at all." He replied without arrogance. "But if they do wish to ignore me and search the barrels, we'll stop them."

"You mean kill them."

"Well we haven't come this far to simply give up and turn Lord Lodge over to them," he replied evenly.

They made slow but steady progress through the forest, not stopping until well after midday. The tortoise like pace of the wagon made taking collective breaks unnecessary, as everyone could stop and then catch up on their own time.

Despite being gifted with more patience than most, even Tiberius was becoming bored. Morgan and Dufresne had been scouting ahead most of the day, and he knew they had been breaking up the monotony by hunting and some fast riding. So when he saw Morgan sitting stoically further up the path, he motioned for him to remain there.

Urging his horse into a trot, he quickly passed his subordinate and ordered him to stay with the wagon. After spending the better part of the day riding slowly through the woods, both he and his horse were happy to be running again. As he moved farther down the path he noticed that Dufresne was nowhere to be seen. However he wasn't too concerned, since he was probably scouting off the path and would appear after hearing his horse.

Tiberius decided to halt for a second and see if this was true. Sure enough, within a minute Dufresne walked out from the thick foliage beside the path leading his mount.

"Anything?"

"Nothing sir," he responded quietly after taking a sip from his canteen. "But it's starting to thin out, we might be getting closer to the end."

"It's been some time since I've travelled this road, but I think you're right. If that's the case, the chances of running into a patrol are as high as they're going to get. You and Morgan should follow the plan we discussed earlier."

Tiberius descended to the ground and walked around, stretching his cramped legs as they waited for the wagon to catch up to them. They heard the wagon before they saw it, making Tiberius cringe at its lack of stealth. Morgan and Kat appeared first, riding ahead and finally the wagon lumbered into view.

"Why are we stopped?" Kat asked nervously as she rode up to Tiberius. "Is there someone ahead?"

"Everything's fine, we're just taking a break."

"No it's not," she retorted, reassuringly touching the butt of the pistol in her jacket pocket. "I can tell when you're lying."

"Everything's fine," Tiberius echoed, ignoring the accusation from the beauty sitting above him. "So try and impress that feeling upon those in the wagon. If something does happen I need everyone to remain calm."

Kat nodded in understanding after a while, though still slightly mad at being left out of whatever plans the men in the long black jackets were making. She decided to take the opportunity to get down and stretch her legs and then followed Tiberius as he walked over to the wagon.

"What's going on?" Jane asked as she dropped the reins and stretched her arms above her head.

"Everything's fine, we're just taking a break."

"Really?" She replied quizzically but then shrugged in acceptance. She knew there was more to what Tiberius said, but she could feel the nervous energy of Maddie sitting beside her. So she decided to try and act calm and unconcerned, hoping it would transfer to the younger girl. She looked over and saw that the sisters were once again talking to each other in low whispers, but both seemed relaxed.

Jane watched as Morgan and Dufresne brought their horses over and tied them to the back of the wagon. They then unslung their rifles and moved into the forest on foot without looking back. She had taken note of the unease in Tiberius' voice and now knew why his men disappeared. They were expecting something up ahead.

"Ok, let's get going," Tiberius ordered quietly as he came up beside Jane after checking on Lord Lodge in the back of the wagon. He gently patted Jane's leg, calming her instantly. "I'll be right ahead of you and if anyone stops us, follow their instructions. Trust me."

Feeling her hands begin to shake she reached for the reins, glad for something to grab onto, something to make her feel in control. She snapped the leather lazily and the wagon lurched into motion once again, heading on an unknown path.

*

"I'm sorry sir, but we've got instructions from Lord Cleaver himself to search anyone travelling through the Raven's Vale."

"This is ridiculous, but search away if you must," Tiberius waved towards the wagon displaying a mixture of annoyance and unconcern.

The two men cloaked in black had appeared suddenly from the sides of the path, making Kat's horse rear and eliciting a scream from Maddie. They called out a challenge that was quickly replied by a challenge from Tiberius. They had approached the group slowly, requiring a better view in the growing dimness of dusk. Despite the presence of Tiberius, they maintained a haughty manner and began questioning everyone.

"I don't know what you're looking for, but I'm also on a mission from Lord Cleaver," Tiberius told one of them calmly. "This wagon of whiskey was hijacked and I'm bringing it back to the Manor."

"Doesn't it usually come from Rivermead?" asked a scar faced guard suspiciously as he started inspecting the wagon.

"Not if it's been hijacked," Kat replied rolling her eyes.

"Now wait just a minute you can't…"

"No you wait," Kat interrupted trying to keep their attention. "This wagon along with me and my sisters were stolen from Rivermead, and all we want to do is go home."

The mixture of the steely gaze from Tiberius and the distraught faces of the women suddenly made the younger guard feel uncomfortable. Their only task was to stop Lord Lodge, who clearly wasn't here. The additional presence of Tiberius made him wary and he was about to wave them through when someone called out from behind him.

"Tiberius is that you?"

Tiberius recognized the voice immediately and waited for the man to come into view. He was one of Malicio's lieutenants and not a friendly face to come across in these woods.

"As you can plainly see," he replied, suddenly on guard. "I've got the whiskey shipment from Rivermead and need to get through this ridiculous road block."

"I heard about your little task. Took you long enough," he sneered as he passed Tiberius towards the wagon. "I see you've picked up some lovely things along the way."

"They were kidnapped with the whiskey," Tiberius replied absently. "What are you looking for?"

"That's confidential," he said as he began tapping the barrels.

Tiberius ordered himself to remain calm, as he watched the wagon get inspected. Beside him he could tell Kat was moving and he reached over to stop her hand as it reached into her jacket pocket. Startled she looked up at him and then stopped moving when he shook his head slightly. Her eyes were on fire and he knew that she would act if she thought anything would happen to her sister or her new friends.

"It's getting dark and we need to get this wagon to the Manor. You can inspect it thoroughly there if you want," offered Tiberius as innocently as he could.

"Fair enough," the leader replied just before he knocked on the last barrel. It took a moment for it to register before he knocked it again. "It's empty!"

"The brigands that stole the wagon drank most of that barrel," answered Tiberius too quickly.

"Is that right?" asked the leader sceptically as he raised his pistol into the air and cocked it. His men followed suit and raised their rifles at Tiberius and the girls by the wagon.

"What the hell are you doing?!" Tiberius bellowed, unhappily staring down the barrel of a rifle.

"I'm going to fire into this barrel unless someone tells me what I want to know!"

"Fine, everyone calm down," Jane said, completely collected. "It was just as he said. Some brigands came into town and stole the wagon of whiskey and kidnapped my sisters and I. They took us across the valley and were going to rape and kill us. Luckily Tiberius and his men tracked them down and saved us."

"Is that right?"

Jane nodded, quickly followed by the other girls.

"Sir," began the young guard slowly, working through a puzzle in his mind as he stared at Jane. "I think I've seen this one before. Something's not quite right."

"I was just thinking she seemed familiar," agreed the leader, before taking a step closer to Jane.

"I used to work at the Manor," Jane answered as calmly as she could. "But I returned to Rivermead some time ago."

"Listen we've answered all your questions and you've checked the wagon…" began Tiberius in what he hoped was an easy tone. He didn't want to provoke a confrontation, but at the same time they needed to get away from the roadblock and continue their journey. He wasn't afraid of these men or being taken into custody if they found Lord Lodge. He and his men could easily handle these three. But he couldn't risk one of the women getting hurt in a sudden armed exchange.

"Stop," ordered the leader pointing his pistol towards Tiberius, cutting off his plea. Something was making the hairs on the back of his neck stand up. It was an uneasy feeling he'd felt before and one that had kept him alive on more than one occasion. But he couldn't put the feeling into coherent thoughts or words as one of his men continued talking.

"What did they say before?" asked the guard with the scar to his companions. "Something about some brigands and the whiskey."

Tiberius knew immediately where these thoughts were leading and he had an explanation ready. But he refrained from uttering it, confident it would only make them more suspicious.

"They said the brigands drank most of the whiskey and that's why the barrel's empty," repeated the young guard wearily, clearly wanting to be anywhere but the forest.

"No, not that."

"But that's what they said."

"I know, but they said something else about the brigands and the whiskey."

"Oh, well I can't remember. Are you sure they said something else."

"Of course I am."

"Both of you shut up," cried out the leader as he lowered his pistol from Tiberius and turned away, desperately trying to order his thoughts. Within a few seconds everything clicked in his mind. "They said Tiberius and his men saved them."

"That's what it was!" Agreed the guard happily, snapping his fingers in triumph. But the feeling was quickly replaced by confusion as he lowered his rifle and turned his head towards his leader. "So where are they?"

The leader of the guards knew the answer before his slow witted compatriot uttered the question. He had been pacing the length of the wagon and was now at the back, staring at two riderless horses hitched there. Their obvious breeding and ornate saddles marked them as steeds from the Manor.

"Son of bitch," he cursed under his breath as he turned his gaze from the horses to Tiberius. Tiberius replied with a quick wink, infuriating him even more.

"They're watching us right now, aren't they?" asked the young guard, now fully roused.

"Of course you idiot!" yelled the leader in exasperation. "They've been watching us this whole time. Haven't they Tiberius?"

"Drop your guns to the ground slowly and take three steps backwards," replied Tiberius calmly, remaining perfectly still.

"He's bluffing," spat the scar faced guard as he kept his rifle raised.

"No he's not!" challenged Kat once more finding her voice. It had taken all her self control to refrain from pulling the pistol out from her jacket pocket when they were first stopped. Days of pent up frustration and anger now had an outlet; the three men standing in front of her. The only thing holding her back was the look Tiberius had given her when they were stopped. She trusted his judgement, in fact she found she trusted him more than she'd trusted anyone in a long time.

"Maybe I am bluffing," allowed Tiberius coldly, ignoring Kat's outburst. "But are you willing to bet your life on it."

"He's not bluffing," insisted the leader with a mixture of admiration and annoyance. "He's not bluffing because whiskey is not the only thing they've got on that wagon. I'd be willing to bet that they've got Lodge smuggled away in there somewhere."

"Even if that were true, the only way you'd get to him would be to kill me first," allowed Tiberius, his steely gaze set directly on the leader. "So, would you also be willing to bet you can raise that pistol, cock it, and kill me with your first shot before two bullets smash into your skull. The tree line is about ten yards away on either side of us. What do you think the odds are of Morgan and Dufresne both missing from that distance?"

"So what do we do now?"

"Like I said, you drop your weapons and take three steps back," Tiberius ordered, keeping his eyes locked on his adversary. "Then we tie up your hands and you tell us why you're hunting Lord Lodge, the Master of the Manor. After that I decide whether I will take you back to the Manor or just shoot you and leave your bodies for the animals, you traitorous filth!"

The leader's hands had been flexing and his teeth grinding throughout the speech. But when Tiberius reached a crescendo with his final insult he lost complete control. With wide-eyed abandon he raised his pistol and screamed something inaudible.

Tiberius would never know what he tried to scream, because two hollow point bullets entered his head and torso milliseconds apart. His body collapsed on itself as the two women on the wagon screamed in alarm.

*

"Things have become much worse than I feared, if such treachery is now possible," Lord Lodge observed as he looked back at the two guards tied to the back of the wagon. After many hours folded into the whiskey barrel, Lodge had insisted on walking beside the wagon as they continued their progress.

True to his word, Tiberius had tied up the two guards when they had dropped their weapons. Also true to his word he left the other body in the woods.

"I'm afraid we didn't learn very much from those two,"

allowed Tiberius, following Lodges gaze backwards as he walked beside him. "Only that they were under orders from Malicio to kill you on sight. That means the order came from Cleaver, nothing we didn't already know or assume."

"True, but we didn't know how far Cleaver's influence had reached. These two men are not part of Cleaver's inner circle, unlike their recently departed leader. We now have to wonder how many others have switched sides."

"I don't mean to interrupt my Lord," interrupted Kat from her saddle above them. "But if you're the Master of the Manor, how did you end up imprisoned and on the run?"

"Call me Victor my dear, we're now compatriots in arms and need not stand on formality," he replied graciously. "The answer to your questions delves into the realm of power and politics. Dr. Cleaver and I have been playing a clever game of cat and mouse for years, and now it seems the rules have changed."

Kat squinted at his enigmatic reply, not really sure what he meant. At first she had been unimpressed by the lanky older man presented to her at the farmhouse as the Master of the Manor. She had expected the most revered, powerful, and formidable person on the island to be more imposing. However in the short time they'd travelled together she quickly realized how Lodge was all of these things without forcing it.

Within an hour their long march through the vale came to an abrupt end as the thick woods ended at a high stone wall. The path continued under a wide columned arch, its white stone glowing in the dusk. Equally spaced torches lit a direct route to the Manor, itself ablaze in light and perched high above them.

"We might be home, but everyone stay on guard," ordered Tiberius cautiously. He then walked over to his men to elaborate. "We'll stay with the wagon, since there's not much cover ahead. Weapons loaded and at the ready."

The group slowly made their way through the immaculately kept grounds of the Manor, the wagon's creaking wheels breaking the silence of the night. Despite the welcome they had received in the woods, the grounds of the Manor were clear of any roving patrols or guards. As they reached the Manor itself, the path split in two; one route going to the main entrance and the other to the service entrance in the rear.

Lord Lodge raised his hand to interrupt Tiberius as he ordered Jane to drive the wagon to the rear entrance. "I am the Master of the Manor and I will not creep in through the back door like some sullen vagabond. I will go in the front."

"Very well," accepted Tiberius, knowing any argument would fall on deaf ears. "Morgan, lead the wagon and the prisoners to the service entrance. Lock them up and then find us."

"What about us?" asked Kat eagerly, thrilled by the rich and imposing surroundings of the Manor.

"We'll go in the back way as well," suggested Jane to Kat's obvious disappointment. "I'll find a room for the girls and we'll wait for word from you there."

"Good thinking," agreed Tiberius, increasing the frown on Kat's face. "Kat, follow Jane's lead. She knows the Manor well and will keep you and your sister safe."

As they descended from their horses and tied them to the wagon, Tiberius noticed that Kat's mood had not lightened by the prospect of safety. She was still frowning and her brow was furrowed like a child angry at being scolded. He stifled a laugh as he moved toward her and she stubbornly avoided eye contact

"Don't scrunch up like that," he said softly. "Your beautiful face might get stuck like that." He was rewarded with an icy glare as she suddenly turned her face towards him. Without missing a beat he grabbed her and kissed her pursed lips forcefully. She reacted immediately, accepting his embrace completely. When he pulled away her eyes were still burning with intensity, but the rest of her face had relaxed into contentment. "Now that's a much better look."

"If you're not too preoccupied," sighed Lodge a few steps away. "I'd like to retake my castle."

"Apologies, lead the way sir," smiled Tiberius as he

walked over to where Lodge and Dufresne were waiting. Once there, all three began their cautious approach to the main entrance.

"I can't help but notice that there's a sister," whispered Dufresne to his leader.

"Don't even think about it."

"But sir, if you can…"

"Sorry," shrugged Tiberius, "privileges of rank."

They quickly reached the massive iron and wood doors of the Manor's main entrance without seeing anyone. With their weapons at the ready, Lord Lodge pushed the doors open and stepped through without hesitation. Tiberius and Dufresne entered immediately after, with their weapons raised and ready to fire.

However the reality they stepped into was anticlimactic, as the Main Hall was devoid of anyone's presence. They waited a few minutes but the eerie silence hung in the vast space. They remained motionless for some minutes, however the ordinarily busy hall remained still.

"The hunt must still be on," Tiberius observed, noting the absence of activity. As the center of the Manor, the Main Hall was never empty for long. "What now sir?"

"I'm tired of playing games," Lord Lodge proclaimed as he stared up at the impossibly high ceiling. "We go straight to Cleaver and end this."

Lodge did not wait for concurrence from his men as he stepped towards the left hand staircase that led to the member's quarters. Tiberius and Dufresne followed him immediately, taking position on either side of him with their weapons at the ready.

They had ascended the staircase and were turning towards the hallway that would lead them towards Cleaver's tower at the rear of the manor, when a lone bang echoed from the far side of the main hall.

"Gunshot," reported Tiberius and Dufresne instantaneously as they raised their weapons, looking for targets.

"It came from the North Wing!" Lodge declared as he turned and started descending the staircase.

"Drummond's office, let's go!" agreed Tiberius as all three quickly retraced their steps down and then crossed the large mosaic floor towards the other staircase.

It took all of their control to refrain from running flat out towards the office outside of the North Tower. This proved even more difficult when they could hear increased shouting as they approached the office.

"You stay back sir," ordered Tiberius when they reached the door. The shouting had died down, but they could hear the low murmuring of voices from inside. "Dufresne will open the door; I go in first, him second, and you follow us."

Lord Lodge nodded, knowing that it was the smart move. He removed a pistol from his jacket pocket, checked it and then nodded to show he was ready.

Tiberius counted to three from beside the door, cringing slightly when Dufresne kicked the door open. Within a second he had passed Dufresne, rifle raised, and entered into the office belonging to the Secretary of the Hunt. He stopped suddenly upon entering, taking in the scene before him. Dufresne had to jump to the side to avoid running into his back.

"What the hell?!" was all Tiberius could muster.

Drummond sat tied to a chair leaning against the wall; his feet flailing and Patrick Pierce standing over him pointing a pistol to his head. A bullet hole was still smoking in the wall, inches from the bound man's head. Liam stood beside Pierce with a giant knife inches from Drummond's eye, the blade glinting menacingly. Sean had pulled the drawers out of the large desk that stood in the middle of the room and was rummaging through their contents. All four men were frozen by the sudden disturbance and looked as if they were posing for a macabre painting. Only MacDuff had actually reacted and was pointing his weapon back at Tiberius.

"Thank God you're here Tiberius!" Drummond cried out, his eyes still locked on the blade inches from him. "You have to save me from these maniacs!"

"Oh shut up," growled McDuff over his shoulder.

"What are you doing back?" asked Pierce turning from Drummond and lowering his pistol. "You're supposed to be getting Lord Lodge."

"And indeed he did," confirmed Lord Lodge, gracefully entering the office as if a man weren't being violently interrogated a dozen feet from him.. Everyone, including Drummond, became quiet as he entered and sat down on an empty seat in the middle of the room.

"What are you doing back?!" Tiberius echoed back at Pierce. "You were supposed to be trailing Colonel Bufford."

Chapter 24

"Lord Pierce, good to formally meet you," Lord Lodge said smiling. "Perhaps you can explain exactly what is going on here?"

"Isn't it clear that they broke in here and attacked me!" squealed Drummond before Pierce quieted him down by cocking his pistol and replacing it against his head.

"Nothing is clear when you or your master are involved," retorted Lodge casually, his curious gaze fixed on Pierce.

"We followed Bufford on the hunt to a meeting with an arms dealer," began Pierce, keeping the pistol in place. "It was pre-arranged and he picked up crates of German made submachine guns and ammunition. We then followed them back through the portal to the Manor."

"And then they disappeared when you followed them in?"

"How did you know?" Pierce asked slightly shocked as he turned to look at Lord Lodge.

"I didn't," he replied evenly. "But presumably you wouldn't be torturing poor Drummond if they hadn't."

"Attempted torture," corrected Liam quietly.

"Drummond here is going to tell us which portal key he gave to Bufford," continued Pierce as he looked back to his prisoner. "We were the first Hunt members that the servants saw exit the North Tower and a quick check of the halls within the tower revealed nothing."

"So they must be in one of the portal anterooms" concluded Lodge in agreement. "And have possibly already taken one of the portals to another time."

"Exactly." Pierce then moved the pistol from Drummonds head and dug it into his right kneecap. "So I'll only ask one more time, which key did you give them?"

"I gave them no key! Check the lock box, none are missing!" protested Drummond angrily, having received some new found courage by the appearance of Lord Lodge.

"He's right, none are missing," Sean concurred from the lock box after searching it.

"You might not have given them a key," allowed Pierce with the pistol still in place. "But there's something you're not telling us. Tell me what you know or you'll walk with a limp for the rest of your life."

"Actually you'll probably lose the leg," Liam corrected. "There are no reliable doctors on this island, except for Lord Cleaver."

"And I doubt Lord Cleaver would scrub up to operate on a mere employee of the Hunt," concluded Pierce smugly, trying to get a rise out of Drummond.

"He would help me!" replied Drummond self-righteously.

"This is getting us no where," announced Lodge wearily. "He clearly does not have any info on Bufford. However he did bring up a good point. Where is your real master, Dr. Cleaver?"

"Why?" Drummond asked, immediately wary.

"We have many things to discuss. Foremost amongst them; why he had me drugged, imprisoned, and ordered killed."

Drummond gulped, having worked at the Manor long enough to know that despite his calm tone, Lord Lodge was furious. "My Lord, I didn't…"

"Before you say another word," Lodge continued, interrupting Drummond as if he hadn't said anything. "Be advised that anything other than your total assistance in this matter will be treated as a direct action against myself and the Hunt. And you will be treated accordingly."

"I understand my Lord," began Drummond, slowly regaining his voice after a brief moment. "I honestly do not know where Dr. Cleaver is, however I was not entirely truthful concerning Colonel Bufford."

"Very well, what have you got to say?"

"It's true I didn't give him the key to a second portal, but I did give him the key to room 2F001."

"That's the door to the portal where the hunt is taking place," observed Pierce impatiently. "Why would you give him that key when you opened the door for everyone to start the hunt?"

"I gave him that key before the hunt was even announced," Drummond answered to Lodge, ignoring Pierce altogether. "A few months ago he asked if he could be let into the hunting grounds beforehand. I know it's against the rules, but the man is unbalanced. I was afraid to say no to him."

"I see," accepted Lodge calmly. "And you don't know where he is now?"

Drummond merely shook his head, eliciting a snort of disbelief from Pierce.

"My Lord, how you can possibly believe him," objected Pierce, confused by Lodge's acceptance. Drummond was clearly hiding something, probably more than they realized, and Lord Lodge sat there nodding. From their last meeting he had thought Lord Lodge had observation and deductive skills bordering on mind reading. But now he was being fooled by a second rate conspirator.

"Lord Pierce, Mr. Drummond knows the penalty for lying to me at this moment," Lodge replied curtly. "If you having nothing to add Drummond, you may leave."

When Drummond shook his head, Lodge motioned Liam to cut him loose. Without wasting time Drummond quickly extricated himself once free, trying to regain his composure as he exited the room.

"Dufresne, follow him," ordered Lodge after the door had

closed, much to Pierce's obvious surprise. "You didn't think I believed him did you."

When Pierce shrugged in reply, Lodge let out a short laugh. "MacDuff please take your men outside and wait for us. I'd like to speak to Lord Pierce and Tiberius alone for a moment."

MacDuff nodded and followed the rest of the Brown pack out into the hall.

"What am I doing here? Why was I recruited into this dreadful mess you call the Black Tower Hunt Club?" Pierce asked as soon as the door closed behind MacDuff. "Something is going on and I want some answers before I blindly continue running around."

"You're here because I needed an outsider I could trust," Lodge answered quickly. "That will have to suffice for the time being, as we don't have time to get into everything."

"Don't have enough time?!" Pierce asked incredulously. "Aren't we outside of time or something like that here? This island has an abundance of time if nothing else."

"True," acknowledged Lodge. "Time does seem to stand still here, but only in relation to the outside world. A threat on this island makes no allowance for that special relationship."

"Fair enough," Pierce grudgingly accepted. "Can you at least tell me what's going on around here?"

"Cleaver is planning something very dangerous and has recruited many allies to his cause."

"But what exactly is he planning?"

"I'm not sure," Lodge allowed uncertainly.

"So you allowed yourself to be kidnapped to find out more information? That's one hell of a risk."

"I agree with Lord Pierce," Tiberius seconded. "What if you hadn't escaped?"

"I thought you rescued him?" Pierce asked, turning to Tiberius.

"I did, after a fashion. We rescued him and Jane when they were captured after escaping the Crows Nest."

"Which can be discussed at a later date," Lodge

interjected.

"Jane?" asked Pierce after hearing her name. "She's in league with Cleaver and can't be trusted. I heard them plotting before."

"She was under my direction at that time."

"If you say so, but she was pretty convincing," Pierce observed doubtfully.

"Which is the reason I used her, because she's good."

"Like you're using me now? So what did you discover from being kidnapped?" enquired Pierce acidly, desperate for an answer of any kind. "Did Cleaver reveal his plans to you once you were in his clutches? Or did you trick one of his subordinates to let some information slip?"

"Unfortunately neither," allowed Lodge. "However I did discover the lengths to which he is prepared to go to achieve his ultimate goal."

"I'm not sure how that helps us."

"Tiberius can confirm to you that for some time Cleaver and I have been battling each other covertly. But this is the first time that it has become violent. By ordering my death he crossed a line that cannot be undone."

"And Bufford, how does he fit into this?" Tiberius asked the other two.

"He's been recruited by Cleaver," answered Pierce before Lodge could. "You said Cleaver has been recruiting allies, well he fits the bill. Plus I don't buy Drummond going along with Bufford's request for the key. There's no way a bureaucrat like Drummond would break the rules so easily, unless he was under orders from his superior. And Drummond is clearly under Cleaver's spell, his reaction to my questions showed that."

"Very good," nodded Lodge appreciatively. "That was my conclusion as well. I imagine Cleaver is using Bufford to distract us, like a magician waving one hand while the other takes your watch."

"Divide and conquer," concurred Tiberius. "So we ignore Bufford and concentrate on the leader?"

"We can't take that chance," replied Lodge vehemently. "Whatever that crazed madman is planning needs to be stopped, even if it's only a distraction. Pierce, you and your men track down Bufford and stop him. This is no longer a scouting exercise; you have your hunting license."

"First I need to find him," Pierce noted sourly. "It's as if they disappeared as soon as they crossed the portal. But that's impossible."

"If you want my advice," Lodge began, lecturing like an instructor. "If you eliminate the impossible, the result however improbable, must be the answer."

"Sounds like a fortune cookie," Pierce chuckled but then stopped immediately. His eyes became fixed and a smile started to creep across his face. "MacDuff!"

Hearing his name called, MacDuff came in from the hall and stood ready for instructions.

"Go back to the anteroom outside the portal from Spain. Check the walls for a passage of some kind."

MacDuff nodded and left the room quickly, excited at having a fresh scent to chase. Within a few minutes he had returned with a big grin across his face.

"Was it behind the wooden chest?" Pierce asked slyly.

"Indeed sir, a hole dug clear through the wall to the anteroom next door."

"Big enough to haul those crates through?" MacDuff nodded in response.

"What made you think of that?" asked Lodge, beaming at his successful pupil.

"It was the only possibility; no keys were missing, they weren't seen outside of the North Tower, and we couldn't find them inside the North Tower. We watched them enter the Villa in Seville and tracked them to the portal within. They had ample opportunity to dig the passage between anterooms because Drummond gave them the key to 2F001. Which door leads to the anteroom beside it?"

"2F003. Marseille, 1835," Tiberius answered immediately from memory. He walked over to the lock box and removed the key, tossing it to McDuff.

"I'll find Bufford and stop him," Pierce promised Lord Lodge as he followed MacDuff to the door. "But you had better have some straight answers for my questions when I get back."

*

"We found him like this," began Dufresne pointing at Drummond's motionless form. "Sitting on that chair and muttering to himself, with that blank stare into nowhere."

"I see," replied Lord Lodge, observing the Secretary for himself. Drummond sat on a plain wooden chair against the wall, his shoulders slumped and his head back, the complete picture of defeat. His expressionless face drooped, with only his mouth moving slightly, muttering incomprehensibly.

Lodge had just entered with Tiberius after being summoned from the Secretary's office by Morgan. Dufresne had followed Drummond's quick retreat from the office straight to Dr. Cleaver's quarter's, with Morgan picking up their trail in the main hall. Together they had followed Drummond around the Manor, seemingly at random, until he arrived at Cleaver's top floor office in one of the towers. Seeing the state Drummond fell into once entering, Morgan had left to get the others.

"Could you make out what he was saying before," Tiberius asked as he leaned closer to the distraught man. "Because he's unintelligible now."

"I think he said; *he's gone, he's gone, I can't believe he's gone*," offered Dufresne trying to remember. "And then he kept repeating *he left me*."

"I fear the reality of his situation has overtaken the good Secretary of the Hunt," mused Lodge as he walked past Drummond and began an inspection of the office.

"Sir?"

"Dr. Cleaver has fled, Tiberius," Lodge answered as he

leafed through some loose pages on the desk. "Leaving his assistant to the wolves, as it were. Obviously the *he* Drummond is referring to is Cleaver, since we're in his office. I imagine all the places he visited before arriving here were Cleaver's haunts within the Manor."

"But how does he know Cleaver has left and gone for good," Tiberius asked looking around the office. "He could be down in Rooks Bay, on his way to the Crows Nest, or anywhere on the island."

"I suspect Drummond knows enough about Dr. Cleaver to recognise the signs. First his engraved surgical case is missing from its normal place of prominence. Second his prized silver plated pistol is also missing. He's never taken these items from this office since arriving. The third sign is that the door was unlocked." Lodge had revealed these things as he toured around the room, finally stopping at the door. "Drummond didn't pick the lock on the door, and Cleaver would have never left this door unlocked unless he no longer had anything to hide."

"If he had nothing left to hide, does that mean his plans are complete?"

"Possibly," allowed Lodge thoughtfully. "However all we can confidently say is that his plans do not require remaining in the Manor, but anything beyond that is pure speculation."

"So what do we do with him?" Tiberius asked as he poked Drummond in the shoulder.

"Take him down to one of the more comfortable holding cells. He'll eventually recover form the shock, and when he does we'll resume Lord Pierce's interrogation. But with slightly less zeal."

"Very well my Lord. May I suggest I gather the remaining hounds of the Black Pack?"

"Good thinking," smiled Lodge briefly. "Gather them together and determine the ones who can be trusted. Anyone you have doubts of will go to the cells with Drummond. The rest will help seek out Lord Cleaver on the island. I'll leave the details to you."

"And their orders if they find him?"

"He's to be brought before me alive and unharmed," ordered Lord Lodge solemnly. "If possible."

*

Pierce emerged from the bath in his quarters, feeling somewhat human after shedding what felt like ten pounds of dust and dirt. The clothes he wore in Spain were already on their way to the laundry and had been replaced by a thick luxurious robe. He slipped it on and dried himself with an equally soft towel as he walked to his adjoining dressing room.

Without any instructions, Melrose had laid out his master's kilt and highland wear, along with the menacing leather hunt jacket. His valet's attention to detail and foresight continued to impress Pierce. He quickly put it all on and was donning the long jacket when Melrose entered, ready for instructions.

"I'm heading to 1830's Marseille with the Brown Pack to hunt down Bufford," Pierce began calmly, surprising himself slightly by his tone. A statement such as this would have shocked Pierce had he heard it in the not so distant past. Not only would it have shocked him, but he would have found it so unbelievable, that he would have ignored it as crazed ramblings. But having heard it come out of his own mouth made him realize how much he had recently changed and made him wonder about what lay ahead.

"Sir?" Melrose asked respectfully, as Pierce seemed to lose concentration mid-sentence.

"Pack a bag with some period clothing," Pierce continued his instructions seamlessly, ignoring his previous thoughts for the time being. "I'm not sure what I'll need, but I trust your judgement. I'm heading down to the Brown Pack's room, so meet me there when you're done."

Pierce followed the now familiar path from his quarters high up in the Manor to the Brown Packs Hall on the main floor. The continued inactivity signalled that the hunt in Spain remained on and that the other Packs had yet to emerge from the portal in the North Tower.

His men were waiting for him in their lair as he closed the stag carved door and entered. They were similarly attired in their highland gear and hunt jackets and a collection of weapons were laid out on the large table. Pierce walked over and inspected the collection of 1830 era rifles, pistols, swords, and daggers.

"It's a shame we can't bring some automatic rifles and some radios," Pierce lamented as he stared down the length of a Baker rifle.

"I've found something I think you might appreciate a bit more than that," offered MacDuff smiling. He reached down and lifted up a long black stick with a bronzed handle, throwing it to Pierce in a smooth arc.

"A walking stick?" Pierce asked as he looked it over. The stick was made out of a single piece of ebony, however it felt light in his hand despite its girth. The handle had a few bronze bands that culminated in a rounded head, engraved with a raven.

"A wee bit more than that," winked MacDuff as he came over to Pierce. "See that small bronze circle on the handle? Push it until you hear a click."

Pierce did as he was told, suddenly becoming aware of the true nature of the item in his hands. When he heard the click he turned the handle, removing a lethal looking three foot blade with a flourish. The steel glinted in the light as he made a few well practiced sweeps and jabs to the air.

"You look absolutely devilish with that in your hands," Sean remarked appreciatively.

"You're right Duffy," Pierce allowed as he replaced the blade in its innocent looking sheath. "This is more useful to me than a gun. So who's got an idea on how we deal with Bufford?"

"This time he's got a head start on us, so we can't track him as easily," observed Sean unhappily.

"But we can still track him?" asked Pierce hopefully.

"Possibly, but it will require a lot of time, probably too much."

"We should have another go at Drummond," Liam offered as he played with his knife. "He must know more than he's telling."

"That's not an option right now," Pierce replied sharply. "Come on, you guys have hunted people with the Manor before, this is the same thing!"

"It's not the same thing."

"Why not?"

"When we've tracked down people in the past, it was on our own time," MacDuff began answering, intentionally changing *hunt* to *track*. "You see we're given a target and we slowly and carefully track and find them. They don't know of our existence and it doesn't end until we find them."

"And in this case Bufford could have completed his plans before we ever get close enough to him," Pierce finished, understanding the difference. "Fair enough, so what we need is a clue or two, something to give us a direction once we cross through the portal. But where are we going to get that around here?"

"His pack is with him, so that option's out."

"Dr. Cleaver, who probably knows what he's up to, has disappeared."

"So who does that leave?" Pierce asked the air as everyone shrugged around the table.

They all turned in unison as the door opened and Melrose entered, carrying a leather and canvas duffle bag. "I've packed your bag for the journey sir. You'll find everything you need for 1830's Marseille, although knowing the season would have helped me narrow things down."

"The valet!" everyone exclaimed at once after the appearance of Pierce's man.

"Of course, how could I be so stupid," Pierce lamented as he tapped his new swordstick on the table. "Bufford's valet has got to know what his master is up to."

"And it shouldn't be too hard to get it out of him, if you'll pardon my saying sir," Melrose offered helpfully. "The Colonel's, shall we say temperament, is not easy on his staff. I've heard his valet muttering about him before. There shouldn't be any trouble getting his assistance."

"Good. You and MacDuff search Buffords quarters for him," Pierce ordered decisively. "Sean, you and Liam search the servant's quarters for him. If any of you find him, bring him back here and we'll have a little chat. If he refuses, tell him it's by order of Lord Lodge. If he still refuses, knock him over the head and forcibly bring him." They all nodded with varying degrees of enthusiasm and quickly left.

Left by himself, Pierce wandered the room lost in thought. There was something nagging him about Bufford, but it was an incorporeal mist in the back of his mind. Every time he tried to reach out and grab it, the thought would slip through his mental fingers. It was something Bufford had said when they first met, but he'd been too dishevelled to take notice of the Colonel's ramblings about horses and Canadians.

After a few minutes without any success Pierce turned his mind to the facts they knew, hoping it would trigger something. He kept asking himself what Bufford was doing with crates of weapons. There were plenty of weapons at the Manor, many newer and better than the ones he'd purchased. Even if he wanted them for his Pack's private collection, which didn't make much sense, he had enough in those crates to supply an army.

An Army! The nagging feeling in the back of Pierce's mind came barrelling out of his subconscious, physically staggering him. It was an old mantra he'd heard many times, but never with the same vehemence and certainty that Bufford had when they'd first met. *The South will rise again.* Even as he said it, his rational mind fought against the possibility of someone taking world war two weapons and using them in the American Civil War. Only a crazed maniac would think that it was possible…

Pierce's train of thought was suddenly derailed when the outer doors burst open and bodies came streaming in. Not only had his men returned, but they also brought the valet, a maid, and one of the stable boys.

The three servants stood at attention before Pierce as he sat down at the large table, his fingers drumming his cane rhythmically.

"I assume these two also have information concerning Lord Bufford?" Pierce asked Sean who stood behind the maid and stable boy. Receiving a nod in reply he instructed Sean to take them to the foyer while he spoke with the valet.

Bufford's valet displayed the same professionalism as Melrose and stood with expressionless rigidity. Pierce realized that a straightforward approach to his questions would yield the same results as any trickery or threats.

"Do you know why you're here?" he began the interrogation.

"I believe you have questions concerning my Lord's whereabouts."

"Correct. Colonel Bufford has plotted against Lord Lodge and is currently conducting activities contrary to regulations of the Manor. We have been charged to stop him and you're going to help us." Sensing the valet's inner struggle, he patiently waited for one side to win out. Pierce was eventually rewarded when the valet's stiff posture seemed to relax slightly and he smiled timidly.

"What do you want to know?"

"What are his plans?" Pierce asked immediately, hoping to confirm his own suspicions.

"I'm afraid he didn't confide them to me, although I can tell you he's in league with Lord Cleaver."

"I see. We know he picked up crates of guns during the hunt in Spain and brought them back to the Manor," began Pierce again hoping for better results. "What does he need them for?"

"I'm not really sure," began the valet concentrating. "He didn't say exactly what they were for."

"What did he say about them?" interjected MacDuff, sensing the valet had something more to say.

"He said something about the guns being the tools of

vengeance or something to that effect," he answered truthfully.

"That's a very strange thing to say," MacDuff remarked, looking to Pierce. However Pierce smiled in reply, in much the same way Lord Lodge would.

"I thought so," replied the valet to no one in particular. "I dismissed it as merely a statement on guns in general. The Colonel's known to go off on tangents."

"What's he doing in Marseille?" Pierce asked patiently, refocusing the valet. "Is he staying in the city or is he going elsewhere?"

"I can offer something more definite there my Lord," he answered brightly as he felt inside his inner jacket pocket. He quickly removed a large purple card with glittering silver trim and handed it to Pierce.

Pierce looked it over and then handed it over to MacDuff to inspect.

"An invitation to a Ball?" MacDuff uttered in disbelief.

"Yes sir. This is actually a copy of the original invitation that the Colonel had made. He intended to invite Lord Cleaver, but he never got a response. So he left it blank and forgot about it."

"Thank you, you've been very helpful," Pierce dismissed the valet, who immediately bowed, and left the room.

"What's that mad-hatter doing at a ball?" Liam asked from the back of the room.

"Who cares," retorted Pierce with growing excitement. "Now we know where he'll be. We can pick up his scent from there."

Chapter 25

Despite the absence of the Hunt Members, the Manor's lower levels continued to hum with activity. The cooks took the opportunity to create new dishes to test on the staff, free from the demands of providing elaborate dinners. The valets and ladies maids were busy cleaning and repairing the clothing of their fashionable masters. The seamstress' worked beside them, creating elegant new dresses and dapper shirts for the members. Everyone used the opportunity to complete the simple tasks that could not be afforded the time when the Manor was full.

Maddie and Kat were still awestruck by the sheer size and magnificence of the Manor as they tried to follow Jane's progress through the busy hallways. It took all of their concentration to avoid knocking into others as they took in every room they passed.

Jane smiled as she looked back at them, hoping she'd get the opportunity to really astound them by going up to the Main Hall. She remembered her first time entering the massive room with its domed roof and mosaic floor, feeling small but not insignificant.

Their progress through the underground maze of rooms and corridors finally ended as they came to a small bedroom with two single beds. A vibrant painting of Rooks Bay and some fresh cut wildflowers spruced up the otherwise utilitarian room.

"This will be your room for the time being," Jane instructed the two sisters. "I know it's not much to look at, but the beds are soft and the blankets are warm."

Maddie sat on the bed briefly, testing out the firmness for herself while Kat put her single bag on top of the small dresser by the door. It contained their few possessions and they both suddenly felt very far from Rivermead.

Jane almost mistook their changed demeanour as disappointment in their lodgings. The room paled in comparison to the richness of the building they had just passed through. But before she reproached them for their ingratitude, she quickly realized that that wasn't the reason at all. Now that they were safe and no longer had to worry about what the next hour might bring, their thoughts were turned elsewhere. Jane had spent nearly her whole life in the Manor and in that time had seen various looks of homesickness in many servants new to the Manor. She knew a temporary cure for the ailment was to distract them and to make them feel at home.

"I don't know about you, but I'm hungry," she stated truthfully, suddenly realizing that they hadn't eaten a real meal in some time. When both girls nodded she led them out of the room in search of the servant's dining room.

They took a different way than before, further disorienting the sisters. However Jane marched confidently ahead of them, able to navigate the Manor blindfolded. After a few left and right turns they entered the staff dining room, its size a reflection on the number of staff employed at the Manor. The lack of windows and the abundance of pillars within the room were the only indications it was underground. The number of pillars made the use of a single long table impractical, so the dining room was dotted with a collection of tables and chairs evenly spaced out.

Jane motioned them to sit down at a table in the corner and went in search of some food in the adjoining kitchen. Because the work hours of the staff revolved around the unpredictable schedules of the members, there was always a pot of soup on and fresh bread available in the kitchen.

They ate in companionable silence in the empty dining room, too hungry to waste time chatting. Within minutes all three had finished their food, slurping their last spoonful of soup. Jane collected the plates and immediately returned with a tea tray, filling three cups with practiced ease.

"I imagine you're anxious to get home," she began, hoping to fill the quiet void that had developed. "You've been through quite a lot."

"It's been one terrible situation after another," replied Maddie at once, shivering in recollection. "I've always been happy in Rivermead, but most of the other girls are always saying they want adventure and excitement. They can have it, they obviously don't know what they're talking about." Jane nodded in acknowledgement, able to see Maddie living quietly in Rivermead and growing old there. However she noticed that Kat displayed none of the same unease of her sister.

Jane saw a kindred spirit in the elder sister, a yearning for action and excitement beyond the humdrum routine of village life. She could tell Kat would not be returning to Rivermead, she'd experienced too much to go back. Jane was also willing to bet she wouldn't even escort her sister back, fearing she'd be stuck there once she arrived. However she didn't broach the subject in case Maddie was unaware of her sister's probable decision.

"So what's it like working here?" Kat asked with feigned disinterest, but failing to hide her fascination.

"It's not easy," admitted Jane frankly, trying to offer a realistic picture. "There are lots of peaks and valleys to the work here."

"How do you mean?"

"Well I can't speak for every position here, but you're either exhausted from the frantic requirements of one of the Hunt events, or you're bored from the routine of daily tasks."

"But it must be a thrill working in such a magnificent environment. This is the biggest and tallest building I've ever seen. I bet I can't even imagine the opulence of some of the rooms in here."

"That's probably true, but I can tell you that the *magnificence* wears off when you have to do the dusting."

Kat frowned slightly at this reply, but Jane could tell it was more from her apparent negative spin rather than disappointment at the reality of the Manor. Luckily she was saved from further elaboration when Kat noticed her sisters repeated yawns.

"You guys must be exhausted, I know I am," Jane offered sympathetically. "I'll show you back to your room."

She retraced their route back from the dining room without any trouble, all of them noticing the decrease in activity. As they opened the door to their room Jane gave them quick directions on where her room could be found in case they needed anything. She then left and walked the short distance to her own room.

When she opened the door a wave of relief, exhaustion, and comfort rolled over her. It had been weeks since she last slept in her room; having bounced around from the pub, to the Crow's Nest, the farmhouse, and campsites in between. She walked over to her bed and collapsed on it, too tired to change and relishing the feeling of her old bed. Jane had been ignoring a tugging feeling within her ever since she'd laid eyes on the Manor upon their return. Listening to the familiar bustle as they walked the halls had only made the feeling stronger, but lying in her bed and smelling the familiar scents now made it impossible to ignore. She was home.

Despite the demanding workload and the indefinable ominous air of the Manor, she realized that she was at home here and wouldn't feel right anywhere else. After years of labouring in the expansive building, she'd come to take it for granted. But after her short absence, she knew she'd never be able to leave. Perhaps she'd been too quick to discourage Kat about the Manor earlier.

A quiet tapping at her door brought Jane back to the present and she swore silently as she forced herself up from the comfort of her bed. A few stiff steps got her to the door where she opened it a crack and faced a surprising guest.

"I can't really sleep, can I come in?" Kat asked from the hallway.

"Sure. What's on your mind?"

"It's this place; at first I thought it was just the excitement of somewhere new. But there's an energy here that I can't ignore."

"Funny you should say that, I was just thinking the same thing," Jane agreed as she sat back down on her bed. She motioned for Kat to sit in wooden chair by her wardrobe. "When we were talking before, I didn't mean to brush you off. I just didn't want to talk about your decision to work here in front of your sister. You haven't told her have you?"

"No I haven't. But I only made up my mind just now. How did you know?"

"Because I feel the same way," replied Jane. "You'd think that after being drugged, kidnapped, imprisoned, and everything else I've been through that I'd be done with this place. But when I got back here, I realized I'll never leave."

"Exactly," Kat agreed enthusiastically. "How can I go back to Rivermead after everything I've seen?"

"And everyone you've met?"

"What is that supposed to mean?" Kat asked innocently.

"I've seen how you look at Tiberius, but more importantly I've seen how he looks at you. It's a way that would make most of the women at the Manor, if not the entire Island, extremely jealous."

"But not you," Kat pointed out perceptively.

"Maybe a little, but I've got my own problems," Jane laughed hesitantly.

"Such as?"

"Such as; he's one of the Hunt Members and we've only talked a couple times. Hell, I don't even know how real my feelings are. I could have built him up in my mind. Besides I'm just a maid, I doubt he even remembers me."

"You're not just a maid, at least not anymore and not to

me" countered Kat, feeling a need to dispel the concerns of her new friend. "Lord Lodge and Tiberius sure don't treat you like a maid. And I don't know of any maids who would have kept their cool like you did at that farmhouse."

"How many maids do you know?" Jane asked with a smile.

"That's not important. But I bet you've always been like this and if that's the case, he'll remember you."

"Maybe," Jane allowed, feeling much better. "But tomorrow I'll put my uniform back on and the next time I see him I'll be dusting the library."

"Well I'm sticking around here and together we'll figure a way to get his attention. I don't think it will be that hard, plus I'm really good at that sort of thing."

*

"I can tell you've got an idea lad," MacDuff warned his master as he led him down a staircase to the servant's level of the Manor. "But why are we dragging Jane into this?"

"Duffy we're not dragging her into anything," Pierce replied tersely. "Jane's up to her eyeballs in this mess. And we need a fifth person for this hunt, more precisely a woman."

"Why a woman?"

"Bufford's going to a ball. You of all people should know that these events are for couples and a single eligible bachelor will stand out unnecessarily. Plus there are places at a ball that a woman can get into easier. We're going to need her to make sure there are no gaps in our surveillance."

"And that's the only reason?" MacDuff asked casually.

"I don't know what you're alluding to." MacDuff only flashed a knowing smile in response to Pierces' denial.

Their boots rang out ominously in the nearly vacant hallways beneath the Manor. Those few servants still working quickly disappeared upon seeing the approaching huntsmen. Members of the Hunt rarely descended to the lower levels of the Manor and when they did it was never a good thing.

"No wonder I've never seen that many staff around the Manor," Pierce noted, breaking the silence between them. They were walking down a long hallway that had multiple staircases leading upstairs.

"All of these staircases we're passing lead up to rooms above; dining room, library, billiard room, salons, and most of the hallways."

Pierce merely whistled in reply, acknowledging the architectural and design skill required to accomplish such a task. Past the hallway they turned into another that clearly led to the main servant's quarters. Numerous doors flanked either side of the walls, all with numbers and personal effects hung upon them. It reminded Pierce of his brief stay in a crowded college dorm.

"It's this one here my Lord," MacDuff pointed out as they stopped in front of a door with a blank chalk board hung on it. "You'd better stand back a bit; we don't want to give the poor girl a heart attack."

Pierce was about to ask what he meant when he realized that it might be a little disconcerting to have the Lord of the Brown Pack banging on her door in the middle of the night. He was still getting used to the idea that he was now more than simple Patrick Pierce.

McDuff knocked gently on the door and was shocked slightly as it opened almost immediately despite the hour. He was even more shocked when it was opened by a beautiful auburn haired young woman.

"Hello," she said as MacDuff took a step back to check the door number, thinking he had made a mistake. But he was relieved when he looked back down and Jane appeared behind the other woman.

"MacDuff what are you doing here?" she asked, ushering Kat back from the doorway. She then inhaled in surprise, seeing Pierce behind him. "Lord Pierce…"

"Sorry to interrupt, the late hour and all, but I need to speak to you," Pierce offered with embarrassment upon seeing Jane blush slightly.

"Well I'll leave you then," Kat said seeing the blush as well, but realized the true nature of its appearance. She gave her friend a quick wink as she passed, "told you I was good."

Jane gave her an annoyed glance as she left and then let the two men enter. They all stood awkwardly in the small room, Jane was thankful that she had not yet changed and glad that nothing embarrassing was out.

"Who was that?" MacDuff asked, trying to ease the tension. "I thought I knew everyone who worked at the Manor."

"She doesn't work here, she's from Rivermead. It's actually a bit of a long story."

MacDuff nodded and motioned for Pierce to begin.

"We're here because I… we need to your help. That is to say…"

"Yes, I'll do it," Jane quickly agreed, cutting Pierce off mid sentence. She immediately began blushing again when she realized he hadn't finished. Any doubts she had about her feelings upon seeing Lord Pierce again were dashed. In fact she found him more appealing than she remembered. She wanted to kick herself for acting this ridiculous and quickly regained her composure. "What exactly do you need me to do?"

"We need you to travel through one of the portals with us," Pierce replied plainly.

"Very funny," she replied, laughing at the impossibility of the request. "What, pray tell, will we be doing there?"

"Hunting down Colonel Bufford."

"This isn't a joke, is it?" She finally uttered after finding her voice.

"I'm afraid it isn't," MacDuff answered gravely. "You can take back your offer if you want. This could get dangerous."

"Why do you want me?"

"You've proven yourself to be very capable," Pierce began uneasily. "You played Dr. Cleaver, helped Lord Lodge escape, and had me completely fooled."

"You fooled?" Jane asked in confusion. "When, how?"

"That first day we met at the pub. I followed you up to

your meeting with Cleaver and heard most of your conversation. I thought you were a pretty face employed by Cleaver to spy on me, or worse."

Jane smiled at the backhanded compliment. She immediately felt like her old confident self and not some blushing schoolgirl. She had done all of those things and realized the opportunity before her. If she was successful her days working as a maid were behind her.

"I'll do it," she stated confidently. "When do we go?"

"That's the spirit lass!" MacDuff exclaimed, slapping his hands in excitement and being rewarded with a beaming smile.

"We'll head up to the Brown Packs room immediately," Pierce informed her. "Don't bother packing anything, I've sent Melrose to find some proper clothing for you, and Sean is gathering all the gear you might need."

Jane merely nodded, trying to remain calm and professional despite the growing excitement within her. Only members of the Hunt and their packs were allowed into the North Tower and the portals within. She might be the first outsider to enter one of the portals only whispered about by members of the staff.

They left her room, waiting a moment as she wrote a note on the board on her door, stating her absence. They then took the nearest staircase upstairs, which opened up behind a menacing suit of armour. Within minutes they walked to the foyer outside the Brown Packs Lair.

"Coming?" MacDuff asked her kindly as both he and Pierce entered the large door.

"Yes, sorry," Jane offered as she followed them in. She had never entered one of the Pack rooms before and was hesitant to cross that line despite her desire. With a determined step she followed them past the door and through the small anteroom beyond.

She was immediately struck by the duality of the main room when she entered it. The tall narrow windows, mounted weapons, and alter-like hearth lent a feeling of quiet reverence. But at the same time there was a warm lived-in quality to the space that was lacking in most of the rooms of the Manor. She realized that since she had never been in here, then it stood to reason that the Manor staff were similarly forbidden, leaving the cleaning to the packs themselves.

The next thing that struck Jane was the laughing from the two men by the table. She recognized them as the Brown Pack Hounds, but couldn't remember their names. The pack members always strode around the Manor with humourless importance. But here were two of them almost giggling like children.

"If you can contain yourself for a second," MacDuff growled at the pair, "we have a guest you need to meet."

"Sean, Liam," continued Pierce, trying to appear in charge in front of Jane. "This is Jane; she'll be joining us on this hunt."

They both smiled at the attractive addition to their troop who had placed herself against the wall on the other side of the large table that dominated the room.

"What's so funny then?" MacDuff inquired as he went over to them.

"We just returned from the forger's with the invitation we got from Cleaver's valet."

"Forger?" Pierce asked with piqued curiosity.

"There's a couple on staff here in the Manor," MacDuff explained picking up the invitation. "We use them to create all the required documentation we need for hunts; passports, licenses, identity cards, and such things. It makes the hunts a little more convenient."

"Makes sense. So you got the forger to put my name on the invitation, what's so funny about that?"

"They put *your* names on the invitation," MacDuff answered after reading the invitation, a smile emerging from his dark beard.

"*Our* names?" Pierce asked, receiving the card from MacDuff and reading it for himself. "The *Count and Countess of Monte Cristo*, very funny. Whose bright idea is this?"

"I thought you enjoyed the works of Alexandre Dumas," Liam replied with an innocent shrug.

"It's not a terrible idea really," offered Sean in defence. "Any guards are less likely to take notice of a minor noble. Plus a married one will not attract the unwanted attention of single women in search of a husband."

"Those are both good points, but don't you think someone will be suspicious of a literary character showing up at the ball?" Pierce asked in exasperation. "Why not just make up a name?"

"Because this is funnier," Liam smiled in reply. "Plus *The Count of Monte Cristo* won't be published for decades where we're going."

Pierce immediately felt stupid for forgetting about the differences in time. However he took some minor solace in the fact that time-travel was still new to him. He was further saved from ridicule when Jane appeared by his side, linking arms with him.

"Well my dear Count, I think this ball sounds like a wonderful time."

Pierce looked down at her beaming face and immediately felt better. He felt better still seeing the slightly jealous looks of Sean and Liam. "The Countess is right, thank you gentlemen."

"Good, you're in character already," muttered Liam sarcastically. "That won't get annoying at all."

"Apart from the invitation, what else have you prepared for the hunt," MacDuff asked Sean looking at the table full of bags.

"A nice collection of period weapons," Sean began, unrolling a heavy canvas bag. A number of rifles, pistols, daggers, and swords were secured in place by leather straps. "I've also packed the usual collection of documentation, coins, and tools."

"Good work," Pierce approved after looking over everything. "I suppose we'll have to change out of our Highland gear for this journey. Everyone get changed and we'll meet back here."

All three men nodded and left through one of the side doors to their rooms, leaving Pierce and Jane alone as they waited for Melrose.

"Why are we searching for Colonel Bufford?" Jane asked, breaking the silence.

"Because he's up to something dangerous and he's abusing the power of this place," Pierce began, explaining everything that had happened in Seville and then their return to the Manor. As he recounted the past days, Pierce was surprised at how much had happened in such a short time. It felt like he'd done more and seen more than he had in the last five years of his old life.

"Will they have these horseless wagons where we're going?"

"Trucks. They're called trucks," Pierce corrected helpfully, remembering that Jane had never left the island. "No, the time period we're going to will seem very similar to what you're used to."

"Thank goodness for that," Jane sighed with relief, having felt anxious after hearing of the car chase though Seville.

"So what's happened here on the island since I've been away?" Pierce asked her easily. "The last time I saw you, you were plotting my removal from the Manor."

"Sorry about that, it wasn't personal," she replied casually, earning a smile in response. She then offered her own story; from the Crows Nest, through the valley, and their subsequent return to the Manor. She had to refrain from smiling when some of the events elicited wide eyed surprise from her audience.

"That's incredible," Pierce acknowledged in appreciation. "I don't think you'll have a problem fitting in with this crew. No wonder Lord Lodge trusts you so much."

"He thinks the world of you as well," Jane replied touching his hand briefly. "I've never seen him take such interest or place such responsibility in a new member."

The sound of a throat being cleared behind them brought both to their feet instantly. They turned to see Melrose standing by the door with two bags in his arms.

"I hope I'm not intruding my Lord?"

"Not at all Melrose," Pierce replied shortly. "What have you got there?"

"Clothes for you and the lady, sir," the valet answered lifting the right and then the left bag in succession. "I took the liberty of obtaining some of Mme Laflamme's clothes from her lady's maid. You look to be about the same size my dear, so hopefully they fit."

"Thank you so much," Jane gushed as she approached, reaching for the bag. After admiring the stunning clothing of the French Lady of the Hunt, she was eager to see what she'd be wearing. "I'd better get changed then."

"I also took one of her nicest gowns for the ball," Melrose winked as he handed the bag over. "You'll look stunning in it."

Jane gave him a small kiss on the cheek and hurried to one of the spare rooms to change.

"Your bag sir," Melrose said with a smile still lingering on his face as he handed Pierce the other bag.

"Don't expect any kisses from me," he grumped taking the bag, realizing he felt a twinge of jealousy towards his valet. But he shook the thought aside, telling himself there was no room for such thoughts with the task that lay before them. Returning from their mission to Marseille was by no means a certainty and he wouldn't risk putting anyone in danger in order to get a kiss from a pretty woman.

Pierce took the same side door as the others, which led to a circular staircase leading up to the floor above. At the top he ran into the others as they left their rooms. They had all changed into period clothes; light or striped pants, high boots, white shirts, waistcoats, and various coloured cravats. However they all kept their brown leather hunt jackets on.

As he moved into one of the spare rooms and removed his own hunt jacket, he marvelled at the versatility of the garment. It really did offer an inconspicuous covering that could be used in any time. This thought then made him amazed that he was once again going to travel into the past. The idea if such an act still made him feel a strange mixture of anxiety and excitement.

The feeling increased as he removed his highland clothing and replaced it with the items from the bag. The boots, breeches, shirt and the remainder were similar to those his men were wearing, but of somewhat better quality. Well, I am a Count, he thought as he inspected himself in the mirror. He wasn't sure if he had done the cravat correctly, but it was basically hidden as he donned his leather jacket.

He left his kilt and old clothing on the bed and picked up his bag with the remainder of his period clothes packed inside. He turned to leave the room and suddenly remembered the swordstick that MacDuff had given to him. He'd put it on the bed when he'd opened the bag.

"Don't want to forget you," he whispered, twirling it in his hand. "I think you might come in handy."

Chapter 26

The sun had just started to burn through the fog that hung lazily in the harbour as Patrick and Liam walked along the pier. Despite the early hour the docks buzzed with activity as sailors, fishermen, and merchants tramped about. Neither man minded the cacophony of sounds and movement, as it provided them a decent amount of anonymity.

They were scouting out the location of the ball, a hotel in the port of Marseille owned by a wealthy businessman. With the end of the Napoleonic Wars, trade between France and North Africa gained importance and the number of ships joining in the lucrative shipping trade grew. As the largest French city on the Mediterranean, Marseille was the hub of all this activity and reaped the rewards. The revitalization of the harbour front displayed this growing prosperity.

Liam lit a pipe while Pierce chomped on an apple, both acting nonchalant as they leaned against some crates and took note of the hotel across the street. It had the same general architecture as the rest of the buildings surrounding the port, but with more grandeur of design.

"Looks like there are only a few points of entry," Pierce observed, noting the cramped collection of buildings across from them. There was little space between each building and sometimes none at all, meaning the doors should only be at the back and front.

"We should check it out, but I think you're right," Liam agreed between puffs.

"You look ridiculous with that pipe," Pierce scoffed as the smoke lingered around their heads. "You don't even smoke."

"I'm just trying to blend in."

"Very nautical. Take a look around back and I'll keep a watch on the front." Liam nodded and slowly knocked the ash out of his pipe and lazily walked away, blending into the crowd.

Once he was gone Pierce turned and looked out over the ship filled harbour. A mass of timber, canvas, and rope filled his view, further displaying the prosperity of the city. The flags of various countries hung limply from the masts of the docked ships, but one in particular caught his attention. It was the stars and stripes of the USA and it popped an idea into his head as soon as he saw it.

A quick glance around the harbour was all it took for him to find his destination and possible lead. The Harbour Master's building sat in a prominent place in the port, as busy as the waterway it controlled.

Once inside he pushed his way past a crowd of captains and ship owners lined up by one of the counters. He stopped to listen and discovered that a ship had run aground by the mouth of the harbour, delaying everyone's planned departures. Most of those gathered around were maintaining their calm, but some were becoming agitated. Continuing past the crowd, it only took a few minutes before Pierce found what he was looking for; a clerk with a large ledger book working alone.

"Excusez moi monsieur," Pierce began after a small cough.

The clerk was busy inscribing some information into his ledger from a document in his hand. Once completed, he looked up at Pierce through a pair of small round spectacles.

"I was hoping you could help me," Pierce continued in his best French.

"If you're here about your ship's departure time you'll have to speak with the Harbour Master, there's nothing I can do."

"No nothing like that," Pierce replied to the obvious relief of the clerk. "You see I'm trying to return to America and was wondering if you could tell me which ships are bound that way."

"Try the shipping companies," the clerk sighed in response as he picked up another document. "I'm too busy and we're not supposed to give out that information."

Pierce reached into his pocket and removed a gold coin and then flipped it onto the desk. The clerk's eyes lit up immediately as he reached out and grabbed it.

"When were you planning on going?" he asked putting down the document.

"Tell you what," Pierce began as he reached into his pocket and pulled out a second coin. "Write down a list of all the ships leaving Marseille bound for America in the next week and you get another one."

"Be back in an hour."

Pierce smiled and put the coin back in his pocket, turned and walked out of the building satisfied by the potential progress. As he walked back to the hotel he could see Liam waiting for him out front, once more smoking his pipe.

"Just the one exit out back," he reported as Patrick approached. "Nothing on the left side, the building on the right is really close, but it doesn't look like there's anything."

"That should make things easy then, only two exits to watch."

"Actually I was just thinking of something while I was waiting here," Liam began slowly. "What if Bufford and his gang try to repeat their disappearing act from the North Tower?"

"What do you mean?"

"What if they realized that two exits wasn't enough and they wanted a back-up?" he explained, slowly reasoning the thoughts as he went. "What if they dug a hole between the buildings through the basement? It's close enough that the foundations might even be touching."

"It's a possibility, but they would have needed time to gain entry into the building and dig inconspicuously," Pierce replied unconvinced. "They only passed through the portal a few hours before us."

"This time."

"This time?" Pierce asked and then immediately understood what Liam meant, upset with his sluggish mind. "Of course, they had the key to the Seville portal on more than one occasion. I just figured it was to lay the ground work for their business there and to dig the connecting hole. But they could have been coming to Marseille as well."

"Exactly, they would have had to come here at least once to get the invitation."

"So there's no telling what they've planned and how much they have prepared," Pierce concurred glumly.

"Not until we check it out."

Pierce nodded in agreement and led the way across the street to the building beside the hotel. It was a plain three story building with evenly spaced windows spread across the façade. It was well kept, with new paint and few cracks visible. Pierce figured the hotel owner didn't mind its proximity to his own building, making it appear more elegant in contrast.

"What's in this building anyway?" Pierce asked as they reached the front door.

"Not sure about the basement, but there's a women's boarding house on the two top floors," Liam winked before receiving a cold stare back. "What? Not all of us got to bring one with us."

"I don't know what you're talking about," Pierce replied sharply after they entered. "And she's not my woman."

"Does she know that?"

Pierce shushed him as he opened the door to the basement, glad at the interruption. Rickety wooden stairs led down into a damp gloomy expanse, dimly light by random grimy windows. The basement floor was made up of hard dirt and littered with old crates, broken furniture, and some large pails of coal.

The two men split up and started following the walls, searching for any clues. Remembering the trick used in the Manor's north tower, they moved any large objects that covered parts of the wall to make sure that there were no holes. After ten dirty minutes of searching, they both met up at the stairs where they began.

"Find anything?" Pierce asked wiping his hands on a rag he'd found.

"Nothing really," Liam answered hesitantly.

"What's wrong?"

"It might be nothing," he started with furrowed brows. "There was a large wardrobe wedged against the wall. I couldn't move it to check behind, but that should mean they couldn't move it either."

"How big is this wardrobe," Pierce asked thoughtfully.

"I don't know, big enough that I couldn't move it," Liam rebuked. "Why does it matter?"

"Clearly you're not familiar with the works of C.S. Lewis." Liam merely stared back in confusion as he pointed Pierce in the direction of the wardrobe.

The wardrobe was indeed a massive piece of furniture, wedged between the dirt floor and a large wooden beam above. It had two large vertical doors at the top with a small drawer underneath. Pierce walked over and inspected the small brass door handles, grinning almost immediately.

"What's so funny?" Liam asked peering at the handles for himself. "They're just ordinary handles."

"More than that, they're ordinary handles with no dust or dirt on them," Pierce explained as he grabbed the right door handle. Very gingerly he pulled it open, his grin doubling as he did so.

"I'll be damned," Liam whistled as he looked through the open door and saw a small hole in the wall.

The hole was actually more of a tunnel, since it was about six feet to the exit on the other side of the wall. It was just wide and tall enough that one person could crouch while walking through it without much trouble. Liam was about to attempt just that before he felt a strong grip on his shoulder. He whipped his head around to see Pierce signalling for him to be quiet.

Both stood listening by the wardrobe for a few seconds before they heard the distinctive sound of footsteps on the other side. This was soon followed by soft whistling and the grating noise of a shovel scraping stone.

"What do we do?" Pierce looked at Liam, they were both shocked that their gamble had paid off. Liam chewed his lip but then immediately flashed a rascally grin.

"Hey you!" he yelled in perfect French through the hole. "What are you doing there?!"

Pierce wanted to slap him for blowing the element of surprise as the man on the other side immediately started running. But instead of the footsteps getting fainter from increased distance, a loud thump sounded through the hole. Pierce shot Liam a questioning look and received a shrug in reply.

The two members of the Brown Pack shuffled their way into the tunnel, their curiosity driving them through the tight space. They emerged to find a bearded man in dirty clothes with a gash on his head. In unison, both raised their eyes from the man's wound to a large iron pipe above.

"I can't believe that just happened," Liam chuckled, checking the man for a pulse.

"He looks familiar."

"He should," Liam replied after finding a pulse and light breathing. He walked over to a wooden stool in the corner by the tunnel and picked something up. "His name's Ivan, one of Bufford's hounds."

Pierce looked up in time as Liam threw what he'd picked up. He caught it before it hit the ground, feeling the distinctive supple grain of leather. Moving over to a small light he could tell it was indeed a long grey leather jacket and similar in style to the two they were both wearing.

"I was hoping we could stop him and interrogate him," admonished Pierce as he threw the jacket back at Liam.

"I didn't think he'd run," Liam countered defensively. "I thought he'd try and talk his way out of it. That's usually what we do on hunts, so as not to arouse unwanted suspicion. So what are we going to do with him?"

"We can't leave him here. He'll just wake up and continue his work."

"And we can't bring him with us; it's too far, he's too heavy, and conspicuous as hell. So that only leaves…"

"No, we can't do that," Pierce shook his head, blanching at the thought of killing a defenceless man.

"He'd probably do it to you."

"That's why we're the good guys," Pierce retorted vehemently. "We don't kill for kicks or convenience. So what does that leave us?"

"What if there was a way to avoid killing him, but also separating him from Bufford?" Liam asked after a brief moment of reflection.

"You've got an idea don't you? Alright spit it out."

The reply was another mischievous grin.

*

The expected scream rang out as they crossed the street from the boarding house. Liam immediately walked over to a pair of nearby gendarmes and proclaimed hearing the screams of a woman being attacked by a drunken sailor in the building. Having heard the screams for themselves, they rushed across the street, eagerly pulling out their heavy truncheons.

It had taken over thirty minutes to pull the incapacitated Ivan through the tunnel and up the stairs to the second floor of the boarding house. They liberated his coin purse and documents after removing most of his clothing. Then as quietly as they could manage, they gently opened one of the girl's bedroom doors and placed him on the floor within. Pierce slammed another door as they nonchalantly left the second floor, intending to wake everyone up.

Everything worked perfectly as they witnessed the

gendarmes drag Ivan out of the building and lead him down the street away from them.

"Ivan doesn't speak French very well, so he'll have a hard time talking his way out of that one," Liam observed happily.

"Nice," Pierce agreed as a nearby clock rung the quarter hour. "Only one last thing we need to do before heading back to the safe house."

Pierce led the way to the Harbour Master's building, leaving Liam outside to wait while he went in. The crowd within the lobby had dispersed and only a few people remained loitering by the front counter.

The clerk was still working through his pile of documents, diligently scratching notes into his large ledger. A folded piece of paper was sitting on the corner of the desk, seemingly of little consequence to the clerk.

Without hesitating at the desk, Pierce walked by slowly, placing a gold coin on the counter and taking the note in fluid simultaneous motions. The clerk calmly removed the coin and placed it in his pocket without looking up or interrupting his work. It was all Pierce could to do keep from laughing at his secret agent manoeuvre as he left the building.

Liam sidled up to him on the street outside and they walked in silence, tired from the morning's activities. Both were relieved that the rising autumn sun did not bring too much heat as they retraced their route to the safe house.

The safe house was a common beige coloured terrace a few blocks south of the port, sitting in the shadow of the imposing Notre Dame de la Garde cathedral. The revitalizing effect of North African trade felt in the port was similarly taking effect here. Widened tree lined streets filled with carriages, wagons, and carts displayed the renewed life of the area. Pierce took all this in and, like at the docks, hoped the amount of activity would provide an adequate amount of anonymity for them.

Without being too obvious, both men looked for anyone familiar or suspicious nearby before entering the front door of the safe house. They had no reason to believe they had been followed or were under observation; however MacDuff had been adamant that they stay alert during their stay. Without any proof to the contrary, they had to act as if Bufford knew of their presence in Marseille. For this reason the first thing the Brown Pack had done upon exiting the building with the portal to the Manor, was to rent out a nearby house. They couldn't risk Bufford running in to them before they were prepared.

Smells of fresh coffee and bread greeted Pierce and Liam as they crossed the entrance and walked into the kitchen. Jane was placing the coffee pot on the table, where MacDuff sat quietly reading a paper.

"You're late," he observed without looking up as he flipped to the next page. "How did it go?"

"It was interesting," Pierce replied, explaining what had occurred after getting a cup of coffee. Sean descended from upstairs in the middle of the discourse, filling the kitchen to capacity.

"Well that's one less thug to worry about at least," he observed hopefully, refilling his own cup.

"I wouldn't be too sure," Pierce countered uneasily. "Liam brought up a good point to me before. Bufford and his men have clearly been here once already."

"If not more," Liam chimed in.

"Yes, if not more," Pierce agreed quickly. "We can't be sure how much they've prepared. He might have hired thugs to work for him. Remember he's a skilled sailor and mercenary in his own right. With that much preparation time, what's the worst case scenario?"

"Worst case?" MacDuff contemplated the question aloud. "He's purchased a ship and crew, who will all be loyal to him. After that he's bribed the local officials, possibly including the gendarmes and local army garrison. He'll have spies everywhere and the muscle to back him up."

"He might even own the hotel this ball is taking place in," Sean added frowning. "That gives him total control of the hunting ground."

"Beautiful," Pierce sighed in desperation. "Anything else?"

"Did Ivan see either of you?" Jane asked quietly, hesitant to enter the conversation.

"Why?" Liam asked, unsure if he had.

"Because if Bufford does own the police, then Ivan has probably been released already or will be soon," Pierce finished for her, visibly impressed with her analysis of the situation. "So if he saw us the game is up, so to speak."

"With the Ball becoming a trap for us rather than Bufford," Jane concurred, pleased to have contributed.

"We can't give up, but we also can't continue blindly," observed Sean succinctly.

"We just went through the worst case scenario," Pierce announced after looking over the sheet of paper from the harbour masters clerk. "I think we can discount some of our fears as to the omnipotence of Colonel Bufford in Marseille."

"Sounds good to me," Liam agreed, recognizing the paper Pierce had picked up on their excursion that morning. "Isn't that what you picked up at the Harbour Master's?"

"Uh-huh," he concurred smiling. "I procured this list from the clerk of the Harbour Master. It should be legit; Bufford might have bribed the master but hardly a lowly clerk. This list contains all the ships traveling to America within the next week, with the corresponding names of the owners and captains for each ship. The names do not match any of the alias' we know Bufford uses."

"Why assume he's bound for America?" Sean challenged doubtfully.

"Where else would a Confederate Colonel with a cargo of submachine guns be travelling to in the 1830's?" Pierce retorted sharply. "His plan must involve bringing these modern weapons to America to be used. So under no circumstances can we allow him to leave the city with those guns. The effects could be catastrophic."

Everyone in the kitchen nodded soberly, understanding the full impact of their mission. It was why those on hunts took such care to only outfit themselves in period clothes and equipment. This attention to detail meant that their presence had very little, if any, impact on the periods they visited. However a watch, telescope, or radio misplaced in an earlier era could have a disastrous effect on the course of human history.

"I doubt he owns the hotel," Liam offered after a brief silence, continuing the groups brainstorming session. "Ivan wouldn't have reacted the way he did if Bufford owned it. He was genuinely surprised and didn't want to be caught digging down there."

"That's true," Pierce acknowledged. "Plus Bufford wouldn't have required invitations to his own ball."

"I accept that he doesn't own a ship or the hotel," MacDuff allowed thoughtfully. "Both of those things would have required an immense amount of time and preparation. However bribing is fairly easy and requires much less time to accomplish. So we must continue with the assumption that any official we come across is potentially involved with Colonel Bufford."

"Agreed."

"Sean take Jane over to the docks and check up on these ships," Pierce ordered, handing over the list he'd acquired from the clerk. "Bufford might not own these ships, but he'll have to use one of them to transport his cargo."

"Me?" Jane responded, surprised at being included and secretly delighted with the idea of helping in a meaningful way.

"Unless you're not up to it," Pierce challenged, testing her resolve.

"Of course I'm up to it!" she retorted sharply. "All I have to do is undo a couple buttons on my blouse and those sailors will tell me anything I want to know."

"Try and be a little more discreet than that," MacDuff suggested behind a wide smile.

"Yeah," Pierce concurred lamely, suddenly feeling jealous of the sailors. He had been secretly annoyed when Lord Lodge had informed him that Jane was not working with Dr. Cleaver. He always felt awkward around women and attractive women like Jane only made it worse. So he had found it easier to deal with her as an enemy agent. But now he felt as awkward as he did when they first met in Drummond's office, despite having turned into a different man in that span of time.

Jane merely flashed a charming smile and shook her black locks in mock reply to both, before leaving the kitchen to prepare.

"Keep an eye on her," Pierce told Sean before he could follow her out. "She's never been off the island before and we'll need her at the ball tonight." Sean nodded in acknowledgment before leaving himself.

"Is it really wise to let her go?" MacDuff asked over a raised cup of coffee.

"I think so. She needs to get used to the environment and I don't want her to feel overwhelmed later on."

"For what it's worth I agree with you," MacDuff agreed as he finished his coffee.

"So how many tests do I have to pass before I get my leadership badge?"

"You caught that did you?" MacDuff replied sheepishly. "I'll follow you, my Lord, because I'm a soldier at heart and that's what we do. But I've also been around long enough to know when to follow wholeheartedly and when to have an exit planned. I suppose I keep prodding you for further insights out of habit. Remember you've only been with us for a short time, considering how long we've been around."

"How long have you been around Duffy," Pierce inquired, his curiosity piqued by McDuff's statement.

"Well I suppose it's hard to determine exactly due to the nature of the Manor," MacDuff answered as he slowly rose from the table and placed his coffee cup on the counter with his back to Pierce. "But I was recruited by Tiberius shortly after the Battle of Bannockburn."

"That was in the 1300's! I saw that in *Braveheart*!" Pierce gasped in shock.

"He looks good for his age don't he?" Liam joked to a disregarding audience.

"Aye, 1314 it was. I followed Robert the Bruce into battle against the English," MacDuff recounted, his highland burr becoming more pronounced. "We won the day and gained our independence. For a time."

"What does that mean?" Pierce asked, confused by the small chuckle uttered by MacDuff.

"A few centuries later I found myself back on the battle field for Scottish Independence. It was at Culloden for the '46 rising with Bonnie Prince Charlie. What a waste."

"I thought you said you were recruited after Bannockburn, what were you doing at Culloden?"

"I went with Tiberius to recruit Sean for the Hunt," MacDuff said, providing some history on another of Pierce's hounds. "He thought it would be easier with a fellow countryman present. We found Sean in Edinburgh, full of rebellious fervour. Well, one thing led to another and I eventually found myself hip deep in smoke and redcoats in Culloden. I followed two very different men into two terribly violent battles, and it was then I really learned that the reason a man makes a decision is often as important as the decision itself."

Chapter 27

Despite the seemingly comfortable surroundings, Drummond knew that his future would be anything but comfortable. He was also not fooled by the innocent looking single bed he was sitting on, or the simple desk and chair he was staring at. He knew all too well that these few pieces of furniture were bolted to the ground and made of strong steel. Standing up he slowly paced the small room, staring at the only thing on the beige coloured walls, a giant mirror. He snorted at the idea of anyone being stupid enough to believe it was a simple mirror. He knew firsthand that it was a two way mirror and he'd be observed like a curious specimen, for this was no guest room, but a cell.

There were many different types of cells in the lower level of the Manor, all for different types of prisoners and interrogation techniques. Drummond had taken a keen interest in them when he'd first arrived and had stood on the other side of the two way mirrors whenever the opportunity arose.

A part of him was thankful that he'd been put in this cell rather than some of the cruder and damper ones. But this thought barely had time to register past the repeating mantra that rang through his head; *he left me, he's gone.*

"He'll come back for me," Drummond whispered hopefully as he sat back down on the bed. He desperately tried to find the reason for his being left behind. Surely Lord Cleaver trusted him and knew his worth? He'd been a faithful ally for years and had proven his worth many times over. So why did he leave without him?

When no answer came to him, Drummond started looking around the cell frantically, his situation becoming clearer. His chest started to pound with anxiety and fear as the beige coloured walls seemingly turned black and crept slowly towards him with silent menace. He fell backwards onto the bed and covered his head, trying to block out the voice in his head with its debilitating message; *he left me, he's gone.*

Drummond could feel his world crashing down on him like the evil walls of the cell he now occupied. He'd been one of the most powerful men at the Manor with access to riches and the power of the portals at his disposal. He was known, respected, and feared throughout the island, free to do what he wished. But more importantly, he'd been an integral part of a group conspiring to take control of the Manor. Being a member of that secret brotherhood meant more to him than the gold he'd stashed in his vault or the women he'd had all over the world.

"I am your rock Lord Cleaver," he whispered as he sat up once more. He knew that they'd come to interrogate him soon, but he wouldn't betray his brothers. He gathered what little courage he had, promising to keep their secrets and prove his worth.

Drummond looked down at the floor and began laughing, lightly at first until it reached a maniacal crescendo. "They can't beat us!"

*

The Hall of the Hounds was a long low ceilinged room directly below the Hunt Room in the older section of the Manor. Unlike the majesty of the grand room above, this one was utilitarian in nature and showed it. Mismatched chairs and tables were pushed up against the battered walls. Smoke hung in the heavy rafters above; some of it from the soot stained fireplaces, but most of it from the hounds themselves. The Hall was used as a sanctum and meeting place away from their masters where they talked, smoked, drank, and fought.

Tiberius walked along the length of the hall, scrutinizing the assembled Hounds of the Black Pack lined up in front of him. There were thirteen of them standing at attention in their long black leather jackets. Unlike their compatriots, members of the Black Pack served the Hunt and Manor in general and were not supposed to owe allegiance to any one member of the Hunt. However, as Tiberius had recently discovered, this was not entirely the case anymore.

After leaving Lord Lodge in Dr. Cleaver's office, Tiberius immediately set about regaining control of the situation at the Manor. Two bugle armed riders were sent out to recall any of the hounds scattered throughout the island. It took a few hours for them to start trickling in from across the countryside and longer still until they were all in the Hall of the Hounds.

Looking at the assembled faces Tiberius saw a mixture of confusion, anxiety, and even some arrogance. He looked down and reviewed the list of names Morgan had given to him moments before. They had continued the interrogation of the two men they'd captured in the Raven's Vale. The list contained seven names, but only one of those names was currently present. Malicio and four other names Tiberius recognized were absent and their whereabouts unknown. The owner of the seventh name was in a shallow grave in the Raven's Vale.

"This one," Tiberius ordered as he pointed the folded list at an arrogant face at the end of the line. His smugness was instantly replaced with the anonymity of a dark black bag, as Morgan quickly shoved it over his head. The bag disoriented him for only a second, but it was long enough for Dufresne to quickly strap his hands behind his back with plastic binders. The bag muffled the screaming protestations of the culprit as he was forcibly removed from the room; however it did nothing to stop the protests of his colleagues.

The metallic sound of a pistol slide rang out; silencing the crowd as everyone's attention was immediately brought back to Tiberius standing in front of them. Weapons were not permitted in the Hall in an effort to keep the inevitable scuffles from turning fatal. The symbolism was not lost on any of them.

"Anyone trying to interfere shall be shot!"

"What's he done then?" demanded one of the men whose allegiance Tiberius was still unsure of. A few others beside him shot inquiring looks with hints of indignation.

"That *man?*" Tiberius nearly spat in contempt. He continued his measured pacing in front of them, removing a silencer from his pocket and methodically attaching it to the end of his pistol. "That man aided in the kidnapping and attempted assassination of Lord Lodge, the Master of the Manor, whom we all swore allegiance to."

Those assembled acknowledged this pronouncement with a collective gulp and remained silent. An event of this magnitude had never occurred before and the level of fury emanating from Tiberius made them all fearful of his wrath.

"Under the orders of the treacherous Dr. Cleaver, Malicio and others participated in this crime," Tiberius continued, no longer willing to call him *Lord* anymore. "If any of you have any information or were involved in anyway, now is the time to come forward. You will not be harmed; however I cannot guarantee that offer will be valid once you leave this room."

Most shook their heads, signalling their ignorance of the situation. A few others admitted to helping the search for Lord Lodge in the mountains to the West; however they'd been told it was to rescue him. Tiberius trusted that they were all speaking the truth. He had doubted that any of those who remained would have acted against Lord Lodge, but he had to ask the question first.

"Very well," Tiberius eventually allowed with something close to satisfaction. He returned the pistol to its holster, significantly easing the tension in the room. "In a case such as this there are no neutral third parties, you must choose a side. Therefore all of you will be expected to follow Lord Lodge's orders, as given by me. There's still room in the cells downstairs for anyone who disagrees or wants to hedge their bets. Understood?!"

"Yes sir!" they answered in unison, without hesitation from anyone.

"Good. You will split into three groups; the first will travel west to the Crow's Nest, the second east past Rivermead to Harrow's End, and the third south to the far side of the Black Loch. Your orders are to track and detain Cleaver, Malicio, or anyone else from the Manor you find. They are to be returned here unharmed if possible."

"And if it's not possible?"

"Then bring back the bodies," Tiberius answered coldly, dismissing them to begin their hunt. As they filed out of the room, Morgan appeared at the door and worked his way against the crowd. He tried to appear calm, but Tiberius had known him long enough to see the small signs of stress and worry. He was immediately wary and waited for the room to empty before digging further. "What is it?"

"It's Drummond sir…"

"Well? Spit it out man!"

"When we took Johann down to the cells, we found him," Morgan replied evenly, but unable to hide his rising sense of guilt. "He hung himself with his shoe laces."

"What?!"

"I'm sorry sir," he apologised sincerely. "We didn't think to remove them or his belt or tie for that matter. It never occurred to us that he'd take his own life." He didn't add that even if they thought he might attempt it, they thought he'd be too much a coward to go through with it. Apparently they were wrong.

"Damn it! He knew more about Cleaver's plans than he let on and he killed himself to save the bastard. Have you informed Lord Lodge?"

"No sir, I thought you'd want to do it."

"Thank you for that," Tiberius replied angrily, but was immediately disappointed with himself when he saw Morgan's reaction. "It wasn't your fault; none of us thought he'd attempt suicide."

Morgan accepted this with a nod, knowing it to be only partially true. "What do you need me to do? Dufresne's in the stables getting our mounts ready for the hunt."

"Organize transport for the girls back to Rivermead. Until we find Cleaver and his minions, the Manor isn't safe for Kat or Maddie."

Tiberius followed Morgan out the door, but headed in the opposite direction to Lord Lodge's office. Unlike Cleaver, Lodge did not have his offices secreted in a tower away from prying eyes. The Master of the Manor's office was located on the second floor where the older section of the Manor met the new, at the very heart of the huge building.

Within minutes he was outside the clean white doors that led to Lodge's office, lounge, library, and sitting rooms. But as his hand grabbed the handle to open the door, he heard his name called out in alarm.

"Sir, wait!" uttered Dufresne breathlessly as he slowed his approach along the corridor.

"More good news?" Tiberius asked dispiritedly.

"I'm afraid so. I was in the stables preparing our horses when a thought occurred to me."

"Which was?" he asked impatiently.

"Well I asked the stable hands which horses Cleaver and his men had taken."

"Good idea," Tiberius agreed, knowing that it would help them in tracking their prey.

"Seemed like it at the time. The only problem was they all looked at me strangely. *Are you sure Lord Cleaver has left?* They asked me. I replied that Malicio and at least four others had also left."

"So what did they say to that?" Tiberius asked, now fully intrigued by the story.

"That may be sir, but they didn't leave on horseback. They took me through the stables and showed me that none of the horses were missing. I think we have a problem."

"To say the least," Tiberius concurred gravely. "Knowing our tracking abilities, they'd have never fled on foot."

"If they left before we returned to the Manor, they might not even know Lodge is back and they're being hunted. Maybe they just went down to the pub in Rooks Bay?"

Tiberius merely raised an eyebrow in disbelief and opened the door to the foyer of Lord Lodge's office. He hoped that his master could shed some light on this new development and take away the uneasy feeling that was growing within him. He also hoped that Pierce and his men were having better luck tracking Bufford.

*

They were.

"I thought she was joking before," Sean laughed to the others gathered around sitting the room. "But she did it; she undid her top two buttons and worked those sailors over good."

"It took a little more than that," Jane replied with a laugh of her own.

Jane had taken on her task to find Bufford's boat with determined zeal, desperate to prove her worth to the others. On the way to the docks she convinced Sean that he'd have to hang back in case any members of the Grey Pack were on the ship and recognized him. He tentatively agreed as they reached the port. Having grown up in Rooks Bay, she was used to sailors and the bustle of dock life. However she was shocked by the magnitude of people, ships, and activity that she encountered when they arrived. The hustle and bustle of one of the busiest ports in Europe was a stark contrast to the sleepy fishing village she was used to.

But the moment only lasted a few seconds before Jane regained her composure and focused on her mission. Seeing a cart laden with apples pull away from one of the ships towards the market, she had Sean buy a dozen of the bright red fruit. He returned with a quizzical look that she merely answered with a wink and smile.

After thirty minutes of searching they found all the ships from the list, still docked and out in the open. Before Sean could suggest their next move, Jane had thrown her coat at him, unfastened the top two buttons of her thin cotton blouse, placed the small basket of apples on her pronounced hip, and strolled over to a group of sailors by the first ship.

She knew a spattering of French from working at the Manor, but this proved to be of little issue. Sailors are really citizens of the world and the crews of most ships reflected this fact. So it didn't take long to find some more than willing to speak to her in English.

"So what did you find out?" Pierce asked hopefully after listening to their story.

"The *Courted Anne*," she replied simply, handing the list back.

"Well done!" clapped MacDuff with pride.

"You found that out with cleavage?" Liam uttered in mock disbelief, receiving an apple in the gut in reply. Smiling, he wiped it off and took a loud bite.

"I even turned a profit on the apples," Jane beamed.

"Those sailors sure were hungry," Sean recalled with a smile of his own.

"How do you know it's the *Anne* Bufford's hired?" Pierce challenged, turning the session back to serious matters.

"Well the crew found out their captain will be replaced, probably by the first mate."

"Go on."

"Yesterday an American showed up, trying to get his cargo on board last minute. But the ship was full and the captain refused, despite the rantings from this gentleman."

"Presumably Colonel Bufford," Pierce allowed.

"However today they discovered that their captain was killed last night and the first mate might be taking over. They're simply waiting for the owner's approval."

"The captain's a known gambler," Sean interjected, explaining the part he discovered at a local bar. "He was accused of cheating in a card game and was killed in a duel."

"Let me guess, the other man was identified as an American. Seems like the Colonel finally got a pistol with a straight barrel. Anything else?"

"The crew was upset because they were supposed to leave today, but now they have to wait until tonight with talk of replacing some of the cargo," Jane continued confidently.

"Well that settles it. Anyone think this isn't the ship we're looking for?" Pierce posed the question to everyone in the room. "Neither do I. Good work you two."

"So what's next, we wait for them to load the boat and then sink it?" Liam asked, looking hopefully between Pierce and MacDuff.

"I don't think it's that simple lad," MacDuff pointed out.

"I agree," Pierce concurred immediately. "There are too many unknowns involved; what if the entire shipment isn't on the boat, what if he's using multiple boats, what if it's a red herring? For us to succeed two things need to happen; Bufford needs to be apprehended and the weapons need to be destroyed."

"That's true; we can't take the chance that one of his men completes the mission. We also can't allow those modern weapons to simply float away and hope nobody makes use of them."

"So we carry on as before," Pierce continued, grateful for MacDuff's support and glad they were thinking along the same lines. "Jane and I attend the ball and watch Bufford. Sean and MacDuff watch the boat and see if those crates get delivered."

"What about me? Want me to play the dark stranger who crashes the party?" Liam offered hopefully.

"Not this time. I've got something special for you," Pierced laughed in response.

"Somehow your laugh is not inspiring confidence."

"We need a boat," Pierce instructed simply, to Liam's immediate confusion.

"Why do we need a boat?" asked Jane, equally confused.

"Who here knows how to sail a ship the size of the *Courted*

Anne?" MacDuff posed to those in the room, receiving only negative replies. "Let's say all the crates are loaded on the one boat and we're lucky enough to arrive before they sail. Let's also assume that we're able to overtake both Bufford's men and his new crew. How many are they?"

"Twenty give or take," Sean answered, slowly realizing the difficulties.

"So we defeat the twenty without taking any casualties," MacDuff continued seriously. "I'd wager that it will be noisy, so we'll probably have gendarmes and soldiers at the ship before we can take care of the entire crew. The only escape route available to us at that point is the *Courted Anne*. Which none of us can sail."

"Why go to all that violent trouble?" Jane demanded, feeling as though she had an easier solution. "Why don't we wait until the ship is loaded and simply blow a hole in the hull? I imagine you gentleman are proficient with all sorts of explosives."

"I'm very proficient in all kinds of things," Liam winked knowingly. "But it won't matter in this case. If we sink the ship in the harbour, it will have to be salvaged and raised, thereby leading to the discovery of the weapons. Sorry Duffy if you wanted to answer that one."

"I'm just glad you've finally caught up with us."

"So that's the goal," Pierce announced firmly. "The *Courted Anne* needs to have all the weapons on board and needs to be sunk outside of the harbour in deep water. The salt water will destroy the weapons before any divers could ever make use of them. Plus Bufford and his men need to be dealt with, either on the ship or before. So you're the experts, how do we accomplish this?"

The question hung in the air as the Brown Pack tackled the question posed by their leader. It was the kind of tactical exercise that energized these men, eager to solve any challenge. Their breadth of experience meant that they had encountered similar situations before and already had ideas that only required minor alterations.

"Did you pack the crossbow?" Liam asked Sean first, receiving a quick nod. "I'll find us a row boat or small skiff. We then modify one of the crossbow bolts and attached a long length of rope to it. We wait for the *Anne* in a narrow part of the harbour, shooting the bolt into the side as it passes. They unknowingly tow us out into the sea."

"That's good, but we'll only have one shot or they're gone."

"The sailors we talked to said they'd be sailing as soon as their cargo is finalized," Sean added positively. "That means at night, so we should be able to get close enough to take the shot without being seen. That also means we'll have a better than average chance at subduing the crew. We silently climb onto the ship from the stern and silently dispatch those on deck. Once they clear the port and they've fully dropped sails, few of the crew will remain on duty. The remainder will be below decks."

"Then it's the simple matter of dispatching Bufford and his men, verifying all the weapons are on board, scuttling the ship and escaping on our little boat."

"Nothing sounds simple about any of those things," Jane offered doubtfully.

"That is disturbing, though not altogether surprising," Lord Lodge replied evenly after hearing the news about Drummond's demise from Tiberius. They were seated in Lodge's study, an antique wooden desk filling the space between them. The desk was free of any papers, making it appear larger than it was. The same could be said for the room itself, the few pieces of furniture within it were covered in white canvas tarps to guard against dust. Apparently the staff had received news that Lord Lodge's return from his illness was tentative at best.

"I'm sorry sir, none of us thought he was suicidal."

"You thought he was too much a coward to take his own

life," Lodge stated with his usual amount of perception, receiving a stiff nod in reply. "It's not your fault; warriors such as yourself have a harder time understanding matters of the heart."

"You don't mean that he loved Cleaver? They weren't… I mean, they didn't…"

"No I very much doubt they were romantically involved," The Master of the Manor replied with a chuckle from Tiberius' obvious unease. "But Drummond was attracted to the power Cleaver held and was devoted to him for the power he received by association."

"It was no secret Cleaver was Drummond's benefactor," Tiberius allowed. "But I had hoped to use that against him. He was obviously left behind and might have been upset enough to tell us something."

"I wouldn't worry too much over what might have been. Drummond probably would have never told us anything, in the forlorn hope that Cleaver would return and reward him for his loyalty."

Tiberius could understand such loyalty as he looked across the table. It would take a significant amount of torture for him to turn against Lord Lodge if he were in a similar situation.

"But that's not all you came to tell me about was it?" Lodge inquired absently as he sorted through a desk drawer. With an exclamation of success he pulled out a long black pipe and tobacco pouch. He expertly filled and lit it as Tiberius began explaining the remainder of the news.

"I've sent the rest of the Black Pack, that is those I trust, to search for Cleaver, Malicio, and anyone else associated with them," Tiberius reported through the growing smoke. "They were split in three and sent to the Crow's Nest, Harrow's End, and the Black Loch. I had hoped one of the groups would come upon their trail."

Lodge merely continued smoking in reply, hardly moving a muscle. From anyone else Tiberius would have found this reaction disconcerting, however he was used to Lord Lodge and knew he wouldn't utter an extraneous word until everything was presented to him.

"But something has come up that makes me think the situation is more complex than before," he continued without waiting for a response. "None of the horses are missing from the stable, neither the ones for riding nor the coach horses. They could have presumably set out on foot, but they'd have to know we'd track them down before they got anywhere safe. From your search of his office we have already determined that Cleaver has left the Manor without plans to return in the near future. So the question is where are they?"

"Indeed and when are they?" Lodge uttered thoughtfully after slowly removing the pipe from his mouth.

"Sir?"

"You said there are no horses missing and you made a good argument against them leaving on foot. So what does that leave? They've escaped through one of the portals in the North Tower."

"But that's not possible," Tiberius immediately dismissed the possibility with hollow conviction. "Is it?"

"It's the only solution that fits the facts."

"But none of the portal keys in Drummond's office are missing."

"Cleaver made copies."

"We would have known," Tiberius offered lamely, his sense of unease growing. Intellectually he knew that Lodge was right, but a part of him wanted to cling to the possibility of another option. He needed an alternative that could easily explain their disappearance and could be dealt with just as easily. But no such answer emerged in his mind, only the knowledge that the portals were indeed the only possible means of their escape. His heart sank at the prospect before them. "They could be anywhere."

"I'm afraid so. Plus with their knowledge and disposition, they could wreak havoc wherever they end up. This is very grave news indeed."

Both men sat in static silence, much like the few pieces of furniture that dotted the large study. On the final leg of their journey to the Manor, Tiberius had actually been optimistic about the future of life at the Manor. He knew there would be a fight with Dr. Cleaver and his cronies, but believed it would have been short and final. With their triumph he and Lodge along with the others could have reformed the Manor and ended the bloodthirsty hunts that dominated their lives. He'd have time to spend in the pursuit of more constructive and pleasing activities. The face of an auburn haired beauty sprung to the forefront of his mind.

But he knew that this would never be possible with Cleaver and his men running rabid throughout time. Although Lord Lodge was the Master of the Manor, he knew that he'd play a leading role in the hunt for the rogue member. He accepted this in silent determination like he'd always done, ever the obedient and trustworthy soldier.

"I'll let the search of the island run its course, in case we're wrong," Tiberius suggested, calmly rising from his seat. "In the meantime I'll have my men and some of the staff search the Manor. Just to make sure they've left."

Lord Lodge remained silent and motionless except for the small puffs he took from his pipe, a smoky shroud beginning to envelope him. His steely eyes pierced the smoke and focused on a myriad of possibilities that only a mind as powerful as his could see. Tiberius quietly left the room without another word, despite knowing that he couldn't have broken Lodge's concentration if he tried.

Morgan, Dufresne, and three others were waiting for him in the hall outside Lodge's office. Tiberius knew and trusted the others and was glad for the increased numbers. The vastness of the Manor would have been almost impossible to search properly with only three. It would still be difficult with six, however he planned to collect a group of footmen, groundskeepers, and groomsmen to further divide the job ahead.

"I just spoke to Lord Lodge and he knows the situation," Tiberius briefed the men as they travelled down the hall towards a staircase that would take them to the servant's area below. "The cursory search of the island will continue in the off chance that they left the Manor grounds on foot. Meanwhile we will organize a search of the Manor itself. We all know there are enough nooks and crannies in this place where a person could hide for a week. But I'm not confident we'll turn up anything."

"What do we do if they're actually here?" Morgan asked as they reached the basement. Tiberius stopped and looked around in a conspiratorial way, waiting for a pair of kitchen maids to pass.

"If we find them," he began with quiet intensity, the words shooting out between gritted teeth. "We give them a warning to drop their weapons and then we shoot them in the face."

"Don't you mean or shoot them in the face?"

"No. I'm tired of these evil bastards running around. This ends once and for all."

Chapter 28

As the carriage lurched along the cobble stoned streets, it was all he could do to refrain from staring at his companion within. Two failed attempts at taking a casual glimpse had already ended with him practically ogling her. So Pierce grudgingly resorted to simply looking out his window onto the darkened street beyond in order to save himself from further embarrassment.

The first embarrassing event occurred earlier in the evening as he waited by the door of the safe house, pacing in a suit Melrose had packed for him. Despite the subtle dark hues of the clothing, the richness of the fabric and expertise of the tailoring displayed his supposed wealth more than any extravagant costume could.

He peered out the front door window as the carriage pulled up, driven by Sean, with Liam riding beside him. He briefly wondered where they found an appropriate carriage in such short notice, but then thought better of it and appreciated their scrounging skills in contented ignorance. The sound of footsteps descending the stairs brought his attention back to the hall and he turned around to inform Jane that the carriage was ready for them. But rather than the pretty but reserved house maid that travelled with them through the portal, a refined and elegant woman was returning his gaze. A flowing black and silver gown, along with elbow length silver gloves, displayed her impressive physical attributes perfectly. Her hair was up in the current fashion and held in place with a pair of silver combs shaped like laurel leaves. She had taken the classical style of the current period and had transformed into a Greek goddess. Pierce's cane and jaw dropped instantly in unison, much to his *wife's* amusement and delight.

"You've dropped your cane sir," MacDuff offered as he approached with Jane's elegant silk shawl. "You look fantastic my lady."

"Thank you MacDuff, but there's no need for that lady nonsense. You've all been more than kind already."

"I wasn't just being kind. You've got to get into character. A Countess has no need to be grateful," MacDuff instructed gently. "You expect preferential treatment at all times."

"Very good, open the door and let's be off," Pierce ordered shortly, trying to regain his composure as he took Jane's hand.

The drive from the safe house to the harbour was short, much to Pierce's relief. Although he had changed a great deal since his arrival at the Manor, he'd just discovered that some things had stayed the same. Shooting another quick glance at Jane sitting beside him he realised that he was a tongue tied mess when faced with women. The more attractive they were, the worse it seemed to be.

With the setting of the sun, the port bared little resemblance to the dirty bustling place of trade from earlier in the day. The workman and stevedores had returned to their homes and those sailors not on duty had escaped to enjoy the lively local establishments. The ships' lanterns twinkled like nearby stars in the harbour, while the lack of electrical light only amplified the power of the true stars above. The moon was not yet full, but still shone brightly in the clear night sky.

The hotel was brighter still, with all of the windows alight and a series of flaming torches out front. A mass of people crowded out front; those lucky enough to have invitations, and those simply happy with observing the party from a distance.

The carriage followed the road along the harbour front, slowing noticeably as it entered the queue of similar carriages disgorging their wealthy riders at the front door of the hotel. There were more than a dozen such carriages in front of them, slowing their progress so that Pierce found himself watching those on foot pass them. Many were couples dressed in their finest, presumably attending the ball as well.

As the carriage inched closer to the hotel, Pierce felt a trembling hand latch on to his. Surprised he looked over and could sense the nerves Jane was desperately trying to contain. The intimidating woman from the staircase had disappeared, but so too had the dutiful servant. He suddenly realised that he was looking at the real Jane for the first time, stripped of the masks she wore for others. He was instantly enamoured and completely at ease with her.

"You're going to be fine," he soothed, lifting her hand and gently kissing the top of it. Much to his relief, a smile broke out across her face. "You're beautiful."

He'd been physically attracted to her from their first brief encounter in Drummond's office, what seemed like a lifetime ago. That attraction had still remained after he overheard her with Cleaver; she was an attractive woman after all, but her appeal had dropped significantly. Pierce had felt he could not trust her, and no amount of beauty could overturn that. But even after Lodge had informed him of her true allegiance, which he believed, something had still felt false about her. Even on the drive to the hotel, when he couldn't keep his eyes off her, he'd felt an inkling of doubt about her in his mind. She wasn't fake or deceitful, but there was something about her bearing that he felt was odd. Now he realized that she'd been putting on an act, trying to appear worldly and confident in the company of the Brown Pack in order to gain their acceptance.

Pierce looked at the real Jane for the first time, the lights from the hotel casting shadows within the carriage. He realized now that she'd hidden herself with chameleon-like ability with projections of what others expected. It was a defence mechanism that he understood all too well himself. But now her true self had escaped and he was enthralled by the excitement, anxiety, fear, and determination that she was now freely displaying. More importantly the look she returned to him seemed to mirror his feelings exactly. For a split second he completely forgot about the Manor, Bufford, Cleaver, Lodge, and everything else outside the carriage.

The sudden stop of the carriage broke the brief moment of respite from duty and the job at hand was once more at the forefront. Without thinking it, they both replaced their open emotional masks and became the characters on the invitation card. They heard Liam drop down from his perch in the back and walk over to the door.

"Are you ready to do this?" Pierce asked, still holding her hand.

She leaned over and gave him a quick kiss on the lips, and then smiling gave him a wink in reply. Pierce wanted nothing better than to grab her and return the favour, but Liam opened the door and was helping Jane out of the carriage before he could act.

There was no red carpet filling the distance between the carriage and the hotel entrance, but that didn't diminish the atmosphere outside. Some of the lesser attendees were lined up patiently with their invitations in hand, eagerly watching those descending from the carriages. Away from the main doors groups of young people stared wistfully through the hotel windows, imagining themselves inside.

If they'd been in Hollywood, Pierce had no doubt that Jane would have attracted every camera in the area and they would have been blinded by the flashes. As it was a collective gasp of envy and desire was let out as they gracefully walked past the crowd towards the front door. Both cut a fine figure in their luxurious black and silver clothing.

Liam fell in step behind them as Sean drove the carriage away. He held the invitation like the dutiful servant he portrayed and merely waved it at the doormen as they approached. The doormen were examining the invitations of those who'd arrived on foot like ill-tempered border guards.

But those rich enough to arrive by carriage were merely waved through to the next level of security.

A tall sparse man in a dark suit greeted them mechanically and asked for their invitation without raising his eyes from the clipboard in his hands. When none immediately appeared he looked up with brief annoyance, quickly replaced by charm as he saw the elegant duo before him. Pierce did not even react to this display, like the cultured aristocrat he was playing, merely raised his hand and snapped his finger.

Liam nearly ran around them and presented the invitation to the greeter, leaving as soon as it was delivered. The man only glanced at it briefly before calling a liveried footman over. He handed the invitation over to the servant, resplendent in crimson and gold and topped with a white wig.

The lobby was decorated with the same colours as the footman and acted as an assembly area for those removing outerwear and other's waiting to make their entrance to the ballroom beyond. The rise and fall of numerous voices crashed like waves within the space, practically drowning out the music from the ballroom beyond. Patrick and Jane followed the footman across the busy lobby, pretending to be oblivious to the stares their passage was drawing. He led them to a counter where a second footman expertly caught Pierce's thrown swordstick, before helping remove their jacket and shawl.

"Does his lordship wish to have any refreshments before entering?" the footman politely asked in French after they'd finished, pointing to the bar across the room.

"Certainement, deux champagnes." Pierce replied in kind. Without waiting for a response he took Jane's hand and led her to an unoccupied salon chair in the middle of the waiting area. Despite the continual arrival of new people into the lobby, Pierce noticed that they continued to attract the most attention from those around them.

"Do you see him or any of his men?" Pierce whispered after they sat down.

"No I don't," Jane replied as she casually scanned the room. Despite the number of people in the lobby, there didn't appear to be any alcoves where someone could hide.

Their drinks arrived swiftly and the footmen remained with them, albeit at a discreet distance. Both had to refrain from shooting their champagne back in an effort to calm their nerves. Everything had gone well so far, but that wasn't easing the tension building within each of them. Nevertheless they slowly sipped their drinks, watching the new arrivals with practiced disinterest. Within a few minutes their glasses were empty and Pierce merely raised his hand and nonchalantly signalled for another round to the footman assigned to them.

These drinks arrived even faster than the first and Pierce could tell the footman was trying to display his worth. Sensing an opportunity to collect an ally, Pierce dropped a gold coin on the footman's silver serving tray as he collected the empty glasses. The servant displayed his tactful professionalism by not reacting to the tip with excitement or shock. He simply nodded with a slight shift of the head.

"I have a request for you," Pierce began after motioning for the footman to come closer. "I'm planning on meeting someone tonight, but I don't want to ignore my lovely wife while I run around looking for him."

"Perhaps I could keep an eye out and fetch you if I find him?"

"My thoughts exactly. He's new to Marseille so his name will be useless to you. But he'll be easy to spot, he's American," Pierce continued, providing a physical description of Colonel Bufford. "One coin, when you tell me he's arrived and another to direct me to him. But don't bring him to me, I don't wish to trouble the Countess with his presence. Understood."

The footman nodded solemnly and left to return the empty glasses to the bar before retaking his position near them.

"You *are* good at this, my Count," Jane whispered as she leaned closer to him.

"I'm not so sure, everyone's still looking at us," he replied cautiously. "I can understand their attention to you, you're a knock-out in that outfit, but I feel like my disguise is wearing thin. It's easy to trick a footman with money, but some of the other guests might not be so easily fooled."

"For such a smart man you can be so clueless" Jane laughed hollowly. "It's been my experience that rich people are easier to trick with money than us mere servants."

"Oh… I forgot…" Pierce muttered quietly, embarrassed by his choice of words. "I'm sorry."

"I'm just teasing, I know you didn't mean it like that," she smiled brightly. "But you don't realize how good you really are at this. You've got this whole place fooled. When I first met you in Drummond's office I didn't know what to make of you. You were a blank sheet, indecipherable compared to the other members of the Hunt. But over time that changed, you've changed."

"Changed how?"

"You might not have noticed how you've changed, since it's much easier to tell from the outside looking in. I hadn't seen you for weeks while I was with Lord Lodge, so I was shocked by the change when you and MacDuff showed up at my room. You weren't the Lord Pierce I'd last seen at the pub, but at the same time you were him, but more so. It's hard to explain, but I feel like you've evolved to become the man you were supposed to be. Not some mindless killer and not some timid bureaucrat. Does that make sense?"

"I guess," he allowed slowly. "I mean, I've developed some new skills since arriving at the Manor. Plus I feel a little more confident after everything we've been through so far."

"Either you're being modest or you have no sense or yourself," Jane retorted to his lame response. "Either way, stop it. Do you know who you reminded me of when you planned our strategy against Colonel Bufford, or when we exited the carriage and arrived here? And sitting there now with such poise?"

Pierce merely looked at her blankly, careful to remain in character as they sat in the lobby full of strangers. He had always blended in to his environment when he wanted to avoid attention from others. But their current cover did not allow for this now, and he felt terribly exposed and uncomfortable as the center of attention.

"You remind me of Lord Lodge," Jane stated shrewdly. "Sure, everyone around here noticed me first, look at what I'm wearing. But the reason they continue to look this way after eyeing my bust line is that they feel the presence of a powerful man."

"But this is an act."

"Great men are powerful because they command attention and respect without trying. Look at how the Brown Pack reacts to your instructions. They all have more experience, skills, and ability than you. But they follow your orders without question."

These thoughts had been lurking at the back of Pierce's mind for some time, but finally surfaced through Jane's persistence. He looked beyond Jane and swept the room with his eyes, noticing more than a few people looking his way with curiosity, admiration, and respect. The truth of Jane's statement both surprised him and filled him with a confidence he'd never known.

Without thinking he leaned over and placed a passionate kiss on Jane's lips. Short enough to be acceptable in their surroundings, but long enough to show his gratitude, confidence, and to show her it wasn't part of the act.

"Shall we enter then, Countess?" he gestured gallantly, rising first and then holding his hand down to her. She happily accepted it and rose to meet him.

From their seats, both had noticed that some of the attendees were announced before entering the ball. They were the rich and influential patrons of the party, the same people who had arrived by carriage like them. The less ostentatious party goers seemed to slink past the announcer, simply happy to gain admittance.

Jane and Pierce crossed the lobby once again, aiming for a doorway flanked by two footmen. As they approached, the music grew louder and a mass of moving figures could be seen beyond. They lined up behind two well dressed couples at the doorway, noticing that it opened up to a small landing overlooking the ballroom. Their footman had discreetly followed their progress across the lobby and had carefully passed them at the doorway to deliver their invitation to the announcer.

Like most balls of importance, a caller was placed at the entrance to announce the arrival of distinguished guests. The names were called in a loud monotonous voice, largely ignored by those present. However it made the people beside the caller feel important and added a regal ambience to the evening.

The two couples before them were the exact target of such flattery; being the honourable Mr. and Mrs. So-and-so. However when Pierce and Jane elegantly stepped onto the landing with dignified indifference, a few people actually took notice. When their names were announced, it sent a minor shockwave through the crowd.

"The Count and Countess of Monte Cristo!" announced the caller with somewhat more verve than usual.

*

From a dark, damp, and dirty alleyway they watched Bufford and his men exit a tavern close to where the *Courted Anne* was moored. A developing mist from the harbour shrouded their feet, making their gliding progress seem ethereal. The four dark spectral shapes moved silently under the faint glow of nearby street lamps, eventually disappearing towards the brightly lit hotel on the other side of the port.

"Well that's the whole Grey Pack," Sean whispered after they had left. "Looks like they were able to bust Ivan out after all."

"Aye."

"I wonder if they're staying at that tavern," Sean mused after a few moments silence. "We could probably pop in and check their room, see if there's anything useful inside."

"If you were Liam I'd think you were trying to get a drink. But that's not a bad idea. We've probably got some time to kill before the shipment arrives and it's loaded on the ship."

"Plus a change of scenery wouldn't go amiss," Sean sniffed and shivered in agreement.

"Aye."

They gladly left the alley and walked across the street to the ramshackle tavern that sat on the harbour front. The building had no doubt initially been a shipping office or something respectable, made of stone and solidly built. However its fall into disrepute was not measured by what had fallen off the building, but by what had been added. A series of additions made of rough wood timbers and planking jutted out from the sides and the second floor, doubling the original building in size. They had already passed similarly built establishments that marked the increased prosperity of the port, and the subsequent need to alleviate the endless thirst of the sailors who brought it.

The dim flicker of lamps and the sound of drunken revellers escaped through the tavern's thick grimy windows as they approached, momentarily distracting them from the prone body stretched out beneath the sill. They sidestepped the drunk at the last minute, forcing a slight detour to the front entrance. This proved lucky a moment later as the solid wooden door forcefully swung open, disgorging another drunken body onto the street.

A myriad of sounds and smells greeted the two members of the Brown Pack as they entered the tavern and walked across the sawdust covered floor. Stale wine and beer fought for prominence with smoke and sweat. Sean and MacDuff were no strangers to this sort of establishment and easily altered their behaviour to fit in. The large room was filled with boisterous men and women, fuelled by booze and the music of a fiddler and an accordion player by the fireplace. Servers circled tables that were filled with singers, story tellers, and gamblers.

"Nice place, let's get a drink first to blend in," MacDuff suggested as they approached an opening along the utilitarian bar. This was not the type of place with mirrors or polished oak.

"What does his Lordship want now?" huffed an older women in a dirty apron as she poured a drink from behind the bar. Much to the surprise of both men, she was addressing them in a quick cockney accent.

"His Lordship?" Sean asked quizzically, wondering if she was actually speaking to them.

"You're one of his men aren't you? You're dressed just like the rest."

"Don't mind him, lass, he's a bit slow," MacDuff offered, quickly realizing that she was talking about Bufford. Both had changed into their long brown hunt uniforms, which were almost identical to the grey ones worn by Bufford's pack.

"A Scotsman is it?" She asked, clearly taken with the large rugged man before her.

"*Scotsmen* and we've come for his luggage. But I suppose we've time for a wee drink first."

She flashed him a toothy smile and turned around to the bottles lined up behind her. While searching for the right bottle, she undid the top button on her shirt and plumped up her bosom with both hands. These were then replaced by a dark green bottle and a pair of glasses.

"A taste of home," she winked, pouring the golden liquid into both glasses.

They each sipped it, unwilling to waste the well aged Scotch. It was indeed the taste of home, the smoky peat almost slapping them across the face with its flavour.

"Another for me and have one yourself," MacDuff saluted after draining his glass and throwing a couple coins on the table. "That'll give us something do while the young one here fetches the bags."

The barmaid took Sean's glass with delight and refilled it along with MacDuff's. After a quick cheers, they each took a sip, heedless of Sean's continued presence beside them.

"Which room then?" Sean interrupted after clearing his throat.

"Number 5, second right at the top of the stairs," She replied, carelessly handing him the key while her eyes remained locked on MacDuff.

Sean smiled to himself, glad that he didn't have the job of charming the aging barmaid. He even had to stifle a laugh after he turned to the stairs and overheard MacDuff continue his task. *So what's a London lass like you doing in a place like this?*

Walking up the main staircase, Sean could tell that it belonged to the original building. It was wide and sturdy, providing a good view of the main bar below. However a few steps after reaching the top, the craftsmanship dropped considerably. Lights from the rooms below shone through gaps between the floorboards, private rooms from the sounds that were emanating. Well this place might as well be a brothel too, he thought.

He reached a door with a crooked 5 on it without trouble. The key slid into the door easily, but took some jiggling to turn until he heard a click. But when he took the key out he noticed a single strand of hair stuck across the door and door frame. Sean immediately stopped opening the door and took a quicker look at the hair. It only took him a second to figure out it hadn't simply fallen there, but had been put in place deliberately. Strands of hair had long been used by operatives to let them know when their doors, drawers, or chests had been tampered with. With a simple lick, human hair could be easily stuck to hard surfaces and would remain until disturbed.

Sean took a mental note to replace the hair when he was finished his search, and to keep vigilant for more tricks left behind. He cautiously opened the door, wondering how far the Grey Pack would go in safeguarding their room. Based on Bufford's normal demeanour he wouldn't have been surprised to find some large bear traps strewn across the floor.

But nothing as blatant as that greeted Sean when he carefully entered the humble room. He was actually shocked that Bufford was staying in such a dreary place. Three small beds with rough blankets were lined against the far wall with a pair of heavy wooden chairs on the opposite side, underneath dirty crooked windows. A dark wooden travel trunk was the only other piece of furniture in the room and didn't seem like it was part of the décor, immediately grabbing his attention.

A quick inspection of the case revealed another hair across a solid brass latch. A second latch had a lock built into it with a small keyhole in the middle. Sean reached into his jacket and removed the tools of the trade for any respectable thief.

Although picking the lock would be no problem, Sean had seen this type before, doing it covertly might. The latch face was polished brass and there were no scratches or scuffs on it, making any mistake with his tools completely noticeable to the owner.

Sean's steady hands went to work, opening the lock cover and then feeling inside for the mechanism with his delicate tools. Despite his experience, it was not an easy task. Hunched over the case, both hands had to work in unison feeling rather than seeing, the tools acting like extensions of his fingers.

Despite the age of the case, Sean could tell the lock was more advanced than it appeared. Locks of the current period were simplistic, some batches produced with the same key so as to be interchangeable. But this lock had more modern aspects to it, forcing him to work harder than he'd expected to. But within a few minutes the lock yielded with a satisfying click.

To use such a lock on a simple case had to mean that whatever was inside was important. Buoyed by this knowledge and from the success of picking a difficult lock, Sean opened the case with unusual eagerness. He flipped the lid open hoping to see something significant or valuable.

But to his instant shock and horror, Sean only saw a trip wire snapping as the lid fully opened and slammed against the wall.

Chapter 29

MacDuff innocently walked up the staircase amid the riotous crowd of the tavern, despite being the cause of the chaos below. He'd spotted some of the sailors from the *Courted Anne* as Sean had walked up the stairs. Sensing an opportunity to potentially disrupt Colonel Bufford's plan, he'd immediately sprung into action. A few more coins to the bartender sent a few bottles of rum their way, despite their existing drunkenness. The bottles were greeted in the spirit of most sailors, with sheer delight and gleeful ignorance as to the source.

MacDuff then spotted another group of sailors in a similarly dishevelled state of inebriation. The difference was that this group had a pair of women at their table, who were probably a convenient mixture of server and prostitute. He watched one of them accept a coin from one of the burly sailors at the table and approach the bar, taking the spot recently vacated by Sean. She passed the coin across and asked for another cheap bottle of booze, receiving no change with it. She accepted the bottle with muttered grumblings about cheap sailors.

With a smile, MacDuff placed two silver coins in front of her before she could leave. She looked up in surprise and immediately displayed a delightful demeanour. MacDuff told her to take the coins and bring her friend over to the crew of the *Anne*. She hesitated for only a moment before noticing that they had plenty of booze and she could keep all of the cash. With a new bounce in her step she grabbed the cheap bottle, signalled her friend, and then joined the new table.

Harsh words were immediately exchanged between the two tables, the two women, and then the bouncers. A fight broke out between the two crews by the time MacDuff reached the stairs. He knew it would envelop the entire tavern by the time he entered Bufford's room, and hoped some of the *Anne's* sailors would end up too hurt to rejoin their ship.

He didn't even bother to see if anyone was watching him as he opened the door to room 5, sure that everyone was either trying to join or escape the fight raging below. He opened the door casually and was about to ask Sean what was taking him so long, but stopped before he could ask.

Sean was simply sitting in front of an opened travel trunk, his eyes fixed in place and his body completely motionless. MacDuff closed the door quietly behind him and gingerly walked over to him.

"What's going on lad?"

"It didn't go off."

"What didn't?"

"The bomb didn't. I can't believe it didn't go off," Sean mumbled into the opened trunk. "I think I just saw my life flash before my eyes."

"You're not making much sense Sean," MacDuff replied calmly before gingerly grabbing his shoulder.

The small amount of human contact seemed to shock Sean back into the current world, eliciting a slow shake of the head and few blinks to clear his vision.

"Sorry MacDuff," he apologized groggily, as if just waking up. "I messed up, but they messed up worse. See this wire by the inside latch?"

MacDuff merely nodded, confused and intrigued by his man's current state.

"Well there's another one on the lid. It was actually one

piece of wire. A trip wire. Well, I snapped it when I opened the lid. I just flung it open like some kid at Christmas. A second after it snapped I heard the click of a detonator, or something like that, and I swear I saw my life flash before me; my parents, friends, the Highlands, Culloden, the Manor, everything."

"But you're still here."

"They forgot to arm the booby-trap. See this small metal attachment? You're supposed to drop some gunpowder in it, creating an explosion when triggered. Luckily for me they forgot."

MacDuff nodded in reply, thankful that Sean was still with him and doubly thankful that their quarry seemed to be slipping. "Anything good inside the trunk?"

"Honestly I haven't moved a muscle since I heard the wire snap."

"Well let's have a look inside," MacDuff rubbed his hands together in anticipation. A booby-trapped trunk usually offered something important.

A quick search turned up nothing useful to their purposes; some clothes, blank parchment and quills, and some other odds and ends. They were about to put everything back, when Sean leaned into the trunk and started scraping the bottom.

"Hurry up if you've found something," MacDuff ordered as the sounds from below started to get even louder and smoke began seeping through the cracks in the floor.

"What's going on down there?" Sean asked as he sat back up triumphantly holding an envelope.

"I might have started a bar brawl in the attempt to get some of the sailors from the *Anne* injured or arrested."

Sean smiled at his mentor and started to carefully open the envelope as MacDuff went back to the door and peered out into the hall. He was shocked to see two large men with equally large clubs running up the stairs

"Matron said the bastard who instigated the fight went up here," the larger one breathlessly informed his companion in French.

"There he is!" yelled the second one seeing the door to

number 5 cracked open. They both sprinted at the door but were unable to reach it before MacDuff slammed it shut.

"Time to get moving!" MacDuff called as he locked the door from the inside. The handle immediately started turning frantically as the goons on the other side tried to get in.

"We're not getting out through the windows," Sean reported from the far side of the room. The two grimy windows were more like portholes and though this might make the sailors feel more at home, they were poorly designed for emergency exits.

Realizing that the door was locked, the men outside put their shoulders into it in an effort to knock it down. Evaluating the workmanship of the room, MacDuff realized it wouldn't hold more than a few solid knocks. He motioned for Sean to grab one of the heavy wooden chairs, while he removed a pistol from inside his jacket and stood against the wall beside the door.

The door flew open with a thunderous crash and the two large bouncers bulled their way in. Prepared for their entrance, Sean immediately swung the chair in his hands across the face of the larger one who was in the lead. The chair splintered on impact, stunning the recipient long enough for Sean to take a second shot with the remaining pieces.

As the first bouncer went down, his companion raised his club with a shout. But before he could take a step towards Sean, the man heard the distinctive click of a cocked pistol and felt the cold steel of a barrel placed against the back of his head.

"Drop the club lad," MacDuff ordered from behind, shoving him across the room after he conceded.

"What are we going to do with him?" Sean whispered as he picked up the club and stood beside MacDuff.

"Shoot him I suppose," MacDuff shrugged in reply, eliciting a sudden wave of fear upon the man on the bed. But their attention suddenly shifted upon hearing a loud crash from below and an increase of smoke seeping up through the floor. "Have a quick look out the door; I've got a bad feeling."

"The bloody place is on fire!" Sean shouted from the hall, seeing flames licking up the wall behind the bar on the level below.

"Today's you're lucky day," MacDuff smiled as he lowered the pistol from the bouncer on the bed. "Take your buddy and get out of here. Being burnt alive is a fate I'd not wish on anyone and I've only got one shot left."

Despite the wave of relief upon their prisoners face, MacDuff kept his pistol ready and walked backwards out of the room. Sean was still in the hallway, looking at the fiery scene from the top of the stairs.

"We're not getting out that way," he said pointing to the front door, now fully engulfed.

"There's got to be a room up here with bigger windows we can get out of. If not we'll make some of our own, most of the walls are pretty thin."

They set off down the hallway at a quick jog, peering into opened rooms as they passed. The first few were similar to room number 5, with small porthole type windows. Amid the thickening smoke and noise within the tavern they almost didn't notice that the hallway took a strange angle and the floor seemed to droop. Initially fearful that the rooms underneath were on fire and ready to give out, they quickly realized they'd reached the rickety additions of the building.

"In here!" MacDuff yelled through a handkerchief covering his mouth, as he entered a room at the end of the hallway. Unlike the other rooms this one was empty; with an obviously uneven floor and a large window. The workmanship was so shoddy that the gaps in the walls were actually helping ventilate the space.

Sean joined MacDuff by the window and together they not only opened it, but shoved it entirely out of the frame. Eagerly taking breaths of fresh air, they watched the descent of the window with surprise as it splashed into the harbour below. The room they now occupied was actually overhanging the dock, thirty feet directly over the water.

"I hope the tide's not going out," Sean observed as they

both swung a leg over the window sill.

"Too late now," MacDuff countered as they both crossed themselves and leapt out into the cold night.

*

"Isn't Monte Cristo a small island without any inhabitants?" inquired the Comte d'Arras, a thin aristocratic looking man with an equally thin moustache. The question was posed with more inquisitiveness than disparagement, in an honest effort to learn more about the mysterious guest. The small group surrounding them leaned in to hear the response, as they were all similarly intrigued.

"Ha, ha, indeed it is," the Count laughed easily in response, taking a sip of his drink before continuing. "There's nothing but sheep and wind on that small rock of an island, to be perfectly honest. The title was bestowed on my Great Grand Father as an insulting joke by a jealous Monarch. Although I think my ancestors and I have had the last laugh."

Everyone laughed in agreement, clearly seeing the wealth of the Count and by the beautiful Countess draped on his arm.

"Tell me your Grace, why haven't we seen you in Marseille before?" asked Madame Dutours, the artificially attractive wife of the army colonel commanding the local garrison. Her husband owed his advancement to his political connections and his wife's socializing, so they were regulars on the cocktail scene.

"We've actually just returned from the orient," Pierce explained vaguely, hoping that it would be sufficient enough to avoid elaborating. He figured that he knew enough about Japan or China to bluff his way past people without televisions or the internet.

"Ahh," accepted the crowd with a mixture of admiration, approval, and some jealousy.

"Darling we've hardly danced at all tonight," reproached Jane playfully, trying to disengage themselves from the growing crowd surrounding them.

"You're right me dear, I've been too busy boring these fine people," Pierce admonished himself with a wink, earning laughing disagreement from everyone. Pierce took Jane's fluted champagne glass and placed it beside his on the tray of a passing footman, freeing his hand to lead her towards the crowded dance floor.

Luckily a slow melodic song was playing, one that didn't require changing partners or specific movements. Neither of them knew the current dances and wanted to keep the illusion of their sophistication.

"So far so good," he whispered to her has they joined in the revolving queue of dancers spiralling around the dance floor. "How are you doing?"

"Me? Fine but it's simple for me, I'm just the eye candy." she replied coquettishly batting eyelashes.

"Well you're filling that role admirably," Pierce acknowledged, catching the quick glimpses of men they passed.

"Are you flirting with me?"

"That depends," Pierce deferred more casually than he felt. "Is it working?"

Jane merely smiled and continued dancing, truly content for the first time in ages. The hotel ballroom had been decorated in opulent splendour; crimson and gold fabric flowed from the ceiling and crystal chandeliers filled the room with sparkling light. Long tables followed the windowed walls looking out onto the harbour beyond and were creaking from the weight of bottles, bowls, and trays of delicious food.

"You can almost forget we're tracking a crazed madman bent on changing the history of the world," Pierce observed, agreeing with the look he read off Jane's happy face.

"Almost," She agreed, and then quickly refocused on the task at hand. "We should move up to one of the tables on the gallery above."

Pierce followed her gaze upwards as they rotated again, shooting a quick glance to the ballroom gallery. Staircases at either end wound up to the second floor dining area opposite the large windows of the ballroom. Tables and chairs were laid out for those wishing to take a break and rest their feet and indulge in some of the fine food provided. It would be the perfect perch to observe the whole room.

The song they were dancing to ended a few minutes later to appreciative applause. Hand in hand they walked towards the closest staircase with poise, the crowd parting naturally for them to pass, like two sharks passing through a school of fish. The comparison made Pierce smile slightly, as they were indeed predators on the hunt.

A waiter at the top of the stairs immediately guided them to a small table by the railing, offering a direct view to the party below. He helped Jane into her seat before taking Pierce's order. Just as before, a small tray of food and bottle of champagne appeared with impressive speed.

"I seem to have hurt my knee while on the dance floor, nothing serious," Pierce told the waiter as he poured their drinks. "Have one of the footmen fetch my walking stick." The waiter nodded professionally and marched off to fulfill the order.

"You weren't limping on the stairs up," Jane noted with slight confusion, worried that they had developed a setback.

"I'm fine," he reassured her conspiratorially. "But I want to have my walking stick with me. Bufford should be making his appearance at any moment and I feel a little naked without it."

"It's certainly a very impressive accessory, but what's so special about it?"

"It's got a sharp surprise within it," Pierce replied cryptically as a footman approached with it in his hands. He accepted it gratefully and flipped the servant a coin for his effort, much to the footman's delight. Once they were alone, Pierce carefully checked to make sure the stick was actually his own. After hearing the quiet click, the handle turned and he pulled it back, revealing a sliver of the sharp blade. Satisfied that it hadn't been switched, he closed it and leaned it against the table.

"Now that is impressive," Jane saluted with her drink,

having never seen a similar weapon before.

"Any sign of Bufford or our footman?" Pierce asked as he took his own glass and peered over the railing.

"Nothing so far," Jane replied after looking around for herself. "You don't think the whole ball thing is a ruse do you? Some sort of red sardine provided to throw us off the scent?"

"Red sardine? Pierce repeated in confusion before letting out a small chuckle. "Oh you mean a red herring! A fake clue is called a red herring."

"Whatever it's called, there's a possibility he won't even show up," she retorted, trying hard to hide her embarrassment.

"I very much doubt it. He needs to meet with the ship owner to get his cargo loaded and a party like this is the perfect place for a discreet meeting. Plus Bufford wouldn't have gone through the trouble of digging a tunnel between the hotel and the building next door if he had no intention of coming here."

"You're right," Jane nodded, having forgotten about the tunnel. "It's just the longer we wait the more nervous I feel."

"It was a good thought," he reassured her with what he hoped was a calming smile. "Don't worry I'm nervous too. But that's good; it means we'll be careful."

They continued their vigil with few words spoken between them. They picked away at some of the food at their table and took tiny sips of their drinks, unwilling to succumb to the influence of the alcohol but wanting to remain in character. Eventually they saw their footman enter the room below, walking the length of the floor attempting to find the Count of Monte Cristo.

It took all of Pierce's patience to calmly sit and wait for the footman to find them and not stand up and frantically wave him over. He could feel the tension and excitement rising within him as their messenger climbed the nearby staircase.

"Well here we go," Pierce muttered to himself, unsure on how the rest of the night would play out. He looked over to Jane, still stunning in her evening gown and realized he had another reason to succeed tonight.

*

The sound of instruments and revellers slowly faded as they walked up a staircase that branched off from the hotel lobby. Pierce kept a straight face as a couple quickly descended past them. From the satisfied look on the man's face and the slightly embarrassed one on the companion, Pierce could tell they were returning from a secret assignation in one of the rooms above.

The footman led him to a hallway on the second level that overlooked the lobby, much less populated than when he and Jane had first arrived. Presumably the hour was late enough that people no longer had to wait to make an entrance to the ballroom.

"I don't understand it," the footman looked around slightly confused. "I followed the man you're looking for when he arrived. He came up the same stairs as we did and was smoking a cigar from this very balcony."

"Well he's not here now," Pierce replied, deliberately putting the gold coin in his hand back into his vest pocket.

"But I was only gone for a moment when I went to fetch you," muttered the footman to himself. "The only place he could really go from here is the manager's office further down the hall."

Pierce looked down a hallway that ran perpendicular to where they now stood, unsure on how to proceed. It was not very long and appeared to only have two doors leading off it, providing no cover in case Bufford were to emerge. Despite being confident he'd discovered Bufford's goals in Marseille, Pierce knew he couldn't risk discovery at this stage. There might be something he missed and needed to monitor the Colonel as covertly as possible to be sure.

However the footman could only think of the gold coin that was in Pierce's pocket, so he took off down the hall. Before Pierce could stop him, he'd tried the door handles at each door. Both were locked and the footman's shoulder's drooped in disappointment.

"The night is not over," breathed Pierce with faked weariness. "That coin is still yours if you can direct me to the American."

Encouraged to know there might still be more money coming his way, the footman straightened up and started to lead Pierce back out. But before they could make it back to the balcony a loud bang rang out from behind one of the doors, quickly followed by a scream.

The footman ran back to the door and immediately started yelling questions through the door while desperately trying to open it. Pierce ran up behind him, and then dropped to his knees to see if he could look through the keyhole. He'd seen this done in movies before and figured that the door was old enough to require a large key.

Amazingly Pierce found that he could see quit clearly through the keyhole, but that feeling vanished once he focused on the scene beyond. Colonel Bufford had a portly gentleman pinned to a desk, one hand around his throat and the other with a pistol to his head. He was red in the face, quietly threatening the man for something.

"What do you see?" the footman asked urgently as he continued to try and open the door. "I can hear voices inside."

"Leave the door alone," Pierce ordered, placing his hand on the footman's arm. One of Bufford's hounds had taken notice of a presence at the door and had started walking over. Pierce watched him turn around and presumably say something to the others before retuning his glance at the door. Smiling, he swiftly removed a pistol from his belt and pointed it at the door. "Down!"

Pierce was just able to pull the footman away before the door splintered from the passage of a bullet. Both men fell against the opposite wall, their hearts pounding from the near miss. The door opened a second later, as the shooter checked his handy work.

"What are you doing here?" the hound from the Grey Pack asked them in rough French as they slowly stood up from the floor.

"What is the meaning of firing a pistol indoors?" Pierce countered back, trying to display the right amount of indignation. He was hoping his costume would be enough to disguise his identity from the gunman. He also hoped that going on the attack would throw the man off enough to ignore his possible identity.

"What are you doing here? Why were you trying to open the door?" He repeated, eyeing them both closely.

"I am the Count of Monte Cristo and this footman was giving me a tour of the hotel, as I've never been here," Pierce began haughtily. "We heard a noise and a scream from inside this room and came to offer assistance."

"This is true?" the Hound asked the footman gruffly.

"It is as his Grace says," the footman replied, still shocked from his brush with danger.

"Very well, you may leave."

"I *may* leave?" Pierce shot out indignantly. "How dare you order me about like a common servant, especially after taking a shot in my direction. I have half a mind to call the gendarme and have you locked up, unless you can explain yourself."

"My apologies your Grace," the gunman muttered, simply wanting these two men to disappear. "I am part of the security for the ball and we discovered a thief in the manager's office. A pistol went off accidently while apprehending him. The gendarmes are actually already on their way."

"I see, in that case we shall leave you to your work," Pierce gallantly agreed before leading the shaken footman back to the hotel lobby. The noise of the party had seemingly hidden the sound of the pistol shot, as they didn't pass anyone rushing up the stairs and found everyone in the lobby as they had left them.

The pair walked over to a quiet corner after Pierce had grabbed a large scotch at the bar. He took a shot before handing it to the footman. The servant quailed from the offer, embarrassed at being served by a noble. But Pierce needed the man calm, so he made him take it.

"We were just under fire together. That makes us

comrades in arms. What's your name?"

"Pierre, your Grace."

"Tell me Pierre, what does the hotel manager look like?" Pierce asked as the footman settled himself, his hands clenched around the cut crystal tumbler.

"Monsieur Dubec? He's tall with a balding head, long nose and glasses."

"The man I saw in there was well dressed and slightly overweight, probably about your height. Do you know who that could be?" Pierce asked lowering his voice slightly as a group of waiters walked past them.

"Did he have a round face with dark hair?" the footman checked, receiving a nod from the Count. "That sounds like the hotel owner, Monsieur Lafayette. What's going on here?"

"I'm not sure, but I fear for his safety. Quietly summon a small group of the staff, the tougher the better, and then fetch Monsieur Dubec. You need to go back up to the office."

"What are you going to do your Grace?"

"I'm going to check on my wife, make sure she's not dancing with any scoundrels or soldiers," Pierce lied with a smile. When the gunman had talked to them in the hallway, Pierce had momentarily seen more of the scene within the hotel office. He'd counted the men inside and had come up one short. One of Bufford's hounds, Ivan to be specific, was unaccounted for and Pierce had a good idea where to find him.

Chapter 30

Pierce silently descended the stairs to the hotel basement, careful to not appear too suspicious if suddenly discovered by someone from the staff. But apart from a well stocked wine cellar, the basement was largely unused. The kitchens, laundry rooms, and servant spaces were above him, between the basement and the main floor of the hotel.

He passed the wine cellar and delved into the darkness, his eyes adjusting just enough to avoid running into the walls. After walking a few yards in the semi-dark he began to hear the faint sound of metal on stone. Following the noise he made his way to a large chamber filled with solid stone pillars.

A small lamp provided just enough light to see a large man clearing stone away from a hole in the wall. He was hunched over with a shovel in his hands, working slow and deliberately. It was Ivan, again working on the tunnel as before. Pierce figured his trip to the prison had delayed the completion of his work, forcing him to continue until the last minute in order to finish.

Taking a few steps back from the door, Pierce took a deep breath before stumbling into the chamber, deliberately knocking into the closest pillar as he did so. His sudden appearance made Ivan jump, but his drunken rambling made the large man quickly relax.

"Out," Ivan pointed at the door sternly, upset at his work being interrupted.

Pierce merely mumbled in reply as he shuffled closer, his rubbery limbs belying the tension he felt.

"Out, now!" Ivan ordered more sternly as Pierce passed him, having a quick look at the hole. It was bigger than when he and Liam had last been there.

"Listen you…" Ivan growled testily as he grabbed the collar of Pierces fancy jacket, twirling him back around from the tunnel. Unlike his companion upstairs, the flash of recognition crossed Ivan's face when got a proper look at Pierce.

However he had no time to react, as the handle of Pierce's walking stick struck him squarely in the groin, dropping him to his knees in an instant. This was soon followed by a knee to the temple, hurling him on to his back.

"No Ivan, you listen," Pierce ordered standing over him, no longer the drunken fool but a member of the Hunt. "The game is up and you're trapped. We've captured everyone but Bufford. If you tell me his plans now, I'll make sure they go easy on you back at the Manor."

Writhing in pain and unable to get up, Ivan merely spat on the floor in response to Pierce's demand. Undeterred Pierce clicked open his swordstick and slowly removed the glinting blade from its dark scabbard.

"You're going to tell me what I want to know, one way or another," Pierce threatened as he lowered the tip of the blade to Ivan's chest. Despite Pierce's past threats to the arms dealer in Merida and Drummond at the Manor, Pierce knew inside he was bluffing. Both those times he'd been pumped full of adrenaline and felt time was running out. However this time he didn't really need the info Ivan had, it would be useful but not really necessary.

"Okay, give me a second," grunted Ivan between breaths as he tried to sit up. The small lantern displayed a small cut on his forehead as he shifted his body over to one of the columns, collapsing back against it after the small amount of exertion.

"Where is Bufford going?" Pierce questioned after Ivan became settled. "How's he getting out of Marseille?"

"A boat, but I don't know which one," he lied easily, feeling the cut on his forehead.

"Destination?" A sneering shrug was all the reply Pierce got.

Pierce wasn't terribly interested in the answers, so he wasn't paying nearly enough attention to Ivan's body language. He didn't notice the small twitches of Ivan's shoulders as he felt behind him for a weapon. Similarly he didn't notice Ivan relaxing after grasping the handle of a small pickaxe.

"You've got five chances to answer my questions," Pierce ordered as his foot came down on Ivan's wrist, pinning it to the floor. He then moved his sword so it was almost touching the thumb. "Where is Bufford going?"

"I don't know!" Ivan yelled as he swung the pickaxe from behind him in a wide arc towards Pierce's legs.

His training helped Pierce sidestep the first attack and then parry the second as the pickaxe came back towards him. Without thinking Pierce immediately counterattacked after the parry, the movement automatic from years of fencing. As Ivan tried to get up, Pierce's blade swiftly travelled the distance from the handle of the pickaxe into the Russians chest.

Ivan had barely enough time to show his shock as the steel instantly pierced his heart. The body fell back to the cold dirt floor, quietly sliding off the thin blade.

"What did you do that for?!" Pierce yelled at the body in front of him, shocked by what had happened. "I wasn't going to torture you, you fucking idiot!"

The shakes came next, triggered from the shock of the sudden violent action that had just occurred. He had to take a few deep breaths in order to steady his hands long enough to replace the sword in its scabbard. The sharp sound from it clicking back into place woke Pierce from a momentary stupor and forced him to face his current predicament.

The fact that Ivan was continuing to clear the tunnel from the hotel to the building next door meant that Bufford still intended to use it to escape. But Pierce couldn't leave the body where it was, it would alarm Bufford prematurely. Similarly, Pierce also wanted to remove their method of escape without tipping his hand to their plan. The answer came a few seconds later, after looking from the body to the tunnel and realized that one solution could solve both problems.

With renewed energy, Pierce grabbed the discarded pickaxe and threw it into the tunnel. He then grabbed Ivan's body from under the arms and dragged him across the floor, careful to watch for any blood that might get on his fancy clothes. It took two heaving shoves to get the body into the tunnel and on top of the pickaxe. Wiping the sweat from his brow Pierce then went in search of the shovel.

The tunnel had been reinforced since the last time Pierce and Liam had been through it. Two medium sized beams ran the distance of the tunnel ceiling, with smaller pieces holding them in place. From the rocky rubble and dirt that surrounded the entrance, Pierce assumed that these additions were made after a small cave-in. With this in mind he hefted the shovel with both hands and started attacking the top beams in an attempt to knock them off the supports.

It only took a few solid whacks for them to fall, landing on the body with a thump. Within seconds the roof of the tunnel started to crumble, until enough debris had fallen to cover most of the body and completely block the tunnel.

Pierce smiled briefly at his small accomplishment, until he saw Ivan's legs protruding from beneath a pile of rock, dust, and dirt. He was instantly filled with guilt, despite the fact it was an accident. He didn't know anything about Ivan, but he felt that the man probably didn't deserve to die like he did. However he wasn't able to linger any longer, as he realized that Bufford and the rest of his men would be heading for their escape route shortly.

Placing the shovel on the floor beside the small lantern, Pierce took one last look at the body before heading for the stairs, fearing that the body count was only going to continue rising.

*

A small crowd had gathered on the second floor balcony outside the hallway to the manager's office. Pierce gently eased his way to the front before being greeted by a large waiter blocking the way.

Pierre the footman was waiting in the hall and waved to Pierce as soon as he saw him. A quick order to the waiter and the man stepped aside to let the Count pass.

"It was as you feared your Grace," Pierre began, his ashen face making the words unnecessary. He led him into the large office, where the hotel owner's body was still draped over the desk and three men were in deep conversation in the corner.

The office blended the aspects of a library and a study, with bookshelves lining two walls and two large desks in the center. There was a lingering smell of gunpowder mixed with that of dust, leather, and alcohol. The room immediately reminded Pierce of his own study at the Manor, eliciting a surprising twinge of homesickness for the comfortable space.

"I returned as you suggested, only to find him like this," Pierre continued, motioning to the body of the hotel owner. Pierce could make out what appeared to be a messy wound in the chest, which in conjunction with the smell, he deduced that a pistol was the cause.

"I guess it doesn't matter how crooked the barrel is if you shove it against the target," Pierce mumbled to himself, figuring that Bufford had finally shot someone.

"Sorry sir?" Pierre inquired in confusion since Pierce had spoken to himself in English.

"Nothing," he replied as he turned from the body to inspect the rest of the room more closely.

The three men were still conversing in the far corner by a window. From Pierre's previous description he spotted the hotel manager as one of the men. He was white as a sheet and barely speaking, probably feeling as though he could have easily been the corpse on the desk.

"Clearly a robbery gone wrong," huffed a tall broad man in a dark uniform covered in gold braid. "Did you keep anything valuable here?"

"Nothing really…" the manager replied slowly, his face contorted in confusion.

"What about in the safe?" Pierce interjected from the opposite side of the room after a quick tour of the space.

"There is no safe," objected the third man; tall, thin, and as expensively dressed as Pierce. "Who the devil are you and how did you get in here?"

"Pardon, that is my fault," Pierre apologised, coming to Pierce's aid. "Gentlemen this is the Count of Monte Cristo. We interrupted the thieves by accident as I gave his Grace a tour of the hotel. He told me to get M. Dubec and gather a group of men together to come back, thinking your brother was in trouble."

"My thanks for your effort," the man said, acknowledging Pierce more warmly. "I am Guillaum Lafayette, poor Jean there was my brother. I don't believe you've met the others here; Colonel Dutours, the army garrison commander, and Monsieur Dubec, who manages this hotel for my brother."

"Now see here, what safe were you talking about?" the Colonel questioned irritably after the introductions were complete.

"That one," Pierce responded calmly as he pointed to a medium sized painting hanging crookedly on the wall. It was a plain oil painting depicting a rather unimpressive coastal scene. "I imagine the thieves didn't have time to straighten the painting after they searched the safe behind it."

"Dubec, did you know of this?" Lafayette demanded as he marched over to the painting and moved it to show a small safe hidden behind.

"I… oh yes, now I remember Jean having it installed," the manager finally answered, seemingly shocked by the safe's sudden appearance. "But he didn't keep anything valuable in there; no money, jewels, or anything like that. Merely some business papers I believe."

"What kind of business papers?" Pierce prodded gently, trying to appear helpful and concerned.

"The deed for this hotel for one thing, plus some other documents," Dubec offered as he opened the safe. He then rhymed off the other documents as he lifted them up from a small stack within.

"Is that all?" Lafayette asked suspiciously when Dubec had finished listing the contents. "I seem to recall my brother owning a ship. I think it had an English name, something he'd won gambling."

"Yes you're right," Dubec confirmed after recollecting his former employer's sudden interest in shipping. "It was named the *Anne* or *Mary* or something like that."

"*The Courted Anne*!" Lafayette remembered suddenly. "But he might not have kept the ownership here. Besides, who would have killed my brother over a ship?"

"I think you're right," the Colonel agreed soberly. "It seems to me as though a gang of thieves entered hoping to steal some money, but when all they found were papers in the safe they shot your brother. My condolences sir."

"I offer mine as well and must take my leave," Pierce added solemnly.

"Thank you your Grace," Lafayette acknowledged gravely.

"Pierre, can you fetch the Countess and have her meet me in the lobby. I think I've had enough excitement for one night." The footman had been loitering by the door and left with a quick nod after receiving the order.

"I appreciate everything you did for my brother tonight," Lafayette continued as Pierce moved to the door. "I fear we might never be able to track down the bastards and bring them to justice."

"I wouldn't be so sure, men such as these will have other enemies. I imagine they'll end up paying one way or another. Good night gentleman."

"Good night your Grace," the men replied in unison as Pierce left the room. The crowd had dispersed from the second floor, allowing Pierce to descend to the lobby without any fanfare.

He only had to wait for a few moments in the lobby before Jane appeared, expertly hiding the concern she felt. Pierre trailed in behind her, but then broke off to fetch her wrap and Pierce's jacket.

"Bufford?" She said shooting him a question look.

"Everything's fine my dear. Thank you Pierre," Pierce acknowledged as the footman approached with their outerwear.

"I hope you had an enjoyable evening madame la Comtesse," Pierre offered sincerely as he draped her shawl over her shoulders. She merely nodded in reply with noble composure.

Pierce shrugged into his overcoat after Jane had been served, flipping another gold coin to Pierre as he led her towards the front door.

"But your Grace, I can't accept," Pierre objected after catching the coin in flight. "I didn't lead you to your meeting."

"Maybe not directly, but now I know where to find the scoundrel."

"The ship?" Pierre asked after a moment's reflection, having listened in on the conversation in the office above. He was rewarded by a knowing wink before the couple turned and left the lobby. "Bon Chance monsieur le Comte."

*

"Bit late for a swim isn't it?" Pierce asked as the carriage rattled along the harbour front.

"Aye it is your Grace," MacDuff responded sarcastically. Both he and Sean were sitting on the backward facing bench in the carriage, shivering slightly under a pair of blankets. "However we also managed to cut the numbers down in our favour. Some of the men from *The Courted Anne* will be in no shape to fight later, let alone get on board."

"Your handy work then?" Jane observed, pointing to a burning building on the other side of the port.

"Indirectly."

"What about Bufford then?" Jane inquired as she turned to face Pierce beside her. "What happened when you left? I was a nervous wreck the whole time you were gone."

"Well I can definitely say they plan on using the *Anne*. Plus I also reduced the numbers in our favour. Ivan is dead," Pierce stated more casually than he felt. He continued to explain the incident outside the second floor office and then his foray into the basement. "So their primary escape route was closed, did you see them leave by the front?"

"We didn't see anything, but Liam had to park the carriage down the street," Sean offered as he dried his hair.

"I don't understand, why go to the trouble of stealing the ownership for the *Anne* and killing the owner?" Jane asked aloud.

"He needed a ship bound for America to move his cargo, but the captain wouldn't let him load it," began Pierce, explaining what he had figured out after discovering the safe in Lafayette's office. "So he killed the captain, hoping the expedition is taken over by someone more inclined to deal with him. Like the first mate."

"But there's no guarantee the first mate will be named captain," MacDuff continued, seeing where Pierce's reasoning was leading.

"Exactly, Bufford needs to get the first mate appointed captain. Something only the owner can do. So he set the meeting for a night the ship owner, who's also the hotel owner, has planned a ball."

"Smart, lot's of people and distractions to offer an inconspicuous opportunity," MacDuff nodded appreciatively. "He built an escape route in case things go south during the negotiations with the owner."

"I'd wager that was also the plan based on the Colonel's record," Sean interjected coldly. "The owner was never going to leave that office alive."

"Very likely. He probably died seconds after signing the ship over to Bufford," Pierce concluded sympathetically. "But this doesn't affect our plan. Did Liam get a boat?"

"It's the only reason we're not swimming in the sea right now," Sean shuddered from the memory rather than the dampness.

"Aye, the current's swift tonight and heading out to sea," MacDuff agreed thoughtfully. "That means our chance of hitting the *Anne* as it leaves port will likely be harder. She'll be moving rather quickly."

The carriage halted abruptly in a more derelict part of the port. The majority of the docks were empty, save for the odd barge tied alongside.

"Welcome to McGillicuddy's tours of Marseille," Liam announced as he opened the door of the carriage. "Please refrain from any flash photography as it will scare the locals. This way to your luxurious cruise vessel."

They all descended from the carriage and followed Liam along the decrepit and rotting dock. Despite the resurgence of the port of Marseille, this was clearly the last section to be overhauled. Thus it was completely empty of any notable ships or their crews. Liam stopped at the end of the jetty, calmly looking out at the harbour and the ships within it.

"So where's our boat?" Pierce demanded as they all crowded together.

"Down there," Liam replied, pointing down a rickety gangplank to a large rowboat haphazardly tied to the jetty fifteen feet below them.

"We're supposed to intercept a sea going schooner in that thing?!" Pierce demanded incredulously.

"It worked well enough the last time I took her out, isn't that right MacDuff?"

"Aye, I suppose we made it back in one piece," MacDuff agreed reluctantly, the uncomfortable memories still fresh in his mind.

"Exactly. I can't work miracles with such a short time frame," Liam concluded, shifting the blame for their sub-par vessel.

"Fine, let's get on board and get in position," Pierce ordered as he led the way down the gangplank.

The vessel was a fourteen foot launch with two banks of oars on each side with a rudder at the stern. A small amount of water sloshed around the bottom of the boat as they all made their way onboard.

"Sir, may I suggest that Sean and MacDuff take the first set of oars and that you and Miss Jane take the second set?" Liam offered as they all boarded.

"Leaving you to steer and thus get out of having to row?" Pierce quickly countered.

"Well I suppose that's true," Liam allowed innocently. "But I do have the most experience traveling on this body of water, plus the pairings work out rather well. Strength wise."

Jane let out a quick snigger, cutting off Pierce's reply. The fact that the damned Irishman was probably right also led to Pierce biting his tongue and sitting down next to Jane on the second set on benches.

"Everyone ready?" Liam asked as the group got settled on their seats. After gripping the large sets of oars, they all nodded assent to Liam one by one. "Altogether then, stroke! Stroke!"

The boat slowly floated away from the jetty and moved into the large harbour beyond. Liam expertly steered against the current, keeping them between the docks and the more open part of the harbour. A few minutes of easy rowing led them close to the entrance to the port, where they soon found themselves rowing against the current to keep from going out to sea.

"You have our weapons?" Pierce asked Liam, getting everyone ready for their task at hand. Liam nodded silently tapping a large duffle bag sitting beside him. "Sean, get your crossbow ready for when the *Anne* passes by."

Sean slowly moved from his seat and delved into the duffle, finally removing some pieces that he quickly assembled into a crossbow. He then pulled out a coil of rope and some menacing bolts. The rope was tied to one of the bolts, which was then loaded onto the cocked crossbow. Sean then moved to the bow of the boat, ready to grapple on to the *Anne* as it passed out to sea.

While Sean was busy with his task, McDuff removed a collection of rifles and pistols from the bag. They all received one of each, along with pouches filled with powder and bullets. Swords and cutlasses were then removed and handed out, so that eventually they all appeared like cutthroat pirates on their small rowboat.

"I want you to stay on the boat," Pierce ordered Jane as they sat waiting while the others busied themselves loading their weapons.

"Why? You don't think I can help?"

"I know you can help," Pierce lied, worried for her safety. "You're going to be our ace in the hole if things go bad. After we get on board I want you to let the boat drift backwards and remain towed behind. If any of us fall overboard, we're going to need you to be ready to fish us out of the water."

Jane nodded with determination, realizing that it was a necessary task and she wasn't being left behind merely because she was a girl. Despite this she was inwardly glad to be staying in the boat. She'd wielded weapons before and well enough to have yielded results beyond getting herself hurt. However she'd never jumped into the chaos that she assumed waited for her comrades once onboard.

"Here it comes! Patrick and Jane, keep rowing!" Liam ordered as the bow of ship emerged from the gloom of the harbour. The vast rigging on the tall masts made the ship appear more imposing from the water level than from the docks and the phosphorescent waves licking off the sleek bow displayed its growing speed. Quickly Liam realized that they were positioned too close and risked discovery if they didn't move. This meant rowing away from the ship in a large loop in order to get the bow pointed back towards the ship as it passed. Sean needed a clear shot at the *Anne* and it had to be from the right angle or their rowboat would capsize once connected.

MacDuff shifted to Sean's vacant seat in order to provide more power to the outside set of oars, thereby turning them faster. Liam had the tiller pushed as far as it would go, desperately turning their boat as the schooner started to pass them. Despite having only set minimal sails, the *Anne* was still moving swiftly out to sea, riding the tidal current perfectly.

"It's going to be close," Sean muttered as the other ship came into his sights. He pulled the trigger lightly as he held his breath, the slight *twing* sound emanating from the string as the crossbow fired. The rope swiftly followed the bolt across the expanse between the two vessels, ending with a quiet thump as it reached its destination. Without hesitating, Sean quickly and expertly tied the other end of the rope to a solid metal ring on the bow of their boat.

They all sat in quiet relief as the schooner passed, waiting to be covertly towed behind. Despite having positioned their boat well, it still shuddered ferociously as the rope became taut, violently wrenching the rowboat from its placid stillness. Unprepared for this reaction, they were all thrown to the floor in a pile of bodies and weapons as the *Courted Anne* dragged them out into the dark rolling sea beyond the safety of the harbour.

Chapter 31

The rowboat disappeared from view as the Brown Pack swarmed up the side of the schooner, careful to keep their heads below the rail. The crew had finished setting the remainder of the sails and the ship's speed perceptively increased. Unlike a trained navy crew, these men sauntered from place to place, unhurriedly completing their menial tasks.

Many were undoubtedly still feeling the effects of their onshore activities and unhappy with the late night departure. Some had the visible signs of a hard fought brawl, with fresh cuts, scrapes, and bruises overlapping less recent ones.

Colonel Bufford's unmistakable voluminous voice carried across the decks, yelling out commands and insults. Pierce snuck a quick peek and saw that the Colonel was pacing the quarterdeck, to the clear discomfort of the man at the wheel. Seeing their target in person cleared any sliver of doubt he had about the current mission. The weapons had to be on board.

They all clung to ropes hanging from the side of the ship as they waited for the watch to change and the top deck to clear of the majority of the crew. It was wet and cold but none of them moved, unwilling to risk discovery and start a gunfight hanging off the side of a moving ship. However after a seemingly endless wait, the noises and footfalls above them faded and only the sound of rushing water and wind remained.

Venturing another look onto the top deck, Pierce could only see three figures left. The new captain had remained behind the wheel while two crewmen walked to the bow. Pierce ducked down and motioned to the others what he'd seen. Nodding in unified comprehension they all started moving to their respective places. Remaining on the outside of the ship, Sean slowly moved to the bow while MacDuff moved to the stern, both keeping their heads down. When they were in place, Liam and Pierce rolled over the gunwale onto the deck. They immediately stood up and casually walked towards the stern, talking in low but not secretive voices.

"...So that was the second time she caught me..." Liam laughingly intoned as they approached the stairs leading to the quarterdeck where the captain was dutifully at the wheel.

"What does the Colonel want now?" The captain asked, too tired to hide his contempt. He'd readily accepted his promotion to Captain from first mate when the new owner had arrived at the dock hours before. However in that short time he'd started to wonder if it had been a mistake. The new owner was much too involved in the running of the ship, despite clearly having a good knowledge of seamanship. These thoughts, along with having not slept in a day, made the Captain confuse Pierce and Liam for Bufford's two hounds. The long leather jackets were just similar enough that the mistake was almost guaranteed in the darkness.

"He wants us to check his cargo," Pierce replied evenly, hoping his voice sounded confident. "Where is it again?"

"Second section on the deck below," the Captain answered immediately, half ignoring them with his eyes scanning the sea beyond them. "You should know that since you watched us load it on board. Wait, you're not..."

Too late to realize his mistake, MacDuff had silently approached from behind him and knocked the Captain out with one fell swoop from the hand guard of his cutlass. He was able to catch the Captain before he landed on the deck, setting him down quietly and then grabbing the wheel.

Liam then left and replayed the previous act with the

crewmen at the bow, only with Sean emerging with stealthy precision to provide the knock out blows. They then returned to the stern carrying the sailors between them. Sean then expertly tied the unconscious men together and draped a canvass tarp over their bodies. Pierce had given them all stern instructions that killing innocent bystanders in their conflict with Bufford was to be avoided.

"So far so good," Pierce whispered in relief. "Next step; Liam up to the crows nest with your rifles for covering fire, MacDuff you stay on the wheel and keep us from crashing. Sean, we're going to check the cargo and then blow a hole in the bottom. Good luck everyone, but remember that this ship can never reach another port."

Sean and Pierce made their way to the forward hatch as Liam scrambled up the rope ladder above them, a pair of rifles strung across his back. They found the hatch easily and started to ease it open as quietly as they could.

"Ever been on a ship like this?" Sean asked quietly, barely breaking the silence of the ship.

"I was on the *Bluenose* once as a kid in Halifax," Pierce replied with a smile. "So it's probably best if I follow you."

As the hatch opened completely, a roar of sound emanated from below, making both men move back from the opening. They could hear yelling, singing, swearing and other such noises from the crew. But a quick glance through the hatch only provided a view of tarp covered bundles lashed down. So they silently descended the stairs to the deck below, mindful of anyone who might appear.

"The crew will be in their mess behind that bulkhead," Sean pointed backwards to where the noise was coming from.

"Really?" Pierce observed sarcastically, the tension of the moment getting to him. He then turned and looked at the cargo surrounding them. "We'll these aren't crates of submachine guns and ammunition."

"No, they should be stored in the section forward of us, according to the captain."

The cargo holds were thankfully clear of people, allowing

Sean and Pierce to continue their journey within the bowels of the ship unobserved. They continued to stop at corners and doors, maintaining their vigilance despite the absence of direct danger.

"Now that looks about right," Pierce observed as they rounded another load. There were six wooden crates stacked on top of each other and lashed to the deck. Sean found a small lantern and risked some light to have a decent look at what they'd found. There was some black stencilling on the second crate, but was upside down and somewhat smudged. "I think this is it, wait… Bingo!"

Pierce had moved to another crate and there he found a much more definitive clue. A large black stamp marked the crate with the notorious image of an eagle holding a swastika in its talons, the evil image of Nazi Germany.

"Want to open it?" Sean asked as he went to remove a boarding axe resting in his belt.

"No I think we're good," Pierce stopped him with a wave. Having finally found the weapons, Pierce wanted nothing more than to send them to the bottom of the sea as quickly as possible. "Find some gunpowder and set it up to blow here. The blast should punch a hole in the hull and with luck set the ammunition off as well."

Sean nodded in agreement and turned to go, having spotted what looked like barrels of gun powder earlier. But he was stopped by the unmistakable sound of a gunshot, followed by another and a rush of feet above them.

"Those aren't even your own crooked pistols," MacDuff laughed in amazement from behind the wheel of the *Courted Anne*. "Turns out you're just a bad shot."

"It was a warning shot you miserable Scot!" Bufford rebuked as he held his hand out for another pair of loaded pistols. He stood at the bottom of the stairs, having just exited the Captain's quarters. "What are you doing here MacDuff and who's with you?"

"You'll find out soon enough you racist bastard!"

"How dare you talk to me in such a fashion!" Bufford yelled back, his face reddening in rage. "You'll answer my questions or I'll have you keel hauled. I am a member of the Hunt and…"

"Not anymore!" Pierce yelled from the other side of the ship, having ascended from the forward cargo hatch. He walked confidently towards Bufford, passing the crewmen who were crowded together. "You backed the wrong horse. Cleaver has fled and Lord Lodge has returned. Triumphant and seriously pissed off."

"And he sent you? The Yankee, sorry Canadian?" Bufford mocked as he turned his attention towards Pierce. "I'm sorry if I don't take your appearance here too seriously. Now if I were staring at Tiberius, that's another matter."

"Well you'll have that chance shortly," Pierce retorted with a grin. "Tiberius and the rest of the Black Pack have commandeered a Navy ship and will be joining us soon."

"Nice try, but I've gambled against better men than you sonny."

Pierce shrugged in response and leaned against the railing. Not sure what he should do next, he decided to see how Bufford would react. He hoped that he would be so shocked to see his plans discovered that it would allow Sean to finish his task.

Before Bufford could continue his verbal assault on Pierce, more yelling and scuffling could be heard from the rear hatch. Seconds later Bufford's two remaining hounds and a crewman led Sean up from below; the look on his face was enough for Pierce to realize he'd been caught prematurely.

"What have we got here," Bufford smiled as he lazily pointed the pistols in his hands.

"We found him in the magazine looking for gunpowder sir," the crewman behind Sean proudly exclaimed.

"Let me guess, you swam aboard to assassinate me, but discovered your powder wet once you boarded?" Bufford laughed, seeing Sean's stoic face flinch. "There's no ship coming and I've captured you all. Ha ha ha!"

"You'll never get away with it," Pierce muttered confidently, momentarily cringing at the classic television dialogue before continuing. "Even if you get those weapons to America, it will be years before the Civil War starts. You'll be an old man, probably dead."

"You think I want to win the war?" Bufford responded incredulously as he walked over to where Pierce was standing. "It can't be done. Didn't Lodge tell you about the nature of time? Some things in history are a constant, they cannot be changed. The more you try, the more time fights against you. The Civil War will occur and the South will lose and a few crates of guns can't change that."

"Then what's this all about?"

"The South will rise again!" The Colonel yelled his response with the wildest eyes Pierce had ever seen. "I will bury those weapons and return to the Manor, where I'll then take my proper portal home."

Pierce then saw the true insanity and genius of the plan. Bufford was correct in thinking he wouldn't be able to turn the tide of the war, even with machine guns. To be of any use they'd have to be mass produced, which would lead to union spies obtaining the specs in order to produce their own. With the Union's greater industrial capacity and population, the Confederate losses would possibly be even greater than before. But if Bufford were to return after the war was over and collect a loyal group of embittered followers, the impact would be much greater. The KKK could conceivably mount a guerrilla war throughout the South, dealing out massive amounts of death and mayhem.

"You think Lord Lodge will just let you come back into the Manor, grab the key to your portal and then let you leave?" Pierce asked incredulously. "After you've conspired with Dr. Cleaver, and broke the rules of transporting goods through time? Tiberius might not be coming with a ship to stop you now, but you can bet he'll be waiting in the North Tower for you to show your face. You might even get to see him before you get a bullet in the head."

"I've been planning this for ages and I won't let some old man like Lodge or trumped up servant like Tiberius stop me!" Bufford growled as he strode over to Pierce, stopping a few feet from him.

Although a few of the ship's crew were armed, none of them with firearms, Pierce could still count and they were easily outnumbered. He probably could have ended the whole affair by shooting Bufford when he first came on deck. But he'd waited too long and now Bufford was too close to him, making it impossible to pull his pistol out and get a shot off. It was still in his belt and not cocked.

"Aren't we armed to the teeth," Bufford observed as he took in all the weapons Pierce had strapped to him. But then his eyes fell upon the black swordstick that Pierce had brought along, unable to leave it in the carriage. He grabbed the bronze head and pulled it from Pierce's belt, twirling it in his fingers. "I think I'll take this as a trophy."

"Didn't your mother tell you to not take things from others," Pierce challenged after getting a signal from MacDuff, still steering the ship. In all the confusion nobody had bothered to replace him at the wheel, as all the crew were still crowded together in a group in the middle of the deck.

"No, she told me to take what I wanted from the weak and you've got to be the weakest Hunt member ever recruited," Bufford laughed as he poked Pierce in the chest with the bronze head.

"Do that again and I'll kill you," he threatened, grabbing the head of the swordstick with his right hand.

"Ha! I bet you've never killed anyone in your life," Bufford scoffed, shoving it against him a second time despite Pierce's grip.

"Not as many as you, you crazy bastard," Pierce shot back. "But I did kill a man tonight. A real moron."

"Really?"

"Ya, some big Russian guy. He thought following your

orders was a good idea," Pierce prodded, seeing the truth dawn on the Colonel. "A real fucking moron."

Bufford let out a wild scream and tried to raise the pistol in his left hand. But Pierce was quicker and with flowing precision he stepped back and removed the blade from its sheath as the ship suddenly lurched to the side.

MacDuff had timed things perfectly, throwing the ships wheel to one side as Pierce had drawn his sword. The crew toppled against each other as he stepped away from the wheel, pulling out his two pistols. His first shot went into one of Bufford's hounds holding Sean, hitting his chest and throwing him overboard. Dropping the fired pistol, MacDuff pulled out his cutlass as some of the crewmen charged the quarterdeck.

The second of Bufford's hounds took a bullet in the gut from Liam up in the crows nest. He'd watched the whole scene below unsure on how to proceed, surprised at not being discovered. He'd thought about trying to sneak into the hold in order to finish Sean's task, but knew he probably wouldn't make it undetected. So instead he'd stayed hidden high above, his rifle trained on the more dangerous Hounds of the Grey Pack.

Surprisingly the Hounds of the Grey Pack had only removed Sean's pistols from his belt when they'd found him. So once they'd been dispatched by his companions, Sean pulled out his boarding axe and a long dagger and charged into the chaos that had erupted on deck.

Two separate battles then formed on the deck of the *Courted Anne* as a sailor grabbed the wheel and righted the ship. MacDuff and Sean took on a group of ten men in a savage fight near the stern. Meanwhile Pierce found himself in a duel with Bufford and the remainder of the crew that had not fled below. He was backed up by Liam, who stayed up above and was methodically picking off targets with his rifles.

Pierce had been lucky that Bufford had pulled out his pistol as MacDuff had rocked the ship. The sudden movement had made the Colonel fire prematurely, enabling Pierce to attack him with the blade in is hand. He was able to make some small jabs along Bufford's arms and chest in quick succession. Bufford used the empty scabbard in his hand to parry these attacks and was the only reason Pierce's thrusts did not result in deeper hits.

Angry at being on the defensive, Bufford threw the scabbard aside and pulled out his own long sword and charged towards Pierce. Undeterred by this change, Pierce maintained his composure and continued fighting Bufford in much the same fashion he had against Sean at their first meeting. Bufford attacked with forceful swings which Pierce avoided or parried easily, then counterattacking with his own quick precise strikes.

Meanwhile the pair at the stern continued their stand. Not wishing the crew any direct harm, Sean and MacDuff tried to refrain from killing any of them directly. They found themselves fighting back to back, covering each other against the greater numbers of their adversaries. Between the two of them they'd managed to wound two and knock out another two; however that still left six men that were now fully enraged by the continued presence of the invaders.

"Just like Culloden!" Sean yelled over the clash of steel as he turned aside a jab from a spear.

"Aye!" MacDuff agreed as he punched a sailor who'd missed him with a wooden club. "Hopefully it will end better this time!"

"I wouldn't count on it!"

"I'll stop shooting you if you stop climbing towards me with swords!" Liam yelled from the crows nest as he aimed his rifle over the side. After hitting two men who'd been trying to join in Bufford's attack on Pierce, those not engaged in the duel had turned their attention to Liam. So far he'd shot two men as they climbed the rope ladders that led above, careful to only wing them. However like their comrades fighting Sean and MacDuff, this only enraged the remainder more. So there were two more quickly climbing up to face him. When they ignored a second of his pleas, Liam shot one of them in the shoulder, dropping him to the deck below in a cry of pain. However there wasn't enough time to reload before the second had reached the top of the ladder.

"I warned him," Liam offered innocently has the sailor swung at him with a knife he removed from his teeth. Liam dodged it easily and brought the butt end of the spent rifle into the man's gut, dropping him immediately. He then delivered a blow to the head, knocking him unconscious. Knowing the fall would kill his attacker; Liam removed the knife, tied him to the mast, and then decided to join the fight below.

The duel below spanned the length of the ship, having started on the bow, they now found themselves fighting up the stairs to the quarterdeck at the stern. Bufford had quickly realized the skill of his opponent and had settled down his wild attacks. Pierce adapted well to the change, but found that his smaller blade was taking a pounding.

"You can't possibly think you can beat me with that toothpick," Bufford goaded after delivering an arm shattering blow.

"I've already beaten you," Pierce rejoined, quickly stepping inwards and slicing Bufford's face. "You're just too stupid to realize it!"

Bufford reacted with brutal force quicker than Pierce was prepared for, catching him in the face with the pommel and splitting his lip. Pierce shook his head clear and spat out some blood, barely prepared for the next attack.

They continued to clash swords, neither one gaining the upper hand until Bufford tripped into the helmsman currently at the wheel of the ship. The contact was enough to knock the sailor off balance, loosening his grip on the wheel and making the ship lurch once again. Pierce took a few steps back to steady himself, finding the distance between him and Bufford greatly increased. Seizing the opportunity, he pulled out a loaded pistol he'd been saving from his belt.

Behind smiling eyes he aimed it squarely at Bufford's center mass as he'd been taught. He waited as the sailor regained control of the wheel, lessening the chance of missing his target. He waited for Bufford to turn and look at him, wanting him to see the bullet coming.

But as he waited, he took a quick glance to the fight below. Despite Liam joining in and the bodies lying around them, his men were still largely outnumbered. A few of the crew had emerged from below decks with better weapons. One of these men was charging at MacDuff from behind as the large Scotsmen fought off two others. Without thinking, the pistol in Pierce's hand shifted smoothly and he fired at the man without blinking. He watched the body crumple in satisfaction, receiving a grateful, albeit surprised, nod from MacDuff.

The satisfaction was shortly lived, as Bufford was once more upon him and as livid as ever. The brush with death had energized the man from Georgia and he pushed his assault on Pierce with more fervour than before. Pierce decided to trade space for time and defended himself as best he could while retreating back to the bow of the ship.

The man Pierce had shot was only the first of the second wave of sailors who returned from the armoury below. Although not great in numbers, their appearance was enough to negate the progress the Brown Pack had made. They continued to fight until four of the sailors raised loaded muskets at them from point blank range.

"Easy lads," MacDuff said calmly as he lowered his weapons, signalling for Sean and Liam to do the same. However with the captain still missing and Bufford fighting with Pierce at the bow, the sailors didn't know what to do next. So they simply covered them with their muskets, too wary to disarm the dangerous men in long dark jackets. "Aye Sean, just like Culloden."

Despite seeing the scene from the bow, Bufford continued attacking Pierce, now fully confident in his eventual triumph.

"Give up and I'll let your men go," Bufford offered as he delivered an easily parried thrust.

"Go to hell!" Pierce countered as he took a step back,

seeing his men's situation for himself. A sudden wave of defeat deflated him as he took stock of the situation. Despite this he knew that he still had to try and sink the ship. He couldn't let her reach America with her deadly cargo. Even if Bufford's plan didn't succeed and he was stopped when entering the Manor, there would still be crates of modern weapons stashed and ready to be found by anyone. The end result could be just as catastrophic as Bufford succeeding in his plan.

"You first," Bufford replied angrily, drawing Pierce's attention back as he removed a pistol from under his jacket. "Seems like you brought a knife to a gunfight sonny."

He cocked the gun while it remained pointing down, taking a few breaths to steady his hands. Their fight had lasted long enough for both men to be exhausted. After a few moments he raised the pistol towards Pierce, who hoped that the Colonel really was a bad shot.

"Nooo!" shouted a scream from behind Pierce, quickly followed by the loud crack of a fired gun. A second shot soon sounded and Pierce heard a whistling pass his ear. Looking behind him Pierce was shocked to see Jane standing halfway out of the forward hatch with a rifle in her hands. Pierce then looked back to Bufford who was kneeling, the smoking pistol still firmly in his grip as he felt a wound on his arm.

"Are you ok?" Jane called from the hatchway. She had dropped the rifle and was shaking slightly, but was otherwise in good spirits. Pierce stared at her with more passion than he'd ever felt in his life. Smiling she looked past him to Bufford, "good, finish this."

Pierce nodded and walked towards Bufford, keeping his eyes on the armed men at the stern. They still had their rifles pointed towards his men, but they were now fully engrossed on the scene at the bow.

"Looks like you brought an empty tube of metal to a sword fight, you bastard," Pierce spat as he marched towards Bufford with determination. Without hesitation he plunged the point of his blade into the Colonel's heart, killing him instantly. Unlike with Ivan, Pierce felt no guilt dispatching Colonel

Bufford. Taking a step back, he felt Jane's body come up behind him.

"We've got to go," Jane offered hurriedly, pointing towards the hatch. "I finished where Sean left off and lit the fuse for the gunpowder. I don't know how long we've got."

"Gentlemen," Pierce called across the deck of the ship as he moved towards the group of men at the stern. He stopped only once to pick up his discarded scabbard, sliding the blade in and turning it back into a walking stick. "I am the Count of Monte Cristo. I apologise for the intrusion upon your vessel and would be grateful if you could release my men."

"You pay for their release," replied a sailor who had taken charge, blood dripping from a gash in his forehead."

"Of course," Pierce replied happily as he started to search in his jacket. With his head turned he whispered to Jane, asking if the rowboat was still being towed behind the ship. When she nodded he told her to get to the railing and get ready to jump over the side. "I've got some gold right here."

Pierce tossed a small bag onto the deck and then motioned to his men. They instantly figured out his meaning and started to slowly back their way towards the rail.

"Now that we have your money, we will take your lives," sneered the sailor as he picked up the bag. But his face instantly turned into a frown when he discovered it was empty except for two dingy coins. As he yelled an order for his men to fire, an explosion from the bow shook the ship. A fire ball shot out from the side and bullets ripped up through the deck like shrapnel.

Unlike the confused crewmen, Jane and the Brown Pack were over the rails like a shot, splashing into the water haphazardly. After surfacing they all swam like mad to reach the rope that was towing their rowboat. They followed the rope to their small vessel, cutting it quickly as the *Courted Anne* started to sink. Pierce helped Jane in first and then they all hauled themselves over the sides, careful to not tip it over.

"Well, I think that went well," Liam offered breathlessly as they all laid strewn across the boat's floor in exhaustion.

Chapter 32

Unsure as to where they were, Liam followed the North Star as they rowed back to shore. Terribly tired from their fight on the *Courted Anne*, the crew of the rowboat made poor progress until the tide turned and pushed them towards the shore. The sun just started to rise when Liam caught the first signs of land. The few landmarks they could see upon their approach were unrecognizable, providing no real clue as to their distance from Marseille.

Liam aimed them towards a safe looking beach and let the surf shove them ashore. What gear they had was bundled up into bags as they struggled along the sand, finally seeing a small cottage with smoke rising from the chimney in the distance.

Claiming they survived a shipwreck, the owner readily accepted their rowboat in exchange for breakfast and directed them to a nearby road that led to Marseille.

"I can't believe our plan worked," Sean uttered after they had all boarded a wagon whose driver agreed to take them to Marseille on his way to the market.

"It wouldn't have worked without our glorious ace in the hole," Liam observed lazily as he shoved a piece of straw into his mouth.

"When did you get onboard?" Pierce asked Jane who had curled up beside him.

"As soon I heard the first two shots I knew something was wrong," she recounted, staring calmly up at the sky. "I pulled our boat up to the ship and climbed up the same way you did. Peaking over the rail I saw Bufford confront you. I wasn't sure what was happening, but I figured you'd been found out and that eventually they'd search the ship and find everyone else. So I lowered myself down to one of the portholes and squeezed in through."

"I saw her out of the corner of my eye after being found in the magazine," Sean continued, still upset at being discovered. "I had a small barrel of gunpowder in my hands, but managed to motion her towards the crates as I was led away."

"That's right. I waited until the coast was clear and then picked up the barrel and a nearby rifle. I moved to the front of the ship where Sean had motioned, but I didn't really know what I was looking for. I was about to place the barrel anywhere when I found the small lantern. The crates beside it were much more modern than any other in the ship, so I figured it must be the right place."

"Clever and beautiful," MacDuff mused in appreciation.

"So then I opened the barrel and made a trail of powder from the ladder by the hatch to the crates. I swapped the barrel for the lantern, doubled back to the hatch and then broke the lantern on the floor where the trail started. It lit up right away and I ran up the ladder."

"Just in time to see Bufford point a loaded pistol at me," Pierce finished for her, amazed by the luck of her timing.

"I was so shocked by the scene that I shot without really aiming," Jane admitted truthfully.

"Now don't be so modest. You aimed to wing him so that Lord Pierce could finish him off," Liam corrected lightly. "The story sounds better that way."

"Exactly," MacDuff agreed swiftly. "Just like a good Hound of the Manor would have done. I daresay you have the talent for it as well."

"You think I could? To be honest I've never been content

being a mere housemaid. I've always wanted more," Jane timidly wished out loud.

"Well you're already an honorary member of the Brown Pack," Pierce observed looking from Jane to MacDuff. "I'm sure something can be done."

"I should think so," MacDuff concurred gruffly. "Seeing as you helped the Master of the Manor escape imprisonment, saved the life of the Lord of the Brown Pack, and was a key part in defeating Colonel Bufford's plans."

Jane blushed slightly after hearing of her exploits listed with admiration by a battle hardened warrior like MacDuff. Leaning back against Pierce's shoulder she smiled in contentment as the wagon bounced along the rutted road towards Marseille.

"Wine anyone?" Liam offered after taking a drink from a dark green bottle encased in woven straw.

"Where did you get that?" Sean asked grabbing it with childish enthusiasm and taking a big gulp before passing it onward.

"There's a case under the straw here. Don't look at me like that Duffy, I put a coin in its place as compensation."

Everyone laughed as the bottle got passed around, the stress of their adventure slowly draining from their bodies. The remainder of the trip was spent in companionable silence as they took in their surroundings, with the steady clip-clop of the horse marking time. A cloudless day greeted them and by the time the sun had reached its zenith, the wagon had reached the outskirts of Marseille.

Unfamiliar with their route into the city, they waited until the driver had reached his destination near the port. Pierce thanked him for the ride and handed him a gold coin from his pocket, surprised that he still had some after their ordeal.

The walk back to the safe house passed by without incident and Pierce was finally able to appreciate their surroundings. Until now he had felt that Marseille was enemy territory and had remained tensely vigilant outside of the safe house. But now with the mission accomplished and Bufford dead, he found the southern atmosphere of the city agreeably relaxing.

Once inside the safe house they hurriedly packed their gear and cleaned all trace of their presence. Within minutes they were once again on the move, walking the short distance to the building that housed the portal to the Manor.

"You still have that thing?" MacDuff asked incredulously once inside. Pierce was tapping his swordstick on the staircase railing as they climbed towards the portal door.

"It's my good luck charm," Pierce replied with a shrug, trying to forget the damage that it had done and the lives it had taken.

"It needed to be done lad," MacDuff said solemnly, knowing the thoughts that were running through Pierce's mind. "You're a good man Patrick. A good man."

One by one they all entered through the portal, with Pierce leading the way. Still unused to the idea of travelling through time and space by merely walking through a doorway, Pierce couldn't help but hold his breath as he walked through the door.

A half dozen automatic rifle barrel's greeted them as they emerged from the portal into the small circular room in the North Tower. Pierce stopped immediately only to have everyone behind him bump into his back.

"Stand down!" ordered Tiberius' familiar voice as he walked through the crowd of armed men. "Lord Pierce, welcome back. Is it done?"

"It's done."

"Very well," he acknowledged without fanfare. Despite Bufford being a deranged madman bent on changing the history of the world for the worst, he was still a member of the Hunt. Protocol had to be maintained. "Lord Lodge would like to see all of you for a quick debrief. I'll have my men take your bags to your rooms."

They followed Tiberius through the North Tower and then across the bridge to the main part of the Manor. The halls were still quiet, prompting Sean to inquire about the hunt.

"The hunt continues," Tiberius answered without looking back. "I think Drummond picked a difficult target on purpose to give Bufford and Cleaver more time to disappear."

"How is that little weasel?" Pierce inquired, remembering their last encounter.

"Dead. He hung himself in the cells downstairs with his own shoelaces." The sombre pronouncement was delivered with equanimity, eliciting a silent response in return.

"Anything else happen while we were away?" MacDuff asked his friend after a few moments as they crossed the Main Hall.

"Dr. Cleaver is missing; my men have searched the island but have not come up with anything so far."

"That's troubling," observed Pierce with trepidation. He was sure that Cleaver had helped or encouraged Bufford in his unsuccessful plan. Therefore it stood to reason that his disappearance was part of a larger and well organized strategy.

Tiberius only made a cursory knock on the door of Lodge's office before opening it, letting everyone enter first. He followed them in, but remained standing by the door. Lord Lodge was reading some documents at his desk, puffing away on his long pipe in deep concentration. He continued like this for a few moments, making Pierce wonder if he should say something.

"Please sit down all of you," Lodge said without looking up before Pierce could speak. After they had all settled in, Lodge finally looked up. Although Pierce had only known the Master of the Manor for a short while, he felt as though the man had aged dramatically since their first meeting. "It is done then?"

"Yes sir," Pierce replied evenly for the group. He then began explaining all that had happened, with other members filling in the blanks as he went. They recounted the discovery of the tunnel and the *Courted Anne*, and their escapades at the ball. MacDuff took up the narrative with his and Sean's adventure in the harbour bar and their timely rescue from the sea. Pierce picked things up again with the discovery at the hotel manager's office and of his encounter with Ivan in the basement.

Lodge remained generally silent, asking the odd pointed questions throughout. He accepted their answers readily, motioning them to continue in order to keep the story flowing as much as possible.

Finally Pierce came to their assault on the *Courted Anne*, and the various roles they played, eliciting a whistle from Tiberius as they finished.

"I suppose I could have brought Bufford back…" Pierce allowed, second guessing his instincts at that moment.

"I'm sure you did what you thought right, lord knows he deserved it," Lodge replied graciously. "He would have only been coming back to a cell in the basement. To be honest I don't know what we would have done with him if you had brought him back."

Pierce nodded grateful for Lodge's acceptance, but not with a wholly clear conscience.

"Well gentlemen, and lady," Lodge corrected swiftly acknowledging Jane. "You have done the Manor and potentially the world a great service. I'm not sure what kind of reward I can offer, but I'm sure we'll come up with something."

When he finished Tiberius opened the door, signalling an end to the debriefing. They all stood up together, but only Pierce refrained from moving towards the door.

"Everyone head up to my room and have Melrose get whatever you want from the kitchen or bar," Pierce called to the group as they filed out of the room. "I'll be up in a bit."

Pierce then sat back down across from Lord Lodge as Tiberius closed the door behind them. He then walked over to a sideboard and poured some drinks without taking orders. He returned to Lodge's desk with three large whiskeys, setting one on the desk and then passing one to Pierce before sitting down beside him.

"You owe me some information," Pierce demanded, before Lodge could speak. "I completed the mission and now I want to know what this place is and what I'm doing here."

"I see," Lodge accepted as he set his pipe down and picked up his drink. He took a miniscule sip and then looked to Tiberius. "How much have you told him?"

"Practically all I know my Lord," he replied, grimacing slightly under Lodge's stern gaze before regaining his composure. "He deserved to know."

"Very well," Lodge accepted stoically, taking another drink before refilling his pipe. "I shall tell you both about the real history of this place and of my real relationship with Dr. Cleaver."

"That would be nice."

"I am not the founder of the Hunt as everyone believes," Lodge continued, ignoring Pierce's sarcasm. "I was recruited much like everyone else here. I had become bored with my life and was recruited by a fellow intellect, a Professor in fact. I had achieved a fair amount of success assisting the Metropolitan Police with some of their cases. However the majority of my time was spent ignoring pleas for help from what seemed like the majority of London. The solutions were so simple that I felt my mind was dulling. Until I faced off against this Professor. He staged a few incidents to see if I was as good at detection as people said. I not only foiled all of his plans, but discovered his existence before he was fully ready to reveal himself. As I was the first recruit to impress him in this way; he immediately offered me a position at the Manor. Bored with my life and with no real family connections I agreed."

Pierce had drained his drink quickly and walked over to the sideboard to refill it, not entirely enthralled with the story to this point, despite it sounding slightly familiar. Tiberius meanwhile had not touched his drink, slightly stunned to be hearing Lodges true story for the first time in their long history together.

"We faked my death, a necessary device due to my small

amount of fame, or in some views, my notoriety. We then travelled to Geneva, where I had my first experience through the portals to this place. The Manor was not as you see it now, but still quite impressive.

"As I said I wasn't the founder or even the first recruit. When I arrived there were six others, all of them thoroughly devious men of poor quality of character. They all had various schemes of world domination to be achieved through the abuse of the power within the North Tower. A number of people had once told me that I would have made the world's greatest criminal if I had ever desired it. I suppose that's what the Professor saw in me and which led to my recruitment. He wanted my powers and skills to aid his destructive plans and thought that I'd adapt to my surroundings."

"He was wrong?" Pierce interjected, his attention growing.

"Very wrong," Lodge shot a quick smile in reply, his clever eyes twinkling in the dim light. "Within a few years I had replaced the Professor as the head of the Manor and had removed most of the others. Realizing that I needed help in order to continue, I recruited Tiberius here, along with some others. The rest he told you."

"Tiberius didn't know how or why you picked recruits as you did. To be honest I don't see any connections either, except that they're all bad people part of nefarious or downright evil organizations."

"I've made understanding the criminal mind my life's work," Lodge began explaining as he leaned back, almost like a college lecturer. "I saw in this place the opportunity for the greatest study of all time, with the added bonus of removing some undesirables from the world. Anyone can commit a crime or atrocity for themselves; personal gain is the ultimate motive. A man steals to become rich; a woman murders her husband so she can remarry. It was this sort of common crime that drove my ennui in London. But here at the Manor I could collect the truly grandiose criminals of all time. So I picked some of the truly malevolent groups of the Western world from which to pluck my specimens."

"I noticed in the Hunt Room that the membership wasn't very culturally diverse," Pierce challenged, setting his empty glass on the table. "No Genghis Khan's, no Pol Pot's, not even an African dictator type. Are they not evil enough to be worthy of you're study?"

"Indeed they are, however I had no insight into their cultures and would have observed them through Western Christian lenses," Lodge continued his lecture. "Despite my travels through the portals, I'm still truly an English Victorian at heart. What I perceive as criminal in an unfamiliar culture, might be completely acceptable to them. I couldn't muddy the waters with this potential bias, so I concentrated on what I knew."

"So you planned on using this place as a giant laboratory with which to study the human condition, vis-à-vis the criminal mind?" Pierce summed up, hoping he had followed correctly.

"Indeed. I've gathered a very good collection of specimens, displaying some of man's worst attributes. Each member of the Hunt was picked to study a certain characteristic."

"Really?" Pierce asked, now fully engrossed and thinking of the Members he'd met. "De la Gena?"

"Religious zealot."

"Zeidt?"

"A soulless capitalist, who will do anything for wealth."

"Sirinova?"

"A misguided scientist, who puts her discoveries above her patients."

"What about Schell, is it just because he was a Nazi?" Pierce asked doubtfully.

"No, it was because he wasn't a Nazi."

"I don't understand."

"I just listed off different personality types that could apply to a number of Nazis. They used the uniform or the organization to fulfill those roles; kill Jews, gain wealth, create super humans, and so on. But Schell represented the true danger and horror of the Nazis. "

"How?"

"Schell was, probably still is, a good man in general. His criminality was that he turned a blind eye to the injustice he saw around him. He followed along, too scared to speak up, while the world burned around him. He represents the good man who allows evil to flourish," Lodge stated sadly, a look of melancholy that was quickly replaced. "And he was meant to be you."

*

"What?!" Pierce exclaimed jumping up from his seat, confused by Lodges' statement.

"Schell was the most recent recruit before you," Tiberius answered for Lodge, finally entering the conversation. "He was supposed to be our ally in the Hunt."

"But his character proved too ingrained. Within a short time I could tell he had become too comfortable with his surroundings to risk anything," Lodge explained calmly. "We have files on all prospective recruits and he appeared to be the best suited to helping us. He had none of the deviant aspects as the others here or those in the recruiting files."

"Wait, I have a file," Pierce observed immediately wary. "What criminal characteristic do I have? What am I doing here?"

"We needed a true ally," Tiberius said first. "Cleaver had become too powerful and was starting to act openly against Lord Lodge. For a place not susceptible to the ravages of time, we were running out of it."

"Ironic isn't it?" Lodge offered lamely.

"Let me see my file," Pierce demanded, as he started pacing the room. "Why am I grouped in with the Spanish Inquisition and the Nazis?"

"You're the mindless bureaucrat," Lodge replied bluntly as his eyes followed Pierce's movements. "That's the personality type that got you a file here. You have no agenda, merely to follow orders as they're laid out to you. You have no creative ideas of your own and wish nothing more than a pat on the head for a job well done."

Pierce stopped suddenly, initially unwilling to hear the truth in the statement. But deep inside, he couldn't deny the possibility it was true. Before arriving at the Manor his life had followed that path precisely. He never questioned orders, merely worked diligently and kept his head down. But he'd never done anything criminal in his life. Nor had he ever ignored or suppressed evidence of wrongdoing by others.

"You were recruited early," Tiberius offered, seeing the confusion on Pierce's face. "We realized that if we recruited you when the file said you'd be most susceptible, it would be too late. Like Schell. But we needed to get someone who had a file here in order to avoid arousing too much suspicion. We even had Cleaver's lapdog do the recruitment."

"We needed someone who could be pushed to greatness," Lodge continued for his trusted aide. "You were the one truly good man in the files and you've proven that."

"So you grabbed me before I went bad?" Pierce asked quietly.

"No, it's not that simple. We brought you here to allow your true self to develop," Lodge countered immediately. "Your true potential was wasting away as you lived your simple life and would have continued to stagnate, slowly turning sour over time."

"I want to see my file."

"I'm afraid I can't show it to you," Lodge rejected swiftly, knowing that the request had been coming. "It contains too much information about your future. You were supposed to be recruited fifteen years later than you were."

"I need to see it!" Pierce banged on Lodge's desk with a closed fist. "I need to know what I become!"

"Why do you need to see it so badly? The man in the file doesn't exist and never will. As such I've destroyed it."

"You did what?!"

"It has been destroyed," Lodge repeated, calmly pointing to a dying fire to the right of him. Pierce ran over to the grate, only to find illegible charred pieces of paper scattered within. "After everything you've done and seen here, Commandant Pierce will never exist. You're life has altered drastically from the path you were on. For the better I think."

"You talk about making things better," Pierce replied icily with his gaze still on the burnt file. "But you're still trying to play God. How bad must I have become for you to think I'm now a better man. Do you know how many people I killed before receiving your letter? Zero. Do you know how many people I've killed since? More than fucking zero!"

"Those were necessary deaths Patrick," Lodge gently responded to Pierce's shouting accusation.

"Necessary for whom? Not for me. If I was back in Ottawa I would have been happily oblivious. So tell me, what was I to become that is so much worse than the killer standing here now?" Pierce made his demand as he walked back towards Lodge's desk, practically shaking in anger.

"When you were supposed to be recruited you would have been a high ranking officer in the Royal Canadian Marshal Service. You were the commandant of a special prison for terrorists in Northern Quebec. The inmates were generally held without full process of the law or their guilt wasn't yet proven in court."

"That doesn't make sense, there is no Royal Canadian Marshal Service" Pierce mumbled in confusion before remembering the black uniform he'd worn. But the uniform alone wasn't enough to convince him completely. "Something like that couldn't happen in Canada, not the Canada I know."

"The Canada you know changed dramatically in the future," Lodge continued, unhappy at having to relay the truth. "A few years after the date Tiberius and Drummond recruited you, a series of bombings took place in Quebec. They were immediately blamed on Islamic extremists angry over language laws and the banning of religious clothing. Anti-Islamic groups sprung up everywhere and the province descended into chaos. However it was soon discovered that the bombings were in fact the acts of radical Quebec separatists, using the chaos and anger to try and take power. The federal government moved in to calm the situation, however it only inflamed things. Think of the FLQ crisis multiplied by a factor of ten. Soldiers, police, bankers, judges, all of them targeted by bombs or ambushed by snipers. The authorities were fairly successful at capturing many of these home-grown terrorist at the beginning. But the criminals soon became just as adept at escaping captivity, with the authorities busy arguing over jurisdiction and unable to track them down.

"Eventually a mid-level public servant wrote a position paper on the creation of a marshal service modelled after the American organization, but with greater power. They would track down and capture fugitives of the law, specialising on the separatists. The difference being that they would also be responsible for the creation and maintenance of special prisons for captured terrorists and fugitives."

"Who would have written such a thing?" Pierce asked incredulously.

"You did."

The two words hung in the air between them for a minute. Pierce couldn't reconcile the story he had just heard with what he knew of his own character. The idea of limiting a person's freedom or liberty was repugnant to him. But a small voice in his head told him that the story he heard had a ring of truth.

"A number of your friends and colleagues had been victims of these escaped terrorists and you were in an angry state of mind. I imagine you wrote the paper in order to burn off some steam and never thought it would be seriously looked at. This was why I didn't want to tell you," Lodge offered apologetically.

"What… What did I do, as Commandant?"

"I have probably already said too much," Lodge said, shaking his head in dismay.

"Tell me," Pierce demanded with quiet determination. The surrealism of asking about his own future didn't register to him as he asked the question. He was too focused on the story, desperately needing to find out what he did. He wasn't even sure where the desire came from. Part of him knew that that future was no longer possible for him. But another part of him worried that it would simply manifest itself in another way if he didn't find out how ruthless he would become.

"You were responsible for all of the inmates placed in the special prison," Lodge began vaguely. But when Pierce shot him a frustrated glance, he continued with more precision. "Your job was to make sure those captured stayed captured in order to be used to provide information on their comrades. Was torture employed? Yes. Did you do anything personally? I doubt it, but I don't know for certain. Those prisoners that did escape were hunted down under your supervision and apprehended with extreme prejudice."

"What the hell does that mean?"

"It means that they were generally killed once captured," Tiberius explained for Lodge who had become silent. "Poor encourager les autres."

"I have to go back," Pierce replied immediately. "I have to go back and fix things."

"There's nothing to fix, it hasn't happened yet. Like Lord Lodge said, Commandant Pierce will never exist and the experiences you've had since arriving will ensure you don't become him in future," Tiberius argued. "We need you here, to recover from this current upheaval."

"Despite the seemingly magical properties of this island, I can't live forever," Lord Lodge declared solemnly to both men. "Patrick, I need you to take over for me when I go. I want you to be the Master of the Manor."

Lodge's wish made Pierce even more conflicted. A part of him wanted to remain at the Manor, swathed in luxurious comfort. But another part of him felt an obligation to the place he called home and its future happiness.

"I have to go back," he repeated thoughtfully. "I understand that my future will no longer follow that old path. But it's not about me anymore. As a young man I grew up proud to be a Canadian. I celebrated our contributions to medicine and science, and our role as peacekeepers. I relished our ability to withstand the hardships of winter and felt a tingle every time I heard Paul Henderson's Summit Series winning goal. But I can't idly sit here in this museum of malevolence when I could be saving my country from itself."

"You can do more good here than returning to your old life," Tiberius continued his arguement. "The terrorist attacks will occur and a similar position paper will be written whether you return or not. But by staying here you can make a positive impact on a much greater scale. Think of all the good we could do from here!"

"Look at how well your good intentions have worked so far," Pierce rebuked angrily. "We barely stopped a madman from ruining history and now there's an evil genius who's gone missing!"

"That's precisely why you're needed. The power of this place cannot be left in the hands of lesser men. But I won't stop your return if that's what you want to do," Lodge allowed with disappointment.

"That's not what I want to do," Pierce objected sadly. "I want to stay here for the rest of my life, living like nobility with the power to travel through time and see history first hand. But if I ignore all the bad things that will happen to my country in order to stay, won't I be just as guilty as Schell in my inaction? And if I stay and try and manipulate history from the North Tower, won't I be just as guilty as Bufford or Cleaver?"

Lord Lodge merely sat silently and continued smoking his pipe in silence, his eyes staring at Pierce intently.

"If you gentlemen have nothing further I'm going to go back to my rooms and get drunk with my friends. I think we've deserved it. I'll make my decision in a couple of days when everything has calmed down and I've had time to think."

Lord Lodge and Tiberius accepted this as Pierce stood up and marched out of the room.

"I told you he was the one," Lodge proclaimed before returning to the documents on his desk.

Chapter 33

The party was in full force as Pierce opened the door to his rooms, feeling as though he hadn't passed the threshold in weeks. The lounge was awash in light, with a fire raging in the hearth. The Brown Pack, along with some of the staff, were drinking and cavorting in the large room, splashing wild shadows across the walls. Melrose stumbled up towards Pierce with a pair of bottles in his hands.

"Drink sir?" he hiccupped, raising a bottle high up for Pierce to drink from.

He took a few gulps of what he figured was very expensive champagne, getting a significant amount on his face. Melrose then moved off towards the study where the sound of more laughter was emanating from.

"Liam's shacked up in your study with about half a dozen of the maids," MacDuff explained gregariously, approaching Pierce with two glasses in his hands.

"Well he's deserved it," Pierce acknowledged, taking one of the offered glasses. "Just don't tell him I said that."

"Never," MacDuff agreed with a smile. "Important discussion with the Master?"

"You could say that," Pierce replied enigmatically. Seeing everyone enjoy themselves in his own expensively appointed apartment made Pierce feel foolish for thinking of leaving. This feeling swiftly became worse as he saw the approaching attractive form.

"Lord Pierce!" Jane exclaimed in greeting, somewhat mockingly. She had her own bottle of champagne in her hand and shoved it into his face as she warped her arm around his neck.

Delighted by her attention Pierce immediately took a swig, relishing the moment. Jane had removed the heavy clothing she'd worn during their assault in Marseille and had changed into a clingy dress. He grabbed her around the waist and decided to have a good time in the present and forget about his impending decision for a while.

"You saved my life," he admitted to her sincerely. "You were magnificent the entire time; at the ball, on the ship, everything."

Without a moments hesitation Jane leaned over and kissed him. Initially shocked by her sudden advance, he got passed it quickly and returned the favour, oblivious to the noise surrounding them. Seeing everyone together and feeling the comradeship with his new friends, Pierce began to seriously doubt a decision to leave.

As the evening progressed, more people filtered into Pierce's apartment; most of them staff of the Manor eager to join in any celebration during the absence of the Hunt. As the rumours started to flow about the demise of Bufford and the Grey Pack, the joyous revelry only increased.

Well after midnight Pierce found himself fairly drunk, talking to a pair of footmen about the rules of hockey. He happened to look up when Tiberius entered the lounge with a beautiful auburn haired woman in his arms. He was instantly intrigued by the companion. She wasn't dressed like any of the servants and wasn't a member of the Hunt. Suddenly he remembered her as the woman he'd briefly met in Jane's room. This was confirmed moments later when Jane flew past him to greet her friend.

"Patrick, this is Kat," Jane began the introductions when Pierce came to greet them to the party. "Kat this is Lord Pierce of the Brown Pack."

"We've met before," Kat reminded her friend. "What a wonderful party sir."

"It's Patrick tonight," he replied warmly. "Come on in and enjoy yourself. But a word of advice, don't gamble with the drunken Irishman in the study, he's probably cheating."

"Come on Kat, we'll get a drink and I'll tell you about my latest adventure," Jane offered excitedly, grabbing Kat by the arm and going to a makeshift bar Melrose had created on the far side of the room.

"Well played Tiberius," Pierce acknowledged as they watched the women talking animatedly together.

"I tried to send her back to Rivermead but she wouldn't go, despite the danger," Tiberius smiled widely while shaking his head. "So she's going to stay, for which I am very glad."

"What's she going to do here? Are Hunt Members and staff allowed to get married?"

"Steady on now!" Tiberius exclaimed as he accepted a glass from Melrose who passed by with a tray. "No need to be hasty."

"Well I can't see her as a maid here at the Manor," Pierce observed, evaluating the firecracker across the room.

"No chance of that," Tiberius agreed with a laugh before turning serious. "That's the newest recruit to the Hunt staff. She doesn't know it yet, but she's going to be trained as a Hound of the Hunt. I told you we're going to change things around here."

"If that's how the new will Hunt look, I might stay after all."

They both laughed, toasting each other before downing their drinks. As Pierce left to grab a new bottle, his attention was pulled towards the door. Morgan had just appeared and was talking to Tiberius rather intently. Within a few seconds Morgan had left and Tiberius walked straight over to Pierce by the bar.

"I need to speak to you and your men urgently," he stated gravely, signalling the severity of the request to Pierce immediately.

Within a few minutes Pierce had gathered the Brown Pack together in his study, expelling the revellers within. They were all somewhat drunk, but were all experienced enough drinkers that they were able to turn their professional switches on quickly.

"The Hunt has returned from Spain," Tiberius announced after they had all found a seat. He was surprised to see Jane present, but figured she'd earned her place among them. "But there's a problem. A number of the members disappeared moments after returning. We believe they are in league with Cleaver and have fled the Manor."

"The island's pretty big," Sean observed, blinking more than usual. "But can track them down easily enough."

"No, they've fled through portals in the North Tower," Tiberius explained with a mixture of anger and embarrassment. "We know which portals have been accessed, but we don't know who used which one."

"Christ, they could be anywhere," MacDuff observed in shock, realizing the full situation. Groups of four highly trained individuals were now running amok throughout history.

"We need you to stay and help hunt them all down," Tiberius pleaded to Pierce who had taken his seat behind the large oak desk.

"What does he mean stay?" Liam asked, clever enough to notice Tiberius' slip.

"He means that I was debating a return to my own time and to leave the Manor behind," Pierce replied to the hurt expressions of his men. The worst was from Jane who looked pained from his admission. "But to be honest I hadn't made up my mind."

"So what are you going to do now lad?" MacDuff inquired intently.

Pierce looked around the room, seeing a collection of hardened warriors looking back at him in anticipation. He could tell they were eager, despite the hardships of the past few days. Even Jane had a fire in her eye that he couldn't ignore.

"I'm going to stay," he finally announced, knowing it was the right thing to do. "And we're going to hunt down every last one of them."